Pamela Evans was bo[...] the Borough of Ealing, London, the youngest of six children. She is married and has two sons and now lives in Wales. She has had eleven novels published, all of which are available from Headline.

Praise for Pamela Evans' previous London sagas:

'A long, warm-hearted London saga' *Bookseller*
'A good story and excellent observation of social change over the past forty years' *Knightsbridge and South Hams Gazette*
'A good traditional romance and its author has a feeling for the atmosphere of postwar London' *Sunday Express*
'Well peopled with warm personalities' *Liverpool Post*
'A heart-warming family saga' *Newtownards Chronicle*
'Very readable' *Bella*

Yesterday's Friends

Pamela Evans

HEADLINE

First published in 1996 by
HEADLINE BOOK PUBLISHING

First published in paperback in 1997 by
HEADLINE BOOK PUBLISHING

10 9 8 7 6 5 4 3 2

ISBN 0 7472 5167 3

Typeset by Avon Dataset Ltd, Bidford-on-Avon, Warks

Printed and bound in Great Britain

HEADLINE BOOK PUBLISHING
A division of Hodder Headline PLC
338 Euston Road
London NW1 3BH

To all the family

Chapter One

The Brooks twins saw themselves as arbiters of justice. Passionately protective of family and friends, Ray and Jack felt duty-bound to look after their own and did so with brute force, being better endowed with muscle than grey matter. Only the foolish or the brave spoke ill of anyone in the Brooks clan within the twins' hearing for they were six feet tall with broad shoulders and big knuckles.

Diehard troublemakers did exist, however, which was how Ray and Jack came to be involved in an incident at the Shepherd's Bush Billiard Hall one Saturday afternoon in the summer of 1956 . . .

This popular meeting place for working men was situated above a gentlemen's outfitters and was a large room filled with individually lit, green baize-covered tables. Clouds of cigarette smoke hung in the shafts of sunlight that filtered through the dusty windows.

Ray and Jack were harmlessly engaged in a game at one of the tables when a conversation between two nearby players caught their attention. 'Have you seen that bird who works in Grover's the chemist's opposite the Green?' asked a young man, a newcomer to the area, as he idly chalked the end of his billiard cue.

'You mean the good-looking, dark-haired piece?' replied his companion, a well-known mischiefmaker.

'Yeah.'

'That's Ruth Brooks,' said the troublemaker with a sly glance in the direction of the Brooks twins, seeing a perfect opportunity to provoke them just for the fun of it.

1

'You know her then?' remarked the newcomer casually, squinting across the green baize with a frown of concentration as he worked out his sporting strategy.

'I know *of* her,' said the agitator, shifty eyes gleaming against his urban pallor, his spotty countenance topped with thickly greased hair and edged by long sideburns. 'Everyone around here knows about Ruth Brooks.'

'Why's that?' asked the newcomer, raising his eyes in idle curiosity.

''Cos she caused a scandal,' he explained. 'Must be about four or five years ago.'

'Sounds juicy,' said the newcomer. 'So, what's the story?'

With slow deliberate movements, the troublemaker positioned himself at the table, pausing before taking his shot, knowing the delay would sharpen his companion's interest. When he was quite ready, he rested the end of his cue on the floor and began speaking in a voice loud enough to be overheard.

'Ruth Brooks was the brainy sort . . . went to the grammar school . . . and not many go there from her street.' He paused, studying his cue, to build the tension. 'Her family were well chuffed, boasted about her all over the town. But they didn't have much to shout about later, when she got herself up the spout and had to leave school.'

'Did she have the kid?'

'Yeah . . . a girl.' He paused thoughtfully. 'I suppose she would be about four by now.'

'Well, stone me.'

'I should steer well clear of Ruth Brooks if I were you, mate,' warned the troublemaker, whose character assessment was based purely on malice because the woman in question had never given him a second glance. 'She's quite a looker, I admit – I wouldn't mind doin' her a favour myself – but I wouldn't wanna be one of a crowd.'

The conversation came to an abrupt end when the

troublemaker's cue was ripped from his grasp and snapped in two over Ray Brooks's knee.

'Have you got a death wish or something?' asked Ray, his tar-black eyes hot and menacing as he towered over the other man, pushing the two halves of the cue into his face for a moment before sending them clattering to the floor.

'I think he must have,' said his brother Jack, standing beside Ray.

'Here, that cue cost money!' admonished the trouble-maker, who was already beginning to regret his recklessness in riling this awesome pair.

'It isn't a good idea to make rude remarks about our sister if you value your property,' Ray informed him.

'Or your health,' added Jack.

'It's a free country . . . I can say what I like about . . .'

'Not about our family you can't . . . not when we're around anyway,' was the reply in Ray's gravel tones.

'Hey, do you mind?' put in the newcomer, glaring at the twins. 'Me and my mate were in the middle of a game and a private conversation. If he wants to tell me that your sister is a slag, he's perfectly entitled.'

An electric silence fell over the room. All games ceased and all eyes were directed towards the disturbance. Through a haze of smoke, the entire gathering watched the twins, a striking pair, tall, dark and identical, with muscles of steel beneath their drape suits.

'We don't allow anyone to insult our sister,' said Ray grimly. 'And if we catch anyone doin' it, we make sure they never do it again.'

'Don't you threaten me,' warned the troublemaker with bravado.

'We intend to do more than that,' said Ray. 'It's a matter of principle, innit, Jack?'

'That's right, bruv.'

'So if you two fellas will oblige us and come outside,

3

we'll finish our business and get on with our game.'

'I'm not going anywhere,' said the troublemaker, looking horribly bilious.

'Nor me,' said the newcomer, also turning pale with fright.

But their arms were twisted firmly behind their backs and they were propelled from the room, ushered forcibly down the stairs and into the street where they were taken to the nearest alleyway and made to suffer for daring to insult a member of the Brooks family.

Ruth Brooks was about to take her lunch hour when Mr Grover asked her to hang on for a few minutes because he had something important to say to her. Having arranged to meet her friend Kitty in the cafe across the Green, Ruth wasn't pleased about the delay but kept her thoughts to herself because Mr Grover was a good employer and very understanding of her circumstances.

'It won't take long, my dear,' he said as they stood among the serried rows of bottles and jars on the shelves in the dispensary, the air faintly scented with wintergreen and coal tar ointment. 'But I'd like you to hear it from me first, rather than anyone else.'

'Hear what, Mr Grover?'

'I'm retiring,' he announced, his gentle blue eyes faded and watery with age behind his spectacles. 'I'm selling the shop.'

This shouldn't have been unexpected since he was well turned seventy but Ruth felt quite shocked by the news. Mr Grover's shop was as much a part of the area as the market and she couldn't imagine his not being around to offer advice and make up 'something that might do the trick' to save someone a trip to the doctor's surgery. Naturally, too, Ruth was concerned about her job.

'I'm really sorry to hear that, Mr Grover,' she replied.

'Surely you don't begrudge an old man a little time to

himself in his autumn years?' he remarked in a kindly manner. A few strands of wispy white hair sparsely feathered his bald head which gleamed in the electric light, switched on even on a sunny day like this. The dispensary had only one small window which was high up and barred for security reasons.

'Of course not,' she said, 'but you'll be greatly missed. You're very well thought of by the people around here.'

'No one lasts for ever and I'm sure my successor will serve the community well.'

'Are you moving away from the area?' enquired Ruth, knowing he'd lived in the flat above the shop on his own since his wife died.

'Yes, I'm going to live near my daughter in Putney,' he explained.

'That'll be lovely for you,' she said with forced brightness as the possible repercussions for her of his retirement registered fully.

'Indeed it will.' He pushed his spectacles on to the bridge of his thin nose. 'But I expect you're wondering about your job?'

'Naturally it's crossed my mind.'

'Well, I shall recommend you highly to the new owner but I can't actually guarantee that they'll keep you on,' he explained. 'If a married couple take it, for instance, they may want to run the shop between them with the help of just a part-timer.'

'Yes, I understand that.'

'But even if that were to happen,' he said with genuine concern, 'I'm sure you'd soon find something else – a bright, hardworking young woman like yourself. There are plenty of jobs about at the moment.'

'Don't worry about me,' said Ruth, smiling despite the knot of tension in her stomach. 'I'll be fine. You concentrate on your retirement. You deserve a rest after such a long career.'

'We all have to stand back at some time.'

'I suppose so.'

'I wanted to make sure you were put in the picture before potential buyers start coming to view the property,' he explained.

'Thank you, I appreciate that.'

'So . . . off you go then now, my dear, and have your lunch.'

'Thank you. I'll see you later.'

As she hurried through the shop, Ruth saw her surroundings through a blur of tears. It was, she had to admit, dismal and old-fashioned despite her attempts to bring it into line with the taste of the 1950s. The solid mahogany counters and wall shelves were piled high with patent remedies for coughs, colds and indigestion; there was malt extract, garden fertiliser, health salts, disinfectant. Tins of baby milk stood in a pile on the floor.

Grover's was overstocked with almost everything except toiletries and cosmetics, of which there were very few. During the four years she'd been working here, Ruth had tried to persuade Mr Grover to allow her to reorganise the shop, to brighten the place up and make space for displays of perfume, fancy soaps and make-up, which would boost the turnover now that people had more money to spend. But her employer had made it clear that he wasn't interested in changing the habits of a lifetime. He was an old man with more interest in pharmacy than business, and he had no intention of modernising his shop at his time of life.

He had allowed her to assist him in the dispensary from time to time, though, which had broken the monotony of counter work. Ruth was an intelligent girl who liked a challenge, which was why she tried to learn as much as she could from Mr Grover about pharmacy.

But now, she left the shop and hurried across the Green, a slim figure in a well-worn summer dress and flat sandals, unstylish compared to others her age who could afford the exciting new fashions. She was undeniably attractive, though: olive-skinned, with sloe-black eyes and curling lashes, her long dark hair tied back with a ribbon.

There was the freshness and brilliance of a perfect summer's day, its clear blue skies soaring over the sunlit suburb which today was vibrant and colourful, the streets thronged with Saturday shoppers eager to spend money on luxury items as well as food in this long-awaited time of affluence. People were pouring off buses and trains and heading for the market.

Teddy Boys were out in force, parading in their Edwardian-style clothes. There was quite a sprinkling of khaki too: National Servicemen home for the weekend. Young women in bright summer dresses or tight skirts and stiletto-heeled shoes with winkle picker toes strutted arm in arm, gazing into the shop windows. The benches on the Green were all occupied by people taking a respite under the trees with their bags and packages as Ruth hurried by.

A naturally exuberant person with a ready smile, today she was unusually subdued. In fact, her full lips were pressed tightly together and her teeth were clenched. Even the glorious sunshine bathing her arms and shoulders failed to soothe her. She was far too concerned with the possible loss of her job to be infected by the atmosphere of energy and enthusiasm around her.

Theoretically she shouldn't have difficulty finding another job at this time of economic upsurge. But how many employers would be willing to take her on once they found out the truth about her circumstances? Even apart from the stigma, they would probably view someone with a child to raise alone as an unreliable prospect. Unmarried mothers were social pariahs in the eyes of many people.

One thing was certain: if the worst happened and she

did lose this job, she'd have to get another one fast. With a child to support, she couldn't afford to be out of work for even a day. She was pale with worry as she approached the cafe.

By contrast Kitty West was in high spirits and bursting to share her good news, which was the reason she'd invited her friend Ruth to join her for lunch.

'You know that interview I went for a few weeks ago – for a job with a new holiday tour operator that's recently started up?' she started saying in a rush as soon as Ruth sat down.

'You got the job?' she guessed.

'I did, I did,' squealed Kitty, her blue eyes sparkling.

'Oh, Kitty, that's wonderful!' said Ruth, concealing her own problems so as not to put a damper on her friend's excitement.

'Yes, it is, isn't it?'

'Come on then,' she urged, forcing herself to sound lighthearted. 'Tell me all about it.'

'Well, I shall get the chance to travel abroad to various holiday resorts,' explained Kitty, who currently worked in the West End offices of a firm of travel agents and, unlike Ruth, didn't have to work on a Saturday.

'As a courier?'

'No, I'll be on the administration side – dealing with hoteliers and managers of apartments as well as sorting out queries for the couriers. I'll be checking out complaints, finding new accommodation for the future and so on.'

'How exciting.'

'I think so,' said Kitty, her face flushed and animated. 'It's only because I'm fluent in French and Spanish that I got the job. The men usually get all the interesting jobs in the admin side of the travel business. Women usually just get to make their coffee and do their typing.'

They each ordered a cheese omelette, though Mr Grover's news had all but killed Ruth's appetite.

'Will you be away most of the time?' she asked, glancing idly around the cafe which had recently been re-vamped coffee bar-style with formica-topped tables, espresso machines and a juke box currently emitting Elvis Presley's latest hit.

'A fair bit over the course of a year, I should think.'

The ache inside Ruth grew. Her day was getting worse by the moment. First she looked likely to lose her job, now her best friend was going away . . .

'Apparently my first assignment will be a trip to Spain, to find out what accommodation is available in a new resort there,' explained Kitty. 'The company is looking for hotels and apartments for package holidays all over Europe. Holidays abroad are becoming really popular.'

'Yes, I've heard about that,' said Ruth, feeling very much out of things. 'We sell loads of sun tan oil.'

The omelettes arrived. Ruth couldn't manage more than a mouthful or two which didn't escape Kitty's notice. Over coffee, she said, 'But enough about me. How are things with you?'

'Okay.'

'How's Jenny?'

'She's fine.' Ruth smiled, her whole face seeming to melt into happiness. 'Well . . . she's adorable actually.'

'I'll pop round to your place and see her before I go home to Hammersmith.'

'We'll go together when we leave here,' suggested Ruth. 'I get withdrawal symptoms if I don't manage to see her in my lunch hour.'

'A hopelessly devoted mother, eh?'

'I admit it.'

Kitty gave her friend a close look. 'So if you and Jenny are both fine, what's the matter?'

'Nothing.'

'Something has to be wrong for you to leave your lunch.'

Ruth knew she couldn't deceive her closest friend.

'Oh, it's nothing really,' she said, making light of it. 'I've just heard that Mr Grover is selling up and retiring, that's all.'

'And you think you'll lose your job?'

'Yeah.'

'Oh, I'm sorry, Ruth,' said Kitty. 'I've been so full of myself, I didn't notice that anything was wrong 'til you left your omelette.'

'Don't apologise. I enjoy hearing your news. I'm pleased things are going so well for you, honestly.'

'You'll soon get another job,' said Kitty reassuringly.

'I hope so.'

'You could even try for something a bit more challenging,' suggested Kitty. 'You *did* get your 'O'-levels, remember?'

'Fat chance of that with the stigma I carry! Honestly, being an unmarried mum is tantamount to being on the game to some people.' Ruth paused thoughtfully. 'Anyway, I need to work near home so that I can see Jenny at lunchtime and be back in time in the evening to put her to bed.'

'Yes, there is that.'

'I'm hoping the new owner will let me stay on at the shop,' she confided. 'It's convenient and I really rather enjoy the job, especially when I'm allowed to help in the dispensary.'

Kitty studied Ruth over the rim of her coffee cup. It infuriated her to see her friend in such a state. Ruth would have been doing something far better suited to her capabilities if she hadn't had to leave school after her 'O'-levels because she was pregnant. She might even have gone to university. The teachers had certainly seemed to think so at the time. Ruth had been the shining light of her year at Redfern Grammar School, a gifted student with a golden future.

But all her youthful opportunities had been destroyed by disgrace and premature responsibility. She'd had a tough time this last five years even though she would sooner die than admit it. Raising a child without a husband was difficult enough in itself, and the attitude of people towards someone in her situation certainly didn't help matters.

What angered Kitty most was the fact that while Ruth's life had been altered irrevocably, the father of her child hadn't suffered in the slightest. But she kept her thoughts on this subject to herself because she knew Ruth was ultra-sensitive about it.

'Let's hope for the best then,' said Kitty in response to Ruth's remark. 'But don't worry. If the new owner doesn't keep you on for any reason, you'll soon get fixed up somewhere else.'

Ruth cast an admiring eye over her friend. Kitty had a pale, delicate beauty and knew how to improve on what nature had already supplied. Creamy beige make-up made her skin glow against her ash-blonde hair which she wore short and feathery. Her blue eyes were enhanced by a generous use of mascara and eye shadow, and she was wearing an Italian-style shirt in cornflower blue with lightweight cream tapered trousers. She had an air of success about her. Kitty had come a long way since she and Ruth had first met as new girls at Redfern Grammar School ten years ago at the age of eleven.

They'd found an instant rapport and been best friends ever since, despite the difference in their backgrounds. Kitty's father owned two grocery shops, and the family lived in their own house in a respectable avenue in the better part of Hammersmith, whereas Ruth's father was a factory worker and the Brooks family lived in a rented house in a working-class area of Shepherd's Bush.

Ruth had always known Kitty would go far. She had the sort of self-assurance that made her stand out in a crowd. She'd stayed on at school to do her 'A'-levels after Ruth had left, which had helped her to get into the travel business. She'd had a reputation for arrogance at school but Ruth could forgive her that because she was such fun to be with. If she got uppish, Ruth told her she was being a pain in the bum and Kitty soon changed her attitude. Ruth thought her air of superiority was probably not deliberate and might have something to do with her being an only child. Whatever her faults, she'd been a good friend to Ruth.

'Don't worry about me,' said Ruth for the second time that day. 'I won't be out of work for long if I do lose this job.'

Kitty chose her next words carefully because Ruth was fiercely proud and resented anything that even hinted at pity.

'Don't you ever feel the slightest bit bitter about the way things have turned out for you?' she asked.

'I sometimes get angry at the way society treats people like me,' Ruth replied, her eyes hardening, her tone becoming brittle. 'But, no, I'm not bitter. Why should I be?'

'Oh, come on, Ruth, this is me, Kitty. You can be honest with me.'

'I am being honest.'

'But when your job is under threat and you have the sole responsibility of supporting a child, surely the unfairness of it all must get to you?'

'How can I even think in terms of unfairness when I have such a precious gift?' said Ruth with utmost sincerity. 'The thing I love most in all the world – my daughter.'

Kitty felt a lump gather in her throat. Ruth was hard up and shabby and stuck in a dead end job with no prospects, but at that moment she seemed rich beyond measure, her dark, velvety eyes filling with tenderness at the mention of Jenny.

Ruth and Kitty had been about as close as friends can get over the last ten years, sharing each other's thoughts and dreams. But although Kitty knew who Jenny's father was, Ruth had never fed Kitty's fevered imagination with the details of events that fateful night when they had both been sixteen-year-old schoolgirls: the night of Jenny's conception.

'There's no answer to that, is there?' said Kitty, humbled by her friend's attitude.

'No, I don't believe there is,' Ruth agreed.

When Ruth got home from work that evening there was an argument in progress. Her mother, Audrey, was holding forth to the twins in the kitchen, having been told by a neighbour that they'd been seen fighting in an alleyway.

Four-year-old Jenny was sitting on her grandfather's lap in the living room, a cosy mixture of the old and the new with its ancient three-piece suite in maroon set amidst contemporary occasional tables and a television set in the corner, its double doors closed across the screen. Jenny was as fair as her mother was dark, a golden-haired, blue-eyed child with dimpled cheeks.

'Gran's cross with the Nunkies,' she informed her mother gravely, using her pet name for her uncles, as Audrey's furious tones rang through the house.

'So I can hear,' said Ruth.

'They must've been very naughty to make Gran shout like that,' said Jenny, tears beginning to roll down her cheeks as she snuggled closer to her grandfather.

'It's nothing for you to worry about, love,' Ruth reassured her, going down on her haunches and gently dabbing the little girl's eyes with her handkerchief. 'Gran isn't angry with you.'

'I don't like it when she shouts, though,' confessed Jenny.

Ruth's father, Dan, an even-tempered and sensible man from whom Ruth and her brothers inherited their dark colouring, said to his daughter, 'You know what your mother's like about the twins fighting. It really gets her dander up. It's time those two packed it in. They're old enough to know better.'

'They certainly are.'

Ruth's protectiveness towards her daughter was so strong it was almost a physical pain. It hurt to see Jenny so upset by adult altercations, of which there were many in this household. Ruth had a warm and loving nature and adored her parents and brothers, but living with them now that she had a child of her own could be purgatory at times as family unity cracked under the strain of too much togetherness and too little privacy.

Much of the friction was caused by Ruth herself as she fought a constant battle to bring up her daughter her own way, without interference. Since rented accommodation was beyond her means, and practically non-existent for an unmarried mother anyway, a place of her own was not even a possibility.

As her mother's fury continued to blast from the kitchen, it began to dawn on Ruth that she herself was to blame for the conflict, at least indirectly.

'When are you two gonna grow up?' Audrey was shouting. 'Twenty-three years old and still scrapping in the street like a couple o' kids, and givin' the family a bad name. It's gotta stop. I won't have it, do you hear me?'

'Calm down, Mum, you'll give yourself a heart attack,' came Ray's deep tones.

'We were only defending our sister's reputation,' added Jack.

''Course we were. Those blokes were asking for trouble,'

Ray said in aggrieved tones. 'The things they were saying about Ruth!'

'We couldn't just stand back and let them get away with it.'

Ruth gave her daughter a reassuring hug and told her to stay with her grandfather. Then she marched into the kitchen, a long narrow room, its dark old-fashioned furnishings brightened here and there by home-made formica worktops.

'Oh, it's you, Ruth,' said Audrey, turning as the door opened. 'I didn't realise you were home from work.'

'You'll have the neighbours in here complaining about the noise in a minute, if you don't keep your voices down,' she admonished. 'And that'll get us talked about even more.'

'Someone's got to make these idiots see sense,' said her mother.

'You leave them to me, Mum, I'll soon sort them out.' Ruth opened the kitchen door leading to the long narrow back garden. 'Come on, you two dumbos. We need to talk.'

Because their sister could be quite formidable in this mood they did as she asked, closing the door behind them.

'Right,' said Ruth in a low but forceful tone, 'how many times must I tell you – I don't *want* you fighting over me. I'm twenty-one years old and quite old enough to fight my own battles.'

'Surely you didn't expect us to let those blokes get away with it?'

'All you did was fuel the gossip and make Mum see red.'

'What were we supposed to do, then?'

'Ignore them.'

'And let people think we've lost our bottle?'

'Better they think that than that you've no brains at all.'

15

'Charming!' said Ray, affronted.

'Cheek!' echoed Jack.

'Well, what do you expect if you carry on like a couple of gorillas?'

They lapsed into an offended silence. Ruth cast her eye over her brothers, so much alike most people outside the family had a job telling them apart. They were extremely good-looking with olive skin and finely chiselled features, their thick black hair heavily greased and brushed forward into a quiff at the front, dark sweeping lashes fringing their eyes. As factory workers, they earned a good wage which enabled them to dress in style too. Although they both attracted a good deal of feminine interest, neither Ray nor Jack could sustain a relationship with a woman for any length of time because of their exceptionally close bonding which tended to make them exclude everyone else.

'Look, you two,' she said in a more conciliatory tone, 'I know you mean well and I appreciate your looking out for me but it only makes matters worse. Don't you think Mum has enough to contend with without your embarrassing her by fighting in public? She's had more than her share of mud thrown at her because of me. Your brawling upsets her and makes me feel guilty. You know what it's like round here – you can't burp without everybody knowing about it! Someone is always bound to tell Mum if you get into a bundle in a public place. If you must fight, join a boxing club. Just don't use me as an excuse for violence.'

'That's gratitude for you,' said Jack gloomily.

The word hit a raw nerve because Ruth had had a bad day and was feeling particularly sensitive.

'Don't talk to me about gratitude!' she said, her voice quivering. 'I'm grateful to all of you, every second of my life. I'm so grateful there's hardly room for any other feelings. I'm grateful to Mum and Dad for letting Jenny

16

and me live here, to you two for standing up for me, to Mr Grover for giving me a job when I've committed the worst sin in the book and had a baby without being married . . . so don't make me feel even more guilty by fighting to protect my good name. I know what people say about me – even now that Jenny's turned four, some of them are still at it. It hurts, of course it does, but I can live with it. But people are never gonna forget if you constantly remind them by brawling in the streets every time anyone says anything about me.'

'Okay, we're sorry if we've upset you,' sighed Ray, who was fond of his sister and could see that she was close to tears. 'We were only trying to help. But we'll try to turn a blind eye in future.'

'Do you really mean that?'

'We'll *try*,' said Ray because he and his brother found self-control very difficult when it came to defending the honour of the family. 'That's the best I can offer.'

'That's better than nothing, I suppose,' said Ruth, hooking her arms through theirs. 'Now that that's settled, let's go back inside and you can make your peace with Mum.'

No sooner had Ruth recovered from that disagreement than another row broke out at tea-time, this time between her mother and herself.

It started when Jenny refused to eat any ham salad or bread and butter and wanted a piece of chocolate sponge cake instead.

'Not until you've eaten some of what you have on your plate,' said Ruth.

'Oh, let her have the cake,' said Audrey. 'It won't do her any harm.'

'She can have cake when she's eaten some of the other things,' insisted Ruth.

'No, I only want the cake,' said the child determinedly,

pushing her plate away and bursting into tears.

'Ah, bless her,' said Audrey, who was a complete pushover where Jenny was concerned.

'Crocodile tears,' said Ruth.

'Don't be so hard on her,' said Ray. 'A bit o' cake won't hurt her.'

''Course it won't,' agreed Jack.

'She's *not* having cake until she's eaten some of what's already on her plate,' insisted Ruth through clenched teeth. 'She's not touched any of it. And will you please stop undermining my authority . . . all of you.'

'Ruth is quite right,' said her father supportively. 'Jenny must learn to do what her mother tells her.'

'What harm can a piece of cake do?' said Ray as Jenny's wailing grew louder.

'The cake isn't the issue,' declared Ruth, trembling with frustration. It was an uphill struggle trying to assert her right as Jenny's mother to prevent her daughter from becoming a spoiled brat. But she had to do it for the child's sake. 'Giving in to her every time she wants something is what this is all about. Apart from ruining her character, she can't live on cakes and biscuits, which is what will happen if we're not careful.'

'I hope you're not suggesting that's what she eats all day when I'm looking after her?' said Audrey sharply.

'Of course I'm not,' said Ruth. 'But we have to be firm.'

'She eats whatever I give her during the day . . . all good nourishing food.'

Ruth was seething but stayed silent to prevent Jenny from hearing any more bickering. When Audrey went against Ruth's wishes and gave Jenny the cake, Ruth almost exploded but managed to contain her rage. However, as soon as her mother left the room to get ready for work at the Rose and Crown, where she did a shift every Friday and Saturday evening, Ruth followed her upstairs to her bedroom.

'How am I ever going to win any respect from my daughter if you constantly disregard everything I say in front of her?' she demanded as her mother sat at the dressing table putting on lipstick.

Audrey turned scarlet, green eyes shining with angry tears in her freckled face. Although a warm-hearted, gregarious woman, she tended to be sensitive and was already feeling emotional because the twins had upset her.

'I've done everything I possibly can for you and Jenny,' she said defensively, her voice wobbling.

'I know that, Mum, and I'm very grateful.'

'What did you know about bringing up a child when you had Jenny?' she continued as though Ruth hadn't spoken. 'Bugger all, that's what. You were still just a kid yourself.'

'That didn't stop me wanting to be a mother to her,' said Ruth, feeling sick, tears welling up inside her. 'But you've never let me take my proper role. I'm twenty-one now and you still treat me as Jenny's big sister.'

'I do my best for both of you,' said Audrey, deeply hurt by the criticism. 'If my best ain't good enough for you, then you'd better stay home from work and look after Jenny yourself.'

'I can't afford to, Mum, you know that.'

'I didn't ask you to go out and get pregnant when you were sixteen,' said her mother, her neck suffused with red blotches as she said things she didn't mean in the heat of the moment. 'But since that's what happened, we've all done what we can to help. The least you can do is to stop being so ungrateful.'

This kind of conversation always ended in the same way, with both of them close to tears and Ruth feeling guilty.

'Mum, I do appreciate everything you do for me, it's just that . . .'

'Oh, go downstairs and see to your daughter,' Audrey interrupted sharply. 'And leave me to get ready for work.'

'I didn't mean to hurt you . . . you do a wonderful job, but . . .'

'There's always a but with you, isn't there?' said Audrey coldly.

'I just want to be allowed to be my daughter's mother, that's all.'

'Go downstairs and get on with being her mother then, and leave me alone!'

With a grinding ache in the pit of her stomach, Ruth left the room.

Audrey left number four Nutley Road and headed towards the Green, past rows of Victorian terraces, weaving her way through gangs of children and narrowly missing a football in her face.

At forty-five she was an impressive figure, tall and busty with green eyes and red hair which she wore in a bubble cut. Tonight she was wearing a navy and white fitted dress and white high-heeled shoes. It was important to make the best of herself for her job at the pub, the punters expected it.

Beneath her smart exterior, however, she was feeling utterly wretched and finding it difficult to hold back the tears. She was certainly in no condition to go to work since a barmaid was supposed to be a cheering influence. Reaching the main road, she crossed over to the Green and sat down on a bench to calm herself, smarting at the memory of the things she'd said to her beloved Ruth. Why had she hurt her when that was the last thing she'd intended?

With a shaking hand she lit a cigarette, drawing on it deeply, only vaguely aware of the people around her on this triangular piece of common land. At this time of the evening most people were at home having their tea. There was a tramp lying flat on the grass under a tree, some boys kicking a ball about, a stray dog sniffing around the litter bin and a couple of young women playing tennis in the courts.

Mulling over what Ruth had said, she could see that she did have a valid point. Jenny had always been the family's baby rather than Ruth's daughter, which was perhaps inevitable given the circumstances. But, yes, Audrey did spoil her granddaughter, if she was perfectly honest.

Her thoughts drifted back to that terrible day when Ruth had told her she was pregnant; it had been all the more of a shock because Ruth hadn't even had a steady boyfriend at the time.

She had insisted that the pregnancy was not a result of rape. She'd told them the name of the person responsible and said he'd gone abroad to live and couldn't be contacted, which was probably just as well with Dan and the twins after his blood. But more than that she wouldn't say. Nothing would persuade her to talk further about Jenny's father.

Although Audrey and Dan had rallied round their daughter, they had both been bitterly disappointed that she'd not been able to finish her education. They'd been so proud when she'd got a place at grammar school. It had given the whole family a boost to have an academic in their midst. The twins, bless 'em, didn't have an intellectual thought between them. Audrey sighed deeply, recalling how Ruth's promising future had all ended in disgrace.

It had seemed sensible for Audrey to look after the baby while Ruth went out to work. She was at home during the day anyway and Ruth needed to be earning. Audrey's only stipulation was that she should be able to continue with her Friday and Saturday evening shift at the Rose and Crown.

Money wasn't her motivation in this. Dan earned a reasonable wage as a metal worker in a factory and the twins paid their way at home. But working as a barmaid for a few hours a week was Audrey's escape from domesticity and she needed it, especially after Jenny was born. As much as she loved her, it was exhausting looking after a young baby again after such a long time. A few hours a week in the convivial atmosphere behind the bar revitalised her.

The argument with Ruth came back to her mind and fresh tears formed. The truth of the matter was that Ruth needed a home of her own in which to bring up her daughter. She needed a husband too. But what chance did she have of either? She couldn't afford a place of her own and there weren't many men around who were willing to take on a woman with a ruined reputation and a young child.

Audrey didn't seem to be having much luck in getting her children married and settled down. The twins seemed doomed to remain bachelors. What woman would want to marry a man who always wanted to be with his brother?

Oh, well, she couldn't sit here all night brooding or they'd wonder where she'd got to at the pub. She stood up and stubbed out her cigarette, blew her nose and headed for the Rose and Crown, resolving to make her peace with Ruth as soon as she got home.

The house was empty except for Ruth and Jenny who was asleep in bed. The twins had gone out chasing women at the Hammersmith Palais and Ruth's father had gone for a pint at the Rose and Crown as he always did on a Saturday night when he waited for his wife to finish work and walked her home.

Ruth was curled up in an armchair in the living room staring at the black and white images on the television set and seeing nothing. As much as she enjoyed having the house to herself, she couldn't help thinking that not many single women of her age would be at home alone on a Saturday night. Kitty certainly wouldn't be. She would have a date of some sort.

She wondered what Jenny's father was doing now. She doubted if he would be spending Saturday night on his own. Not someone like him. Thoughts of him stirred her emotions and set her pulses racing – even now, after five years. She knew she would never see him again but she would not forget him. How could she when she saw him every day in her daughter? She had secretly wept for him but she hadn't blamed him or been bitter. Why should she? He was the loser. He didn't have Jenny.

Her thoughts drifted back to the earlier tension within the family. Her mother was a well-meaning soul who did her best in an almost impossible situation for which Ruth was to blame. Ruth hated to hurt her but sometimes she had to, for Jenny's sake.

It occurred to her then that a different sort of woman from her mother might see her offspring as a collective disappointment, having sons who were incapable of staying out of trouble and a daughter who had presented her with a bastard grandchild.

Just allowing the word to take shape in her mind stabbed at Ruth's heart. It also forced her to face up to the fact that that was how the outside world regarded her daughter.

What did the future hold for Jenny? At present she was safe in the bosom of a loving family, sheltered from the harsh reality of life outside this house. But next year she would be going to school. The family couldn't protect her then from the cruelty of playground talk.

Ruth's head throbbed from the tension of the day and worry for the future. She deeply regretted the trouble and disappointment she had already caused her parents, and was desperately anxious about the agonies yet to come for her daughter, growing up in a world that had no place for someone who didn't slot neatly into the established order.

Suddenly a burst of spirit shone through Ruth's gloom. Being negative wasn't going to help. She must concentrate all her energies into easing Jenny's path through life and making sure she had plenty of joy and opportunity. Somehow, too, she must make amends to her parents for disappointing them so badly.

Chapter Two

On Friday afternoons before the shop got busy with prescriptions from the late surgeries, Mr Grover made up enough basic medicines from his own formulae to last about a week. The liquid ingredients for the nostrums were carefully measured in a large jug and poured into huge brown Winchester bottles. Ointments were also produced and stored in big jars. If there was time, non-prescription tablets were counted into small bottles ready for sale.

In between attending to customers, Ruth assisted him in this operation. She'd become so familiar with the procedure she could make up standard cough and stomach medicine herself, though the law said that Mr Grover had to be present to supervise. She found this work most interesting, possibly because chemistry and biology had been her best subjects at school.

One warm Friday afternoon in late summer when they were busy with the nostrums in the dispensary, Mr Grover received a telephone call from the estate agent asking if he could bring a prospective buyer to view the property.

As the shop had been on the market for some time and Mr Grover was impatient to retire, he told the agent he could bring his client around as soon as he liked.

'It isn't really convenient having someone nosing around when the shop's open for business,' he confessed to Ruth. 'It's unsettling for the customers and difficult for us to concentrate. But the chap wants to see the business in action, apparently. The agent says he's a qualified pharmacist and not just a businessman looking for an investment.'

'Sounds promising.'

'Mmm, that's what I thought, so let's hope he likes what he sees.'

'I'm sure he will,' she assured him, hiding her own feelings in her eagerness to reassure an old man who needed to take things easy. 'A thriving little business like this will soon be snapped up.'

They were just finishing the weekly nostrums when the sound of the bell sent Ruth hurrying into the shop, her dark good looks emphasised by her starched white overall. There was a sudden flurry of business – a woman for a bottle of Dettol, another for some Drene shampoo and a home perm kit which they didn't stock, and an elderly lady who wanted something for an eye irritation.

'I'll ask Mr Grover to come and have a chat with you,' said Ruth kindly, nodding towards one of the chairs they kept dotted about the shop for customers' use. 'Have a seat. He won't be long.'

When Ruth returned from the dispensary with her employer, the shop was packed to the doors as doctors' waiting rooms emptied. While Mr Grover dealt with the eye irritation, Ruth worked her way through the queue until she came to a smartly dressed man carrying an attaché case who told her he was from the estate agent's.

'Oh, yes, we are expecting you,' she said courteously.

Turning to the man beside him, the agent explained, 'This is Mr Paterson. He's come to have a look at the property.'

Her eyes widened in surprise for Mr Paterson was very different from her current employer. He was youngish and slim with rich brown hair, razor cut in the latest Italian style, and compelling shandy-coloured eyes. Stylishly dressed in a pale grey continental cut suit and dazzling white shirt, he was a knock-out. Probably in his late twenties, guessed Ruth.

'Is anything the matter?' he enquired, looking at her

with a lazy smile. 'Have I got cabbage on my teeth or something?'

'Sorry,' said Ruth, embarrassingly aware of her scrutiny and adding rather unnecessarily, because she was flustered, 'I'm Mr Grover's assistant. My name's Ruth.'

'Glad to meet you, Ruth. I'm Larry,' he said easily.

'Pleased to meet you.' Ruth was stiff with embarrassment. 'I'll go and tell Mr Grover that you're here.'

She hurried into the dispensary to get her employer who asked her to hold the fort while he paid attention to the visitors, which she did with her usual pleasant efficiency. She was heartened by the fact that the prospective buyer was alone. The presence of a wife would almost certainly mean the end of Ruth's employment here.

She'd only been taken on in the first place because Mr Grover's wife had died. This shop didn't have the volume of business to warrant two full-time assistants as well as the owner. But surely if there was a Mrs Paterson and she was going to be working with her husband in the shop, she would have come with him to look at the place? Knowing that her future here hung in the balance, Ruth's nerves were jangling.

Audrey and her granddaughter were queueing at the greengrocery stall in the market for the weekend fruit and vegetables. The weather was hot and sticky; not a breath of wind stirred the trees on the Green or the shop awnings. Fat bluebottles buzzed greedily around the nearby cooked meats stall and the greengrocer was fighting a losing battle swatting the wasps away from his juicy ripe plums. The market was swarming with people and queues trailed from every stall. The pungent smell of fish, fruit, rotting cabbages and cheap perfume hung heavy in the stagnant air.

'I wanna go home, Gran,' said Jenny, who was too hot and bored with dragging round the shops in the Friday afternoon crowds.

'Not long now, love,' said Audrey, who had also had enough and was dying to get home for a cup of tea and a sit down.

'I'm hungry.'

'I'll get you something from the cake shop when we've finished here,' she said because she always treated Jenny to something nice when they were out shopping.

'Can I go and look at the toy stall while I'm waiting?'

'No, not now, darlin'. You stay here with me in case I lose you in the crowds. Gran won't be a minute.'

Slowly they inched towards the front of the queue, Audrey clutching a shopping bag in one hand and Jenny's hand in the other. She amused herself by watching a trader demonstrating a supposedly 'magic' kitchen appliance and gathering a lot of interest. Another spieler was working the crowd with artifacts at 'give away' prices. Several of Audrey's acquaintances passed by and stopped to exchange pleasantries.

'Yes, love, what can I do for you?' asked the stall holder as her turn came at last.

'Two pounds o' carrots, please, and a cauliflower,' she said, letting go of Jenny's hand for a moment while she pointed to the one she had chosen and opened her shopping bag ready to fill it with her purchases. 'That one there . . . that's it.'

'The caulies are lovely today.'

'Yeah, they look nice,' she agreed. 'Just the job to go with the Sunday joint.'

'Anything else, love?'

'Yeah, I've a list as long as my arm today,' she said. 'I need a couple o' pound of apples and plums and some . . .'

She looked sideways, instinctively checking on Jenny, her heart lurching when the child wasn't by her side. Don't panic, she told herself, scanning the immediate vicinity, she'll only have wandered over to the toy stall.

'Your apples, love . . .'

But Audrey had gone, pushing through the crowds to the toy stall only to find that Jenny wasn't there. Frantic, she asked the nearby stall holders if they'd seen her. No one had. Someone's gone off with her, she thought, paralysed with fear and damp with sweat. Forcing her legs to move, she hurried to the end of the market then turned and headed back in the other direction towards the Uxbridge Road, searching the crowds for a mop of golden hair.

'Wotcha, Audrey,' said a neighbour. 'How's it going?'

'Have you seen young Jenny anywhere?' she gasped.

'Yeah, she's outside the cake shop, looking in the window,' she said. 'I thought you were inside and she was waiting for you.'

'Oh, thank God.'

Audrey was weak with relief as she dashed past the shops behind the market stalls, passing a butcher's, a greetings card shop, an emporium selling leather goods, a greasy cafe exhaling the steamy odour of fried onions. Sounds buffeted her: the shouts of the traders; the clamour of the punters. A tube train rumbling overhead on the viaduct alongside the market seemed to beat through her brain like a hammer blow.

She almost shouted for joy when she saw Jenny's blonde head bobbing through the crowds just past the cake shop.

'Jenny!' she called. 'Jenny . . .'

Apparently oblivious of her grandmother's calls, the child headed on towards the main road. Even from behind, Audrey could see that she was bewildered. She was peering this way and that in search of her grandmother. By the time Audrey emerged, panting, from the market, she'd almost caught up with her.

'Jenny,' she called again, just yards away from her now.

But the volume of the street noise drowned her cries. Sick with fear, Audrey moved even faster to get to Jenny before she reached the kerb, terrified that in her anxiety she would forget what she'd been taught about the road. She was almost within touching distance of her when the worst happened – Jenny stepped out.

'Come back, Jenny!' screamed her grandmother.

But the child carried on to the other side, Audrey's voice obliterated by the roar of traffic. Suddenly there was a screech of brakes as a car pulled up sharp and Jenny fell to the ground, disappearing under the bonnet.

Larry Paterson was certainly showing a serious interest in the business, Ruth noticed. He'd spent a long time in the shop and dispensary, thoroughly inspected the small staffroom, the office and stockroom, and was now upstairs looking at the living accommodation with Mr Grover while Ruth took care of things down here.

A couple of local yobs came in, swaggered noisily over to the counter and asked for a packet of contraceptives. Guessing that their main reason for the purchase was to embarrass her, Ruth was determined not to give them that satisfaction. Ignoring their puerile sniggering, she opened a drawer under the counter where these items were discreetly stored and took a packet out, put it into a paper bag and handed it to the youth who had made the request. She took his money and handed him his change with steely composure, bracing herself for the vulgar remark she knew would come.

'You wouldn't have been left holding the baby if your boyfriend had had some of these,' he said with an insolent grin.

'Get out!'

'That's what you should have said to him,' said his companion, and they left the shop roaring with laughter.

Ruth felt sick. This sort of thing still upset her even though she was used to it. Realising that Larry Paterson had come into the shop from the door behind the counter, and must have heard everything, only exacerbated her humiliation.

'Just some local riff-raff,' she explained, her cheeks burning. 'They'll say anything to draw attention to themselves.'

Before he had time to reply, a neighbour of Ruth's, Mrs Barton, came into the shop.

'Well, well, I didn't expect to see you here,' she said.

'Why not?'

'Because I thought you'd be at the hospital, of course.'

'Hospital?' she said, her heart beating wildly.

The woman's eyes gleamed with relish. She was the neighbourhood gossip and enjoyed nothing better than being the bearer of dramatic news.

'Your Jenny's been knocked down by a car,' she informed Ruth gravely. 'They've taken her away in an ambulance.'

Without even stopping to remove her overall or tell Mr Grover she was leaving, Ruth rushed to the staffroom for her handbag and tore out of the shop like a woman possessed.

'She's a bit shaken up but apart from a few bruises and a grazed knee where she hit the ground, she's fine,' said the doctor an hour or so later in the casualty ward of Hammersmith Hospital where Jenny was lying on a bed, having been examined and had a dressing put on her knee.

Ruth and her mother were with her, Ruth holding her hand and stroking her hair to soothe her. Audrey was standing aside, her face ashen and tear-stained. Seeing Jenny fall in front of that car had been the worst moment of her life.

'Thank God for that,' said Ruth.

'She's a very lucky girl to have got off so lightly, Mrs Brooks,' the doctor said with a hint of admonition.

31

'Miss,' corrected Ruth.

'Sorry, I just assumed . . .'

'Most people do, don't worry about it.' She had far too much on her mind to care about that slip and had only corrected him out of habit.

'The driver of the car must have excellent responses to have been able to pull up as suddenly as he did,' the doctor remarked.

'Yes,' agreed Ruth. 'It was a good job he wasn't going at any sort of speed.'

'Because it's a built up area,' muttered Audrey numbly.

'Fortunate indeed,' agreed the doctor.

'I've told my daughter over and over again not to go in the road,' said Ruth, her voice thick with anguish. 'I've taught her her road drill, time after time.'

'I'm sure you have but she obviously didn't remember it today.'

'No.' There was an awkward pause. 'So can we take her home?'

'There's no reason why not,' he said. 'Keep your eye on her for a day or two, though. She might have a delayed reaction.' He turned his attention to Jenny, frowning. 'And no more running into the road, young lady.'

She shook her head sheepishly. She was very pale, obviously still in a state of shock. From what they could make out, she'd been in a panic when she'd lost her grandmother in the market and had been trying to find her way home when she'd run into the road.

'I'll put her on a lead if necessary to stop her wandering,' said Audrey, smiling weakly.

'Good idea,' said the doctor, without smiling. 'She might not be so lucky a second time.'

Later on that day the incident was given a thorough post-mortem as the Brooks family had tea in the living room which they used as a dining room too, the best sitting room being at the back of the house. The events of the day had been too much for Jenny who was fast asleep in bed.

'The driver wasn't to blame at all, then?' said Dan.

'Definitely not,' declared Audrey, who thought she was to blame for the accident and had been castigating herself ever since.

'He must have been tearing his hair out, though, until he knew she was all right,' said Dan, dipping a piece of sausage into a pool of brown sauce.

'Yeah, the poor bloke was in a terrible state,' said Audrey, too upset to eat much but attempting some mashed potato. 'I've never seen anyone as relieved as he was when we told him she wasn't badly hurt.' She forced a grin. 'Apart from Ruth, that is, when she got to the hospital and found out that Jenny wasn't badly injured.'

'Phew, you're not kidding!' she said emphatically. 'When Mrs Barton came into the shop and said Jenny had been knocked down, I nearly passed out cold.'

'I bet you did,' said her father.

'It was enough to give anyone a heart attack, hearing about it like that, Ruth,' declared Audrey. 'I intended to ring you at the shop from the hospital as soon as I had any news. Trust Mrs Barton to beat me to it, the interferin' old cow!'

'I just rushed out without even stopping to tell Mr Grover,' said Ruth, remembering. 'There was a prospective buyer there too.' She made a face. 'If that one goes ahead and buys it, I'll be out of a job for sure. I mean . . . an unmarried mother is bad enough, but one who goes off and leaves the shop unattended is beyond the pale.'

'Mr Grover thinks very highly of you, I do know that,' said her father encouragingly. 'A lot of people use his shop rather than the other chemists in the area because you are so helpful and have such a nice way with you. He told me so himself when I met him in the street the other day.'

'That's nice to know,' she said, smiling. 'Anyway, if I do lose the job, I'll just have to get another one sharpish. What happened today couldn't be helped.'

Audrey let out a deep eloquent breath and held her head as though in terrible pain. 'Jesus . . . when I think what might have happened to Jenny. And all because of me.'

'Now then, love,' said Dan. 'No point in blaming yourself.'

'I was looking after her,' Audrey said grimly. 'She was in my care.'

'Stop tormenting yourself, Mum,' said Ruth. 'It's all over now.'

'I shan't let go of her hand for even a second when we're out in future,' she announced.

'You have to do your shopping,' said Ruth sensibly, even though her protective instincts were in overdrive. 'We'll have to ram it home to her about not going into the road.'

'Phew, I don't think I can face going to work,' said Audrey. 'I feel too drained.'

'Have a night off then,' suggested Dan. 'I'll pop round the pub and let the guvnor know as soon as I've finished my tea.'

'Thanks, Dan,' she said, relaxing slightly. 'Tell them I'll be in tomorrow night as usual.'

'Will do.'

Audrey turned her attention to the twins. 'I suppose you two are going out boozing, as it's Friday night?'

'No, we've got a heavy date as it happens,' boasted Ray, the leader of the two inseparables.

'We?' said Audrey, narrowing her eyes suspiciously. 'I hope that doesn't mean you're both going on the same date.'

'We are, you know,' Jack informed her, stifling a grin.

'You're both taking one girl out!' exclaimed Audrey, sighing and rolling her eyes in disapproval. 'Oh, really! Surely even you two can see that that's taking brotherly love too far?'

'There are *two* girls.' Ray exchanged glances with his brother and they both burst out laughing. 'They're twins, as a matter of fact.'

'I don't believe it!' said his mother, smiling with relief.

'At last you've found the perfect solution to your love life,' giggled Ruth. 'A permanent foursome. You two need twins or best friends to go out with. At least they can keep each other company while you two enjoy yourselves.'

'That's probably the only way I'll ever get you off my hands,' said Audrey, her sense of humour returning after the trauma of the day. 'If a pair of twins take you on.'

'Do you take this man . . . and his brother . . . as your lawful wedded husband?' laughed Ruth.

But something had caught Ray's attention in the street and he was staring out of the window.

'Blimey, now that's what I really call a motor car,' he said as a silver-grey Lagonda drew up outside the house 'You don't see many of those round here.'

'Cor, I'll say you don't!' agreed Jack.

'Who do we know in this street who's likely to have visitors who can afford one of those?' enquired Ray.

'No one that I know of,' said Dan.

'Perhaps our landlord's gone all flash and traded in his black Austin?' suggested Jack lightly.

Ray's curiosity got the better of him and he stood up and went closer to the window, peering out from behind the net curtains.

'Well, we'll soon find out who it is 'cos he's coming in here.'

'He never is!' said Audrey.

Even as she spoke there was a knock at the front door.

Ray went to answer it and they all waited to find out who the stranger was. When he came back he looked puzzled.

'He says his name is Paterson,' he told them in a hushed voice. 'He's come to see Ruth. I asked him to wait in the other room.'

'I hope you offered him a cup of tea?' said Audrey.

'Give us a chance, Mum.'

'Paterson,' muttered Ruth thoughtfully. 'That's the name of the chap who was looking at the shop this afternoon.' She stood up, her cheeks flaming with agitation. 'But what on earth does he want with me?'

'Dunno, Princess,' said Ray. 'So I suggest you go into the other room, find out and put us all out of our misery.'

'And don't forget to offer him a cup of tea,' said Audrey.

'Oh, do give over, Mum,' replied Ruth impatiently.

Larry Paterson was sitting in an armchair when Ruth entered the room but stood up immediately and smiled at her.

'Hello,' she said enquiringly.

'Hi.'

'You must have thought it very bad of me this afternoon, rushing off and leaving no one to cover for me in the shop,' she said, wondering why she felt the need to justify herself since he wasn't her employer and she'd already apologised to Mr Grover on the telephone.

'It was perfectly understandable under the circumstances.' He looked concerned. 'How is your little girl now?'

'In bed and fast asleep, with nothing more than a few bruises and a grazed knee – after frightening us all to death.'

'I'm so glad.'

She narrowed her eyes quizzically. 'Mr Grover told you where I live, did he?'

'Yes, I called at his place just now on a matter of

business,' he explained. 'As you're so near, I thought I'd drop in.'

'That's nice of you.'

'If you hadn't left in such a hurry this afternoon, I'd have taken you to the hospital in my car,' he said as though to prolong the conversation. 'It was parked just around the corner.'

'I didn't stop to think.'

'No, of course you didn't. Anyway, after you left I made myself useful in the shop,' he explained. 'I don't think Mr Grover is quite up to running the place on his own.'

'It's difficult with the dispensary and the shop to look after single-handed,' she said defensively. 'He gets quite flustered if I'm not there.'

'So I noticed.'

'Lucky for us you had the time to stay on and help out,' she said.

'I'm on a few days' leave at the moment,' he explained. 'I'm the manager of the Oxford Street branch of Berry's the chemist's.'

'I see.' She paused thoughtfully. 'So did you come especially to ask about Jenny?'

'Yes.'

'That's very kind of you and I appreciate it.'

'Not at all.'

Ruth became acutely aware of her surroundings. The sitting room was nicely furnished and comfortable. With five wage packets coming into the house every week, the Brooks family certainly weren't paupers. But they were ordinary working-class people and this room reflected that with its bulky furniture, polished lino floor with rugs, and an assortment of cheap ornaments. Ruth was so used to it, she hadn't noticed just how humdrum it was until Larry Paterson's stylishness made it seem noticeably dowdy and lacking in taste.

Audrey came into the room and Ruth introduced them.

When her mother offered him a cup of tea, Ruth hoped he wouldn't accept. He was so out of place in her home she felt uncomfortable and couldn't wait for him to leave.

'Mr Paterson has to go now, Mum,' she said hopefully. 'He only called in to find out how Jenny is.'

'How kind,' said Audrey, looking at him with undisguised admiration for he was a very impressive figure. 'Are you sure you haven't time for a cup of tea, Mr Paterson?'

Much to Ruth's annoyance, he said, 'I'd love one, thank you, Mrs Brooks.'

'Sit yourself down then, love,' she said. 'I'll only be a minute.'

Having finished their meal, Ruth's father and the twins came in to give the visitor the once over. Ruth made the introductions, thinking how rough and ready the men in her family looked compared to him. Not that she thought this in a disparaging way. Quite the opposite, in fact. Larry Paterson was the odd one out here. Her father and brothers were working men who'd been in a factory all day, big, muscular and wearing basic working clothes, while Larry Paterson looked as though he'd just walked out of the window of a men's outfitters. Compared to them he looked rather effeminate with his perfect features and well-cut hair.

'So, you're thinking of buying Mr Grover's shop then?' said Ruth's father.

'That's right.'

'Grover's a nice old boy,' said Dan, adding pointedly, 'He thinks the world of Ruth, you know. Relies on her completely. He told me what a good worker she is only the other day.'

Larry looked at Ruth who had turned scarlet at this blatant attempt to promote her before a possible new employer.

'I'm sure he does,' said Larry, giving her a sympathetic smile as though guessing how she was feeling.

'Aren't you supposed to be going out, Dad?' she reminded him meaningfully, dreading that he would stay and embarrass her further. 'I thought you were going to tell Mum's boss that she isn't going into work tonight?'

'Yeah, I am . . . but not yet awhile.'

'Oh.'

'That's a classic piece o' gear you've got outside,' said Ray to Larry.

'Pardon?' said Larry, baffled for a moment by the jargon. 'Oh, you mean the car.'

'What else?'

'Do you like it?'

'Do mice like cheese?'

'It isn't bad, is it?'

'*Not bad?*' exclaimed Jack. 'It's a bleedin' masterpiece!'

'Jack and I are saving for a car, aren't we, bruv?' said Ray.

'Yeah. It won't be anythin' like yours, though. We might manage a second-hand Ford on HP if we can cut down on the booze and get enough for the deposit.'

'What a good idea, to get one between you,' said Larry, who didn't let the fact that he was out of his depth with these tough men impair his ability to charm. 'So long as you don't fall out over whose turn it is to use it.'

'Not much chance of that,' put in Audrey, bustling on to the scene with a tea tray. 'These two are practically joined at the hip, so taking turns won't come into it.'

Larry laughed heartily and put them all at their ease. 'I'm sure that isn't true, is it, boys?' he said lightly.

'Almost,' said Dan, making himself comfortable on the sofa near the visitor.

As her mother settled into a chair, too, and looked set to make Larry Paterson's visit into a full-blown social event, Ruth's heart sank.

'I thought you two were going out?' she said to her brothers.

'And so we are.' Ray grinned knowingly at Larry. 'We've got a date with a couple of right little crackers.'

'Oh, well, don't let me hold you up then.'

'I suppose we'd better go and get ready, slap on some of the old aftershave,' said Ray. 'To help us get lucky.'

Ruth thought she would die at this vulgarity.

Ray thrust his hand forward as though Larry was an old friend. Smiling, Larry stood up to shake it.

'Well, it's bin really nice meeting you, mate,' said Ray, shaking his hand with such vigorous matiness, Ruth could almost hear Larry's bones cracking. 'Might see you again sometime.'

'You might at that.' Larry shook hands with Jack too. 'Well, have a good time, boys.'

'It's Friday night,' said Ray with a meaningful grin.

'Say no more then, eh?' said Larry.

'That's right,' agreed Jack.

Much to Ruth's relief, Larry didn't re-establish himself in the armchair. He finished his tea standing up and said, 'Well, I must be making tracks. Mustn't take up any more of your time.'

'Stay as long as you like, son,' invited Dan warmly. 'We enjoy company, don't we, Aud?'

'Ooh, not half,' agreed his wife. 'Another cup of tea?'

'You're very kind but I really must go,' said Larry, to Ruth's great relief.

She went to the front door with him to see him out.

'Thank you for coming,' she said. 'I appreciate your concern about Jenny.'

'It was a pleasure.' He looked at her thoughtfully. 'Actually . . . while I'm here, perhaps I should tell you that I've decided to go ahead with the purchase of Grover's shop.'

'You have?'

'Yes. That's why I called on Mr Grover this evening,' he explained. 'I wanted to clear up a few points. Having done that successfully, I've made my decision.'

Her heart lurched.

'Oh.'

'And I'd very much like you to stay on and work for me.'

'Really?'

'Yes, really,' he confirmed. 'So, what's your answer?'

'Thank you, I'd be delighted,' she said, smiling.

Her job was safe! He couldn't possibly know what a blessed relief that was.

Chapter Three

Driving home to his flat in the West End, Larry Paterson was feeling pleased with himself, having decided to go ahead with the purchase of Grover's shop, and also having secured the services of the old man's assistant.

Larry knew the value of Ruth Brooks. Having seen her in action, he believed Grover when he said she was good for business. As well as being popular with the customers, she was apparently a favourite with the local GPs, with whom she was in regular contact regarding prescription queries. Apparently they directed their patients towards Grover's.

Ruth had a way with her, there was no doubt about that. Her lustrous dark looks hadn't eluded him either, for Larry had a keen eye for a pretty face. But her usefulness to him as an employee was his main concern since he was already fixed up in the personal department.

He needed an employee who would work hard and take responsibility. Ruth Brooks would do both, he was certain of that. If he was any judge, she would willingly take on more than was normally expected of a shop assistant. Her 'special circumstances', as Grover put it, would make the job so essential to her she'd do everything she could to hang on to it. She was obviously intelligent and accustomed to assisting in the dispensary, which would be a great help to him too. The more work she took off his shoulders, the better he would like it.

Being the mother of a young child could make her unreliable but he was confident that her other attributes would more than compensate for that.

All things considered, it had been a good day. He was glad he'd acted on impulse and gone to visit Ruth Brooks at home. It had got their working relationship off to a good start. She seemed awfully nice and he was looking forward to working with her.

It would be good to be his own boss at last. Thank God he could give notice at Berry's now that his decision was made. Even as manager of his own branch, he'd still had to report to his superiors about the slightest thing.

Fortunately, his father had rescued him from this unsatisfactory state of affairs by dying and leaving him enough money to set up on his own. Larry would have been even happier if the legacy had been sufficient for him not to have to bother about earning a living but his father hadn't been *that* rich. Anyway, running his own show with the help of an industrious and grateful assistant had to be a vast improvement.

The son of a stockbroker, Larry had never had to struggle for anything. He'd received an excellent private education which had secured him a place at university, where he'd had a fabulous time socially and, by some miracle, still managed to get his pharmacy degree. He'd walked straight into a job at Berry's because his father had contacts on the board. Similarly, his promotion to manager had been more or less automatic.

His parents had been well into their forties when Larry had been born and his widowed mother now lived quietly by the sea in Sussex, playing bridge with her cronies most of the time. She was a great old girl of whom he was very fond, especially as she made so few demands on him.

He viewed the future with optimism. Grover's shop should give him a reasonable income with no one but himself to answer to. The business had the potential to do a whole lot better than it was doing now, which appealed to him so long as it didn't cause him too much effort. Although Larry liked to maintain a certain standard of living, he found work very much of an inconvenience.

Ruth could hardly believe how much her working life had altered since Larry Paterson had taken over from Mr Grover in the autumn.

Now, as Christmas approached, regular customers might have been forgiven for thinking they'd come into the wrong shop. The store that had once been gloomy and uninviting now sparkled with a festive welcome and a wide range of attractive goods for sale.

Having been given a completely free hand in the shop, including the layout and the ordering, Ruth had reorganised everything so that standard items like cough sweets and corn plasters no longer dominated the display area. This gave her space for toiletries and cosmetics. Naturally, they still stocked a wide range of patent medicines but they were now on the counter and the shelves behind it.

In the centre of the shop was a table covered with Christmas paper and gift sets. Bath cubes wrapped in cellophane, boxed talcum powder and soap sets, perfume presented in Christmas crackers – some boxed by the manufacturers, other packed by Ruth herself. There was also a glass display cabinet containing cosmetics.

The takings had been boosted by these new innovations, as had Ruth's self-esteem. Every day Larry, as he insisted she called him, gave her new responsibilities on which she thrived. Instead of being merely a shop assistant, she was now working on her own initiative and practically running the retail side of things. Her sound ideas and hard work brought in so much extra business, they'd even had to take on a Saturday girl and Larry was talking about a part-timer in the New Year.

As well as trusting her to deal with wholesalers and to do more in the dispensary than she'd ever done with Mr Grover, he'd even asked for her help with the paperwork.

It was a pity she wasn't a qualified pharmacist because she wasn't allowed to dispense even the most basic medicine or sell it if he wasn't on the premises.

Although she worked extremely hard all day, Ruth still found it necessary to stay late at the shop quite often, filling shelves and clearing paperwork. This meant she'd had to make arrangements with the family to look after Jenny until she got home. But they were so delighted with her new interest in the job they were only too happy to help.

Now, on a December morning, she took a prescription to Larry in the dispensary, gratified to see a queue of people waiting to pay for purchases from the gift table.

When the shop eventually emptied, Ruth made some coffee in the staffroom and took a cup into the dispensary. Larry invited her to bring hers in and join him. He often did this. It gave them a chance to discuss business.

'The Christmas gifts are selling like hotcakes,' she informed him brightly, perching on a stool near him at the workbench.

'So I've noticed,' he said, looking pleased. 'You're doing a great job, Ruth. I don't know what I'd do without you.'

'I'm sure you'd manage,' she said modestly, though flattered by his appreciation. 'But thanks anyway.'

'Making up some of the gift sets yourself was a brilliant idea,' he complimented her. 'You're proving to be quite a businesswoman.'

'I'm glad of the chance to put my ideas into practice,' she said. 'Mr Grover never let me do anything different. He wanted the shop to stay as it was.'

'That's understandable at his age,' said Larry. 'He was winding down.'

'The more I get to know about pharmacy, the more interesting I find it,' she remarked casually. 'Maybe I would have gone in for it if I'd stayed on at school. I was always

46

good at science. Perhaps one day I'll do a course as a dispenser.'

'Oh, really?' Larry wasn't sure if he liked that idea. Although it would be a tremendous help to him if she could do more in the dispensary, a qualification might dampen her enthusiasm for mundane shop tasks like shelf filling and sweeping the floor. 'I couldn't spare you to go to school on any sort of day release scheme, though. Not with there being just the two of us here.'

'I realise that,' she said. 'I meant evening classes.'

'Oh, I see.'

'I wouldn't be able to take on anything like that for ages yet, though,' she explained. 'Not until Jenny is quite a bit older. My spare time is all taken up with her.'

'Yes, I suppose it would be.' He took a sip of his coffee and looked at her thoughtfully. 'And on the subject of your spare time, I appreciate your working late so often this last couple of months.' His wide mouth curved into a devastating smile. 'And I shall be increasing your salary in the New Year as a token of my appreciation.'

'Oh, that is good news,' she said, beaming, her cheeks flushed with pleasure. 'Thank you very much indeed.'

'Don't mention it,' he said. 'It's no more than you deserve.'

She really was the most attractive female, he thought. Those gorgeous dark eyes played havoc with his emotions.

The shop bell tinkled.

'Oh, well, I might have known I wouldn't get to finish my coffee in peace,' she said, but went into the shop smiling – something she seemed to be doing rather a lot of lately.

'You're positively glowing,' observed Kitty when the two friends met for lunch the Saturday before Christmas. 'So . . . what's his name?'

'There isn't anyone.'

'Well, *something* must have happened to you,' said Kitty,

who hadn't seen Ruth for a while because she'd been abroad. 'I haven't seen you this happy for a very long time.'

'There isn't any one particular thing,' explained Ruth. 'But if I'm happy I suppose it must be because I'm enjoying my job so much more now.'

'And all because of the handsome Larry Paterson,' said Kitty, who had been introduced to him when she'd called at the shop to see Ruth when he'd first taken over.

'That's right. Honestly, Kit, he's given me so much more responsibility,' she said excitedly. 'It's wonderful. I'm never bored now. In fact, the days simply fly past.'

'I hope he's paying you for all the extra responsibility?'

'Yes, he's giving me a salary rise in the New Year.'

'Good.'

'He's terrific to work for,' enthused Ruth. 'I feel as though I have a completely new job.'

'And he's gorgeous with it, too,' remarked Kitty. 'And unattached. Is there any chance of your getting off with him?'

'Of course not.'

'Don't you think he's attractive then?'

'I'm not blind,' pronounced Ruth, 'but I shouldn't think he even sees me as a person. I'm simply an employee.'

'And bosses have been fancying their workers since time began,' Kitty pointed out.

'Well, he's never indicated anything of that sort to me,' she declared. 'So let's change the subject, shall we?'

'Okay.'

'How's your job?'

'Fabulous,' said Kitty. 'I'm off to Paris in January.'

'Lucky you!'

'I know.' She gave a wicked grin. 'And I've met a super new man.'

'Tell me more.'

'I met him at a party,' she said. 'Tall, dark and thirty

48

something. He's a high flyer at a merchant bank.'

'Sounds like your type.'

'My type?'

'Well-heeled.'

Kitty chuckled. 'I like to do things in style, I admit it . . . Actually, I have some other news too.'

'Oh?'

'I'm moving into a flat of my own.'

'With the new boyfriend?'

'You're joking!' she said. 'My parents would have a fit if I did that. No, it's just that I feel it's time I was out on my own. I need freedom and independence. Know what I mean?'

'*Do I?*' said Ruth with emphasis. 'I could do with some of that.'

'We've reached that age.'

'Mmm.'

They finished their mixed grills, chatting generally. Over coffee, Ruth said, 'The big news in our family is that the twins are both courting strong.'

'Get away,' said Kitty with a grin. 'I didn't think the women had been born who could prise those two apart.'

'The girls are twins too so they go out in a permanent foursome.'

Kitty's laugh soared above the general hubbub. 'How very convenient! Trust those two to get something like that organised.'

'They both seem really serious, too,' Ruth told her. 'They even brought the girls home to Sunday tea the other week.'

'Well, well, love really is in the air then,' said Kitty.

For everyone except me, thought Ruth, but said, 'Yes, it certainly seems like it.'

The next day Larry made a surprising suggestion.

'As it's Christmas and it's traditional for people who

work together to recognise the festive season, I wonder if you might like to have dinner with me tomorrow evening?'

'I'd love to,' said Ruth, more thrilled by the invitation than he could possibly imagine. Her smile faded however as she realised she couldn't accept. 'But I can't, I'm afraid.'

He looked very disappointed. 'You already have a date?'

The only dates she ever had were the sticky ones with stones in. But she just said, 'No, but I do have a young daughter.'

'I hadn't forgotten,' he said smoothly, 'but I thought perhaps your parents might babysit for you for the evening?'

'Well, I suppose they might if I were to ask them,' she told him. 'But I don't want to put on them. They do so much for me already.'

'Ah, yes, I understand,' he said, feeling more dejected than he ought.

'Thanks for asking me though,' she said graciously. 'It was a kind thought.'

'Thanks aren't necessary,' he said. 'I'm just sorry you can't make it.'

'Are you telling me that you refused an invitation out to dinner with Larry Paterson just because of Jenny?' said Audrey incredulously that evening when she and Ruth were in the kitchen washing the dishes after supper.

'That's right,' confirmed Ruth, drying a dinner plate and putting it in the wire rack over the gas stove.

'Are you soft in the head or something?'

'Come off it, Mum,' said Ruth. 'I can't just go swanning off of an evening when I have a little girl to consider.'

'You know perfectly well that we'll look after Jenny for you,' she said. 'If it happens to be when I'm out at work, your dad will do it.'

'You and Dad already do more than enough for me,'

said Ruth, whose guilt complex was more or less permanent. 'Anyway, I'm not with her all day so I like to be around for her in the evenings. I don't have any choice when I have to work late but I wouldn't feel right about leaving her if I was going out for pleasure.'

'You could put her to bed before you go out,' suggested Audrey. 'It won't make any difference to her whether you're in or out since she'll be asleep.'

'Mmm, I suppose I could do that,' said Ruth, but she still sounded doubtful.

'When was the last time you had a night out?'

'Oh, about 1951, I think,' said Ruth with a wry grin.

'Exactly,' said Audrey, who thought it was high time her daughter had some fun. 'So if you want to accept your boss's invitation, you can go ahead with my blessing.'

'It's too late now,' she said. 'He'll have made other arrangements.'

'There's no harm in mentioning the fact that you can go after all, though, is there? Just in case he hasn't.'

'I suppose I could have a word with him about it tomorrow.'

Ruth sipped her coffee feeling pleasantly relaxed, having had several glasses of wine with her meal. They were dining in the restaurant of a West End hotel and had had a festive meal of turkey and all the trimmings.

'I'm very glad you were able to make it after all,' said Larry.

'Me too,' she replied, her eyes shining with pleasure. 'I'm having a lovely time.'

He'd seemed delighted when she'd told him she could accept his invitation after all. Finding something suitable to wear had been more of a problem because the few newish things she had were strictly practical. She had nothing dressy at all. She'd finally settled on a plain white blouse and black skirt with a red cardigan. It was a very ordinary outfit but Larry had been most complimentary about her appearance, especially her hair which fell loose to her shoulders.

She hadn't felt this lighthearted since those heady days at Redfern Grammar. She'd forgotten what it was like to have fun. Larry was very good company and Ruth felt completely at ease with him, despite their different backgrounds. The fact that it was a one-off event made it even more of a treat.

'Perhaps in the New Year we can have a sale of toiletries to boost business,' she said, eyes bright with enthusiasm as she looked at him across the table.

'Good idea.'

'Business is always very slack after Christmas.' She looked thoughtful. 'And later on, if things continue to go well, perhaps you might even consider some modernisation? Our shop fittings are positively archaic.'

'Mmm.'

'A lot of chemist's shops have streamlined, contemporary fittings these days, don't they?'

He chuckled softly. 'Ruth . . . Ruth,' he said in a way that made her feel *so very* special, 'don't you ever stop thinking about work?'

Since theirs was a working relationship, she'd assumed he'd want to talk business. But he seemed to prefer to talk about her and had asked all sorts of personal questions.

'Of course I do,' she said. 'But I thought you'd want to talk shop . . . since that's our mutual interest. I mean isn't that what this evening is all about?'

Larry knew a lot of beautiful women. His present girlfriend, Lorna, was lovely and never let him forget the power that conferred on her. So to meet a pretty girl who was unaware of her looks was a real novelty.

Much against his better judgement he was finding Ruth increasingly captivating. The fact that she had a past sharpened his interest, especially as she was so mysterious about her daughter's father, the man who could be said to have ruined her life, though Larry suspected that Ruth didn't see it that way, devoted as she was to Jenny.

There was a pluckiness about Ruth that excited him. He'd never been out with a woman who had a child before. The mere fact that she was a mother gave her an air of experience, but there was an innocence about her too, somehow.

'No, not really,' he said in answer to her question. 'This evening is about its being Christmas, and our getting to know each other better.'

'Do you make a habit of getting to know your staff personally?'

He thought about that. Lorna had been on his staff at Berry's. She still worked on the counter there. He'd had brief affairs with other subordinates too. It was a mistake for a manager to get involved in this way but he'd always been weak when it came to beautiful women. He hadn't originally intended to have anything more than a working relationship with Ruth, but the more he saw of her the more attracted to her he became. Christmas had given him the perfect opportunity to set the ball rolling.

'Not usually,' he lied with practised ease, leaning across and squeezing her hand. 'But as there's only the two of us, I think it's a good idea, don't you?'

Her mood changed instantly as the blatant suggestiveness of his action made her painfully aware of the real reason for his invitation. She was disappointed. She'd expected better of him. How could she have been so gullible?

'You've got me all wrong,' she said coldly, her eyes never leaving his face. 'Just because I got into trouble when I was at school, doesn't mean I make a habit of it.'

'Of course not,' he said with feigned affront, annoyed

with himself for rushing things. 'Have I suggested that you do?'

She finished her coffee, eyes narrowed on him suspiciously. 'Do you deny that you took me out to dinner this evening with the sole intention of sleeping with me afterwards?'

That was exactly what Larry had had in mind but he said coolly, 'I think you're the one who's made an error of judgement, Ruth. My motive in asking you out is entirely honourable.'

'Oh.' He was convincing enough for her to doubt herself and feel embarrassed. 'I'm sorry. People tend to misjudge me . . . because of my situation.'

'Are you a little over-sensitive, perhaps?' he suggested.

'Probably,' she admitted, feeling very much at a disadvantage now. 'But not without good reason. People can be very cruel.'

'Those louts who came in the day I came to view the shop, for instance?'

'I've had more than my fair share of that sort of thing, yes.'

'Well, I don't happen to have the yob mentality,' he said, sounding really offended.

'No, of course you don't.' Trust her to get it all wrong! This was what came of being so inexperienced with men. 'I really am sorry.'

'Apology accepted,' Larry said, giving her a forgiving smile, pleased with himself for using his mistake to his own advantage. 'So let's change the subject, shall we?'

She nodded and he ordered more coffee.

'Are you doing anything exciting over Christmas?' he asked.

'I find Christmas exciting in itself,' Ruth told him, relaxing again.

'Really?'

'Oh, yes,' she said exuberantly. 'Especially now that

Jenny is old enough to understand about Santa Claus. I just can't wait for Christmas morning when she opens her presents.'

He found himself unexpectedly infected by her enthusiasm. 'It sounds like fun. Kids are what Christmas is all about.'

'Definitely. It's like having a second childhood for me,' she said, 'because I live it all again through Jenny.'

'I can imagine.'

'What are you doing over the holiday?' she enquired conversationally.

'I'm spending Christmas with my mother in Sussex.'

'That will be nice,' said Ruth. 'It's a family time.'

'It certainly is,' he said, failing to mention that he'd be back in London on Boxing Day to meet up with Lorna. Given his growing attraction to Ruth, he was glad he'd kept his relationship with Lorna to himself this past few months.

'I always used to be taken to the pantomime on Boxing Day as a child,' she said wistfully. 'Jenny's getting to the age to be able to enjoy something like that now.' She paused thoughtfully. 'I think I might take her next year.'

Larry could hardly believe his ears when he heard himself saying, in an inviting manner, 'Are you doing anything special on Boxing Day this year?'

'Not really,' she said. 'Just lazing around recovering from the excesses of Christmas Day, I expect.'

'Would you and Jenny like to go to a pantomime with me?' he asked.

She stared at him in surprise.

'I could try to get tickets.'

'Well . . .' She was stunned. 'But what about your mother?'

'Oh.' He speedily gathered his wits. 'She'll probably have had more than enough of me by Boxing Day. So if you and Jenny would like to come to the panto . . .'

'I'd love to, and I'm sure Jenny would too, but I doubt if you'll get any tickets for Boxing Day this close to Christmas.'

'You just leave it to your Uncle Larry,' he said with the confidence of someone who knows that most things are obtainable, if you are prepared to pay over the odds for them.

Larry was sitting in the stalls of the London Palladium watching Norman Wisdom charm an audience as Aladdin. Sitting beside Larry was Jenny and on the other side of her Ruth, both of them enraptured by the colour and gaiety of the show.

Jenny had got a bit fidgety earlier during some topical adult jokes but for the most part she was captivated. To Larry's amazement, this gave him a great deal of pleasure. He even found himself responding to the party atmosphere in the auditorium.

His experience of children was practically nil but Jenny seemed rather a nice little thing as kids went. Since he wouldn't get anywhere with Ruth unless he got along with her daughter, it was in his interests to make a friend of Jenny which, to his astonishment, was proving to be quite easy.

He could hardly believe that he was pursuing Ruth with such ardour. It had already caused trouble with Lorna when he'd broken their date for today, even though he'd told her he had to stay on in Sussex because his mother wasn't well.

So why was he, a contented bachelor, sitting here amid a crowd of rowdy, vociferous youngsters? Why was he shouting and screaming with the rest of them, when he could be enjoying a much more peaceful and adult Boxing Day with Lorna? He glanced at Ruth, who was leaning forward slightly in her seat, her eyes fixed on the stage in concentration. His heart turned over and he knew the answer. He was falling for her in a big way, despite his good intentions. Larry's biggest problem was that he was completely in thrall to his instincts when it came to women. Once the chemistry stirred he was helpless.

As Aladdin left the stage, a troupe of glittering chorus girls danced on, high kicking and grinning in unison. The show then progressed at a fast pace in traditional style with the usual riotous audience participation and a glittering grande finale which caused a great deal of 'Ooohing' and 'aahing'. Jenny got so excited at one point, she dropped her Dolly Mixtures on the floor. Larry found himself comforting her by telling her he'd buy her some more after the show.

Ruth leaned across her daughter and put her hand on his arm. 'It's kind of you to offer but there's no need,' she whispered.

'I'd like to just the same,' he replied, burning at her touch.

When they finally emerged into the bitter streets, after he'd purchased the promised sweets in the foyer, he said, 'Well, Jenny, did you enjoy the show?'

'It was lovely, Uncle Larry,' she chirped, skipping along between them, clutching their hands. 'I liked Aladdin best.'

'Yes, he was good, wasn't he?' said Larry with a smile in his voice. 'Did you like the pretty dresses the ladies were wearing?'

'I thought they were lovely.'

'It was a wonderful afternoon, Larry,' said Ruth, smiling at him over Jenny's head. 'Thanks ever so much.'

'I'm glad you both enjoyed yourselves. I did too,' he said, holding her glance and feeling the full force of her appeal. 'And it isn't over yet. Time for refreshments, I think. I know a hotel where they do an excellent afternoon tea.'

'You're spoiling us,' said Ruth.

'It's my pleasure,' he told her, and really meant it.

* * *

'So what do you reckon Larry Paterson is up to with Ruth?' Ray Brooks asked the family at tea-time that same day.

'I'm hoping he isn't up to anything other than giving her and Jenny a pleasant afternoon out,' said Audrey sharply, passing a plate of turkey sandwiches to Jack's girlfriend Peggy, an attractive, warm-hearted blonde who fitted in very well with the Brooks family.

'That's a bit naive, innit, Mum?' remarked Ray, offering his girlfriend Pat a thick wedge of Christmas cake. 'I'd like to know exactly what he's playing at.'

'Why should he be playing at anything?' asked Pat, a mirror image of her twin sister but a bit more outspoken.

'Isn't it obvious?' said Ray. 'He's well-educated and well-off. Ruth's a hard-up unmarried mother who works for him. I mean . . . ask yourselves. Why is he bothering with her when he could have someone of his own class?'

'Ruth isn't thick,' Audrey reminded him hotly. 'She went to the Gram, remember. She can hold her own in any company.'

'Yeah. She's a clever girl, is Ruth,' agreed Dan defensively. 'She's done wonders with that shop of Paterson's. You wouldn't know it since he took over from Mr Grover.'

'Surely you're not suggesting that Larry Paterson is going out with Ruth because he's impressed with her ability to run a shop?' said Ray.

'There's no call for sarcasm,' admonished Audrey firmly. 'Anyway, he isn't going out with her, as such. He's only taken her and Jenny to a pantomime, for heaven's sake.'

'Oh, wake up, Mum. Larry Paterson's a man with an eye for the women, you can tell that by the way he dresses and the car he drives,' Jack stated categorically. 'And Ruth's a good-looking girl. It's obvious what he's got in mind. This afternoon's outing is just the beginning.'

'I thought you two seemed to like him when he first came to the house.'

'That was before he started showing a personal interest in Ruth,' said Ray.

'You shouldn't judge other people by your own standards,' said Pat. 'Not all men are just after one thing.'

'That's right. You tell him, Pat,' said Audrey, who was secretly hoping that something romantic would develop between Ruth and her boss because it would be so good for Jenny and her. 'I'm sure Larry Paterson has every intention of behaving properly towards Ruth. And it's up to us, the family, to support her if he continues to take an interest in her and wants to take her out again . . . without Jenny, perhaps, the next time.'

'Your mother's right, boys,' agreed Dan predictably.

'I agree with you too, Mrs Brooks,' said Peggy who was eager to make a friend of Audrey because she was very keen on Jack. 'It can't be easy to go out courting when you've a kiddie to look after. Jack and me don't mind baby-sitting, do we, Jack?'

'I s'pose not,' he said.

'That goes for Ray and me too,' announced Pat, who was also hoping to become part of the Brooks family before very long.

'Thanks for the support, girls,' said Audrey, delighted that the twins had found girlfriends who fitted in so well with the family and weren't afraid to speak up for themselves. Ray and Jack had calmed down considerably since Pat and Peggy had come on to the scene.

'Okay, so we're all willing to help out by baby-sitting,' said Ray gruffly. 'But if Larry Paterson does anything to hurt Ruth, he'll have Jack and me to answer to.'

'Too true,' agreed his brother.

Audrey was pouring tea from a large brown pot. She slammed it down on the table and looked from one to the other of her sons.

'If either of you two spoils things for Ruth by poking your brotherly nose in, you'll have me to contend with,' she declared formidably. 'Is that clear?'

'But if he starts messing her about, Mum . . .' began Ray.

'Keep your noses out, do you understand me?' she roared.

'Yes, Mum,' said Ray, with a sigh of resignation. 'We hear what you're saying.'

'Good. Because if anyone is going to put Larry Paterson right on the subject of Ruth,' she said, turning her attention back to the teapot, 'it's going to be me!'

Chapter Four

Ruth sat in the back of the car on the way home from the West End, an arm around Jenny who had been lulled to sleep by the movement of the car.

The afternoon had been nicely rounded off with tea amid potted palms and a pianist playing at a grand piano. The penny-thin, crustless sandwiches had borne little resemblance to the rough-cut wads Ruth was used to at home, and they had also been served with an assortment of mouth-watering cakes and pastries.

Now, as they drew up outside Ruth's place, Larry switched off the engine and turned to her, speaking in a whisper.

'Is Jenny still asleep?'

She nodded.

'I'll carry her into the house.'

'Thanks,' she hissed. 'I might be able to get her to bed without waking her.'

'Okay.'

'And, Larry . . .'

'Yes?'

'We've had a lovely time. Thank you so much for everything.'

'No need to thank me . . . the pleasure's been mine,' he said softly.

Ruth led him upstairs to the bedroom which she and Jenny shared and he carefully lowered the sleeping child on to her bed. The room was in darkness except for the landing light shining in.

'You go on downstairs,' she said in a hushed voice.

'I'll join you when I've settled her down for the night.'

'Okay. But don't be too long . . . 'cos I'll miss you.'

'I'll be as quick as I can.'

They smiled at each other in the half light, mutual attraction drawing them together. He hadn't intended their first kiss to happen at this precise moment and it took them both by surprise, all the sweeter for its spontaneity. Ruth felt weak with pleasure and longed for more.

She didn't move for a few moments after he'd slipped quietly from the room but stood quite still, luxuriating in the afterglow. Then she began carefully undressing her sleeping daughter, ready to ease her between the sheets.

Downstairs, Ruth's parents were treating Larry to some Brooks hospitality. The twins and their girls had gone out for the evening, so Audrey and Dan had been watching the quiz show 'Double Your Money' on the television but had turned the set off out of courtesy to their visitor. As it was Christmas time, the fire had been lit in the back sitting room which was where Larry was being entertained.

'Sit down and make yourself at home, mate,' said Dan warmly.

'Thanks very much, Mr Brooks,' said Larry, settling down on the sofa.

'You will stay and have a Christmas drink with us, won't you?' invited Dan.

'That's very nice of you,' said Larry, his face wreathed in smiles because he could still feel the touch of Ruth's lips on his.

'What's it to be then?'

'I'll have a small whisky if you have some, please, Mr Brooks.'

'At Christmas we have more booze than a brewery,' Dan told him companionably. 'It's the only time we do any drinking indoors, though. I prefer to go down the pub, myself. You don't get the same atmosphere at home.'

Larry nodded politely.

Dan looked enquiringly at his wife. 'What are you having, love?'

'A sherry please, Dan,' she said, smiling. 'And perhaps you could bring some cheese straws in with you when you bring the drinks?'

'Will do.'

Glad to be alone with Larry, Audrey seized the opportunity for a few quiet words.

'You enjoyed the show then, Larry?' she said, shifting forward slightly in her seat and leaning towards him.

'Yes, very much,' he said, feeling rather unnerved by the directness of her gaze.

She cleared her throat and leaned even closer.

'While we've got a few minutes to ourselves, son,' she said in a confidential manner, 'there's something I think I ought to make clear.'

'Oh?'

'You will have noticed that us Brooks are a very close-knit family.'

'Yes, I had noticed it.'

'And Ruth means everything to us.'

'I can imagine,' he said, having a fair idea where all this was leading. 'She's a real credit to you and Mr Brooks.'

'We think so too.' Audrey sniffed and looked him straight in the eye. 'That's why we don't want her to get hurt.'

'I can understand that,' he said, feeling trapped.

'She's already had one serious setback and is no stranger to heartache,' Audrey continued in a firm manner.

'Yes,' he said, clearing his throat nervously, 'I know she hasn't had it easy.'

'So if anyone is thinking of leading her up the garden path then doing the dirty on her, I'd advise them against it.'

'Really?' he said innocently.

'Oh, yes,' she said with emphasis. 'In fact, I'd go so far as to suggest that they don't take her out at all unless they have her best interests at heart.' She paused thoughtfully, chewing on her bottom lip. 'You see, us Brooks are the warmest people on earth to those we like and trust. There's nothin' we wouldn't do for our friends. But let anyone cross us and they'll soon get to know just how awkward we can be. Do you get my drift?'

He didn't enjoy being threatened, especially by a woman. But he wasn't going to protest, not when she had the mighty twins in her corner.

'Oh, yes, I get your drift all right, Mrs Brooks,' he said smoothly, managing to conceal the fact that she had put the fear of God into him. 'You've nothing to worry about so far as I'm concerned, I can promise you that.'

'Good. So long as we understand each other, I'm sure you and I will get on like a house on fire.' Audrey smiled briefly before throwing him a shrewd look. 'There's just one more thing . . .'

'Yes?'

'Ruth would be very annoyed with me if she knew I'd spoken to you along these lines, so I'd appreciate your keeping quiet about it.'

'I won't breathe a word,' Larry was able to say with complete honesty, simply because he wouldn't dare.

She grinned broadly and affected a complete change of mood.

'Smashing. So now that the formalities are out o' the way,' she said cheerfully, 'we can relax and enjoy a friendly drink together.'

Ruth was both surprised and disappointed when Larry changed towards her suddenly. Having seemed so keen on Boxing Day, she'd expected a warm welcome when she arrived at work the next day. But he was unmistakably offhand.

'Jenny was still chattering about the pantomime when I left home,' she told him cheerfully, hanging her coat up in the staffroom while he slipped into his white coat.

'Was she?'

'Yes. I think Mum's gonna be sick of hearing about it by the end of the day.'

'Really?' he replied. She tried not to hear his tone, telling herself she was imagining his lack of interest.

'Talk about verbal diarrhoea,' she said, trying to encourage him to respond. 'My daughter has more rabbit than a dumpling stew!'

'I'm glad she enjoyed herself,' said Larry, eyes not quite meeting hers.

'We both did . . . I told you several times.'

'Yes, I know.' He looked down, fastening the buttons on his white overall.

'You seem a bit quiet this morning,' she said. 'Is anything the matter?'

'No,' he said crisply.

'Oh.'

'But now that the holiday's over, it's time to settle down to work.'

She smarted at his abrasive tone, especially as she was the one who did most of the work and certainly didn't need reminding of her purpose for being here. Still finding it hard to believe that anyone's attitude could alter so dramatically, she wondered if his change of mood was not being aimed at her personally. Perhaps he was just feeling a bit below par after the holiday. She decided to put this theory to the test by giving him an opportunity to invite her out again.

'A lot of people don't feel as though Christmas is over until after New Year's Eve, do they?' she said meaningfully. 'Some people celebrate the New Year in a really big way.'

'I expect some of them do,' he said brusquely, and

glancing at his watch added, 'It's time to open up now, Ruth.'

She frowned darkly. She really didn't need to be told when to open the shop, and Larry was well aware of that.

'There's still five minutes to go,' she pointed out coolly.

'Never mind that,' he said in an efficient manner which was completely alien to him. 'The doctors are back in their surgeries this morning so we'll be inundated with prescriptions as well as everything else. You know what it's like the first day back after Christmas. There's always a rush on things like Aspro and Andrew's Liver Salts. In fact, there are people already waiting outside so we might as well let them in and get started.'

'Just as you like,' she said, giving him a look of angry bewilderment before going out into the shop and turning the Closed sign to Open. Her eyes were brimming with tears as she unlocked the door.

It was obvious what this was all about. Yesterday had been a one-off for Larry and he didn't want her getting any ideas to the contrary. How could she have been so stupid as to think their outing had meant something to him just because it had to her? Lack of experience was the easy answer to that. But she could have sworn something special had happened – for them both. As she had obviously been mistaken, she would make damned sure he knew she wasn't expecting anything more from him.

Burning with humiliation and conscious of the dragging sensation of disappointment in the pit of her stomach, she went into the dispensary where Larry was busy checking the stock of nostrums on the shelves.

'I've opened the shop and the place is packed to the doors already, so it looks as though we're in for a hectic morning,' she announced in her most businesslike manner.

Without waiting for him to answer, she turned and marched back into the shop to attend to the waiting customers.

* * *

Larry sat on a stool at the workbench and stared gloomily into space. Having had the reality of the situation spelled out to him so menacingly by Ruth's mother last night, he'd been thrown into turmoil. Being ordered either to get serious or back off altogether was a new experience for Larry and he'd found it most intimidating. He certainly didn't fancy being beaten up by the Brooks twins if it didn't work out between him and Ruth.

If he did carry on seeing her, he would have to play it straight or find himself in some back alley one dark night with a broken neck. At the moment he was besotted with her but how could he be sure he'd still feel the same in a few months' time, or weeks for that matter? He knew himself only too well – he was a man of wild enthusiasms and intense passions that grew cold without warning. Was he ready to settle down with one woman? Because if he wanted Ruth Brooks, that was what it would amount to.

This whole thing was straight out of a second-rate gangster movie, he thought irritably. All the ingredients were there: the gorgeous girl, the clannish family, the brawny brothers hovering in the background ready to jump on him the minute he stepped out of line. Frankly, he was beginning to wish he'd never set eyes on Ruth Brooks, against whom other women seemed dull in comparison, even Lorna – *especially Lorna*.

He was recalled to the present by the sound of Ruth in the shop, speaking to a customer in the gentle, slightly husky voice that he could listen to for ever.

Appearing at his side she handed him a prescription. After reading it, he walked across the room and looked in a drawer to check they had the item in stock.

'You can tell the customer it'll be ready in a few minutes,' he informed her smoothly.

'I guessed you'd say that, as you haven't had time to gather a backlog,' she said evenly.

She left the dispensary, chin up, her long hair swinging. His hand was trembling slightly as he counted pills into a bottle.

Later on, when the shop was quiet, Ruth brought his coffee into the dispensary as usual, but left hers in the staffroom.

'Not much doing on the non-medical side today,' she remarked chattily because she had decided that the best way to keep her dignity was to behave normally. 'Everyone's broke after Christmas.'

In an effort to put things back to how they'd been before the holiday, she gave him a friendly smile, otherwise the atmosphere between them was going to be intolerable.

He tried to look away from her because he didn't trust himself. But he simply didn't have the strength of will.

'Ruth?' he said, his eyes meeting hers.

'Yes?'

'I was wondering if you'd like to come out with me on New Year's Eve?' he heard himself say.

Her eyes widened in astonishment. 'Oh, do stop messing me about, Larry,' she snapped.

'I'm not.'

'Oh, but I think you are,' she said tartly. 'One minute you're all over me, the next you don't want to know. I've no time for all this blow hot, blow cold business.'

'Sorry.'

'Don't apologise,' she said sharply because she needed to know exactly where she stood with him. 'Just don't take me for a fool.'

'That's the last thing I'd ever do.'

'So why was I given the big freeze this morning?' she asked.

He looked very sheepish. 'I was in a foul mood, I'm sorry.'

'So am I.'

'Am I forgiven?'

'I might consider it.'

'Please?' he said in his most persuasive manner.

'All right then, I suppose we all have our off moments.' She gave him a hard look. 'But I'd rather you were straight with me, Larry. We had a lovely time yesterday and got on really well together. But it *was* only an afternoon out. If you'd rather leave it at that, that's fine with me. Don't ask me out again just because you think that's what I'm expecting.'

'I really do want to spend New Year's Eve with you,' he assured her promptly. 'So please say you'll come?'

'Well,' she said melting inside but trying not to sound too eager, 'it depends on whether or not I can get a sitter for Jenny.'

'But you'd like to come?' he said, almost boyish in his eagerness.

'Yes, I'd like to come,' she said, smiling into his eyes.

'Wonderful.'

Now that the decision was made Larry felt jubilant. There was no turning back. He'd break it off with Lorna and play it for real with Ruth. It was the only thing he could do because he simply couldn't give her up.

Ruth's happiness was so acute as she stood with Larry in the crowds in Trafalgar Square, waiting for the chimes of Big Ben to ring out the old year, it had an ephemeral feel to it, as though it might end at any moment.

They'd had a long and romantic candlelit dinner in an intimate little place in the backstreets before strolling here to join in the fun. The West End was a riot of excitement and celebration, Trafalgar Square heaving with revellers determined to have a good time. People in party mood swarmed over the steps around Nelson's column; others had climbed up on to the bronze lions. A few daring souls were making merry in the floodlit fountains.

'Are you cold?' asked Larry, his arm around her. Both of them were wearing thick coats.

'No, I'm much too excited to notice the weather.'

'Excited because it's NewYear?' he asked, his face close to hers.

'Because of everything.'

'Are you happy?'

Ruth turned to him, seeing his clear-cut features gleam in the fluorescent lighting. 'I think you already know the answer to that.'

'I just wanted to make sure.'

They were standing at the back of the square, slightly away from the boisterous crowds but near enough to be involved as the countdown to midnight began. At last came the moment they were all waiting for: the chimes. As the echo of the last thunderous boom died away and everybody welcomed in the New Year by cheering and kissing one another, Ruth was so overcome by the occasion, her eyes filled with tears.

'Happy New Year,' she said, laughing and crying simultaneously.

'Happy NewYear, Ruth,' said Larry, kissing her deeply on the lips.

The crowds were forming into rowdy circles for 'Auld Lang Syne', the atmosphere filled with emotion and camaraderie. Ruth and Larry joined in with gusto.When it concluded with a loud communal cheer, Larry drew her away from the crowd.

'Marry me, Ruth,' he said, looking right into her eyes.

Her mouth dropped open. 'Don't tease me about something as important as that, Larry,' she admonished.

'I'm not teasing you, Ruth,' he told her gravely. 'I've never been more serious about anything in my life.'

'You can't be?' she said, hoping it was true, despite herself. 'It's much too soon.'

'Not for me it isn't,' he said, as surprised as she was by this turn of events.

'Surely you don't really mean it?' she said in astonishment.

He looked into her face, swathed in a scarlet muffler against the frost, her skin glowing, her dark fringe shining damply in the night air as she observed him with a wary smile. He'd had no prior intention of asking her to marry him and had been driven to propose by the strength of his passion for her. But having acted on impulse, marrying her now became the most important thing in his life. If Larry wanted something this much, he just *had* to have it.

'Yes, I really do mean it,' he said. 'Please say you will?'

Excited and flattered but knowing she must keep hold of herself, she said, 'I think you and I had better go somewhere a bit quieter and talk about this some more.'

'Oh, come on, Larry, let's be sensible,' said Ruth, sitting beside him in the front of his car which was parked in a side street.

'I don't want to be sensible,' he said with glorious recklessness. 'I'm in love with you and I want to marry you. That's all there is to it.'

As wonderful as it was to hear him say it, she was determined to stay in control.

'We've been out together three times and you want to marry me?' she said, desperately trying to hang on to her rapidly diminishing common sense. 'We hardly know each other.'

'That isn't true,' he objected. 'We're together all day at the shop.'

Yes, he did have a valid point but she still felt compelled to add, 'Can you imagine what my parents would say if I went home and told them we're getting married?'

'You're over twenty-one,' he reminded her. 'You don't need their permission.'

'No, but I'd like their blessing.'

He thought Ruth's parents would probably be overjoyed at the idea of offloading their daughter into a marriage which would give her and Jenny a respectable place in the community. But recalling his conversation with her mother, he also thought he would be more comfortable with the family's blessing than without it.

'And they'd say you were rushing into it, I suppose.'

'Of course they would,' she said. 'And they'd be right.'

Putting his forefinger on her cheek, Larry gently turned her face towards him.

'But it's how you and I feel that matters,' he said. 'Can you honestly say that you don't feel the same way about me as I do about you?'

She did – she did! She wanted to throw herself into his arms and tell him she'd marry him tomorrow. But things were moving too fast. She had responsibilities.

'That isn't the point,' she said. 'Marriage is a huge commitment.'

'It's what people do when they love each other, though, isn't it?' He leaned over and kissed her lingeringly. 'It's what I want us to do. We're both single and of age, so why not?'

'Oh, if only things were that simple,' she said. 'But even aside from the fact that I need more time to get to know you better, I've my daughter to think about.'

'I'd be good to her,' he said softly. 'I think you know that.'

'Yes, I do know that.'

'So?'

'Let's give ourselves a little more time,' Ruth suggested. 'Just to enjoy getting to know each other better.'

'Okay. If that's what you really want,' he agreed with reluctance. 'But be warned, I've no intention of allowing you to keep me waiting for very long. I shall pester the life out of you until you agree to name the day.'

Kitty gave Ruth a knowing look when they met for lunch one Saturday at the end of January.

'If you tell me this time that there isn't a man behind this new radiance of yours, I won't believe you!'

'And you'd be right not to.'

'Your boss, I bet?'

'That's right. Oh, Kitty,' she said, her eyes sparkling with happiness, 'he's completely changed my life.'

'Tell me about it.'

'He's asked me to marry him.'

'Good God!'

'Well, don't sound so thunderstruck,' reproached Ruth, over-reacting to Kitty's unconcealed astonishment. 'I know most men are put off by the fact that I'm an unmarried mother but surely it isn't *that* surprising that someone would want to marry me?'

Larry Paterson had struck Kitty as the type for an affair rather than marriage, which was why she was so surprised. But that was the last thing Ruth would want to hear so she said, 'Don't be so silly, of course it isn't. It's just that . . . well, you haven't known him long. It seems a bit sudden.'

'Yes, I know,' Ruth admitted, smiling again. 'That's why I've asked him to give me more time to think about it.'

'Good idea.'

Ruth shook her head as though she still couldn't believe what was happening to her. 'But honestly, Kit, he's really pushing the boat out to get me to set the date. Flowers, chocolates, meals in classy restaurants . . . He certainly knows how to make a girl feel good.'

'It sounds wonderful.'

'Fortunately, Mum and Dad are being very co-operative about baby-sitting.'

'I'm so pleased for you, Ruth.'

'Thanks.'

But there was a nasty little suspicion at the back of Kitty's mind. She wondered if perhaps charm came too easily to Larry Paterson. Having been taken out of circulation at such an early age, Ruth was naive when it came to men, unlike Kitty who had had lots of boyfriends and was feeling especially cynical about men at the moment – and for a very good reason as it happened. But how could she spoil her friend's happiness by mentioning her doubts? It wasn't as though she herself knew Larry well enough to make a considered judgement, and he did seem to be very good for Ruth.

'He certainly seems to have done wonders for you.'

'He makes me feel like a million dollars,' she enthused, her face lighting up at the thought of him. 'And he's wonderful with Jenny. She thinks the world of him. I wouldn't even consider marrying him if she wasn't happy about it.'

'Wedding bells are on the agenda then?' surmised Kitty.

'If things go on as they are, definitely,' declared Ruth.

'I really hope it happens for you, kid,' said Kitty sincerely.

'It'll be so good for Jenny to have a daddy and a proper family life,' said Ruth. 'Especially as she'll be starting school soon. It'll certainly save her from a whole lot of grief – you know how cruel kids can be.'

Kitty was thoughtful. 'So long as you don't let Jenny's welfare be your incentive to marry him.'

'As if I'd do that!'

'You wouldn't be the first,' countered Kitty. 'I should think it's all too easy for a woman in your position to be tempted to accept a marriage proposal because she needs a place of her own and a father for her child. You could be influenced by that factor without even realising it.' She paused, looking at her friend. 'Let's face it, Ruth, there isn't much you wouldn't do to make Jenny's life easier.'

'That's true enough,' she admitted. 'And that's what so great about this whole thing: that I've fallen in love with a man who loves me back and is willing to be a father to Jenny.' She grinned. 'Anyway, I still haven't said yes.'

'Let me know when you do.'

'You'll be the first. After Mum and Dad, of course.' Ruth paused thoughtfully. 'Anyway, enough about me. How are things with you and the merchant banker?'

Kitty frowned. 'That's all over.'

'Oh, I'm so sorry,' said Ruth. 'And there's me going on about Larry.'

'There's no need to be sorry,' said Kitty in a brittle tone. 'I had a narrow escape.'

'What happened.'

'The bastard was married,' she said in a light tone that didn't quite ring true. 'I'm right off men at the moment. It'll be a long time before I trust any damn one of them again.'

'I see,' said Ruth, guessing that Kitty was more upset than she would admit.

'I'm not sure it's quite decent to feel as happy as I do at this moment,' said Ruth one Sunday afternoon a few weeks later as Larry flopped down on a park bench beside her, exhausted from a game of chase with Jenny who had at last found a playmate of her own age and was playing ball on the grass nearby.

'Don't worry about whether it's decent or not, just enjoy it,' he said, breathless from the exercise, his cheeks glowing from the wind which had blown his hair into attractive disorder.

It was a glorious February day, crisp and bracing, with a sharp breeze and bright sunshine shining from a steely blue sky.

'Everything's so perfect, I'm not sure I deserve it.'

'Of course you deserve it,' said Larry who never even considered such things. 'Why on earth shouldn't you?'

'Oh, I don't know. I suppose I've still got a guilt complex . . .'

'You think you have to keep paying for that one mistake?'

'I don't regret it for myself because to do so would be to regret Jenny and I wouldn't be without her,' she said. 'But I do still feel bad about letting my parents down.'

'They think the world of Jenny and wouldn't be without her either.'

'I know that,' she agreed. 'I still let them down, though. Apart from the scandal, there's the fact that I didn't finish my education. They had such high hopes for me.'

'You could drive yourself mad with that sort of attitude,' he said. 'You should put the past behind you.'

'That isn't such an easy matter, though, is it?'

The mistakes of the past didn't trouble Larry one iota. He'd not given Lorna a thought since he'd told her it was over between them. Once a thing had ended, it wasn't even worth thinking about in his opinion. The present was what mattered.

'Maybe not. But you have to make yourself do it. Hanging on to the past is a pointless exercise. Now is what matters, Ruth,' he told her gravely. 'Now and us. You, me and Jenny and our life together.'

'Yes, I know.'

'Marry me, Ruth,' he breathed softly into her ear.

'Larry, I . . .'

The intimacy of the moment was shattered by Jenny scampering over to them to say that her new friend had gone home with her mother. She wanted to know if Ruth and Larry would go over to the swings with her.

Becoming suddenly aware of the chill in the wind, Ruth said, 'All right, darling. But not for very long. It's getting cold now and we have to go home for tea soon. So let's not have a fuss when it's time to leave.'

Jenny treated her to one of her most winning smiles.

'Just for a little while, then, Mummy,' she promised.

Something about the expression on her daughter's face as she looked up persuasively, reminded Ruth of Jenny's father so vividly, she groaned softly.

'What's the matter?' asked Larry in concern. 'Do you have a pain or something?'

It was a kind of pain – an ache of nostalgia – a moment of regret for something that had gone for ever: the throbbing sweetness of first love. Larry was right, though. She must put the past behind her and make the most of the considerable blessings she had in the here and now.

'No, I'm fine. Someone must have been walking over my grave,' she told him, shivering as she stood up and clutched her daughter's hand.

'That's all right then,' he said, rising and taking Jenny's other hand.

'And the answer to your question,' said Ruth, looking at him with a gleam in her eye, 'is . . . yes, I would be honoured to marry you.'

'Oh, Ruth, that's wonderful,' he said, beaming at her.

They were both smiling as they walked across the grass to the children's playground with Jenny hopping and skipping between them.

Chapter Five

Ruth and Larry had a spring wedding at the register office and a hotel reception afterwards. Larry's mother came up from Sussex and some of his friends were there too, so it wasn't totally dominated by the Brooks family.

Looking beautiful in a cream suit with sage-green accessories, so perfect for her dark looks, Ruth set off the slim-line look with stiletto-heeled shoes with sword-sharp toes. She carried a posy of spring flowers and wore her hair in a French pleat beneath a wide-brimmed cream hat with trailing green ribbons, the wedding tableau completed by Jenny in a peach-coloured satin dress carrying a basket of flowers. It was the next best thing to the traditional church wedding Ruth had always dreamed of and she enjoyed every moment.

Larry insisted on a honeymoon despite her doubts about leaving her daughter. They flew to Spain for a week in the sun while Jenny stayed with her grandparents. Going abroad for the first time was a terrific thrill for Ruth. The sunshine and gaiety dispelled all inhibitions and she positively wallowed in the romance and sexual abandon of being newly married.

But it was when they returned home and began their life together in the flat above the shop that she was at her happiest. She had no regrets at all about marrying Larry so quickly.

It was bliss to be in her own place, running the household and making a home for the three of them. For the first time *ever* she truly felt like an adult, in control of her own life and in charge of her daughter's upbringing.

The accommodation was on two floors. It had a separate street entrance next to the shop as well as a shop entrance in the hallway at the bottom of the stairs. An old property with sash windows and high ceilings, it comprised a living room, sitting room and kitchen on the first floor, and two bedrooms and a bathroom upstairs.

Ruth wasn't happy with the decor. It was far too dismal and old-fashioned for her taste. Larry had furnished in contemporary style but done nothing about Mr Grover's ageing wallpaper and sludge-coloured paintwork, which made the flat dark and claustrophobic. The fact that Larry was such an untidy individual meant that Ruth moved into a tip.

However, he gave her a free hand to get the flat as she wanted it, only too pleased to have the problem attended to without any effort on his part. Ruth got busy with wallpaper and paint and transformed the living room single-handed. Larry had never picked up a paintbrush in his life and made it clear that he had no intention of doing so now.

'You've done wonders, darling,' he said, seeing the room uplifted with walls in pastel shades above a warm red carpet. 'You should have got a decorator in to do it, though.'

'There's no need when I can do it myself and save us some money,' she said cheerfully. 'By the time I've finished, you won't know the place. I'm going to do it from top to bottom.'

Which meant a hectic time for her because she was working harder than ever in the shop all day. While she was still under school age, Jenny continued to stay with her grandmother while Ruth was working, but she made sure she gave the little girl plenty of attention as soon as she was free, despite the domestic chores and the decorating. Ruth's workload in the business continued to swell as Larry passed an increasing amount of responsibility over to her.

The fact that she was running Larry's business as well as his home, while he did as little as he could possibly get away with, didn't bother Ruth too much. Hard work was nothing to her and she enjoyed being in a position of responsibility after the tedium of being just a shop assistant to Mr Grover. Naturally, as Larry's wife, she now felt more personally involved since the shop was their family business, and was keen for it to do well.

Life was good that summer as the three of them lived in harmony together and Ruth and Larry became closer as a couple. Larry was a passionate and considerate lover, a good father to Jenny and an affectionate husband, even if he did put upon Ruth outrageously. His irresistible charm and the fact that she was in love with him made it easy for her to turn a blind eye to his faults.

Ruth had very little spare time, though, and crawled into bed in a state of exhaustion at night. As well as keeping the paperwork up to date, she kept the shop immaculate with every pot and bottle dusted and shining. While Larry relaxed in the evening, she was usually filling shelves in the shop, working in the office, or struggling with the decorating. She sometimes reproached him about not pulling his weight but it didn't make a scrap of difference.

It was a happy routine for all that and they had a lot of fun. Sunday was their family day and they usually took Jenny out somewhere – to the park or the river, before tea at Nutley Road. Sometimes they went further afield in Larry's car – to the country or the seaside for the day.

Jenny thrived in this stable atmosphere. Even when Ruth was working in the evenings, the child was secure in the knowledge that her mother was on the premises if she needed her and her Uncle Larry was usually around.

In September when Jenny started school, Ruth didn't know who was the most eager for that first schoolday to end – herself or Larry.

'So you're a schoolgirl now then, sweetheart?' he said

that evening as Jenny sat on his lap before bedtime.

'Yes.'

'What did you say your teacher's name is?' he asked.

'Miss Brown.'

'Is she nice?'

'Not as nice as Mummy.'

'Oh.'

'I've got a lovely friend called Mary who sits next to me, though.'

'That's good. So you'll be seeing her again tomorrow then.'

'Am I going again tomorrow?' she enquired doubtfully.

Larry exchanged glances with Ruth who was sitting beside them on the sofa.

'Yes, you'll be going to school every day,' said Ruth. 'Won't that be fun?'

'Oh, I'm not sure if I want to go *every* day,' she said as though she had a choice.

Neither of them had the heart to disillusion her at this point.

'Well . . . it'll be fun to see your friend Mary again tomorrow anyway, won't it?' said Larry diplomatically.

'Yes.' She looked up at him. 'Will you read me a story?'

'You want me to do your story tonight instead of Mummy, then?'

'Yes, I want you to do it, please, Uncle Larry,' she said.

'Okey-dokey.' He smiled. 'Off you go and find a storybook.'

Ruth felt a rush of happiness that made her eyes smart. It warmed her heart to see the two of them getting on so well together.

'I've had the most brilliant idea,' Ruth announced to Larry over a snack lunch in the flat one day in December.

'Another one?' he said, because his wife seemed to be

an endless source of brainwaves to improve the business.

'You know that the draper next door is selling his shop.'

'Yes?'

'Well, why don't we take it on and extend our premises?' she suggested. 'We desperately need more shop and storage space . . . we're bursting at the seams now that our turnover has increased so dramatically.'

'That's true.'

'We could make the two shops into one and have the new section for toiletries, cosmetics and other non-medical items,' she said, growing keener by the second. 'We could even think about having a self-service section.'

He finished his cheese on toast, sipped his coffee and lit a cigarette, observing her thoughtfully. 'He's selling it complete with accommodation over the top, though, isn't he?'

'Yes . . . but it's only a small, one-bedroomed flat and we can make very good use of it,' she said with enthusiasm.

'You think so?'

'Definitely. What we don't need as living accommodation can be used to store stock. We could knock both the shops and the flats into one big property.'

'The idea does have possibilities, I must admit,' he conceded.

'Our business is doing really well,' she said with the confidence of someone who looked after the office work and knew just how much their profits were rising. 'So we won't have any trouble getting an additional mortgage.'

'Mmm.'

Seeing the light in her eyes confirmed what he already knew – that he had made the right decision in marrying her. Not only did she keep him happy in bed and provide him with entertaining company out of it, she also kept a comfortable home and practically ran his business, lock stock and barrel. Apart from the actual pharmacy, and a lot of that he was able to delegate to her under his supervision, she took care of everything. She had almost trebled Grover's turnover.

The situation suited him perfectly. Having a business that did more while he did less was his idea of heaven. And his conscience was clear about transferring so much of the responsibility to Ruth because she thrived on it. Theirs was the ideal partnership. She enjoyed work and he didn't so they were both happy.

He was under no illusions as to his own limitations as a businessman. Without Ruth, the shop would have just about managed to stay afloat, providing him with enough to live on and that was about all. He had neither the drive nor the initiative to increase trade as she had.

Their personal life together was satisfactory too. They got on well and had a lot of laughs. Despite his earlier doubts, Jenny had proved to be no problem at all. He'd been driven by passion to marry Ruth but he had no regrets. As well as pleasing him as a business partner, she still excited him as a woman.

'So what do you think?' she said.

'Basically I think it's a very good idea . . .' he said slowly.

'I can sense a but?'

'But it will take a lot of organisation and hard work to set it up.'

'Since when has either of those things worried me?' she said.

'Oh, well, if you're prepared to take it on, Ruth,' he said, leaning back and relaxing as he inhaled on his cigarette, 'we'd better think seriously about putting an offer in for the premises next door then, hadn't we?'

The extension to the shop opened the following April after four months of gruelling activity for Ruth who organised everything herself. They managed to continue trading despite the chaos caused by the presence of the builders.

'You've worked miracles,' said Larry when it was finished.
'Thank you,' she said.

He hadn't lifted a finger to help which had been infuriating at times. But, determined to see the project through, she'd managed without him and been given the satisfaction of knowing that the finished result was entirely the result of her own hard work and ideas.

The renovated and enlarged version of Paterson's Pharmacy was much more streamlined, with a new glass shopfront, tiled floor and modern shopfittings. The shop was open-plan with two departments, each with its own entrance. There was a counter area in the original premises and a small self-service section in the new part which stocked a host of non-medical items. Upstairs they had gained a bedroom and a spare room which they used for storage.

They decided that the time had come to employ a full-time assistant to help Ruth in the shop while Larry continued to limit his efforts to the dispensary.

'Well, we've certainly come a long way in a year,' she said to him over dinner in a restaurant on their first wedding anniversary.

'Indeed.'

'It's been a very happy year for me,' she told him, sipping her wine. 'I've enjoyed every moment. Thank you.'

'It's I who should be thanking you,' he said softly.

'We've proved a lot of people wrong anyway,' she remarked. 'There were plenty who thought we were rushing things and wouldn't last six months, let alone a year.'

'And we'll continue to prove them wrong.'

'I hope so.'

'We'll celebrate our silver wedding . . . and our golden . . . and whatever comes after that.'

'Will you still love me when I'm old and grey, that's the question?' she giggled.

''Course I will. You'll be the loveliest oldie in London,' he said in a way that melted her heart. He raised his glass. 'Here's to us and to many more years together.'

'I'll drink to that,' said Ruth, chinking her glass against his.

Audrey was very upset about the race riots that had broken out in the Notting Hill area, during which several people had been badly hurt.

'A dreadful business,' she said to Ruth one autumn evening when she called in to see her parents, having left Larry looking after Jenny. 'What is London coming to?'

'You tell me,' said Ruth with a solemn shake of her head.

'A gang of youths started it, apparently . . . demonstrating and throwing petrol bombs as well as milk bottles,' said Audrey. 'They say the streets around Notting Hill are strewn with broken glass and debris.'

'I heard they were throwing bombs and bottles at the police as well as black members of the public,' commented Ruth. 'And the blacks retaliated with iron bars.'

'It's a bit too close to home for comfort,' said Audrey.

'All the customers have been talking about it,' added Ruth. 'People are very shocked.'

'They're bound to be. It's enough to scare anyone to death, knowing that there's such violence on the streets . . . on their own doorstep.'

The two women were in the kitchen. Audrey was pouring tea, Ruth was sitting at the table. Her father and brothers were watching television in the other room.

Audrey handed her daughter a cup of tea and sat down at the table, resting her chin on her laced fingers.

'Anyway, how are things with you?' she asked, as though she hadn't seen her for ages when they actually met most days.

'Fine,' said Ruth, unable to stifle a yawn. 'Wonderful in fact.'

Audrey cast a studious glance over her daughter, noticing the pallor, the shadows under her eyes and the general look of exhaustion.

'You look worn out, though,' she remarked.

'That's a permanent state with me at the moment,' she said brightly. 'We always seem to be so busy lately.'

'You mean *you're* always so busy,' corrected Audrey with more than a hint of disapproval.

'What do you mean by that?'

'I mean that I haven't noticed Larry working up much of a sweat.'

'That isn't fair, Mum,' objected Ruth, immediately on the defensive. 'Larry and I are a team.'

Her mother stirred her tea thoughtfully. She was delighted at the way things had turned out for Ruth and Jenny in that they were no longer outcasts from society and had a proper family life with Larry. Audrey liked Larry. He was a real gentleman. But he wasn't a worker. In fact, she'd go so far as to call him bone idle.

'In theory you're a team, yes, but you run that business single-handed,' she said. 'You're carrying Larry.'

'That can hardly be the case since he is the qualified pharmacist,' Ruth reminded her, fiercely loyal to her husband. 'The business couldn't function without him.'

'He looks after that side of things with your help, I'll grant you that much,' said Audrey. 'But he does bugger all else. If it hadn't been for you, that shop would still be as tatty and run down as it was the day Mr Grover left.'

In all honesty, Ruth couldn't deny it but devotion to Larry wouldn't allow her to admit it without making an excuse for him.

'That's only because I'm the one with all the ideas,' she said, telling herself this was true and she wasn't just evading the issue.

'You're also a willing work-horse,' declared Audrey. 'Don't get me wrong, Ruth, I like Larry, I think he's a smashing bloke. But any fool can see that he doesn't pull his weight.'

'He's very good to Jenny and me.'

'*And you're very good to him,*' said Audrey with emphasis. 'You mustn't let gratitude blind you to your own worth.'

'Meaning?'

'It's only natural that you are grateful to Larry for rescuing you from the shame of being an unmarried mother and all that it entails,' she said, 'but he's the one who should be grateful to you now, for all you've done for the business, not to mention the home. But the more you do, the more he'll let you do. As nice as he is, he's an idle bugger.'

'All this because I'm feeling a bit tired,' said Ruth, who felt duty bound not to criticise her husband to anyone else even if she did occasionally echo a mild version of her mother's sentiments to Larry himself.

'I'm your mother . . . if I can't speak my mind, who can?'

'Okay, point taken,' said Ruth. 'But Larry's a good husband even if he isn't the most willing worker in the world.'

The conversation was halted by the appearance of the twins, dressed up ready to go out.

'How's it going then, sis?' they asked almost simultaneously.

'Fine thanks, boys,' she replied. 'Are you two going out courting?'

'Yes,' said Ray.

'It's about time you got married and out from under Mum's feet.'

The two exchanged knowing glances.

'Funny you should say that,' said Ray with a wide grin, "cos the girls are thinking along similar lines.'

'And giving us a load of earache about it an' all,' said Jack.

'So what do you plan to do about it?' asked Ruth lightly.

Ray looked at Jack who nodded approvingly.

'We're having a double wedding,' declared Ray. 'That's what we're doing about it.'

Ruth and her mother gaped at them.

'You're kidding?' said Audrey.

'We're not,' said Jack.

'I suppose now is as good a time as any to tell you,' said Ray with a broad grin. 'We're planning on getting married sometime next year.'

Attracted by the outbreak of excited conversation, Dan appeared from the other room and the kitchen erupted into a riot of congratulations.

Kitty phoned Ruth quite early in the New Year to say that she'd met a fabulous new man.

'He's a pilot,' she said.

'Ooh, I say . . . how very romantic novelish.'

'I met him in Paris.'

'Even more Mills and Boon,' said Ruth. 'Is he French?'

'No, English. He lives just outside London, near the airport.'

'How did you meet?'

'We were staying at the same hotel,' explained Kitty. 'He was on a stopover between flights, I was checking the hotel out for my company. We got talking in the bar.'

'Was it love at first sight?' asked Ruth jokingly, because Kitty usually made light of her numerous love affairs.

'I don't know about that but I'm desperately in love with him now,' she confessed, sounding unusually sombre.

'He sounds special.'

'He is . . . *really special*.'

'Oh, Kit, how exciting.'

'I'd like you to meet him, Ruth.'

'Bring him over to lunch one Sunday then,' she suggested.

'Thanks, I'd like that.'

'How about Sunday fortnight?'

'Lovely.'

'Come about twelve-thirty for lunch at one o'clock,' said Ruth. 'We'll look forward to seeing you both.'

Tim Barrett was exactly the sort of man Ruth would expect Kitty to fall for. He was charming, witty and devastating to look at. Wearing a black polo-necked sweater under a light grey jacket, he was tall and muscular with an athletic gait that made him seem almost to glide when he walked. Brown curly hair topped his clean-cut features and a pair of warm brown smiling eyes.

Ruth took an instant liking to him and perceived a difference in Kitty the minute she saw her. She seemed unusually serious, more intense and less frivolous. Ruth could feel the electricity sparking between her friend and Tim.

'So, how do the two of you manage to see anything of each other if you're always travelling in different directions?' said Ruth, over the meal of roast beef with horseradish sauce.

'With difficulty,' said Tim, turning to Kitty beside him and exchanging an intimate smile with her. 'But we manage. We aren't working all the time, remember.'

'I suppose you have to work weekends, though?' said Ruth looking at Tim.

'Oh, yes,' he said. 'But not every one which is why I'm able to be here today.'

'A huge responsibility, flying a plane,' remarked Larry conversationally. 'All those lives in your hands.'

'Yes, it is a big responsibility,' agreed Tim. 'That's why I like to keep myself fit, so that I'm on the ball.'

'The airline is hot on health and fitness, I should imagine?' said Larry.

'Yes, we have regular medical checks but I try to keep on top form anyway.'

'How did you get on last week in that terrible fog?' enquired Larry chattily, to keep the conversation moving.

'All flights were cancelled,' said Tim. 'The airport was at a complete standstill.'

'They say it was the worst winter fog in this country since the great peasouper of 1952,' remarked Ruth.

'Yes, I read about that in the paper,' replied Tim.

Conversation was no problem because they all got along so well. Tim showed a polite interest in the pharmacy business, they touched on the recent and tragic death of American pop star Buddy Holly, and Jenny entertained them with chatter about the current hula-hoop craze and how the older girls at school held competitions in the playground to see who could keep their hula-hoop spinning around their waist the longest.

After lunch they all went for a walk in Ravenscourt Park. Jenny walked in front with the men who delighted her by lifting her and swinging her between them. The weather was cold but dry with intermittent bursts of sunshine escaping from behind banks of racing clouds.

'You're really serious about Tim, aren't you, Kitty?' said Ruth as the two friends lagged behind the others.

'Yes, I'm afraid so.'

'Don't sound so worried about it.'

'My feelings are out of control, Ruth,' she explained. 'I love him so much it hurts and there's not a damned thing I can do about it.'

'Why should you want to do anything about it?'

'Because I've never felt like this about anyone before and it scares the hell out of me.'

'But he seems very keen on you,' said Ruth reassuringly.

'Yes, he is at the moment.'

'Then what are you worried about?'

'Living without him if it doesn't work out,' said Kitty.

'It hasn't been like this for me with any boyfriend I've ever had before.'

'I see.'

'Have you had the feeling that something's so perfect it can't last?'

'Yes, I felt like that when things first got serious between Larry and me,' said Ruth. 'And we've been married for nearly two years. I think it's probably quite normal to feel like that when you're intensely happy. It doesn't mean that it's going to fall apart or anything.'

'I hope not.'

'Forget your fears and enjoy it.'

'I am doing. And I can tell you one thing, kid,' declared Kitty, 'I'll marry him like a shot if he asks me!'

'Do you think he will?'

'I'm absolutely banking on it,' she said, and they walked towards the men who were now pushing Jenny on the swing.

The twins got married that summer. Being a double wedding of twins, jokes about the double patter of tiny feet abounded.

It was a very happy occasion, though. The two brides were radiant in white and Jenny was a bridesmaid in pink along with three of the brides' relatives. The reception was in a hotel in Hammersmith and was a jovial affair with a sit down meal and dancing to a band.

Kitty and Tim, who had got engaged at Easter, weren't able to make it because of working commitments. But Kitty telephoned Ruth the week before the wedding to tell her that there would be another special occasion soon because she and Tim were planning to get married in the autumn.

But now both the happy couples were leaving for their honeymoon, amid showers of confetti and bags of risqué wedding banter.

Audrey was awash with emotion after they'd gone.

'I shall miss that couple o' daft buggers around the place,' she told Ruth tearfully.

'They'll only be living down the road in Hammersmith,' she reminded her. 'They'll be calling on you so often, you'll be glad to send them home to their wives.'

'I suppose so,' her mother agreed sensibly. 'It's just that . . . well, you've all left home now. It'll be strange with just me and your dad.'

'It will be nice for you to have some time to yourselves.'

'Yeah, yeah, I know,' she sighed, but didn't sound convinced.

As though aware of his wife's feelings, Dan appeared at her side.

'Let's go and have a dance, shall we, love?' he suggested.

'I'd like that, Dan.'

Seeing the affection that had survived so many years together, Ruth had to rummage in her handbag for a hanky.

'Don't you start crying too,' admonished Larry playfully at he swept her on to the dance floor. 'I thought a wedding was supposed to be a happy occasion.'

'It is,' she said. 'It's also a very emotional one.'

Because it was good manners to mingle with the other guests at a wedding reception, Ruth found herself dancing with the uncle of the brides, a middle-aged man known to all as Uncle Ted. They chatted generally and when they got on to the subject of Ruth's occupation, he seemed very interested.

'Useful things, chemist's shops,' he said. 'I often go to the one near us when I'm poorly, to save a long wait in the doctor's waiting room.'

'A lot of people do,' she said. 'But pharmacists can only offer limited advice. For anything serious, they'll advise you to go to see your doctor.'

'There's a rumour going round that our local chemist's is selling up, as a matter of fact,' he informed her.

'Really?' said Ruth, her interest immediately aroused.

'Mmm. They say the chap's retiring.'

'Is it a big shop?'

'No, but I reckon it's a little goldmine, 'cos it's right near the doctor's surgery.'

'Where is this shop exactly?'

'In the Redston Road parade,' he explained. 'Just a few minutes' walk from Hammersmith Broadway.'

'That's really interesting,' said Ruth thoughtfully.

A few nights later, when Ruth got into bed beside her husband, she said, 'There's a chemist's shop about to come on the market in Hammersmith, near a doctor's surgery.'

'So?'

'So if we want to make an offer before it goes on the market officially, the vendor will knock off the fee they would have had to pay to the agent.'

Larry, who had been sitting up reading, put his book down on the bedside table.

'You're remarkably well informed,' he said, turning to her with a querying look.

'Someone told me about it at the twins' wedding and I went to see the owner of the shop in my lunch hour today,' she explained. 'I didn't want to say anything to you about it until I'd made a few enquiries and had something definite to say.'

'You're a ruddy marvel, do you know that?' he said.

'You like the idea then?'

'It's certainly worth thinking about,' he told her.

'My thoughts exactly,' she said, settling back against her pillows. 'We'd have to put a manager in, of course, a qualified pharmacist.'

'Mm.'

'But opening another shop seems the logical next step for us.'

'Yes.'

'I wonder if it might make more sense, though, for us to take on someone qualified to work with me in this shop while you manage the new one?' she suggested. 'So that the customers can get to know the new owner. At least until the business is up and running. We can always change things around later on if we want to.'

'Good idea.'

'Shall I get an appointment for us to go and look at the property together?' she suggested with enthusiasm.

'Yeah, why not?' he said, but they both knew that his going along was just a formality. Ruth would organise the new project as she organised everything else in their lives.

'Good. I'll deal with it first thing tomorrow morning.'

Turning to her and reaching out, he said, 'And in the meantime, come here, you gorgeous and clever woman . . .'

Chapter Six

Finding someone suitable to work with Ruth in the Shepherd's Bush shop proved to be more of a problem than they'd expected. The purchase of the new business was progressing smoothly and they were hoping to take over in time for the Christmas trade. But for this to be possible they had to find a qualified pharmacist.

The lack of takers was caused by the job's being that of joint manager with Ruth. All the applicants so far had been men who saw the presence of a woman in a non-subordinate position as a threat.

'If only I was qualified, we wouldn't have this problem,' said Ruth, who found herself wishing with increasing fervour that she could run the shop on her own. 'It's a blasted nuisance.'

'Yes,' agreed Larry, 'but there's nothing we can do about it so we'll just have to use a locum to tide us over if we don't find someone in time for the takeover.'

'It's the only thing we can do.'

'Anyway, another applicant phoned just now while you were busy in the shop,' he told her. 'I've arranged for him to come along tomorrow evening after we've closed, for an interview.'

'That *is* good news,' she said with renewed hope. 'Did he sound promising?'

Larry picked up a scrap of paper from the workbench in the dispensary where this conversation was taking place.

'He's well qualified and experienced anyway,' he informed her, consulting his notes. 'He's working in a big

West End chemist's at the moment. Goes by the name of Vince Todd.'

'Oh, really!'

Larry threw her an enquiring glance. 'Sounds as though you know him?'

'I used to know someone of that name when I was at school,' she said. 'But I shouldn't think it's the same one.'

'Probably not,' agreed Larry without much interest. 'Todd is a common enough name.'

It was the same Vince Todd. A tall, gangling man, firmer featured and more self-confident than the youth she remembered, but the same unassuming, thoroughly good-natured bloke he'd always been. Not in the least handsome or hunky but terribly nice.

'Ruth . . . Ruth Brooks?' he said, with a query in his voice as he tried to match this beautiful woman with the sixteen-year-old schoolgirl she'd been when he'd last seen her.

'That's me.'

'It's great to see you,' he said, beaming. 'You're looking wonderful.'

'Thank you. You look well too.' She smiled warmly. 'It's really good to see you again, Vince,' she said, showing him into the office and inviting him to sit down.

'It's been a long time.' He paused, narrowing his eyes in thought. 'It must be about eight years.'

'Yes, it would be about that.'

Seeing Vince again wasn't disturbing to Ruth but the memories he evoked were extremely unsettling.

He gave her a lopsided grin. 'So you went into pharmacy then?'

'Oh, no,' she corrected, forcing her wayward thoughts to stay firmly fixed in the present. 'I'm not qualified.' She glanced towards Larry who was sitting at the desk waiting, rather impatiently, for the interview to begin.

'This is my husband Larry. He's the chemist. I run the business side of things.'

The two men shook hands and Ruth explained to Vince that they were about to open another shop.

'So if you were to join us, you'd be working with me, not Larry,' she explained. 'You and I would be running this branch of Paterson's together, though obviously you'd be in charge of the dispensary.'

'Oh, jolly good,' he said with unfeigned enthusiasm.

'That isn't a problem, then?' she said. 'I mean, you wouldn't mind sharing the responsibility with a woman?'

'Not at all,' he said heartily.

'Can we begin the interview?' interrupted Larry, who was irritated because he disliked having his working day extended. He wanted to go upstairs to the flat to relax.

'Yes, I suppose we ought to make a start,' agreed Ruth.

They went through the usual procedure, Ruth conducting the interview with minimal input from Larry. Vince, who was still a bachelor, was looking for a position with more of a community feel to it than the one he had at present.

'Working in the West End can be a bit impersonal. Naturally, we get a lot of passing trade,' he explained. 'I'd like to feel I belong in a job . . . get to know the regulars and their families.'

'You'd certainly get plenty of opportunity to do that here,' said Ruth. 'Most of our regulars have been coming to us for years.'

Eager to put his feet up in front of the television, Larry brought the proceedings to a speedy halt after the main points had been dealt with. He thanked Vince for coming and said they would let him know their decision as soon as possible. Then he hurriedly departed to the flat, leaving Ruth to see Vince off the premises.

'Do you still see Kitty West?' he asked as they made their way through the shop.

'Yes . . . we're still close friends.'

'How is she?'

'Fine. She's done very well in fact,' Ruth informed him proudly. 'She's in the travel business. Goes abroad quite a bit.'

'Married?'

'She's getting married in a couple of weeks' time, as a matter of fact . . . to a pilot.'

'Ooh, very impressive.' He made a face. 'I was quite smitten with her at one time . . . a schoolboy crush.'

'Yes, I remember.'

'We've all done a lot of growing up since then, eh?'

'Indeed we have.' She paused, wishing against her better judgement to extend this journey into the past.

Opening the shop door, she was greeted by a current of cool air, the earthy scent of autumn on the Green spoiled by the choking miasma of exhaust fumes. Traffic was still fairly heavy in the tail-end of the rush hour.

'Well . . . I'll look forward to hearing from you about the job then,' he said, lingering in the doorway.

'Yes, we won't keep you waiting more than a day or two.'

Her emotions hovered on the brink of turmoil as she struggled to suppress the question that had been aching to be asked ever since she'd clapped eyes on Vince Todd an hour ago. Temptation finally proved too much.

'Do you ever hear from Paul Stoneway?' she asked with feigned casualness.

'No . . . we lost touch after we left school,' he answered with a look of regret.

'Really? I *am* surprised.' She felt a pang of disappointment at the lack of news. 'And you were such good pals too, weren't you?'

'We were best mates,' he agreed. 'It's a pity we didn't stay in touch 'cos I liked Paul. He was a lot of fun. But that's life, isn't it? You drift apart when you grow up and go your separate ways.'

'I think men are lazier about keeping in touch with old friends than women are,' she remarked. 'Women seem to have closer friendships.'

'Quite possibly. It's all too easy to let things slide, though, whatever your gender, when you're trying to make your way in the world,' said Vince, who rarely had a bad word to say about anyone as Ruth remembered it.

'Yes, you move on, make new friends, change your opinions.'

'Exactly. When I went away to university, Paul had already gone abroad. I was busy with my new friends and time slipped by. I couldn't write to him anyway because I didn't know where he was. He said he'd drop me a line at my parents' place when he had a permanent address in Australia. He never did. I suppose he just never got around to it. Too busy with his new life, the same as I was, I expect.'

'Yes, that's probably it.'

'Anyway, Ruth, it's been really good to see you again,' he said, stepping into the street, the squeal of tyres and the roar of a motor bike rising above the general din. 'Give my regards to Kitty when you see her. She probably won't remember me, but still . . .'

'Of course she'll remember you . . . and I'll pass your message on.'

'Just one last thing, Ruth?'

'Yes?'

'I really fancy this job and if you were to decide to take me on, I'd make absolutely certain you didn't regret it.'

She looked at his face, so open and full of hope, and saw a man who exuded honesty and reassurance. He had straight brown hair and warm, caramel-coloured eyes. Although his skin was clear and his features strong, his face was too long and lean to be handsome. His clothes were conservative – a grey suit and white shirt.

'So far as I'm concerned the job's yours,' she said, expecting Larry to agree with her if only to save him the bother of interviewing anyone else. 'But it isn't just up to me.'

'I understand.'

'We'll let you know in the next couple of days and that's a promise.'

'Okay.' He moved back slightly. 'Cheerio for now, then.'

'Cheerio, Vince,' she said, feeling better for having seen him because he was such a nice person, but shaken by the emotions he had unwittingly aroused.

'Vince Todd! You're gonna be working with *Vince Todd*!' exclaimed Kitty the following Sunday afternoon when Ruth and Jenny were at her flat in Holland Park Avenue. They had come for the final fitting of their dresses for the wedding at which Jenny was to be bridesmaid and Ruth Matron of Honour.

'There's no need to sound quite so shocked,' said Ruth.

The dressmaker had finished her work and left. Jenny was watching Captain Pugwash on the television in the living room while the two friends chatted in the kitchen over a cup of tea.

'But he used to be the biggest creep at Redfern Grammar School.'

'Only in your eyes,' Ruth protested. 'He was nice . . . still is.'

'What's nice got to do with it?'

'Everything when you're considering someone for a job in a chemist's shop.'

'Well, yes, of course it's important from your point of view,' conceded Kitty with a wicked grin. 'But nice wasn't on my list of priorities as a sixteen year old with a sudden invasion of demanding hormones.'

'I suppose not,' laughed Ruth.

'Fancy him turning up again after all this time,' remarked Kitty.

'It isn't too surprising when you consider that we're all from this part of West London originally, albeit Redfern Grammar had a wide catchment area.'

'True.'

'Anyway, he asked after you and sent you his regards.'

'Lucky me,' said Kitty, pulling a face. 'He always fancied me rotten.'

'I remember.'

'I had to spell it out loud and clear for him that night . . . to make sure he got the message – that I didn't fancy him.' She paused with her tea cup in mid-air. 'He was about as tempting as smallpox.'

'I hope you weren't mean enough to use those words to him, Kitty,' said Ruth with a wry grin at her friend's cruel turn of phrase.

'Give me some credit, Ruth. But I had to be firm with him 'cos he was dead keen.' She bit her lip ponderously, wondering if she dare ask the question that had been on her lips ever since Ruth had mentioned the reappearance of Vince Todd. She decided to take a chance on it. 'And talking of that night . . . is Vince still in contact with the last member of the foursome?'

'No . . . they didn't stay in touch.'

'Well, well,' said Kitty, managing to suppress a string of abuse about the person in question, knowing it would upset Ruth. 'Don't they even exchange Christmas cards?'

Ruth shook her head. 'Apparently not. Vince doesn't have an address for him.'

Tension tightened at the mention of Paul Stoneway. Kitty hastily changed the subject.

'So you think Vince is right for the job then?' she said.

'I can't be certain until he actually starts work, of course, but I'm impressed with him. He has all the necessary qualifications and exactly the right sort of personality to communicate with the customers,' explained Ruth. 'And, above all, he isn't going to be fighting with me for authority every step of the way. He seems quite happy to work with me and not over me. He knows his stuff but isn't the least bit pushy, unlike the other applicants.'

'Did any women apply for the job?'

'Not a single one. There are female pharmacists around but not nearly so many as there are men,' Ruth told her friend. 'Not enough women are encouraged to get qualified.'

'It must be annoying that you're not qualified yourself?'

'Very,' she admitted. 'Now that I'm so deeply involved with pharmacy, qualifications would be really useful.'

'One day perhaps . . .'

'Not a chance,' she cut in. 'The most I can hope for is a course at evening class to become a dispenser, maybe later on when Jenny is older and I have some spare time. But to qualify as a pharmacist means "A" levels . . . which I don't have.'

'If things had turned out differently . . .'

'But they didn't, did they?' put in Ruth quickly to deter any further discussion on the subject. 'So I have to do my best with what I have, which is a hell of a lot.'

'So when does Vince start?'

'Next month when he's worked out his notice at his present job,' she said. 'The week after your wedding, in fact.'

'I shall have to call in at the shop sometime to say hello to him,' said Kitty. 'See if he's a bit less soppy than he was at eighteen.'

'Well, be kind to him if you do,' warned Ruth lightly. 'I don't want you upsetting my colleague.'

'As if I would,' said Kitty wickedly.

'Anyway, I'm sure you're going to have more important things to do with your time as Mrs Tim Barrett than calling in to take the mickey out of Vince.'

'You're right,' agreed Kitty. 'I won't be round this way so often either as I'm gonna be living out near Staines.'

'Exciting, eh?'

'Not half,' she enthused. 'Tim . . . now he really *is* a man!'

'I'm glad it worked out.'

Kitty's expression became deadly serious.

'So am I, Ruth,' she said gravely. 'I'd have fallen apart if it hadn't.'

Kitty's wedding was predictably lavish, her parents being comfortably off. There were church bells and organ music and a reception at a classy hotel. Not for Kitty the traditional long white gown, though. She wore one of the short, trendy wedding dresses with a stand-out skirt stiff with layers of lace and chiffon, and a frothy veil with clouds of tulle billowing around her face.

She and Tim made a handsome couple and were obviously devoted to each other. Ruth enjoyed the occasion, if perhaps a little less exuberantly than Jenny who was feverishly excited about being a bridesmaid again. The Brooks family were there en masse and having a whale of a time.

Ruth wondered if she and Kitty might begin to drift apart. The newly weds had bought a house near Staines because it was convenient for the airport for Tim. Kitty wouldn't be coming into central London for work either because she'd got a job in a travel agent's close to where she was going to be living, a position which didn't entail being away from home. Travelling abroad on her own had lost its appeal for the besotted Mrs Barrett.

Friends of the couple were mostly airline types who talked about exotic places, hilarious parties and infidelities among their colleagues. Ruth felt very much an outsider among them.

But, oddly enough, she found herself needing to reassure Kitty about their friendship later on when she was getting changed to go away on honeymoon.

'You and I go back a long way,' Kitty remarked as Ruth helped her off with her wedding dress in the bedroom at Kitty's family home.

'We certainly do.'

'I enjoy my new friends . . . they're great fun,' continued Kitty.

'Mmm.'

'It's important to me to have a busy social life,' she explained.

'You've always needed that sort of thing more than I have,' said Ruth, hanging the wedding gown up while Kitty slipped into a suit.

'But you're still my closest friend and I don't want that to change just because I'm going to be living further away.'

'Neither do I, so we won't let it happen,' said Ruth, noticing tears glistening in her friend's eyes.

'I'm glad you've said that,' said Kitty, dabbing her eyes with a handkerchief. 'After all, Staines isn't far. And I'll be coming up to town as often as I can. I'll have to, to see my parents.'

'Don't worry . . . if I don't see you for a while, I'll be on the phone to find out why,' said Ruth, hugging her.

'Yes, there's always the phone . . .'

''Course there is.'

'I'm so happy, Ruth,' said Kitty, tears trickling down her cheeks.

'I should hate to see you when you're miserable, then,' laughed Ruth though she, too, was dangerously close to tears.

The force of their emotion manifested itself in giggles, tearful uncontrollable laughter which released the tension and rose in loud shrieks and guffaws. Kitty's mother, who was sorting out wedding presents downstairs, called up to remind her that she did have a plane to catch: to Paris, where the couple had first met.

'I'll cover for you in the shop, Ruth, while you go and collect Jenny from school,' said the amiable Vince one afternoon the following spring.

'It's awkward for me to get away when Madge isn't here,' said Ruth, referring to their assistant who was currently on sick leave. 'You have more than enough to do in the dispensary.'

'I'll manage . . . don't worry,' he assured her. 'Off you go then. You don't want Jenny to be hanging about outside the school.'

'Thanks, Vince, you're a gem.' She grinned. 'I don't know what I'd do without you.'

'Flatterer!' he joked. 'Go on . . . go and get your daughter.'

'I think I'll go in the car,' she muttered to herself. 'It'll be quicker.'

Ruth drove the short distance to the school in the estate car she and Larry had decided she needed for business errands now that he wasn't around during the day to do them in his car. Fortunately she'd learned to drive quickly and passed her test first time. As well as being useful in a multitude of ways, this meant she was able to save money for the business by taking advantage of the cash and carry warehouse that had just opened for some of the shop's goods, instead of relying on wholesalers for everything.

Thinking back on the last six months since she'd been working with Vince, she thought what an asset he'd proved to be, a true friend as well as a diligent and reliable colleague. Nothing was too much trouble for Vince – no person too tiresome nor task too demeaning. He was certainly a darned sight easier to work with than Larry had been because Vince did his share, which meant that Ruth wasn't bone tired every single night.

As well as keeping abreast with scientific developments which gave him a first-class technical knowledge of pharmacy, Vince was also popular with the customers. He had endless patience and never hurried them when they wanted to discuss their ailments, though he was quick to spot danger signs and advise them to see their doctor if necessary. She smiled, recalling an embarrassing incident recently when a man had insisted on showing him a boil on his buttock, right there in the crowded shop.

His caring personality spilled over into his private life, too, from what Ruth could gather. He seemed to be a magnet for people whose lives were in crisis. Those with troubled marriages or difficult mothers or accommodation problems, all flocked to Vince's door. But there was no special woman in his life, much to his regret.

'I'm everyone's friend and nobody's lover,' he confessed wistfully.

'You'll meet someone one day,' Ruth told him, and meant it because he had so much to offer. He was no heart throb it was true, but neither was he physically repulsive. Ruth came to the conclusion that he was one of those kind souls whom people use as a crutch when they are low and promptly discard when they are feeling better. He was a bit *too* accommodating and people took advantage of him.

The fact that there was not, and never would be, anything other than platonic friendship between Vince and Ruth made theirs a comfortable working relationship with no sexual undertones to complicate matters.

Kitty, who was enjoying married life with Tim in Staines and saw Vince only briefly when she was in town and called at the shop to see Ruth, still thought he was a twit of the highest order.

'I don't know how you can stand having that long streak

of congeniality around you all day,' she announced to Ruth one day when they were having lunch together.

'Why?'

'All that niceness would drive me round the bend. A man needs a bit of wickedness about him to make him interesting.'

'Maybe, but as a friend and colleague, Vince is perfect,' Ruth had countered.

Recalled to the present as she approached the school gates, Ruth greeted her daughter and settled her into the car then made her way home. On the way back to the shop through the backstreets, she caught sight of her mother trudging back from the shops, weighed down with bags.

'I told you I'd take you to the supermarket in the car to shop once a week, to save you lugging all the shopping home nearly every day,' said Ruth in mild admonition as her mother settled into the back of the car.

'Yeah, so you did, love,' said Audrey, sounding unconcerned. 'But you know me: I enjoy wandering down the shops and having a look round the market. I like to have a chat along the way too.'

'I won't nag you,' said Ruth, 'but the offer's there if you want it.'

'Okay. Actually, I'm glad I've seen you 'cos I've got some news,' said Audrey excitedly, leaning forward so that Ruth could hear.

'Ooh, what's happened?'

'The twins are both gonna be dads.'

'You mean Pat and Peggy are *both* pregnant?' exclaimed Ruth.

'Yeah. And that isn't all . . .'

'Don't tell me they're both expecting at the same time?'

'They are . . . both the babies are due at the end of August.'

'Well, I'll be blowed!' said Ruth. 'Some sort of twin telepathy has been at work.'

'Are the Nunks getting some babies?' enquired Jenny curiously.

'Yes, love,' said Audrey, smiling at her beloved granddaughter. 'You're gonna have two little cousins soon. Won't that be exciting?'

'Ooh, yes. Perhaps the aunties will let me take the babies out for walks in the pram,' she said in happy anticipation.

Larry didn't seem the least bit interested in Ruth's news about the forthcoming new additions to the Brooks family.

'Don't you think it's the most amazing coincidence, both Pat and Peggy expecting at the same time?' she said, brushing her hair in front of the dressing-table mirror before going to bed. Larry was already there, reading.

'No, not really. That sort of thing often happens with twins,' he replied impatiently. 'It's a recognised fact.'

'It'll be great fun for the babies growing up together, though, won't it?' she said trying unsuccessfully not to be hurt by his brusque manner. 'It'll be just like having another set of twins in the family.'

'Mmm.'

'Mum says she feels as though she's permanently seeing double,' Ruth remarked casually. 'Since Pat and Peggy came on to the scene.'

This time he didn't even bother to reply but immersed himself determinedly in his book, making it obvious he found her conversation boring. Puzzled, Ruth smoothed some cold cream over her face and got into bed beside him.

'You seem a bit touchy,' she said. 'Is anything wrong?'

'No.'

'Have you had a bad day?'

'Not especially,' he snapped.

'Vince and I have been rushed off our feet,' she said chattily, hoping he would come out of his sour mood if she ignored it. 'There's some sort of a tummy bug going around. The doctors must have got writer's cramp doing so many prescriptions.'

He didn't reply.

She snuggled against him, burying her face in his neck. Larry was a very passionate man. She knew what he needed to cheer him up.

'Not now, Ruth,' he said sharply.

'Playing hard to get, eh?'

'Not at all,' he snapped.

'Oh.'

'I'm just not in the mood.'

And much to her dismay, he put his book down on the bedside table, switched off his light and turned on to his side with his back to her.

They had had their share of disagreements during the three years they'd been married, the same as any other couple, but they'd never slept back to back. And Larry didn't usually reject any physical initiative from her. Quite the opposite, in fact, for he was insatiable in that department. Now it was as though he couldn't bear to have her near him.

'What's the matter, Larry?'

'Nothing.'

'Why are you being so hateful then?'

'Oh, don't be so childish, for God's sake,' he rasped.

'Is it me?' she persisted, hot tears swelling beneath her lids. 'Have I upset you without realising it?'

'No. Just leave it, Ruth, will you?' he said with an eloquent sigh.

'But, Larry . . .'

'I'm feeling very tired,' he said. 'I want to go to sleep.'

'Goodnight then.'

'G'night.'

Stunned by his coldness, she turned off her bedside light and lay back against the pillows, staring into the darkness, her heart racing with worry, her mouth dry with fear. Larry wasn't given to moods – he was normally quite easygoing so long as he got his own way. Or he had been until recently, she thought, realising that he had been rather offhand towards her this last few weeks. Not quite so vile as he'd been tonight but definitely pre-occupied. She'd been so busy running the business and the home, this fact hadn't fully registered until now.

Something must be worrying him. She wondered if he was finding it a strain running the Hammersmith shop without her to do most of the work. Perhaps he was feeling resentful towards her because of this. He hated having too much work and responsibility and relied on her to ease his burden. This wasn't so easy now that she wasn't at his beck and call all day long.

Whatever he had on his mind, she knew instinctively that it wasn't something that was going to disappear overnight. She also knew that it concerned her personally and wasn't just some minor problem outside their relationship. She lay awake until the small hours turning it over and over in her mind but came to no definite conclusion. She found she was frightened of losing him. She couldn't bear that!

Larry's assistant Wendy smiled adoringly at him when she took his morning coffee into the dispensary, set out attractively on a tray with a plate of fancy biscuits.

'There you are . . . nice and milky with two sugars,' she said in a soft intimate voice. 'Just the way you like it, Mr Paterson.'

'Now what have I told you about that, Wendy?' he said in a playful tone, looking straight into her eyes. 'My name is Larry and that's what I would like you to call me. "Mr Paterson" makes me feel so terribly old.'

'You're not old, Mr . . . er, Larry,' she said with assumed coyness. 'Not at all.'

'I am compared to you,' he said, for he was thirty-two

and she was just eighteen. 'You must think I'm positively ancient.'

'Never,' she breathed, leaning over to remove the coffee cup from the tray and set it down on the workbench with the biscuits, her white cotton overall rustling as she moved. 'I would never think that about an attractive man like you.'

Wendy had been working with him at the Hammersmith shop for about a month. She had replaced the assistant he'd inherited from the previous owner who hadn't been suited to the job in as much as she hadn't been willing to do anything beyond serving at the counter.

A forthright middle-aged woman, she'd complained bitterly about having to carry out tasks she considered to be outside her duties as a shop assistant, like staying after hours to clean up and fill the shelves. She'd also objected to doing more than she'd ever had to do before in the dispensary. She'd finally resigned in a fit of pique after being asked to get some paperwork ready for Ruth who looked after the office work for both shops.

This new assistant was quite different. Not only was Wendy eager to please, she also had a pretty face and a figure that did wicked things to Larry's libido. Even better, she was obviously attracted to him. He found himself longing to get to work each morning and was becoming increasingly besotted with her every day that passed, a process he enjoyed enormously. He'd always found the thrill of a potential new love affair irresistible. Just as he had when he and Ruth had first met.

Ruth . . . Oh, dear. What was he going to do about her? They'd had a lot of good times together and he'd enjoyed his marriage for the most part. But now that there were more exciting opportunities for the taking, she bored him. Their relationship had run its course. All passion for Ruth had died the minute he'd felt the chemistry with Wendy. What on earth had possessed him to be so hasty in getting married, he couldn't imagine. He'd always known in his heart he would never settle for one woman indefinitely.

He decided to cast all thoughts of his wife out of his mind. This wasn't difficult because Larry had never been troubled by conscience. Shedding the past in favour of the glorious present was no problem to him at all.

'Wouldn't you, Wendy?' he said in reply, taking her hand and putting it to his lips.

'No, Larry, I never would,' she said. 'I think you're wonderful!'

'The feeling is mutual, my dear,' he sighed, slipping his arms around her and holding her close. 'I can promise you that.'

Chapter Seven

In mid-August the two eagerly awaited additions to the
Brooks family arrived, two weeks early and within an hour
of each other, in the maternity ward of Hammersmith
Hospital. Both were boys; both had their fathers' dark
colouring. Pat and Ray named their son Tom; Peggy and
Jack settled on Gary.

'I bet they'll be a right couple of tearaways, just like
their fathers used to be,' Ruth said jokingly to her mother.

'God forbid,' said Audrey, rolling her eyes at the
thought. 'One thing's sure to happen though, they'll grow
up more as twins than cousins.'

'Bound to,' agreed Ruth, 'as their parents are always
together.'

One evening at the end of August Ruth was at home
alone. Jenny had gone with Audrey to visit the new mums,
who were now out of hospital with their offspring. Larry
wasn't in. He was rarely at home these days.

The weather was hot and stormy with low, mud-
coloured clouds and the smell of rain in the air. Ruth
had finished her meal and was sitting by the open window
in the living room, reading an article in the newspaper
about the imminent introduction of parking tickets and
traffic wardens. They'll be about as popular with the
motoring public as a petrol price rise, she thought
gloomily.

Finding concentration difficult under the weight of
her problems, she put the newspaper down and stared
idly out of the window. There was a scene of high activity
on and around the Green as people went out for their

115

evening entertainment, many of them cutting across the eight-acre area of grassland, dry and balding now in the August heat.

Larry was supposed to be meeting an old chum from university for a meal out. Last night it had been a different old friend; the night before that he'd been working late at the shop.

Or so he'd told her. But she guessed he was seeing another woman and was certain it was his assistant, Wendy. Ruth could sense the closeness between them when she called at the Hammersmith shop and it was like a knife in her heart. Part of her wanted to confront him with her suspicions with furious desperation, the other part was afraid to know the truth. She was clinging to the hope that it was just a casual affair that would run its course and peter out if it was left alone without interference from her.

Her husband was a very attractive man. Ruth had known all along that he wouldn't lack for opportunities to be unfaithful. She just prayed to God it wasn't serious. After all, Wendy was a lot younger than him. She'd probably tire of him quite soon.

Hearing someone come in at the front door, she was startled because she hadn't been expecting Larry back so soon. She knew it was him because her mother would have rung the bell.

'Hello, love,' she said, getting up to greet him as though everything was normal between them. 'I wasn't expecting you home for a while yet.'

'No.'

'Have you had anything to eat?'

He nodded.

Their eyes met briefly before he looked away. He was obviously uneasy. Ruth stiffened with fear as she realised with chilling certainty that he was about to make a confession.

'We need to talk,' he said, standing with his back to the unlit hearth.

She moistened her parched lips, heartbeat thundering erratically in her ears.

'There's someone else, isn't there?' she said, praying he would deny it.

'Yes, I'm afraid there is,' he said, staring at the floor.

'Oh.' The nagging ache of suspicion was as nothing compared to the agony of having her worst fears confirmed. It was as though every last vestige of vitality and self-confidence was being physically dragged from her, leaving her broken and lifeless. 'Is it Wendy at the other shop?'

'Yes.'

'I suspected there was something going on when I saw you together.'

He raised his head and looked at her. 'I'm sorry, Ruth,' he said, but didn't sound particularly contrite.

'So am I.' She took a deep, shuddering breath. 'But what happens now?'

'I want to marry her.'

She stood rooted to the spot, trying to gather her wits.

'Marry her!' she exclaimed at last.

'That's right.'

She was not prepared for this. Playing around was one thing. But leaving her to marry someone else . . . she just couldn't take it in. Her legs felt so weak she collapsed into the nearest armchair.

'It may suit you to put it out of your mind, Larry, but you are already married to me.'

'Divorce shouldn't be too much of a problem,' he said in the insouciant manner of someone who knows they are in a position of power.

'Divorce?' she echoed dumbly.

'Yes, I'll admit adultery. I can hardly deny it as Wendy is pregnant. She's willing to be cited as co-respondent.'

Ruth winced. This really was turning the knife. She had wanted to have a child with Larry but he'd been dead set against the idea. He'd said they needed more time together . . . just the two of them and Jenny. But she'd suspected that he didn't want the inconvenience of having a baby around.

As though reading her thoughts, he said, 'It was an accident. It was the last thing I wanted. But as it's happened, I shall have to do the decent thing.'

She stared at him incredulously. 'But what about me, Larry? What about doing the decent thing by me, your wife?'

'You'll be all right, Ruth . . . you're tough . . . one of life's survivors,' he said in a tone she could only describe as matter-of-fact. 'Wendy's very young and vulnerable.'

'And I don't feel pain, I suppose?' she said through clenched teeth.

'You'll cope, you've done it before,' he said lamely.

That hurt. By God it did.

'Hardship doesn't make you immune to heartache, you know,' she told him.

'You'll get by without me.'

'How do you think Jenny's going to feel?' she said. 'She's grown fond of you.'

This seemed to catch him off guard and he didn't reply for a few moments.

'Obviously I don't want to hurt Jenny any more than I want to hurt you,' he said, soon regaining his composure. 'But she'll get over it. Life moves on and takes us with it. It isn't as though I'm Jenny's real father. And as I'm going to be having a child of my own soon . . .'

A storm of rage lashed through her at the sheer callousness of the man.

'Have you no sense of responsibility at all?' she demanded, leaping up and staring at him, her eyes bright with fury. 'These are people's lives you're messing with.'

'I *am* being responsible,' he stated categorically. 'I'm taking steps towards marrying the woman who is carrying *my* child.'

'What about Jenny and me?' she cried, her voice quivering with emotion. 'Don't you have any feelings for us?'

'What you and I had was good, Ruth . . . very good, in its time,' he informed her with hurtful carelessness. 'But, as I said, life moves on and things change. My future lies with Wendy now.'

His words stung with the bite of acid, seeping through her body in an agonising tide. A cry of pain rose up in her throat and she couldn't suppress it. Nor could she control the need to lash out at the cause of her torture. She threw herself against him, groaning and beating her fists against his chest.

'Oh, for God's sake!' he rebuked her in a superior manner, extricating himself as though she was an embarrassment to him. 'Is all this drama really necessary?'

'How could you do this to me, Larry?' she sobbed, on the verge of hysterics and far too upset to bother about her dignity. 'How could you betray me in such a cruel way?'

'Grow up, Ruth. I'm not the first married man to fall in love with someone else and I certainly won't be the last,' he said impatiently. 'It's life . . . it happens all the time.'

'And that's supposed to make me feel better, is it?'

'It might, knowing you're not the only woman in the world this has happened to.'

Her fury drained away as she realised with bruising certainty that she'd lost him – that all the discussion in the world wasn't going to change anything, because what he had once felt for her had gone for ever. It hadn't been strong enough to withstand his own fickle nature.

'Oh, get out,' she said wearily. 'Just go and leave me in peace.'

119

'Sure I'll go,' he agreed, speaking in a slow and deliberate manner. 'I'll move in with Wendy for the time being . . .'

Something in his tone made her look at him questioningly.

'But obviously you'll be the one who'll be leaving here eventually,' he continued calmly. 'On a permanent basis.'

'Me . . . leaving?' She looked bewildered. 'But this is my home, mine and Jenny's.'

'Only because you're married to me, which you won't be for much longer,' he informed her harshly. 'The property is mine. If I no longer want you to stay, then out you go.'

Before she could marshal her thoughts sufficiently to respond to this body blow, he was pounding down the stairs.

Weakened by shock, she sank into an armchair, overwhelmed by pain and misery as she digested this devastating turn of events. In her heart she'd known all along that Larry was weak and selfish but had accepted him as he was because she loved him, allowing him to take advantage of her because of her strong feelings for him.

The strength of her love made the disillusionment all the more complete as the tide turned. She felt robbed and cheated. She despised him for exploiting her then making her feel worthless. The pain went deep. She couldn't cry – she couldn't move. She was totally demoralised, as though her self-esteem had been punched out of her by Larry's fist.

She was recalled to the present by the sound of the doorbell. Managing to pull herself together sufficiently to set her face into a smile, she went downstairs to let in her mother and Jenny.

'Are you all right, love?' asked Audrey, noticing her daughter's greyish pallor.

''Course I am.'

'You look a bit peaky.'

'This stormy weather has given me a bit of a headache, that's all,' lied Ruth.

'Are you sure that's all it is?'

'Certain,' she bluffed. 'I'll take some aspirin in a minute.'

Her mother would have to know the truth soon enough, as would Jenny. But not now. Ruth couldn't face telling anyone tonight.

After a sleepless night, Ruth got up feeling sick at heart and achingly weary but knowing she mustn't let her own pain blind her to the practical side of all this. Having been forced back into the role of single mother, she had to be strong for Jenny. She must do everything she could to prevent her daughter losing more than just her stepfather.

As soon as the morning rush of prescriptions was over, she left Vince in charge of the shop and drove over to Hammersmith where she found Larry in the dispensary finishing off a prescription for cough linctus.

'I'm here to find out if you were serious about my leaving the flat?' she said, coming straight to the point. 'I can't believe you actually expect me to get out.'

At least he had the grace to look a little sheepish.

'Well . . . er, yes, I was serious,' he said, scratching his cheek in agitation. 'I need the accommodation for myself and Wendy and the baby.'

'But I'm your wife. That flat is my home . . . mine and Jenny's.'

'The property is in my name,' he pointed out, his voice hardening. 'Obviously I don't expect you to move out tomorrow but I'd like you to find alternative accommodation as soon as possible.'

'Surely you wouldn't turn Jenny and me out, not after all we've been to each other?'

'Spare me the melodrama, Ruth,' he admonished in the most patronising manner. 'You'll hardly be out on the street, will you? Not with a family like yours behind you.'

'That's beside the point.'

'Your parents will be only too pleased to have you and Jenny living at their place again, especially now the twins have left home.'

Ruth had gone beyond pain and was in a state of numb disbelief. This was so awful, it must be some sort of a nightmare.

'I'm not even going to ask my parents if we can move in with them,' she heard herself say. 'The flat is our home and that is where we are going to stay.'

'I think not.'

She was standing just inside the dispensary door. He was standing by the workbench, looking at her with pure arrogance now, any trace of compunction having disappeared.

'I must say I expected better treatment than this from you, Larry,' she said.

In reply he shrugged his shoulders.

'I've really worked at that business,' she continued. 'A business that I came to think of as our family business . . . and partly mine.'

'I won't deny you've worked hard.' He sighed, his manner becoming slightly more conciliatory. 'Look, Ruth, I didn't want our marriage to fail . . .'

'You're not making any effort to make it succeed though, are you?'

'You wouldn't want me to carry on being married to you, knowing I was in love with someone else, surely?'

'In love?' she exploded. 'It's nothing more than lust.'

'You can call it what you like but I know how I feel.'

'It strikes me that you fall in and out of love as the mood takes you,' she said. 'As a married man, you should

122

have had more control of your feelings.'

'Maybe I should. But this has happened and we both have to accept that,' he said. 'Obviously, I will be obliged to pay maintenance to you and I'll not shirk my duty so far as that's concerned. But I need you out of the flat.' He cleared his throat. 'And obviously I won't want you to stay on in the business.'

'So I'm to lose my home *and* my job just because you've been behaving like a dog on heat?' she said, shaken to the core by this added blow.

'You're an intelligent woman,' he said. 'You won't have any trouble finding another position. I'll give you a reference.'

That was the last straw. If anything was needed to shake her out of her self-pity it was this giant-sized piece of condescension.

'Considering it was I who built your business into what it is today, that's very big of you,' she said sarcastically.

'There's no need for you to take that tone . . .'

'There's every need for me to take that tone,' she interrupted angrily. 'I've carried you this last four years . . . well, ever since you took over from Mr Grover to be exact. It was my ideas and hard work that trebled the turnover. It was me who worked late while you were loafing about in the flat of an evening. You just sat back and enjoyed the extra cash as our profits rose, *because of me*. And now I'm about to lose three major parts of my life in one fell swoop: my husband, my home and my job.'

This was proving to be more difficult that he'd expected. He'd known that Ruth wouldn't be overjoyed, of course, but hadn't expected her to be this forceful. He hadn't anticipated any real problem in ending his marriage, especially as her brothers were no longer a threat to him. These days, the twins were far too busy being family men to give him any trouble. It was just Ruth's attitude that was so damned tedious. All he wanted was to get shot of her so he could get on with his life with Wendy.

'You won't come out of this completely empty-handed, you know,' he pointed out blandly.

'Oh, no?' she said, narrowing her eyes at him. 'You tell me what I've gained except a whole lot of pain and humiliation?'

'As I've said, you'll get maintenance payments from me,' he reminded her.

'You don't have a choice about that, since it's the law,' she pointed out.

'Many a man ignores that law.'

'That's irrelevant.'

'Regular maintenance isn't all you'll have had from me,' he said spitefully. 'Don't forget I gave you and your child respectability. You won't lose that. Better to be a divorcee than an unmarried mother so far as your standing in society is concerned.'

'My God, Larry, you have a cruel streak in you,' she rasped, eyes brimming with tears as she remembered that magical New Year's Eve when he'd proposed to her.

Who would have thought their fairy-tale romance would have come to this – a slanging match about economics? Who could have guessed that the sweet-talking hero who had showered her with gifts and pursued her relentlessly until she agreed to marry him could have turned out to be such a bastard?

There were no words to express what she felt for him at this moment. So she turned and left, saying nothing more.

Much to Ruth's relief, it was time to shut the shop for lunch when she got back to Shepherd's Bush. Jenny was at her grandparents' house, this being the school holidays, so Ruth was spared the effort of putting on an act for her.

Desperately in need of a friend, she invited Vince up to the flat for a bite to eat. It was easier to talk to someone who was less personally involved than the family, somehow, and out it all came in a painful torrent.

'I run this shop and do all the administration for the other one,' she said after she'd given him the full story, 'and now I'm going to be booted out of my job and my home. It's so bloody unfair, especially when I built this shop up into a thriving business single-handed while Larry sat back and did as little as he could get away with.'

Vince listened to everything she had to say, remaining calm.

'I think you're entitled to some compensation,' he said.

'So do I but I won't get it,' she said. 'Everything is in Larry's name. I won't be entitled to anything except maintenance payments.'

'You should be given a damned sight more than that,' was Vince's definite opinion. 'Surely Larry must see that?'

'Even if he did, he would never admit it because it wouldn't be in his interests to do so,' she said. 'Honestly, Vince, I've seen a side of Larry I never dreamed existed.'

'The fact is, he has two thriving shops because of you, so you should have your fair share.'

'If fairness came into it, I should have this shop,' she said. 'But justice isn't on the side of the woman when a marriage breaks up.'

'Frankly, I think you should go all out to get this shop,' said Vince, surprising her.

'Oh, now you really are entering into the realms of fantasy!'

'I mean it,' he said. 'Larry has two successful shops, both of which are the direct result of your hard work and initiative. He should do the decent thing and sign this one over to you, keeping the other one for himself and the new woman in his life. That's hardly going to leave him in poverty, is it?'

'Can you imagine Larry agreeing to that?' she said gloomily.

'If he was forced to by law, he would have to,' said Vince.

'Take him to court, you mean?'

'If he won't do the right thing without that, then, yes,' said Vince.

'Oh, Vince, it seems so dreadfully hard and clinical,' she said. 'I *have* been married to the man for four years.'

'Exactly . . . which is why you should be treated decently. After all, he's the one who wants to end the marriage, not you. You've done nothing wrong.'

She knew he was right. It wasn't just her own quality of life that was at stake here. Jenny was going to suffer if they were reduced to living in rooms, because Ruth was determined not to impose on her parents a second time. They'd raised their family and were entitled to some peace and quiet at this stage in their lives.

'But before you do anything at all, you need to have a chat with a solicitor and find out if you have a case.'

This put the whole thing into perspective, bringing her right back to earth.

'Solicitors cost money,' she said.

'Is that a problem?'

'It could be. I take what cash I need from the business for general household and personal use and I've managed to save a little from that over the years,' she explained. 'But I don't think I can afford a court case, especially as I stand to lose my income soon. Things will be really tight for me when that happens. Don't forget that I have a daughter to support.'

'If you win the case, Larry will have to pay your costs.'

'Even so . . .'

'You could enquire about legal aid,' he suggested. 'But if you're really stuck, I could lend you some money. As a bachelor, I've saved quite a bit over the years. If you win the case – and if there's any justice in the world, you will – you won't have a problem paying me back.'

'I really appreciate the offer, Vince, but it's all getting frighteningly dramatic,' she said, wringing her hands in despair. 'Who would have thought it would come to this? Two people who once loved each other fighting something out in court.'

'It won't be pleasant,' he said sympathetically. 'But you'll just have to toughen up, for Jenny's sake as well as your own.'

As the bleak future became horribly clear to her, she decided that she wasn't prepared to take the role of victim for a second time. Maybe she couldn't mend her broken heart but she could fight for what she was entitled to.

'You're absolutely right,' she said with a surge of determination. 'Why should I make it easy for him by slipping conveniently out of his life just like he wants me to, without a fight? I'm going to stand up for my rights.'

'That's the spirit.'

She looked at her watch. 'It's time to open the shop.'

He glanced at his wrist. 'So it is.'

She raised her hands in a gesture of helpless bewilderment.

'So what happens now?' she said. 'Am I supposed to carry on working in the shop as the discarded wife of its legal owner, a man who wants me out in his own good time?'

'Who's going to do it if you don't?' Vince wanted to know. 'I'm busy in the dispensary and Madge can't manage the shop on her own.'

'A good point,' said Ruth. 'Larry hasn't got round to thinking about this side of things yet, I shouldn't think.'

'You're needed downstairs in the shop,' emphasised Vince. 'Larry isn't going to be able to conjure up an extra pair of hands immediately, is he? It'll take time to find someone to look after things the way you do.'

'Mmm.'

'Anyway, you need to stay with the job if you're going

to be taking over the business,' he suggested. 'You don't want it to go downhill, which it will do if you aren't around to make sure that doesn't happen.'

'That's a bit premature . . .'

'I'm just being positive, Ruth, which is what you must be.'

'You're right.' She tapped her chin with her thumbnail, a determined gleam coming into her eyes.

'So what are you going to do?' he pressed.

'I think the best thing I can do is to give Larry a ring and suggest I carry on here as normal for the time being.'

'That should keep him off your back while you get some legal advice.'

'Yes, and if I know Larry, he'll be only too relieved for me to carry on, no matter how much he wants me out of his life.'

'He does like things to run smoothly around him, doesn't he?'

'With the least amount of effort on his part,' added Ruth with a wry grin.

'Yes.'

'And Wendy doesn't seem the type to step in and organise everything for him like I did. If I'm any judge, he'll want me to stay around in the shop until it suits him to get rid of me, especially as he won't have to see me very often.'

'Well . . . Madge and I can manage in the shop while you go and see a solicitor,' offered Vince. 'I think you should do that without further delay.'

'You're right,' she said. 'I'll get an appointment to see someone as soon as possible.'

'Good.'

Ruth looked away and blinked back the tears. Having a positive attitude was all very well but it didn't take away the pain.

Chapter Eight

'Does your husband own the property outright, Mrs Paterson?' asked the solicitor, a white-haired, dapper little man with a confident manner which Ruth found reassuring. 'Or is there a mortgage on it?'

'There's a mortgage on it which is covered by the income from the shop,' she explained.

'And you'd be prepared to take over the repayments . . . if the business were to be handed over to you?'

'Of course,' she replied, shoulders aching with tension, eyes sore and itchy from having been awake all night. 'And obviously my husband would have no further financial responsibility towards me, so he wouldn't be badly off, especially as he will still have our other shop.'

He nodded, adding something to the notes he'd been making throughout the interview.

'The living accommodation above the Hammersmith shop is quite spacious and currently rented out on a short-term lease,' she continued. 'So my husband could live there when the tenants move out, if he wishes. It will save him the bother of re-letting. And since I wouldn't require maintenance from him, he would be quite well placed financially.'

The solicitor tapped his pen on the blotting pad, observing her closely.

'You seem to be more concerned about his welfare than you are about your own,' he said, liking this spirited young woman.

'I only want to be fair,' said Ruth. 'I want nothing to which I'm not entitled.'

'The law as it stands at the moment doesn't protect women in your situation, which is why so many ex-wives find themselves facing hardship when a marriage breaks up,' he remarked.

'And that is why I'm being forced into court,' she said. 'I really believe that it's wrong for me to be rendered homeless and jobless when I've worked hard to build a business that was considered to be our joint family concern until it suited my husband for it to be otherwise. I have a daughter to support and it's my duty to secure the very best standard of living I can for her. She's already going to suffer the loss of her stepfather. I want to protect her from further suffering.'

'I can understand how you must be feeling, my dear,' he said, leaning back, linking his fingers together and resting them on his stomach in a relaxed manner. 'But it would be much less distressing for you personally if this matter could be settled out of court.'

'I agree. But I doubt if my husband will change his mind unless he's forced to by the law.'

He tapped his thumbs together and pondered the matter.

'It's a question of proving that you've made a substantial contribution to your husband's business over a period of time,' he explained. 'The accounts will show the rise in turnover but they can't prove who is actually responsible.'

'It's common knowledge among the staff and customers that I run the business,' she said. 'The local doctors are also aware of my position, as are the wholesalers with whom we do business.'

'Mmm.' He pondered for a while. 'It sounds to me as though you have quite a strong case. But leave it with me. I'll have a chat with my colleagues and get in touch with you again in a few days.'

While Ruth was out at the solicitor's office, Kitty called at the shop.

'I've been to visit my mother and thought I'd call in on the offchance of seeing Ruth before going home,' she explained when Vince told her that Ruth was out. 'Do you know if she'll be long?'

'She should be back at any minute.'

'Oh.' Kitty looked at her watch and seemed doubtful as to whether she would wait.

'I was just going to take a tea-break, actually. Do you fancy joining me?' he invited. 'Ruth shouldn't be long.'

'Well, I . . .'

'Come on through to the back,' he urged because he thought Ruth needed her best friend at this traumatic time. 'I'll put the kettle on.'

'I don't really have the time to hang about,' she said. 'I have to get back to Staines.'

Vince's expression became grave.

'To be honest, Kitty, I'd really appreciate your waiting 'til she gets back,' he said, 'because I think you're the one person in the world she'll be really glad to see right now.'

'Why? Has something happened?' asked Kitty, looking worried.

'Let's go into the back.'

Puzzled, she followed him into the staffroom and sat down in an armchair while he put the kettle on and told her about Ruth's troubles.

'I'm probably gonna be in dead trouble for telling you,' he said, 'but I think she's really going to need her friends.'

'You did right to tell me, Vince,' said Kitty. 'Ruth and I have been closer than sisters and I want to know when she has a problem. I had my doubts about Larry from the start. He was just a little bit too charming, somehow.'

'I hardly know the man,' confessed Vince. 'I've seen very little of him since I came for an interview which he sat in on. Paterson's is run by Ruth so far as I'm concerned.'

'Exactly,' said Kitty. 'And he wants to take away her home and her job . . . it's scandalous.'

'I think so, too.'

They drank their tea in thoughtful silence until Vince was summoned into the shop by Madge to advise someone with a wasp sting.

'I'm sure Ruth won't be long now,' he said on his return.

'Don't worry, Vince . . . I'll wait no matter how long she is,' Kitty told him. 'Now that you've explained the situation.'

'How come you're not working today?' he remarked chattily.

'I've a day's leave owing to me. I thought I'd use it to come into town.'

'What, no store bags?' he teased. 'Don't tell me you haven't been shopping?'

'No chance of that,' she laughed. 'The merchandise is in the boot of my new Mini.' When he raised his eyebrows she added, 'A present from my husband who spoils me rotten.'

'How are things out airport way?' he asked casually. 'Still living the high life?'

'Hardly the high life,' she corrected pleasantly. 'But we do have a hectic social life . . . it seems to be pretty general in the travel business.'

'Sounds like fun.'

'Not your sort of thing, though,' she speculated.

'Maybe not, but that doesn't stop me being interested,' he said. 'I find human beings a constant source of fascination.'

'Is there anyone special in your life at the moment?' Kitty asked lightly.

'No, no one to share my life,' he said with mock sorrow.

She observed him studiously. Although he didn't ring any bells for her, she had to admit that more hideous men than Vince managed to get fixed up. He had a nice fresh complexion and lovely warm eyes.

'I expect someone will come along eventually,' she said reassuringly. 'Probably when you're least expecting it.'

'I usually attract people who are going through a bad time and need a shoulder to cry on, that's my trouble,' he told her. 'When I've helped them recover their faith in themselves, they move on . . . without me.'

She felt a pang of conscience for once having been so hateful to him. 'I was rotten to you that night, wasn't I?'

'I have had happier evenings.'

'I'm sorry.'

'Apologies are hardly necessary,' he assured her. 'It was a very long time ago, and all part of the process of growing up.'

The conversation was halted by the appearance of Ruth, looking pale and exhausted.

Kitty stood up, opening her arms. 'Vince has told me what's happened.'

'Oh, Kitty,' said Ruth, feeling the comfort of her friend's arms around her. 'I don't think I've ever been more pleased to see anyone.'

Without a word, Vince made a diplomatic exit into the dispensary.

'I don't believe I'm hearing this,' exploded Larry a few days later when he came to the flat to collect his belongings and Ruth took the opportunity to tell him what she planned to do about her future. 'You want me to sign this shop over to you?'

'That's right.'

'You must be off your rocker!'

'Not at all,' she said. 'The solicitor said I have a very good case.'

'*Solicitor?*' he bellowed, turning crimson with rage. 'You've already been to see a *solicitor*?'

'Yes, I have.'

'Well, of all the underhand tricks,' he thundered. 'If you think you're going to steal my business from me, you're in for a big disappointment.'

'I've no intention of stealing anything,' she said. 'I made the business what it is today and you know it . . . besides, I'm willing to take over the mortgage payments.'

'Oh, really?' he snorted with withering sarcasm. 'That's jolly decent of you.'

'It seems fair enough to me,' she said, managing to keep a hold on herself. 'You'll still have the Hammersmith shop. Our assets will be more or less split down the middle, that's all it means.'

'*Our assets?*' he growled. 'When were they ever *our* assets? Everything is mine.'

'Legally, yes,' she agreed. 'But morally they belong to both of us, as a married couple.'

'Rubbish! I own the lot and there isn't a damned thing you can do about it.'

'You evil bugger,' she gasped, hardly able to believe this was the same man she had married. 'Four and a half years ago you bought a small, run-down chemist's shop that was barely ticking over. Now you have two big thriving shops, and all because of me. Anyway, you and Wendy will still have a lucrative business even if I do have my share.'

'You scheming bitch!'

'I only want what I'm entitled to,' she insisted. 'One day the law might protect women who find themselves in my position . . . in the meantime we discarded wives have to fight for what we can get.'

'Oh, spare me the plug for women's rights,' he said. 'You'll get nothing, do you understand – nothing at all.'

'It would be better for us both if this was settled out of court, Larry,' she continued, determined not to crumble in front of him though she was falling apart inside. 'If we go to court and I win, you'll have to pay my costs as well as your own. A case like this will be bad for business too. People will be shocked to hear what their smooth-talking, neighbourhood chemist is really like. There are plenty of chemist's shops for the public to choose from in Hammersmith. They don't have to use yours.'

He shook his head as though in disbelief. 'My God, how you've changed,' he said grimly. 'Butter wouldn't melt in your mouth when we first met. I was really taken in.'

Ruth was stunned by his powers of self-deception. He had obviously managed to convince himself that he was the victim in all this because he didn't have the guts to face the truth.

'If that isn't the pot calling the kettle black, I don't know what is,' she countered. 'But if I've changed, you're the cause of it. You're the one who wants to end our marriage. You're the one who's committed adultery. The divorce will be punishing enough; fighting this other business out in court will be hellish for us both.'

He didn't reply but continued to drag his clothes out of the wardrobe and drawers and stuff them into a suitcase. Ruth went downstairs to make some coffee because seeing him prepare to leave made her want to cry. Even now, after all the pain he had caused her, it still made her heart ache to watch him putting the final seal on the failure of their marriage by moving his things out of the bedroom – a room full of tender memories which obviously meant nothing to him.

She was in the kitchen waiting for the kettle to boil when he appeared. His mood had changed – become more conciliatory, like a spoiled child trying to get his own way.

'Look Ruth . . . neither of us wants this to go to court,' he said in a wheedling tone. 'So what do you say to my giving you a cash settlement?'

'You really don't understand what all this is about, do

you?' she said with a slow shake of the head. 'This isn't only about money. This is about decency and showing me some respect.'

'Oh, God . . .'

'You can sneer, but I've made the shop what it is today and I want to continue to run it and live here in the flat with Jenny. I enjoy the job and I'm damned good at it. I give more than just a service to the customers and that helps me to make a contribution to the community as well as the bank balance. And as I'm willing to take over the mortgage, I can hardly be accused of robbing you blind.'

'Not much,' he snorted.

'You'll still have a good income to keep you and Wendy . . . an income from a business you wouldn't have at all if it hadn't been for me,' she pointed out. 'I found the Hammersmith shop, negotiated for the purchase and set it up. You didn't lift a finger to help.'

With a deep, eloquent sigh, he said, 'I was really hoping that the end of our relationship could be settled more amicably.'

'You're got some front, Larry,' said Ruth. 'You break my heart and threaten to rob me of my home and livelihood, and you expect me to disappear from your life without so much as a whimper . . . and just a cash payment to keep me quiet? Oh, no, it isn't on. I've told you what I want and I'll settle for nothing less.'

'Bitch!'

'Just for once in your life be honest with yourself,' she implored him, 'and you'll see that I'm not asking for anything to which I'm not entitled.'

He left the room and she heard him stamp back upstairs, presumably to finish his packing. She took her coffee into the living room and stood by the window staring across the Green, idly watching the trees swaying in the afternoon breeze, their leaves already tinged here and there with the fiery tones of autumn. The weather had sharpened with the passing of August and people wore sweaters and jackets and moved faster with the renewed energy that autumn often brings.

Jenny had started back at school yesterday after the summer break. Vince and Madge were looking after things downstairs so Ruth was free to deal with the depressing matter of her failed marriage.

The most terrible part was having to stand her ground and be firm with Larry when all she really wanted to do was to throw herself at his feet and beg him not to leave her. She didn't *want* to have to threaten the man she had loved enough to marry with legal action; she didn't *want* to make demands on him. But all her instincts cried out against letting him treat her so shabbily.

She turned at the sound of someone entering the room.

'All right, you win,' he said coldly. 'Tell your solicitor that I'll sign the shop and flat over to you whenever he wants.'

'Oh, Larry, I . . .'

Now she was overcome by guilt, as though she was to blame for the failure of their marriage. His attitude made her feel as if she were being greedy and taking something from him to which she was not entitled.

'Well, I can't hear you cheering?'

'No.'

'I don't know why not. You've got what you want, haven't you?'

'What I want is my marriage to continue,' she corrected. 'But as that apparently isn't possible, I need a means of survival for myself and my daughter, who incidentally is going to miss you dreadfully.'

A flicker of remorse came into his eyes. 'Yes, I'm sorry that Jenny has to be hurt.'

'Will you want to see her, now and then?' she asked, hoping to save Jenny from total rejection.

He pondered on this. 'No . . . I don't think that would be a good idea.'

Sensing that he was experiencing a moment of regret, Ruth decided to make one last attempt at reconciliation, not because she was weak but because she couldn't turn off her feelings for him just because he had stopped loving her.

'It doesn't have to end this way, Larry,' she said, her tone softening and becoming tender as she moved slowly towards him. 'Even after everything that's happened, I'm still prepared to try to patch things up between us.'

Seeing her advancing towards him, he was struck with horror. He wanted to distance himself from her with all possible speed because emotional scenes and clinging women were abhorrent to him. His time with Ruth was over and he wanted a clean break. This shop was a small price to pay if it meant he need have nothing more to do with her. His life was with Wendy now and Ruth must be made to realise this.

'Can't you get it into your head, woman,' he said, determined to destroy any shred of lingering hope, 'I don't want to patch things up with you? It's over. I don't love you any more.'

Surely there could be few words more painfully demoralising and they penetrated to the very depths of her being.

'In that case, Larry,' she said, managing with a supreme effort not to break down in front of him, 'the sooner arrangements for a divorce are underway, the better.'

'I couldn't agree more. I'll get on to it right away. In the meantime, you can instruct your solicitor to prepare the documents for the transfer of this property into your name,' he said. 'I'll be staying at Wendy's place until the flat over the shop becomes vacant. But tell your solicitor to address all correspondence to me at the Hammersmith shop.'

'I'll do that,' she said briskly. 'And I'll continue to run things here until the business becomes legally mine.'

'Fine.'

A few minutes later he left. Ruth felt utterly destroyed, longing to weep with the sheer pain of it all but too tense for tears. How could a marriage made in heaven have ended this way? Was there anything she could have done to prevent it?'

Even as the doubts flooded in and she began to castigate herself for failing to hang on to her man, she knew in her heart that the woman hadn't been born who could satisfy Larry indefinitely. She wondered how long it would be before he betrayed Wendy in a similar fashion.

Somehow she managed to rally herself sufficiently to go back to work.

That evening Ruth had the difficult task of telling Jenny that her stepfather had moved out and would no longer be a part of their lives. Jenny had got used to not seeing much of Larry since he hadn't been home a lot lately but was still hurt and bewildered by his final departure.

'Has he gone because he doesn't love us any more?' she asked, her huge blue eyes glistening with tears in her small white face.

'I'm sure he hasn't stopped loving *you*, Jenny,' Ruth told her kindly, 'but he's found someone else he'd rather have as a wife than me. It happens to grown-ups sometimes.'

'Oh.'

'But you and I will still live here in the flat and I'll be working downstairs the same as I always do,' Ruth told her reassuringly. 'So things won't change that much.'

'Nothing will be the same though, will it?' she said, adding vehemently, 'I hate Uncle Larry for going away and leaving us.'

'I know, darling,' said Ruth, hugging her daughter as

the child's tears began to fall. 'But we still have each other and I'll make everything all right for us, you'll see. We'll soon get used to not having your Uncle Larry around.'

'We'd like to see Mr Paterson, please, dear,' said Ray Brooks the following Saturday afternoon to the counter assistant in the Hammersmith branch of Paterson's.

'Who shall I say wants him?' asked Wendy, looking at the two large men whose presence seemed to fill the shop.

'Tell him Ray and Jack Brooks would like a few minutes of his time.'

She went to the dispensary, returning a few moments later with the message that Mr Paterson was too busy to see them at the moment.

'Is that right?' said Ray slowly, his dark brows rising. 'Well, you just go and tell your boss that if he ain't out here in five seconds flat, we'll be in there after him.'

'He'll wish he'd done as we asked then,' echoed Jack.

Wendy was about to go and deliver the message when Larry appeared in the shop, having been hiding behind the door listening to the conversation.

'Hi, boys,' he said with bravado. 'What can I do for you?'

'Outside, mate,' said Ray pointing towards the street door. 'We're going for a little walk, just the three of us.'

'I'm afraid not,' said Larry, managing to hide his terror. 'I'm too busy to leave the shop just at the minute.'

Ray glanced around the shop which was full of people. He leaned close to Larry and said in a low voice, 'Unless you want your dirty linen washed in public, you'd better come outside.'

Hastily making his excuses to Wendy, Larry followed the twins into the street where they 'encouraged' him to go with them to a narrow alleyway behind a row of houses and pushed him up against a high wall.

'We've heard you've not been treating our sister right,' said Ray.

'They say you've been playing away and want shot of Ruth,' added Jack.

'These things happen, boys. You're men of the world . . . you know how it is.'

'These things only happen if you let 'em happen,' said Ray.

'Come on, boys, you're no angels . . . you know what it's like.'

'The only thing we know about you is that you've not been playing it straight with Ruth,' said Ray. 'And that offends us. You hurt our sister and you hurt us. Isn't that right, bruv?'

'Not half,' Jack replied in gravel tones.

'We understand you're gonna be signing the Shepherd's Bush shop over to her?'

Larry nodded.

'I should bloody well think so too, after all she's done for you!' said Ray. 'And just in case you're thinking of not following through on that deal, we're gonna give you a small sample of what we'll do to you if anything like that was to happen.'

'I won't let her down . . . ouch! Hey, lay off . . .' he gasped as a string of well-aimed punches hit home.

Ray stopped hitting him and drew back slightly, his dark eyes never leaving Larry's pale, staring countenance.

'That's nothing to the beating you'll get if you pull a fast one on Ruth as regards that property,' he warned.

'I-I won't, I promise,' stammered Larry.

'You'd better not,' warned Jack.

'And another thing,' announced Ray with a threat in his voice, 'we don't want our sister to know about this little get together.'

'She'll give us a lotta grief if she finds out we've been to see you,' said Jack.

141

'So you keep quiet . . . not a word,' commanded Ray, giving Larry one last smack on the jaw for good measure. 'Is that clear?'

'Not a word,' he stuttered.

Leaving the terrified man slumped against the wall, blood trickling from his nose, his face suffused with red blotches which would soon turn blue, they walked away.

It was her determination to make a stable life for Jenny that kept Ruth going in the dark days that followed Larry's departure. Even when she sank to the depths of despair within herself, she kept it hidden for her daughter's sake.

Time passed. Every day life went on even though she was personally shattered. Work, motherhood, family commitments – all had to be attended to regardless of her broken heart. She clung tenaciously to activity to get her through each day. She was desperately lonely, though, despite having people around her, and was constantly tortured by feelings of failure.

'You've nothing to blame yourself for,' said Kitty one day when Ruth admitted her feelings to her friend. 'Men like Larry are incapable of being faithful to one woman for any length of time. Wendy probably won't last any longer than you did.'

Superficially Ruth could accept this, but a broken marriage cut deep and was a difficult thing to come to terms with. Her self-esteem had taken a serious battering.

Kitty was a good friend, always at the end of the telephone if Ruth needed to talk. Living outside London and being deeply immersed in her own marriage, however, it wasn't possible for the two women to get together as often as they would have liked. Ruth's independent nature prevented her from becoming too reliant on friends and relatives, anyway. She brushed aside their concern, assuring them that she was fine.

Vince was a tower of strength – always there for her

with a cheerful word and a sympathetic ear, constantly illustrating to her why people turned to him in times of trouble. His reassuring presence was as comforting as a cushion to an aching back. But no matter how supportive people were, Ruth was still on her own, feeling cold and empty inside.

Divorce proceedings were underway but it was going to be a lengthy process, apparently. The formalities over the property came to a much speedier conclusion. But when Ruth became the owner of the shop, she felt no sense of triumph, just the satisfaction of knowing that justice had been done and a deeper commitment than ever to the business. Now, even more than before, she regretted her lack of qualifications which would have been such an asset.

Because of this, Vince was especially vital to her as a colleague as well as a friend and she dreaded that he might eventually want to move on. There were other pharmacists she could employ, of course, but the working relationship she and Vince shared was special and would be hard to repeat with anyone else, based as it was on mutual respect and friendship.

When Larry had been gone for two years, Ruth decided to guard against the possibility of losing Vince by offering him a partnership. She was delighted when he accepted. It was good to have someone she could trust to share the responsibility.

By 1963 Ruth was really beginning to feel as though her broken marriage was behind her. The whole thing had been a painful episode that must stay in the past while she moved forward, albeit with a void inside of her that family and friends couldn't fill.

If Ruth lacked romance in her life, she certainly gained no shortage of pleasure from Jenny who followed in her mother's footsteps and won a place to Ruth's old school.

'Oh, I'm so proud of you, love,' she said, dancing round the room when Jenny came home from school with the letter containing the good news. 'You'll love it at Redfern Grammar.'

And you'll reach your full potential too, she vowed silently, you won't be silly enough to blow your chances like I did.

The entire Brooks family was thrilled to have this second academic in their midst. The Saturday after the news came through, they gathered at Nutley Road for a celebration. It was an impromptu affair, a real family occasion. The twins were there with their wives and offspring, now boisterous three-year-olds always up to some mischief, which surprised no one given who their fathers were. Congratulations in abundance were offered to Jenny and glasses were raised. Audrey and Dan promised to buy her a new bicycle to reward her for all her hard work.

Lying awake in bed that night, Ruth found herself at ease and happy, a feeling she hadn't experienced for a very long time. Life wasn't at all bad for her now. There wasn't a man in the picture but there were many other good things. She had a lovely daughter, a caring family, friends she was fond of and an interesting job. Plenty, in fact, to be grateful for.

Her divorce would become absolute soon. Appearing in court hadn't been a pleasant experience but because the divorce hadn't been contested, it hadn't been as bad as it might have.

A distant noise startled her out of her thoughts. It must be Jenny going to the bathroom, she thought, immediately tensing as she realised that the sound was further away than that. It was coming from the ground floor – *from the shop*. Sitting up and listening intently, she had just identified the sound of the shop door rattling when the muffled tinkle of breaking glass set her heart thumping.

With nerves jangling, she swung out of bed, dragged on her dressing gown and slippers and headed for the stairs, grabbing the broom on the way. Creeping downstairs carefully, holding her breath, she halted by the door into the shop, listening to someone moving about in there. Without stopping to think, she charged in and switched on the light to see two youths with Beatle fringes at the till.

'Blimey!' said one of them when they saw Ruth standing in the doorway behind the counter.

Trying not to show how frightened she was, she forced herself to step towards them brandishing the broom, treading through broken glass. 'I've called the police,' she lied, wishing she'd been less impulsive and dialled 999 instead of tackling the situation herself.

'Liar,' said one.

'We ain't stupid,' said the other.

'You'll see . . .'

'Tell us where the money is, missus, and we'll be on our way,' said the youth.

She did not reply but noticed that the shop door was swinging open, the treacle and brown paper they'd used to break the glass lying on the floor among the debris.

'Tell us where it is,' he demanded again, moving closer to her.

'In the bank,' said Ruth, waving the broom at him, not at all sure how she was going to get help since she couldn't get to the telephone in the dispensary and the streets were deserted at this time of night. 'You don't think I'd have cash on the premises overnight, surely?'

Fearless in his determination, the youth snatched the broom from her and threw it on the floor.

'Don't believe you,' he said, hitting her across the head with his fist. 'Give us some dough and we'll go.'

Reeling from the blow, she fell against the wall, banging her head and grazing her arm.

'Oh, Gawd, there's a copper coming,' said his mate, looking out of the door.

'Quick, scarper,' said Ruth's attacker, and the two of them rushed from the shop straight into the arms of someone on the way in.

'Phew, am I pleased to see you, officer,' gasped Ruth, holding her sore head. 'Thank goodness for the copper on the beat.'

Although the incident had no serious consequences, Ruth was unnerved by it and reminded of the vulnerable position she was in as a woman on her own with a child living above a chemist's shop. She dreaded to think what might have happened to Jenny if she'd been woken by the noise and come to her mother's assistance.

Ruth wasn't the only one who was perturbed by the situation.

'You could have been seriously hurt,' warned her mother the next day when she called to see Ruth, having heard about the break-in through the local grapevine.

'There was no real harm done, I'm just a bit shaken up.'

'You might not be so lucky next time,' declared Audrey with concern. 'And it's no use saying it won't happen again because it might. I really think you should rent the flat out to a married couple and get a place off the premises for you and Jenny to live in. You're not safe without a man here at night. There's more crime on the streets than there used to be.'

Moving off the premises was the logical thing to do, Ruth admitted that. But she didn't want to move out, not for the time being anyway. Living on the job was very convenient when you had a child to look after. It meant she was around when Jenny needed her – always here when she got in from school or was at home sick or on holiday. Jenny was no longer a small child but neither was she old enough to be left alone for any length of time.

Another reason Ruth wanted to stay put was a recalcitrant streak in her nature which meant she didn't take kindly to the idea of being driven out of her own home by people with no respect for the law or their fellow citizens. She'd fought hard·for this place and she wasn't about to leave it at the first sign of trouble.

Audrey's answer to this argument was: 'All right, so it wouldn't be so convenient for you to live away from the job but at least you'd sleep easier in your bed at night. And so would the rest of us.'

'I could get some extra strong locks put on the doors,' suggested Ruth.

'They'll soon get through those if they're determined enough.'

'And I'll put steel shutters across every bit of glass when we close at night,' she promised.

Audrey didn't look too impressed. 'That would be something of a deterrent, I suppose. But I still don't like it,' she said. 'It was different when Larry was living there with you.'

'I've been on my own for three years,' Ruth pointed out. 'And this is the first time anything like this has happened.'

'It might not be the last, though,' said Audrey. 'I don't want to scare you, love, but we have to be realistic. As well as villains after money, youngsters are so keen on getting high on drugs, a chemist's shop is a prime target.'

'Yes, I know.'

'You'll move off the premises then?'

'I'll give the matter some serious thought,' was the most Ruth would agree to.

The next morning, Ruth took some time off from work to drive across the river to Battersea. That evening she and her daughter walked round to Nutley Road. When Audrey opened the door she smiled a welcome at her visitors, her expression changing comically as she lowered her gaze.

'Blimey . . . a dog!'

'Well spotted, Mum,' laughed Ruth.

'This is Ringo,' said Jenny proudly, stroking the head of the golden labrador she held on a lead, who was fidgeting and straining, wanting to leap all over Audrey in an affectionate greeting.

She looked at Ruth through eyes narrowed with suspicion. 'What's it doing here? And, more to the point, whose is it?'

'It isn't an it, it's a he, and he's ours,' said Ruth, looking down at the exuberant creature. 'I collected him this morning from Battersea Dogs' Home. He's going to look after us, protect us from burglars. And we're going to look after him in return.'

'A guard dog?' said Audrey weakly.

'I'm told he'll make an excellent one,' explained Ruth. 'So you can sleep easy at nights now, Mum. We all can.'

'A burglar alarm would have been easier . . . and a damned sight less messy about the house,' declared her mother.

'It would have cost a fortune and still wouldn't have made us feel safe,' Ruth argued.

'Ringo will scare off burglars, won't you, boy?' said Jenny adoringly as the hound sniffed around her grandmother's doorway, wagging his tail, eager to elicit Audrey's friendship so that he could slobber all over her.

'But we're not dog people in this family,' said Audrey disapprovingly. 'None of us knows anything about them.'

'Jenny and I are leaning fast,' said Ruth, fondling Ringo's ears. 'Aren't we, boy?'

'What sort of a name is Ringo for a dog, for Gawd's sake?' tutted Audrey.

'You can blame Jenny for that,' said Ruth. 'She named him after some pop musician.'

'He's in a group called the Beatles, Gran,' said Jenny. 'You must have heard of them? Everybody's heard of the Beatles.'

Audrey looked thoughtful, still wary of letting them over the threshold with their energetic new lodger. 'I think I might have heard something about them as it happens,' she said absently. 'Were they on the telly the other night . . . four lads from Liverpool?'

'That's right.'

'Are you gonna keep us on the doorstep all night?' interrupted Ruth.

''Course not. I suppose you'd better bring the blessed thing in to show to your father,' Audrey consented at last. 'But that animal had better not leave anything behind on my clean floor.'

'Don't worry, he won't,' Ruth assured her.

'He'd better not. Any accidents and he doesn't get through the door a second time,' she said, but there was a smile in her voice. A dog in the family. Well, that really was a turn up for the books.

Chapter Nine

Paul Stoneway sat by the window of his fourth-floor hotel room, looking down into the misty London street, grey and gloomy after twelve years of Australian sunshine. But exciting too, somehow, and curiously endearing to an expatriate reunited with his home town after a long absence.

Nothing was quite the same as London in a November fog, he thought, watching the hazy tail of headlights moving at a crawl in the shifting, swirling vapour. It had an atmosphere all its own: the acrid smell, the muted street noise, the traffic in chaos against the backdrop of dark old buildings.

The familiar winter confusion, that would probably irritate him when the novelty of being back had worn off, seemed very precious to him at this moment. London was in his blood. Wherever he went in the world, it would always be his spiritual home.

The hotel near Marble Arch was extremely comfortable. Paul certainly had no complaints, especially as his bill was being settled by the Shaldrake Drug Company with whom he was about to take up a position as Sales Manager for London and surrounding areas. This hospitality was on offer to himself and his wife, Leila, until they found a suitable house.

They'd arrived in England a week ago and had spent most of the time since then house hunting. Leila was out looking at a place in Chiswick this very afternoon as a matter of fact. Impatient as ever, she'd gone to view the property on her own rather than wait for him to get back from a meeting with his soon-to-be boss. Paul frowned, wondering how she was managing in the fog.

As though reading his thoughts, his wife walked in.

'I was just thinking about you,' he told her. 'Wondering how you were getting on in this thick fog.'

'It took me for ever to get there 'cos the taxi had to go at snail's pace,' she said with a fearsome scowl, taking off her coat and scarf and draping them over a chair. 'And I thought I'd never get back, we were going so slow.'

'What was the house like?'

'A dump.'

'Really?'

'Yes, really. The place needs knocking down,' she declared, flopping on to the bed and emitting an expressive sigh. 'And that goes for London as well. I'd forgotten just how filthy and crowded it is.'

'Bags of character, though.'

'Oh, yes, it's got that all right,' she admitted in a derisory tone. 'But what about all the ugly tower blocks that have sprung up while we've been away?'

'Yes, they're awful.'

'That's an understatement!'

'Actually, though, I've just been thinking how glad I am to be back,' Paul remarked casually. 'It's a strange thing because if you hadn't been so keen to come back to London, I'd have happily stayed on in Sydney. But now I'm here, I realise just how much I've missed it.'

'I think I must have been remembering the place through rose-tinted spectacles or something,' she confessed gloomily, 'because I certainly don't remember it being so tatty.'

'All cities have their shabby parts,' he defended. 'It's probably the weather that's making you notice the worst bits. You'll feel differently when the sun's shining. In the meantime, shall I ring down for some tea?'

'Yes, please, dear.' She got up and went over to the

dressing table where she sat down and brushed the thick auburn hair which fell loosely to her shoulders. 'I certainly need something to warm me up. I'll have a hot bath, too, when I've had a cup of tea.'

Paul went over to the telephone. He was a tall, muscular man with blond hair and sapphire-blue eyes, their brilliance emphasised by the richness of his tan. He ordered tea for two then went and stood behind his wife with his hands on her shoulders, speaking to her in the mirror.

'We have to make a go of it here, love,' he said, 'as I've landed such a good job with Shaldrake's London operation.'

'I know that, Paul,' she answered, her green eyes meeting his. 'But you must admit everything seems very grey and dismal?'

'Only because it's November.'

'We used to get some pretty grim summers too, as I remember it.'

'Well, I just love the place, for all its faults and awful weather,' he said, unable to hide his enthusiasm. 'The minute we landed I felt at home, as though I really belong here.'

'Lucky you.'

'Perhaps that's why it took me so long to settle in Australia – because my heart was so firmly rooted here.'

Paul was surprised by his reaction to being back because he'd done well in Australia. Although hampered by chronic homesickness for the first two years, he'd finally managed to settle and built a successful career in pharmaceutical sales, reaching the position of Sales Manager at Shaldrake's in Sydney, in charge of a large sales team.

It had been for Leila's sake he'd decided to apply for the position of Sales Manager in London when he'd seen it advertised in the company magazine. She'd wanted to come back to England ever since he'd known her, even though her parents had put down roots in Australia.

He sometimes wondered if Leila was capable of being content anywhere. Discontented by nature, she was a restless creature whom he never seemed able to satisfy. Although their marriage worked well enough, he was constantly aware of something missing between them, a closeness they just didn't seem able to achieve.

At some point in the future he hoped Leila might share his wish to start a family. But children certainly weren't on her agenda at the moment. There was no special reason for this so far as he knew. She just didn't want to have a baby. The new contraceptive pill had been welcomed by her with open arms because it put her in a position of control. 'It's about bloody time something was invented to give a woman the right to choose whether or not to become pregnant,' was the way she'd put it. But Paul hadn't given up hope for they were both still only thirty.

'It could well be the reason,' Leila said in reply to his last remark. 'I thought my heart was still here until I actually got back. But it's early days. I'll get used to it. I shall have to, won't I, as your job's here now.'

'Things will seem a lot different when we get into our own place.'

'Yeah, sure.'

He went back to his armchair by the window, idly watching Leila as she changed out of her green woollen Chanel-style suit into a pink fluffy dressing gown ready for her bath. She was just as sexy now as the day he'd married her ten years ago, with her bright hair and terrific figure.

They'd met at a party in Sydney when they were both going through a particularly harrowing period of homesickness. Initially drawn to each other by physical attraction, they had soon discovered they had other things in common. They were both from London and had emigrated to Australia at about the same time; both had been taken as teenagers with their parents. A mutual longing for their native England was a powerful bond in their adopted country.

Would they have married in such haste, he wondered, if they hadn't both been feeling so wretched at that time? Would they have got married at all without that need to cling to someone with the same roots?

A knock on the door heralded the arrival of a waitress who walked briskly into the room pushing a tea trolley and smiling coyly at them. She was young and slim with dark hair tucked under the cap of her black and white uniform. It was her huge dark eyes to which Paul responded so powerfully, though, because they reminded him of a girl he'd known briefly just before he'd gone away. He drifted off into recollections of that sweet summer night before he'd sailed to Australia ... and winced as he recalled how torn he'd felt then.

'The sandwiches look good,' Leila was saying as she put a cup of tea on the table near him, the girl having left the room. 'Do you fancy one?'

'Not really,' he said, forcing himself back to the present. 'So you go ahead and have as many as you like.'

'I mustn't have much to eat before a bath,' she said. 'But these little things aren't big enough to fill a fly.'

They got back to the subject of their future accommodation while she ate.

'Once we find a house we like, we should be able to move in without delay as we don't have a property to sell,' said Paul, for they had sold their house in Sydney before leaving.

'I hope so. Hotel life has its advantages in that you get everything done for you,' said Leila, 'but I want my own things around me. And if we don't find something before you start work, I'll have to find a place by myself.'

'We've still got a week ... we can look at a lot of properties in that time.'

'True.' She sipped her tea. 'But I'm hoping to find the

time to visit some relatives in North London before I get too taken up with moving in. I promised my mother I would do it as soon as I could after we arrived.'

'Sure.'

Leila finished her tea, dabbed her mouth with a napkin and said, 'Well, I'm going for a nice long soak in the bath.'

'Okay.'

Sitting alone by the window in the gathering dusk, the street now barely visible through the thickening mist, Paul's thoughts turned to the friends he'd heard nothing of for twelve years. It wasn't idleness or lack of interest that had prevented him from putting pen to paper but the agony he had suffered trying to make Australia his home. The only way he had been able to cope with the crippling homesickness was to cut himself off from England and his friends.

In those early days abroad, thoughts of London had filled him with such longing he had had to blank them out as a means of survival. He'd considered it his duty to his parents to make a new life down under because it meant so much to them. Attracted by the advertisements put out by the Australian government, they had left England in genuine hope of finding a better life for their family than post-war Britain had to offer. They had even delayed their departure so that Paul could sit his 'A' levels and finish his last term at school. It was just as well they had because he wouldn't even have been considered as a sales representative for a drugs company without those qualifications.

Twelve years was a long time, his friends would have moved on by now, he thought sadly. But his spirits rose again as he realised that although they would have moved on, their parents might still be at the same addresses. On impulse, he went over to the telephone, dialled Directory Enquiries and was rewarded with one of the numbers he needed.

'Hello . . . is that Mrs Todd?'

'Yes, speaking.'

'It is? Oh, that's wonderful! My name's Paul Stoneway, I'm an old friend of Vince's – you might remember me?'

'Paul, of course I remember you . . .'

After they'd exchanged a few basic pleasantries, he said, 'The thing is, I've lost touch with Vince and would like to contact him. Can you tell me where I can get hold of him?'

'I certainly can,' Mrs Todd said. 'Do you have a pen handy?'

The newspaper that Paul was reading on the tube the following afternoon was full of reports of President Kennedy's assassination. Even though Paul and Leila had seen horrific accounts of the shooting on the television in the hotel lounge last night after dinner, it still shocked him to read about it. Shot in the head in an open car. God, what a terrible thing!

Something as earth-shattering as that made you feel very insignificant in the scheme of things, he thought. It certainly put his own situation into perspective. The fact that he was on his way to see his old pal Vince again seemed trivial in the light of the ghastly events in America, which would be deeply felt all around the world.

But, for all that, Paul's excitement refused to be entirely quelled as he got off the train at Shepherd's Bush, glad that Vince's mother had supplied him with the address of his friend's place of business as well as his home. It was more convenient to pay him a visit this afternoon while Leila was in North London visiting relatives rather than waiting until the evening to see him after work. Paul hadn't telephoned because he wanted to surprise him.

Yesterday's fog had cleared but it was raining as he strode purposefully out of the station with his newspaper stuffed into his raincoat pocket. It was cold and windy and the rain blew into his face but Paul barely noticed it as he headed for the Green, overcome with nostalgia.

Hardly able to control himself at the thought of seeing Vince again, he hurried on with a spring to his step. That was the good thing about blokes – they didn't take offence if you lost touch. Whereas women were funny about that sort of thing.

The shop was light and airy and a woman in the self-service department directed him towards the medical section. 'Mr Todd will be in the dispensary,' she said.

Another young woman in a starched white overall appeared from the back of the shop and stood behind the counter.

'Can I help you?' she asked pleasantly.

'I'd like to see Vince Todd, please,' said Paul with a hint of an Australian accent. With his attention focused on the back of the shop where he presumed the dispensary would be, he barely spared the assistant a glance.

When she didn't reply, however, he looked at her to find her staring at him with her mouth open in an expression of utter astonishment . . .

Emotional upheaval was what Paul experienced as he stared back at her, dry-mouthed, heart racing. She'd changed a lot from the sixteen-year-old girl he had known. Her hair was short and stylish now, her make-up immaculate, her features firmed into womanhood. But the eyes were the same. Oh, yes, he'd know those eyes anywhere.

'Ruth!' he exclaimed, his whole face lighting up with joy. 'Is it really you?'

'Paul . . . Paul Stoneway?' she said, eyes wide with surprise, voice quivering slightly as she struggled with this emotional onslaught. 'I just don't believe it.'

He put his hands to his head.

'I'm having difficulty believing it myself. When I came

looking for Vince, I never dreamed I'd find you here too.'
Somewhere among his scrambled thoughts was a feeling
of surprise to see Ruth working behind a shop counter.
She had shown such high academic promise as a girl.
'Do you work for him?'

She grinned, a little stiffly because she was still in shock.
'Not exactly,' she said. 'It's my shop actually but Vince
and I work here together . . . we're business partners.'

'Oh, I see.' How stupid of him not to realise. It should
have been obvious that she was just the sort to qualify in
pharmacy.

'Anyway, come on through to the dispensary,' she
invited through parched lips. 'I'm sure Vince will be
delighted to see you.'

She left the two men in the dispensary, heartily shaking
hands and back slapping, and went back into the shop,
hoping there wouldn't be too many customers until she
had calmed herself. Her heart was knocking hell out of
her ribs and her legs were so wobbly she could hardly
stay vertical. Seeing Paul again after all this time had
wrought havoc with her feelings. Long suppressed memories now surfaced with such heartstopping brilliance, it
was like walking into an hallucination.

Her thoughts drifted back to a summer evening in
1951, the night that had changed her life so irrevocably . . .

The evening was warm, with a soft breeze that felt like
velvet to the skin. The mellow tones of Nat King Cole
drifted out through the open windows into the garden
where the party guests were talking, laughing, fooling
around.

Inside the house, couples were smooching in the half-
light. The atmosphere was heavy with youthful sexuality,
the romantic mood boosted by the unusual occurrence
of alcohol being freely available without adult supervision.
Ruth had noticed quite a bit of snogging taking place in

the hall and on the stairs when she'd gone to the bathroom to wash her hands.

She and Kitty were standing near the record player, drinking Babycham and getting sillier by the second. All the guests at this end-of-term party, apart from Ruth and Kitty, were from Redfern Grammar's Upper Sixth and had left school that day, the last of the school year. Fifth formers Ruth and Kitty were only there because Kitty played netball with an older girl whose party it was, in a house near Ravenscourt Park.

'Fancy her parents going out and letting her have a party without them,' said Kitty. 'Not many parents would do that.'

'Mine certainly wouldn't!'

'Nor mine.'

They drank some more and giggled a lot until Kitty sobered them up by saying, 'Don't stare now, Ruth, but Paul Stoneway is looking this way.'

'At you or me?'

'I hate to admit it, kid, but I think it's you,' said Kitty.

'I think it's me too,' she said, her skin prickling with excitement. 'I noticed him having an eyeful just now.'

'Do you fancy him?'

'Not half . . . he's gorgeous.'

'Not much point in getting to know him, though,' said Kitty. 'I've heard he's emigrating to Australia with his family tomorrow.'

'Aah, what a shame,' said Ruth. 'Just my bloomin' luck.'

'Looks like my luck's even worse,' giggled Kitty. 'That drippy mate of his is trying to give me the eye . . . he'll be lucky!'

'Vince Todd isn't drippy,' said Ruth. 'I think he's quite nice.'

'Do me a favour,' protested Kitty. 'I'd sooner kiss the cat's bum.'

'If they want to team up as a foursome with us for the

rest of the evening, will you go with Vince, just for tonight, though?' begged Ruth. 'Only I'm really keen on Paul Stoneway. I've been fancying him like mad all term.'

'You and plenty of others,' said Kitty. 'He must be the most fancied boy in the school. School captain . . . best sports allrounder . . . and dead sexy with it.'

'I know,' sighed Ruth.

'He usually goes for the older girls.'

'Mmm.'

'But he's definitely got his sights set in your direction for tonight, by the look of it,' remarked her friend.

'Do you really think so?'

'We'll soon find out 'cos he's coming this way – with that dozy mate of his in tow!'

'You will stay with his mate, won't you?' Ruth asked again. 'If Paul wants to stay with me . . . please, Kitty?'

'Oh, all right,' she agreed with reluctance. 'But only because it'll be the last time you'll ever ask me . . . it can't happen again as Paul's going abroad tomorrow.'

'Hi, girls,' he said, looking even more attractive out of school uniform, in tapered trousers and a summer shirt.

'Hi,' they said in unison.

'Fancy a dance, Ruth?' asked Paul.

'You know my name?' she said, thinking how handsome he was with his fair hair and blue eyes and lashes longer than any film star's.

'I made it my business to find out.'

That sounded promising, thought Ruth, living for the moment and never mind about tomorrow when he went away.

'I'd love to,' she said, and they joined the other smoochers in the small space in the middle of the room.

'I've seen you around at school,' he said, moving back slightly to look at her.

'I've noticed you too.'

'I'm glad to have the chance to get to know you, at last.'

'You're going away tomorrow, though, I hear?'

'Yep. We're sailing from Tilbury tomorrow afternoon. We'll be at sea for several weeks.'

'How exciting.'

'Yeah, isn't it?'

'Your parents must be very adventurous to do something like that,' she said. 'I don't think my mum and dad will ever move out of Shepherd's Bush, let alone go across the world.'

'The adverts about the golden opportunities out there were very enticing,' he explained. 'To them anyway.'

'What are you planning on doing there?' Ruth asked, finding herself becoming more interested in him by the minute.

'Not sure yet. I'll see what's on offer when we get there. They want people in a wide range of jobs, apparently. It depends what my exam results are like too. They'll be out by the time we get there. I'll write and ask the school to send them on as soon as I have an address.'

'You're not hoping to go to university out there then?'

'No, I want to start work . . . preferably in something that entails meeting people,' he explained. 'But good grades will be useful, whatever I go for.'

'I'm sure you'll find what's right for you,' she said, smiling at him.

'I hope so. It's a long way to go to be disappointed.'

'Yes.'

'You'll be staying on at school, won't you?'

'If I pass my "O"s.'

'That's a foregone conclusion from what I've heard,' he breathed into her ear, bodies melting against each other as they moved slowly to the music. 'A little bird told me that you're top of your form on a regular basis.'

Her position in class was the last thing on her mind at

this moment but Ruth said, 'Thanks for the vote of confidence.'

When the music ended they drifted back to where Kitty and Vince were standing. They all had more drinks and Ruth and Paul danced some more. By now Ruth was quite dizzy with happiness. The most popular boy in the school wanted to be with *her*. This had to be the most exciting night of her life!

Dusk was falling and somehow she and Paul were out in the garden, kissing under the lilac tree, its flowery scent heady with evening dew. He told her she was beautiful.

'I wouldn't have agreed to go to Australia if I'd known I was going to meet you.'

'I'm having such a wonderful time, Paul,' said Ruth, trying not to think too much about his imminent departure. 'Do you think it's the drink? It's the first time I've really tried alcohol.'

'It isn't the drink,' he said. 'It's us . . . you and me.'

Such heartfelt phrases were nectar to a sixteen-year-old girl and Ruth lapped them up.

'Oh, Paul,' she sighed, completely in thrall. 'You say the sweetest things.'

'I mean every word,' he said, and he did – *he really did*. So much so that the thought of going away tomorrow was beginning to hurt.

They went back inside and danced and talked and kissed and got to know each other better. As the evening progressed, Paul was all that mattered to Ruth, everyone else paling into insignificance. She was vaguely aware of Kitty on the periphery, complaining bitterly about being lumbered with Vince Todd.

'He's following me around like a pet puppy,' she wailed. 'I'll have to be really rude to him if he doesn't get the message soon. And if he thinks I'm gonna let him see me home, he's got another think coming!'

In the event they did leave the party as a foursome.

'I can't get rid of him,' Kitty whispered to Ruth when they reached the point where they were to go their separate ways. 'I wish he was going to Australia tomorrow instead of Paul.'

She couldn't have wanted that more than Ruth, who was far too caught up in her own miracle to be overly concerned about the other couple. She was glad when Kitty and Vince left and she and Paul were alone, walking through the streets with their arms around each other, stopping every few minutes along the way to kiss and whisper sweet things to one another.

'I love you, Ruth,' he said.

'I love you too.'

When they came to an overgrown bomb site that was out of the light, they slipped eagerly into the shadows . . .

'I shouldn't have let that happen,' said Paul later as they sat together on his jacket on a hillock covered with rose bay willowherb, their eyes now used to the pale light from a crescent moon.

'I don't regret it,' she said.

'I'm glad.'

'I won't be pregnant, though, will I?'

''Course you won't,' he said, inexperience leading him to believe this to be true for Ruth wasn't the only one to lose her virginity tonight. 'I made certain of that.'

'Thank goodness for that,' she said, trusting him completely.

They fell silent, holding hands, both deep in thought.

'I'll have to go home soon . . . my mum and dad will be going spare,' she said. 'It's well past midnight. They said I could be late as it was a party, but I don't think they meant this late.'

'I can't bear to leave you.'

'I feel the same.'

'It was *really* special tonight, wasn't it, Ruth?' he asked.

'Yes . . . *really* special.'

'If only I wasn't going away . . .'

'Do you think you'll ever come back?' she asked, looking at him, his clean-cut profile discernible in the moonlight.

'I doubt it,' he said softly, wanting to be honest with her. 'Australia is on the other side of the world. And the idea of going is to make our life there, not think about coming back.'

'The timing just isn't right for us, is it, Paul?' she said sadly.

'No.'

'We're too young. We don't have the power to change anything.'

'Worse luck!'

'I still have to finish my education,' said Ruth with a wistful sigh. 'I've been told I could go to university if I work hard. And you have to make your way in the world.'

'Mmm.'

'I'm not even going to suggest that we write to each other,' she said. 'That would only make things worse . . . knowing we're not going to see each other again. We have to finish growing up and make our lives as adults.'

'I'll never forget you, though, Ruth,' he said with great sincerity. 'Or tonight. Ours might be the shortest love affair in the history of the world but I shall treasure every second of it in my memory for ever.'

'Me too,' she said, tracing the outline of his features with her fingers.

Eventually, and with great reluctance, they stood up and began to walk slowly towards Ruth's home, arms around each other.

'I'll come in with you and tell your parents it's my fault you're late home, if you like?' he offered when they turned into Nutley Road.

'Thanks for offering but you'd better not,' she told him.

'Why not?'

'The sparks are bound to fly and I'd rather you weren't involved.'

'I'm quite willing to take the flak with you,' he said.

'I appreciate your being such a gentleman, but don't let's spoil the memory of a wonderful evening.'

'As you wish.'

'Better not come any further,' she said. 'In case they're at the window.'

'Okay.'

They clung together in a last bitter-sweet embrace, hardly able to tear themselves apart.

'Goodbye, Paul.'

''Bye, Ruth.'

Then he walked away and began the long sad trek home to Acton, having missed both the last bus and train.

Ruth turned the key in the lock and went inside to face the music. Nothing her parents could do or say could touch her tonight, though. She was far too deeply immersed in her own emotions. She'd been brought up to believe that what had happened between her and Paul tonight was wrong and would make her feel cheap. But instead of that she felt beautiful and loved.

Knowing that she wouldn't see him again hurt like mad. How could it do otherwise? But it didn't take away the magic of this evening or what she felt for him. She'd known from the start it would be nothing more than a one-night stand and they would go their separate ways afterwards. But what she and Paul had between them would go with her into the future, to comfort and sustain her. It was something priceless and she would never forget it. She knew instinctively that he felt the same.

Ruth was recalled to the present by a sudden flurry of activity. A flood of customers came into the shop at the same time as Vince and Paul appeared from the dispensary.

Ruth and Vince served the customers while Paul hovered behind the counter nearby watching them. Ruth was sixteen years old again, feeling his eyes on her and loving it, her body ripe and craving for his.

No sooner had they cleared the queue than the shop door opened again and in walked Jenny, home from school. Cheeks glowing from the cold and her hair damp from the rain, she had a red and black school scarf slung casually around her neck, her satchel over her shoulder, her fair hair tumbling over the collar of her navy blue school raincoat.

'Hi,' she said breezily, glancing towards her mother.

'Hello, love,' said Ruth, smiling at her. 'Had a good day?'

'Yeah . . . you?'

'Fine.'

'I'm starving,' said Jenny, her youthful exuberance filling the shop as she headed for the door behind the counter on her way upstairs, unbuttoning her raincoat as she went. She looked at Vince and Paul who were blocking her path. 'What's this, some sort of men's meeting?'

'Jenny . . . this is Paul Stoneway,' intervened Ruth. 'He's an old school friend of Vince's . . . and mine too, really.'

'Hi,' said Jenny casually.

'Paul is just back from Australia.' Ruth glanced towards him. 'This is my daughter, Jenny.'

She smiled at him, said she was pleased to meet him and offered her hand.

'Australia, eh?' she said, obviously impressed. 'Wow!'

He grinned at her youthful enthusiasm.

'You were at Redfern then?' she said.

'That's right.'

'I'm in my first year there,' she said, and beamed with pride.

'Enjoying it?'

'You bet.'

Seeing them together, Ruth thought the conspicuous likeness must be as obvious to everyone else as it was to her. Her personal feelings about seeing Paul again were swept aside by concern for Jenny. Ruth wanted nothing from Paul for herself or her daughter, but there was another question to be addressed here . . .

Was it her duty to tell them that they were father and daughter, or would it be better to say nothing? Jenny could get hurt if the truth came out.

God, what a mess. There was serious trouble ahead – she could feel it!

Chapter Ten

'Why don't the three of you have a proper reunion?' suggested Jenny, startling Ruth out of her thoughts. 'You could go out for a meal together and talk about old times. Perhaps you could invite Aunt Kitty along too as she was at Redfern.'

'Aunt Kitty?' enquired Paul.

'Kitty West that was,' explained Ruth. 'She's Kitty Barrett now, though.'

'Oh, I remember Kitty,' said Paul heartily. 'She was with us the night before I went away.' He gave Vince a matey grin. 'Gave you a bit of a hard time as I recall.'

'That's Kitty,' said Ruth, unnerved by all this talk of the past. When Jenny was younger she'd been told that her father had gone away before she was born, and up until now had shown no interest in learning more about it. But Paul's unexpected appearance reminded Ruth that her daughter was getting to an age to be more inquisitive.

'Sounds to me as though you've a lot of catching up to do,' said Jenny, who was very perceptive for her age. 'And you can't do it here in the shop with customers coming in and out.'

'I quite agree,' said Paul, eager to follow up any suggestion that would give him the opportunity to see Ruth again. Purely for old time's sake, he told himself. Where was the harm? It was only natural he would want to know what had been happening to the woman he'd once loved so briefly. She was divorced apparently, he'd learned that much from Vince, but Paul wanted to know more about her. 'So what say we all get together one evening soon?'

'I can't go out and leave Jenny on her own,' Ruth excused herself, because the whole situation spelled danger with a capital D.

'Mu-um,' admonished Jenny. 'You know very well I can stay with Gran and Granddad.'

'There you are, Ruth . . . problem solved,' said Paul, sounding pleased.

'I'm not sure about Kitty,' said Ruth as a delaying tactic. 'She does have her husband to consider.'

'I have a wife to consider but I'm sure she isn't going to object to my meeting up with a few old friends for a chat one evening.'

So he was married! This made her even more inclined to stay silent about Jenny. The sudden appearance of a love-child probably wouldn't be welcomed by a married man, especially if he and his wife had a family of their own. Ruth couldn't risk Jenny learning he was her father if there was any chance of his rejecting her. She'd suffered enough when Larry left.

'Anyway, I'm going upstairs to get something to eat,' said the girl.

'There's some fresh scones in the larder,' said Ruth, who usually took a short break upstairs in the flat with her daughter when she got in from school. 'I'll join you in a few minutes.'

'Okay,' said Jenny breezily, and disappeared through the door.

Seconds later they heard shrieks of pleasure accompanied by loud woofs.

'Jenny and the dog always make a terrific fuss of each other when she gets home from school,' Ruth explained.

'She's a great kid,' observed Paul. 'You must be very proud of her.'

'I certainly am.'

A sudden rush of customers filled the shop.

'Well, I'd better leave you people to your work,' said Paul, going round to the front of the counter. 'But let's get together soon, okay?' He looked at Vince. 'I'm staying at the Lambert Star Hotel in Marble Arch. Give me a bell and let me know when you can all make it . . . the sooner the better.'

'Will do,' said Vince.

'See you, Ruth,' said Paul, smiling at her. 'It's really good to meet you again.'

'S'long, Paul,' she said, engrossing herself in a customer's needs.

'Paul Stoneway's back in London?' was Kitty's astonished reaction to the news when Ruth spoke to her on the telephone on the evening of the next day, after Jenny had gone to bed. 'I don't believe it.'

'I had difficulty believing it myself when he appeared in the shop out of the blue like that,' said Ruth.

'Well, well, what happened to the wonderful future he was going to have down under?'

'He told Vince he came back because his wife couldn't settle there,' Ruth explained. 'He's married to an English woman, apparently.'

'You can believe that if you like,' said Kitty cynically because she still thought Stoneway was a rat for leaving Ruth. 'My guess is he failed miserably out there.'

'Well . . . he's staying at the Lambert Star, all expenses paid until they find a house, according to Vince, and he's starting work as Sales Manager for the firm he worked for in Australia. That doesn't sound much like failure to me.'

'Mm . . . well, I suppose not,' Kitty was grudgingly forced to agree. As Ruth's staunchest defender, Kitty would have been pleased to hear that all was not well with the callous bugger who had left her friend in the lurch.

'Anyway, he wants the four of us to get together one evening.'

'Whatever for?'

'For the sake of old times, I suppose,' said Ruth. 'Because we were all together the night before he went away.'

'And I'm expected to team up with Vince again, I suppose?' Kitty said sourly. 'And how do you think Tim will feel about that?'

'There won't be anything like that,' Ruth was quick to assure her. 'It's just a meal out and a chat. Paul's a married man now, anyway.'

'I hope you're going to tell him?' said Kitty after a short pause.

'Tell him what?'

'About Jenny, of course,' she announced stridently. 'It's about time he made some sort of a contribution.'

'I'm not sure whether to tell him or not, actually,' confessed Ruth. 'It's a delicate matter . . . and needs careful thought.'

'What's there to think about?' enquired Kitty sharply. 'He's her father but he's never paid a penny towards her keep.'

'How could he when he didn't even know she existed?'

'He should have made it his business to find out what had happened to you after taking such a dead liberty,' exclaimed Kitty. 'Anyway, now's your chance to tell him . . . and force him to face up to his responsibilities.'

'It isn't a simple matter,' said Ruth. 'Jenny is my only concern.'

'Exactly . . . there's no excuse for him not to acknowledge his daughter now.'

'She could get hurt,' said Ruth. 'Paul's a married man . . . he might not want to know about a child from the past.'

'In that case you'll just have to remind him of a few

home truths then, won't you?' said her friend aggressively. 'That he's her father, whether he likes it or not, and it's about time he helped you to support her.'

'I don't want help from him.' Ruth was adamant. 'I've managed to support her all this time, I'm damned sure I can carry on doing so until she's old enough to support herself.'

'That isn't the point though, is it?' pronounced Kitty. 'He shouldn't be allowed to get away with it.'

'People could get hurt if this isn't handled carefully,' Ruth pointed out. 'Jenny in particular . . . but there's also Paul's wife.'

'She isn't your problem,' continued Kitty in dogmatic mood. 'But Jenny is and she has every right to know the truth about her father. And he has the right to know about her, for that matter.'

'Mmm.' That was something that Ruth had been wrestling with ever since Paul had come back into her life. But she needed time to give it more thought. She had to make sure it was the right thing for Jenny. 'Well, I'll give it a while longer before I decide what to do.'

'If it was me I wouldn't hesitate, not for a second.'

'But it isn't you, is it?' said Ruth sharply. 'So you'll just have to let me be the judge of what's best.'

'Oh . . . suit yourself then,' said Kitty with obvious pique.

There was a heavy silence.

'Anyway,' said Ruth, with a hasty change of subject, 'what about this reunion Paul wants? He seems very keen. He's asked Vince to make the arrangements. So do you fancy it?'

'I suppose it won't do any harm,' said Kitty thoughtfully. 'I'd like to see what Stoneway has turned out like.'

'He's even more gorgeous than he was as a schoolboy!'

'That's a pity, I was hoping he'd deteriorated into a mess . . . I'd like him to get some sort of a comeuppance.'

'Vince is suggesting Friday evening,' said Ruth, ignoring her friend's malice towards Paul because she knew it was born of loyalty to herself. 'Does that suit you?'

There was a pause, as though Kitty was thinking it over.

'Yeah, that'll be okay,' she said at last. 'Tim's flying and will be away overnight so it'll help me to fill the time.'

'I'll tell Vince to make the arrangements with Paul then.'

Paul suggested an Italian restaurant near his hotel that he and his wife had tried.

Kitty drove to Ruth's and left her car there while Vince, ever the gentleman, drove them to the restaurant. It was a cheerful, colourful little place with scarlet and green table linen, raffia-covered Chianti bottles strung down the emerald green walls, a profusion of indoor plants and a stubby red candle on each table.

Initially the atmosphere was a bit starchy as no one knew quite what to say, but the wine soon loosened their inhibitions and conversation became easy, apart from a certain hostility towards Paul shown by Kitty. Inevitably, most of the talk was about school – friends they'd known, teachers they remembered, and a general update for Paul on his three companions.

'Well, everyone,' he said when they were replete with steak cooked Italian style followed by a gooey chocolate pudding, 'here's to us . . . yesterday's friends reunited.'

Glasses were raised to this. Ruth was beginning to feel lightheaded so decided to ease off on the wine afterwards, unlike Kitty who was noticeably squiffy and still knocking it back. Both women were wearing fashionable shift dresses with long sleeves. Ruth's was red with gold braid around the sleeves and a vee-neckline; Kitty's was black and sparkly. Whilst Ruth wore her dark hair short and bouffant, Kitty's fair mane was in a simple Vidal Sassoon-type bob.

'To old times,' said Ruth.

'We mustn't wait twelve years to get together again,' said Paul.

There was a general murmur of assent.

Kitty turned to Paul. 'Did your wife mind being deserted tonight so you could go out with your old school chums?' she asked.

'I haven't deserted her,' he explained, meeting the challenge in her eyes, puzzled by her cool attitude towards him. 'It's the other way round, actually. She's staying with relatives tonight.'

'Who's looking after the kids?'

'We don't have any.'

'Oh . . . I bet you didn't even tell your wife how you'd be spending your time, did you?' said Kitty accusingly.

'Of course I mentioned it,' he said, frowning. 'Why wouldn't I?'

''Cos of Ruth, of course,' she said, sounding much the worse for wine. 'Wives usually take a dim view of husbands meeting up with their old flames.'

'Kitty . . .' reproached Ruth, smarting with embarrassment.

Paul gave Kitty a defiant smile. 'My wife is a reasonable woman. She knows there's no threat to her in my meeting up with someone I haven't seen for twelve years.' He smiled at Ruth. 'Even if she has grown up to be a most beautiful woman.'

She decided on a swift change of subject to ease the troubled atmosphere.

'So tell us about this new job of yours, Paul?' she suggested.

'Yes, do that,' said Vince, noticing how uneasy she was.

'There's nothing much to tell really. Basically, I'll be doing the same as I was at Shaldrake's in Sydney,' he said. 'Looking after the Sales Team. Keeping them motivated, making sure those orders keep on coming in.

I've worked my way up from the bottom. Done my share at the sharp end.'

'It's quite a coincidence, your going into a branch of pharmaceuticals,' said Vince. 'I mean, with Ruth and me both being in pharmacy.'

'Maybe we were all good at the science subjects,' said Paul.

'You didn't go to university, though,' remarked Vince.

'No, I'd had enough of book learning when I left school,' Paul explained. 'You were always the brainy one, Vince.'

'Yeah, worse luck.' He made a face. 'I'd have sooner been the sporty type like you . . . the one all the girls were after.'

Paul threw back his head and laughed. Ruth thought how handsome he looked in a black shirt and light jacket in contrast to Vince who was strictly traditional in a grey suit and white shirt.

'I'm sure that isn't true,' said Paul modestly. 'But those were the days.'

'Long gone but not forgotten, eh?' remarked Ruth lightly.

'We all seem to have done quite well for ourselves anyway,' said Paul, and turned his attention to Kitty to make sure she wasn't excluded as she was the only one of them not working in pharmacy. 'Your job sounds interesting.'

'Yeah, it has its moments,' she replied in a slurred voice.

'And Vince and Ruth are both pharmacists,' he continued, glancing at them.

'I'm not a pharmacist,' Ruth was very quick to point out.

'You're not?' he said in surprise. 'But aren't you and Vince partners?'

'Yes, but I'm not qualified,' she explained. 'The shop came to me in a divorce settlement.'

'Oh, I see, I just assumed . . .' Paul was thoughtful.

Jenny was already quite grown up which meant Ruth must have been young when she'd had her. 'Gave up the idea of university in favour of marriage and motherhood, did you?'

Before Ruth had a chance to reply, Kitty blurted out, 'University was ruled out for her when you went to Australia leaving her pregnant, you rotten bastard! She couldn't finish her education because of you.'

Ruth turned ashen, shocked into silence. Paul looked dumbstruck. Vince's heart went out to Ruth who looked stricken.

'Oh, don't look so innocent, Paul Stoneway,' said Kitty, her voice rising as the rage that had simmered within her for so long was finally given a voice. 'You knew the facts of life and what happens if precautions aren't taken.'

'I . . .'

'The truth must have been obvious to you since you've been back,' she cut in. 'You've seen Jenny, you must have seen the likeness and done a few calculations.'

'I hadn't, as it happens,' said Paul, looking bewildered.

'Well, it bloody well should have . . .'

'Kitty, please stop,' begged Ruth. 'You've said enough.'

'Oh, no, I haven't,' she said, completely impervious. 'It's time he knew what you've been through because of him.' She glared at Paul. 'Have you any idea how Ruth suffered after you left? And I'm talking about the early 1950s, remember. People didn't hang loose about unmarried mothers then. Oh, no! There was no such thing as sexual liberation then. Ruth was insulted, gossiped about, expelled from school, and generally shat on by anyone who fancied having a go at her. That's what was happening to my best friend while you were sunning yourself on the other side of the world without a care.'

Kitty's voice was loud and people were beginning to look in their direction.

'That's enough, Kitty,' warned Ruth.

'You talk about us getting together as old friends,' she ranted as though Ruth hadn't spoken. 'Do you think we're thick or something? You couldn't give a toss about anyone except yourself, Paul Stoneway. You only wanted us all to meet up to make sure we got to know how well you've done for yourself.'

'Come on, Kitty,' intervened Vince in a firm voice. 'You've had too much to drink. I'll take you home.'

'I'm not going anywhere, least of all with you.'

'Shut up and do as you're told for once in your life,' said Vince in a tone of authority Ruth had never heard him use before. 'You and I are leaving before you do any more damage.'

While Kitty was still dumbstruck at this uncharacteristic display of masterfulness, Vince asked the waiter for her coat which was produced with speed. As Ruth and Paul looked on in astonishment, he dragged Kitty to her feet, draped her coat around her, gave Ruth and Paul a knowing wink and marched Kitty from the restaurant.

'Well, I don't believe I just saw that,' gasped Ruth.

'Nor me,' said Paul. 'I didn't know old Vince had it in him.'

'Neither, I suspect, did Kitty.'

They both managed a polite smile but the atmosphere was too highly charged for either of them to do more than that. An awkward silence ensued. Ruth didn't know how best to tackle the complications that Kitty had left behind her.

'The trouble is,' she said to break the silence, 'Vince was in such a panic to remove Kitty, he forgot about me. I came in his car too. So I'll have to get a taxi . . .'

'Don't worry, I'll arrange that for you. But don't go yet. We need to talk.'

'Yes, we do,' she agreed. 'Fortunately Jenny's staying at my mother's tonight so I don't have to rush off just yet.'

'I'll order some more coffee, then.'

'Thank you.'

'I'm still in shock,' said Paul, looking at her across the table when the waiter had taken their order. 'I just can't believe it. I feel terrible about leaving you in that predicament. I honestly thought it would be all right. I thought I'd taken . . . Oh, well, such is the arrogance of youth.'

'You don't seem too peeved suddenly to find that you have a daughter?'

'I'm still a bit dazed,' he admitted with a half smile. 'But I'm dead chuffed too. My wife Leila doesn't want children.'

'I didn't intend you to find out about it in such a public way,' Ruth explained. 'I hadn't even decided whether to tell you at all. I could murder Kitty for interfering.'

'You mean, you were going to keep it from me?' he said in an accusing tone.

'If I thought Jenny might be hurt in any way by the truth coming out,' said Ruth in a hard voice, 'certainly I would keep it from you.'

'But I wouldn't hurt her,' said Paul emphatically. 'I want to make it up to you both for all the years I wasn't around. I want to be a father to Jenny. Surely you wouldn't deprive me of that? Surely I have a right . . .'

Now Ruth was angry.

'How dare you lecture me about your rights?' she protested. 'Jenny is *my* daughter. I gave birth to her and have looked after her and supported her for the past eleven years. She was already five years old when I got married and I continued to support her during my marriage because my husband was lazy and left everything to me. Your part in Jenny's existence is purely a matter of biology. You are a stranger to both of us. I want nothing from you and certainly don't need you to tell me what I should or shouldn't do when it comes to Jenny. She is my only concern in all this . . . I won't have her hurt.'

'I've told you I won't hurt her.'

'It could happen through thoughtlessness,' she said as the waiter poured the coffee. 'Okay, so you think that having a ready-made daughter is a neat idea because your wife doesn't want children at the moment. But where would Jenny stand if Leila were to have a change of heart and decide she does want a family after all? You wouldn't want to know about Jenny then.'

'I'd like to think that I wouldn't be that shallow,' replied Paul. 'Jenny would still be my daughter, however many other children I might have. I don't want to be in her life just because I want a child – *any child*. I want her because she's my own flesh and blood. It still hasn't sunk in properly but it feels good, *very good*. I know it'll take time but I want to get to know her.'

Ruth sipped her coffee, mulling over the potential problems.

'That's all very well but how do you think your wife is going to feel about a child from your past suddenly coming into your life?' she said. 'She could be jealous and hurt Jenny without your even knowing about it. Jenny is an outgoing child but she's also quite sensitive. She's already had one painful experience when my marriage broke up and she lost her stepfather. I'm not going to allow that to happen again.'

'You're not going to tell her who I am, then?' said Paul grimly.

'I didn't say that, but I don't want to tell her yet and must ask you not to do so either,' said Ruth. 'Not until I've decided if it's the best thing for her.'

He fell silent, stirring his coffee and gazing into the cup. Then he glanced up and met her eyes. 'For what it's worth, Ruth, I'd never have gone away and left you if I'd known you were pregnant. And if I'd known about it when I was there, I'd have got back to England somehow.'

'Words are easy,' she said, more as a general observation than a criticism. 'Do you really believe that's true?'

'I've no way of knowing for sure, of course,' he said earnestly. 'I was young and impetuous. But I would like to think I would have done the decent thing by you.'

'That's something we'll never know for sure.'

'True.' He drank his coffee, looking at her thoughtfully. 'It wasn't a question of "out of sight, out of mind", you know,' he added. 'I wanted to write to you but we'd agreed not to stay in touch. And I was so damned homesick for the first couple of years, it was easier if I didn't think about home at all, especially you. Eventually, I managed to settle to Australian life and got married. Writing to you seemed pointless after that.'

'Mmm.'

He looked hard at her. 'So how did you manage? It must have been hellish for you.'

'The worst part was telling my parents,' she said. 'They had such high hopes for me.'

'They must have been devastated?'

'Yes . . . but once they were over the shock, they were wonderful. And, of course, once Jenny arrived, we were all besotted. None of the rest of it mattered after that.'

'At least you had plenty of family support, then?'

'Yes. Actually I didn't feel bitter towards you, not even at first.' She grinned with a hint of wickedness. 'Well, I could hardly claim to have been raped, now could I?'

'Not as I remember it,' he said, his eyes meeting hers as he grinned.

'And it was a mutual agreement not to keep in touch so you couldn't be blamed for not knowing the situation,' she explained. 'But other people didn't see it that way.'

'I bet my name was mud?'

'I'll say! The family and my friends, most of all Kitty, felt murderous towards you. But although I was a victim in other people's eyes, I considered myself to be a winner because I had Jenny. You had left me with a blessing, not a burden. So far as I was concerned you were the one who lost out, not me.'

'I see.'

'The only thing I do regret, though, is not being able to finish my education. Especially now that I have a pharmacy. It would be so much easier for Vince and me if I was qualified. We could think about opening another shop then, without having to employ someone qualified from outside. I've learned a lot about pharmacy over the years and can do the dispensing, but the law says I can't even serve a customer with medicine unless there's a qualified chemist on the premises.'

'I see,' muttered Paul in a small voice, looking very guilty.

'And even after all this time, I still feel as though I let my parents down,' Ruth went on. 'They were so proud when I got into grammar school. No one in the family had ever done anything like that before. And I shattered their dreams.'

'With my help.'

'I won't deny your part in it,' she said, again with a touch of devilment in her eyes, 'but it's over and done with now. We were just kids hungry for everything life had to offer. No point in raking it up and dishing out blame after all this time. The important thing now is what to do about you and Jenny.'

'Yes.'

'I can't prevent your telling her that you're her father,' she said, 'but I'm begging you not to say anything to her until you are quite certain you can make a commitment to her. Once you start along the path to fatherhood, there's no way back without hurting Jenny. You need to speak to your wife. If she objects to your seeing Jenny then there's no point in starting because, one way or another, she will be the one to suffer. I simply can't risk having her rejected by you.'

'*She* might reject me.'

'Yes, she may well do that . . .'

'What shall I do if that does happen?'

'Be patient with her,' Ruth advised. 'Give her time. It could be that you'll have to accept she doesn't want anything to do with you.'

'God, I hope not, Ruth,' he said, impulsively reaching across and clutching her hand. His fingers felt cool and strong and produced shock waves of sexual desire that both confused and excited her. 'Now that I've found her, I do so want to get to know her.'

'Think carefully about what you'd be getting into, and discuss it with your wife,' said Ruth, moving her hand away reluctantly. If they were going to be seeing each other on a regular basis because of their daughter, things needed to be kept formal. 'When you know you can make a full commitment to Jenny, let me know and we'll talk about it again.'

'I'd like to start doing my share financially right away,' he offered.

'That won't be necessary,' said Ruth quickly. 'I can manage.'

'I'd like to help though,' insisted Paul. 'You've carried the burden on your own for long enough.'

'I'm sure we can come to some arrangement about it,' she said, 'but not for the moment. Now I really must go home. I have to be up early for work in the morning.'

'I'll get them to call you a taxi,' he offered, smiling at her.

Physically he had changed almost beyond recognition, his features having hardened with manhood. His skin had lost its boyish bloom, his face and neck had thickened, he even had a slight feathering of lines around his eyes. But she could see the old boyishness in his smile – the smile she'd seen so often since on Jenny's face. After all this time, Ruth was still very attracted to him.

But she had more serious matters on her mind than Paul's undeniable sex appeal. His ability to be a part-time father to her daughter in particular . . .

'I don't care what you say, Vince Todd,' argued Kitty as they drove out of the West End and headed for the suburbs, 'it needed saying. Paul Stoneway has got to be made to face up to his responsibilities.'

'I'm not denying that. But it wasn't your place to tell him . . . and in such an embarrassing way, too,' he reproached her. 'Poor Ruth didn't know where to put herself.'

'Someone had to say something,' said Kitty, belligerent with booze.

'That was for Ruth to decide,' he said angrily. 'It's a personal matter between her and Paul, and none of your business.'

'What's got into you all of a sudden to make you so stroppy?' she asked drunkenly. 'It isn't like you at all.'

'*You* are making me stroppy,' he said. 'What you did was beyond the pale.'

'Dunno what makes you think you have the right to criticise me.'

'Someone has to put you right,' was his forceful reply. 'You mustn't interfere in other people's lives, it just isn't on.'

'Ruth isn't just other people. She's my closest friend.'

'All the more reason for you to be sensitive to her feelings. Don't you think she's had enough trouble in her life without you poking your nose in where it isn't wanted?'

'It's because she's had trouble that I want better things for her, said Kitty. 'That man is the father of her child and he ought to know it.'

'He does now, thanks to you.'

'What I did was right,' she said. 'Ruth's too soft . . .

she wasn't sure whether to tell him, would you believe!'

'She had her own reasons for being hesitant,' said Vince. 'She was probably worried about how it will affect Jenny. Anyway, Ruth should have been given the chance to tell Paul in her own time. You were well out of order, Kitty.'

'Oh, shut up,' she said. 'You're a twerp of the highest order . . . always have been.'

'And you're a spoiled and selfish brat,' he retorted.

'Don't you dare speak to me like that!'

'Oh, for God's sake, change the record, will you?' he said irascibly. 'The sound of your voice is really getting on my nerves. If you can't hold your drink, you should leave it alone, not put it away like there's no tomorrow.'

'You always were too good to live,' she retorted. 'That's what really gets up my nose about you – the fact that you're such a saint. Trust you to stick to lemonade on a night out!'

'And who would have been your chauffeur if I'd got tanked up?'

'Have you never heard of taxis?'

Lapsing into silence, Vince concentrated on the road ahead, eventually pulling up outside a small block of flats in Fulham.

'Why are we stopping here?'

'This is where I live and where you're staying tonight,' he informed her briskly. 'And don't worry, I'll be sleeping on the sofa.'

'I don't want to stay here . . .' whined Kitty.

He turned off the engine and glared at her.

'Now listen to me, woman,' he said in a tone that defied argument. 'I am not going to drive all the way to Staines with you in this state . . . and likely to throw up at any minute.'

'Bloody cheek,' she retorted. 'I'm not going to be sick.'

'One of the pitfalls of getting drunk, I'm afraid.'

'I'm *not* drunk.'

'Oh, no . . . only paralytic. Anyway, you said your husband is on duty overnight, so you don't have to go home until tomorrow.'

'My car's at Ruth's place,' she said sulkily. 'Take me there and I'll drive myself home.'

'Don't be so bloody ridiculous, you're in no condition to drive.'

'I'll stay at Ruth's then.'

'And who's going to let you in?' he rasped. 'Ringo the dog? Ruth isn't home and Jenny is spending the night with her grandmother.'

'I'll ring for a taxi . . .'

'Oh, I've had just about enough of your nonsense,' roared Vince. 'Can't you stop thinking of yourself for one single moment? Not only have you ruined the evening for all of us, but now you want to make me feel obliged to drive you all the way out to Staines when it isn't even necessary. This may come as a surprise to you, but you are not the only person in the world.'

She'd never known Vince to be so assertive and wasn't sure how to handle him.

'Oh, all right then,' she said aggressively. 'I suppose I'd better do as you say.'

'Ungrateful bitch,' he fumed, getting out of the car and going round to the passenger side to open the door for her.

'I don't feel well, Vince,' she said, suddenly pathetic as she stood up and her legs buckled.

'I don't suppose you do after all the wine you've poured into yourself,' he said, but his tone had softened despite himself. 'Here, take my arm to steady yourself.'

With Kitty leaning heavily on him, they walked towards his flat.

When Kitty woke up the next morning, with a raging thirst and a set of cymbals clashing in her head, she found a note from Vince to say that he'd gone to work and she was to help herself to anything she needed.

A great deal of strong black coffee was consumed, she took some aspirin, then got bathed and dressed and rang for a taxi to take her to Ruth's to collect her car. She'd have lunch with her friend before she drove home to Staines, she decided on the way to Shepherd's Bush. Now that everything was out in the open with Paul, Ruth would probably be grateful to her for speaking out.

She was astonished, therefore, to find that Ruth was very angry indeed.

'You had no right to say anything,' she said over coffee and sandwiches in her kitchen, Jenny having stayed at her grandmother's for lunch. 'You knew I was still undecided about what to do. The booze was obviously responsible for your behaviour but that's no excuse.'

'But the truth had to come out sometime,' Kitty pointed out. 'And at least it saves you having to pluck up the courage to tell him yourself.'

'*Pluck up the courage – me?*' fumed Ruth incredulously. 'Have you been blind this past twelve years or something?'

'What do you mean?' Kitty was quite bewildered by this onslaught.

'I've brought up a child on my own whilst putting up with every insult known to humankind, been through a broken marriage, and built up a business more or less single-handed. After surviving all *that*, I certainly don't need anyone to speak up for me!'

'You were being hesitant . . .'

'Not because I was afraid of telling Paul,' she explained heatedly, 'but because I wasn't sure if it was the right thing to do. I discussed this with you on the phone . . . don't you ever listen to any voice but your own?'

'I thought he ought to know . . .'

'If I had made that decision, I would have told him in my own good time,' bellowed Ruth.

'I still can't see what all the fuss is about.'

'Jenny is *my* daughter and this is *her* life you're meddling with. What makes you think you have the right to interfere?'

' "Interference" you call it?' said Kitty, deeply hurt by this attack which she thought completely unjustified because she really did have Ruth's best interests at heart. 'I did what I did because I care what happens to you . . . I thought that was what friendship was all about.'

'Friendship?' blasted Ruth. 'You call what happened last night friendship?'

'Yes, I do.'

'Do you realise how serious the consequences of what you did could have been?' she enquired. 'Supposing Paul was the sort of man who wanted to make things awkward for me? I could find myself with a custody battle on my hands or some sort of legal demand for access.'

'Oh, don't be so ridiculous,' scorned Kitty in full flow, 'as if any court would even consider giving custody to a man who'd had nothing to do with his daughter until she was eleven years old.'

'They wouldn't . . . you're right,' agreed Ruth. 'But that isn't the point. I'm just trying to make you see how dangerous it is to meddle with other people's lives.'

'I acted out of friendship and I don't regret it,' said Kitty, flushed with anger. 'I probably wouldn't have said anything if I hadn't had so much to drink but I'm not sorry it happened.'

Ruth pushed her food aside. 'You just can't admit you're wrong, can you?'

'Okay, I'm wrong,' said Kitty, her tone contradicting the statement. She stood up, scowling, leaving her food untouched. 'If that makes you feel any happier.'

'It doesn't.'

'I can tell you this much, though,' said Kitty through clenched teeth. 'It will be a very long time before I do anything for you again.'

'Thank God for that,' said Ruth. 'I can do without those sort of favours.'

'Then you can probably do without my friendship too,' said Kitty, who was hurting inside and wanted to hurt Ruth back. 'As it means so little to you.'

'Don't be silly,' said Ruth, shocked by what she was suggesting.

'I won't be silly enough to think we're friends in future,' declared Kitty, ashen now but for two small spots of colour staining her cheeks. 'I don't know why I've bothered with you all these years.'

'Kitty . . . now come on . . .'

'I don't need you,' she said in a tight voice, her eyes hard with anger.

'This is getting out of hand . . .'

'I've plenty of other friends, real friends,' she continued in a thick voice. 'People who appreciate what I do for them.'

With that she stamped into the hall, dragged her coat off the rack and pulled it on in a rage. Ruth followed, feeling wretched. Although she was caught up in the heat of the moment, Ruth sensed that any attempt at conciliation from her would not be a good idea right now because it would only give Kitty licence to be intrusively protective of her again in the future. They both needed to calm down before this matter could be properly resolved.

'I'll give you a ring,' said Ruth at the front door.

'You can dial my number 'til you're blue in the face but I won't speak to you,' declared Kitty. 'So far as I'm concerned, you and I have come to the end of the road.'

'Please, Kitty . . .' began Ruth.

But her voice tailed off as Kitty marched out to her car without another word, leaving Ruth with a gnawing ache in the pit of her stomach. She had been through a massive emotional upheaval recently and this was just about the last straw. She closed the door and went slowly upstairs.

'Oh, Ringo,' she said, stroking the dog's head as he rested it on her lap when she sank, weeping, into an armchair. 'Why is my life so full of painful complications?'

Chapter Eleven

Having given a lot of thought to what Ruth had said about the serious commitment of taking on fatherhood, Paul was feeling nervous that evening as he sat down to dinner with his wife. He was about to take the first step by telling Leila about his newfound parenthood. She'd only just got back from her relatives and this was the first chance he'd had to speak to her about it.

'How did the reunion go last night?' she asked, spreading her napkin over her lap when they had been served with their soup.

'It was okay.'

'Your enthusiasm is overwhelming,' she said ironically, breaking her bread roll and nibbling a piece. 'Was it a bit of a let down?'

'No . . . it was fine.'

'Why the long face then?' she enquired with a sharp look. 'Don't tell me London is losing its charm for you already?'

'Well . . . er . . . actually . . .' he began, dreading telling her but anxious to get it over. 'Something rather important came to light . . . something I need to talk to you about.'

'Oh?' She frowned, putting down her soup spoon. 'Sounds as though it's something I'm not going to like, so get on with it.'

He told her all about Ruth and Jenny.

'Well, it's a bit of a bombshell to say the least,' she said.

Although worry was clearly discernible in her green eyes, she wasn't as outraged as he'd expected.

'It was a bombshell to me too,' admitted Paul. 'I can still hardly believe it.'

Giving him a shrewd look, she said, 'You're pleased to have a daughter, though, aren't you?'

He nodded. 'I'm sorry, Leila, I know this is expecting a lot of you but I want to spend some time with Jenny . . . to get to know her. I'd like to be a father to her if I can, albeit only on a part-time basis.'

Leila waited to be consumed with jealousy and felt nothing much except slight annoyance at the threat of some personal inconvenience. This reaction didn't surprise her too much because she didn't understand her feelings for Paul any more than she understood the rest of her psyche. She liked the man, was even quite fond of him in her way, but he didn't make her life complete or remove the inner sense of isolation that had plagued her throughout her adult life and which she'd hoped marriage would cure.

She dared not delve too deeply into her complicated emotions because that would mean facing up to the powerful longings that shamed her, desires she suppressed and pretended she didn't harbour. But the feelings were there, however much she denied them. They frustrated her and made her restless, which was why she could never be at peace anywhere. The grass was always greener somewhere else for Leila because she was always trying to escape – from herself.

'I can understand that,' she heard herself say, feeling curiously detached from the situation.

'You can?' He was amazed how well she was taking it.

'I think so,' she said, wondering where she herself was going to fit into this equation. 'But what do you want me to do?'

'Just give me your approval. I'd like to be able to spend some time with Jenny without upsetting you,' he explained, surprised to realise that he didn't want Leila involved with his daughter. It seemed right, somehow, to keep this new dimension to his life separate from his marriage.

'Mmm,' she muttered non-committally.

'Ruth insisted I talk to you about it before she'll consider telling Jenny the truth,' he explained, hoping to guide Leila towards giving him some sort of agreement. 'She doesn't want me to start something that I won't keep up.'

'Sensible woman.'

'From what's been said, I think she's had a tough time one way and another,' he said. 'And Jenny is her whole life.'

'And you're my whole life, Paul.' Her marriage wasn't great but it was all she had. She didn't make friends easily, which meant she relied on Paul for her social life. His job already made enough demands on him outside of normal business hours. She didn't want their personal arrangements constantly upset by the added responsibility of a child. 'Obviously, I don't want your new parental responsibilities to disrupt our life together.'

'I'm aware of my duty to you, Leila,' he said, 'but I feel I have a duty to Jenny too. I feel I owe her, and Ruth.'

'What about money?' she asked. 'Does Ruth want you to do your share financially?'

'Quite the opposite,' he said. 'She wants nothing from me. I'm the one with all the demands. I'm the one who wants my rights as Jenny's father. Ruth is very wary about the whole thing. She's afraid I might take it on, then lose interest when the novelty wears off.'

'Is she afraid I'll make it difficult for you?' asked Leila.

'Yes, she is.'

'And what if I do, Paul?' she probed. 'What if I object to your having this child in your life? What then?'

He met her eyes, his face set. 'I would still see Jenny,' he told her gravely. 'It's something I really believe I have to do. Please try to understand.'

'Does all this stem from a sense of duty?' she asked, continuing with her soup.

He thought about this carefully because he wanted to be honest with her. Pretence at this early stage wasn't fair to her and would only lead to trouble later on.

'I suppose duty does come into it,' he said, 'but there's more to it than just that.' He broke his bread roll and picked up his soup spoon. 'I really *want* to be a father to her. It's all to do with her being my own flesh and blood. Knowing I'm Jenny's father feels like nothing else I've experienced before. I can't explain it.'

She sighed impatiently. 'I suppose I should be grateful to this Ruth person for providing you with the child I won't give you.'

'That's up to you,' he said, hoping this wasn't going to develop into a row.

They fell into a thoughtful silence while they finished their soup and the waiter cleared their dishes ready for the next course.

Leila wasn't bothered by the idea of having to share his affections with someone else. It was only the possibility of being inconvenienced that bothered her.

'I've no objection to your seeing your daughter as such,' she said. 'So long as you make sure my life isn't ruined by it.'

'Don't worry, Ruth will only allow me limited access anyway.'

'We'll just have to see how it goes then, won't we?' said Leila, because she knew she had no choice. 'But don't expect me not to give you hell if my life is turned upside down every other week.'

'Of course not.'

'Well . . . now that that's settled, can we talk about something else?' she suggested as the waiter served their main course.

'Sure.'

'I've had a good look through the property details that came in the post this morning and there's a place near Chiswick that I'd like us to take a look at.'

'We'll go and see it as soon as you like,' said Paul, guilt for burdening her with the consequences of his past sins making him eager to please. 'And if we like it, I'll do everything I can to get us moved in without delay.'

'You'll be very busy getting to grips with the new job for a week or two, though, won't you?' she reminded him.

'That's true. But I'll find time to get us housed, don't worry.'

'I'm sorry I couldn't make it last Monday,' said Paul, sitting in an armchair in Ruth's living room with a cup of coffee one Monday evening a week or so later. The coal-effect electric fire Ruth had had installed for convenience in the big old-fashioned hearth exuded a cosy glow.

'Don't worry about that,' she said. 'Any Monday night will do.'

Paul was feeling much less relaxed than he was trying to appear and talking too quickly and too much.

'I wanted to get here but it was the first week in my new job and by the time I got away from the office, Jenny would have been home from her Girl Guides meeting. I'll be glad when things settle down at work. Phew! What with that and the house we're buying . . .'

'You've found a place then?' said Ruth, herself feeling very tense and nervous. It was not an easy thing, having to share her parental role after so many years.

'Yes, a little house in Chiswick,' he said through dry lips. He was nervous about the commitment he was about to take on, desperately keen to do his very best for Jenny but unsure of his ability for he knew next to nothing about children. 'Leila will be in her element furnishing it. We sold most of our stuff in Sydney . . . thought we'd make a new start rather than have it all shipped over.' He paused suddenly. 'Sorry, I seem to have developed a serious case of verbal diarrhoea. You wanted us to have a chat while Jenny isn't at home?'

Paul had telephoned Ruth after his discussion with Leila, to say he wanted to move things on with Jenny. Wary about the whole thing but disinclined to come between father and daughter, Ruth had suggested she and Paul get together, without Jenny, for a discussion before they broke the news to her. She explained that a Monday evening would be the best time because that was Jenny's night for Girl Guides.

'Well, obviously I'm anxious as to how she will take the news,' Ruth said now.

'I'm terrified,' confessed Paul.

'And I think it's very important that we work out exactly what we're going to tell her . . . er . . . about us.'

'Us?'

'In relation to how she came about.'

'You think it would be easier for her if she thought we'd had a love affair that lasted longer than one night?'

'Exactly,' she said, warmed by his understanding. 'I hate telling lies, especially to my daughter, but I think a fib would be kinder on this particular occasion . . . a one-night stand has such a tacky ring to it somehow. We don't want her to think she's the result of anything seedy.'

'Ours wasn't a one-night stand . . . not in the usual sense.'

Ruth sipped her coffee to moisten her dry mouth and met his eyes.

'No, it wasn't,' she said softly.

'But no one else could possibly understand the magic of that night and how we felt then,' said Paul huskily.

'True.'

'I've often thought about it,' he said. 'It was as though we were possessed.'

'Yes.' She put her coffee cup down on a small table

and stared into her lap to avoid the look in his eyes, which she found disturbing. 'I think we should tell her that we'd been going out together for a while before you went away. That need be the only deviation from the truth.'

'I'll go along with that.'

'She probably won't even want to know the details yet,' said Ruth, 'but she will want to know at some point and it's as well if we're as one on this as you are going to be spending time with her without me around to prompt you.'

'Sure.'

'Also,' Ruth continued, 'I shall have to tell my family that you're back. They'll find out from Jenny anyway.'

'Great,' he said. 'I'm Jenny's father and I want the world to know it.'

'You might change your mind about that if you have cause to meet the family,' said Ruth with a wry grin. 'They're bound to give you a hard time. It's all in the past so far as you and I are concerned but the Brookses have memories like elephants when it comes to someone not doing right by one of their own. Kitty isn't the only one who would like to see you rot in hell . . .'

'It'll take more than the wrath of your folks to put me off, I can promise you that,' said Paul stoutly.

'That's what I thought you'd say.'

'So . . . is there anything else you think I should know before we take the plunge?'

'Yes. I'll only agree to your seeing her so long as it doesn't interfere with her school work or any of her other commitments. And only if it's what she wants.'

'Fair enough.'

'Good.'

'When shall we tell her?'

'A weekend would be best . . . in case she needs time to recover before school. It'll be a shock for her, whichever way she takes it,' said Ruth. 'How about this Friday evening?'

197

'I'll check with Leila but I think it'll be okay.'

'Perhaps it'd be best if you came for a meal so that you and Jenny can break the ice before we tell her why you've really come?'

'Great.'

'Seven o'clock then?'

'I'll look forward to it.'

Ruth visited her mother in her lunch hour the next day to bring her up to date with what had been happening, rather than have her hear it from Jenny at the weekend.

Having heard the story, Audrey Brooks stared at her daughter in disbelief.

'That bugger's turned up out of the blue and you're being civil to him?' she exploded.

'What's the point in being otherwise?' said Ruth. 'I've nothing against him.'

'*Nothing against him!*' Audrey expostulated, raking her red hair with her fingers distractedly as she leaned against the sink waiting for the kettle to boil. 'Have you gone soft in the head or something?'

'No.'

'The bloke clears off to Australia, leaving you in trouble, and you've nothing against him?'

'That's right.'

'You must be mad!'

'I've told you before . . . he didn't tie my hands behind my back.'

'He still took advantage of you.'

'You weren't there, Mum.'

'Even so, I still say you're mad to give the bloke a civil word, let alone dinner.'

'Okay, so I'm mad . . .'

'It's a wonder he admitted paternity,' snorted Audrey. 'It's only your word against his.'

'He wouldn't be so eager to have Jenny in his life if he

had any doubts about that, would he?'

'I suppose not,' her mother was forced to agree. 'But you make sure he pays for all the years you've struggled on your own, my girl. Squeeze whatever you can get out of him.'

'He's only too keen to help financially,' explained Ruth calmly, 'but I don't particularly want money from him.'

'That's just plain stupid.'

'I don't need it.'

'Oh . . . I didn't know you were related to the Rockefellers?'

'Now, now, don't be sarky.'

'Well, you're your own worst enemy sometimes,' protested Audrey. 'I mean . . . is your shop doing so well that you can turn money away when you've a growing child to raise?'

'No, but I can easily afford to carry on supporting Jenny on my own. I've managed to do it this far, and I've no intention of handing responsibility over to Paul just because I've agreed for Jenny to be told the truth about him.'

'And how's Jenny gonna feel about his sudden appearance in her life?'

'I honestly don't know,' confessed Ruth. 'But I can't deprive her of the chance to meet him and get to know him. It wouldn't be fair.'

'It's all so damned civilised,' said her mother. 'I'd want to slit the bugger's throat if I was in your shoes.'

'I want it to stay civilised, too,' said Ruth. 'It'll be easier for all of us.'

'I doubt if it will, though,' sniffed Audrey, pouring boiling water into the tea-pot. 'Human nature isn't that simple. There's trouble ahead . . . you mark my words.'

'I'll just have to get on and deal with it then, won't I?' declared Ruth. 'As you very well know, I'm no stranger to trouble.'

* * *

'I bet it's fabulous in Australia, isn't it, Uncle Paul?' chirped Jenny on Friday evening as the three of them dined on spaghetti bolognese in Ruth's living room, with the fire glowing in the hearth and wine on the table. 'One of the girls at school has an auntie who lives there. She brought some photos to school once to show us. It was lovely scenery, and ever so sunny.'

'It's sunnier than here certainly,' he informed her. 'And there's lots of open spaces and some great beaches.'

'I'd like to travel abroad for holidays when I'm older,' remarked Jenny chattily.

'Going abroad for holidays is quite commonplace nowadays,' he told her. 'But it was unheard of when I was your age.'

'That was when people lived in caves, wasn't it?' teased Jenny, her small face alive with mischief.

'Cheeky miss.' Paul grinned, enjoying the joke. His daughter was quite enchanting. Ruth had done a good job.

Ruth smiled too. In fact, it would have been a very happy gathering, had she and Paul not been so apprehensive about the task in hand.

'If it's so nice there, why did you come back to London?' wondered Jenny.

'My wife wanted to come back,' he explained. 'But since we've been back I've realised that there's no place like home.'

'Oh.' She didn't have the maturity to hide her surprise. 'You're married then?'

'Very much so,' he said. 'My wife and I are in the process of buying a house here . . . in Chiswick.'

'Oh,' she said again, and Ruth realised she'd thought Paul was here with romantic intentions. 'I thought . . .'

'More spaghetti, Paul?' asked Ruth to ease an awkward moment.

'Not for me, thanks.' Apprehension had killed his appetite.

'Do you have any children, Uncle Paul?' asked Jenny casually.

'No.'

Ruth's heart lurched. She knew the perfect moment had arrived and caught his eye to indicate this.

'Well, when I say no, what I actually mean is . . .' Paul faltered.

'The thing is, Jenny,' assisted Ruth, before she too found it difficult to continue.

Jenny looked from one to the other.

'What's the matter with the two of you?' she asked casually, twirling spaghetti around her fork only to have it slither back on to her plate.

'Well, actually, love, Paul is here this evening because we have something important to tell you,' said Ruth.

'Oh?' Jenny waited for her mother to continue, her fork poised in mid-air.

'Well, you know that Larry wasn't your real father, don't you?'

'Yeah . . . of course.'

Ruth looked at Paul and he took over.

'Larry wasn't . . .' He paused then said in a rush, 'But I am . . . I'm your father, Jenny.'

She turned pale and swallowed hard, looking from Paul to Ruth and back to Paul again.

'You?' she said, staring at him in bewilderment.

'That's right.'

'Oh,' she said, scrutinising his face as though searching for some sort of confirmation.

'I'd like to get to know you, Jenny, if that's all right with you?' he said tentatively.

Whey-faced, Jenny put down her fork and sipped some water.

'If you're my father, why haven't you wanted to do that before?' she enquired.

'I had to go away to Australia . . . before you were born.'

'Like Uncle Larry had to go away?' she said in a flat voice.

'No, it wasn't like that,' said Ruth, wondering if they should have postponed telling her until she was older and more able to cope.

'Are you going to be living here with us?' Jenny cut in before Ruth could finish.

'Of course not, Jenny,' explained Ruth in an effort to help things along because the atmosphere was so tense. 'Paul has just told you that he has a wife.'

'But I'd really like us to see one another some weekends, Jenny,' he said quickly. 'Go out together . . . get to know each other better.'

As though he hadn't spoken, she turned to her mother, blue eyes clouded with worry in her paper-white face.

'I've got a headache, Mum,' she said, pressing her fingers to her temples as though to prove it. 'Can I go to my room, please?'

'But you haven't finished your meal.'

'I don't want any more, thank you,' she said with heartbreaking politeness. 'I just want to go and lie down.'

'All right, love,' agreed Ruth, surprised at this reaction. She'd expected anger and bewilderment, she'd even thought there might be tears, but this show of stoicism was far more worrying.

Jenny stood up, a small, slight figure in a navy blue sweater and denim jeans. 'G'night, Uncle Paul,' she said unemotionally, almost as though the previous conversation had never happened.

'Good night, Jenny,' he said hoarsely. 'I hope you feel better soon.'

'Thanks.'

Ruth and Paul sat at the table in silence, listening to her footsteps on the stairs.

'I think you'd better go,' said Ruth, anxious to comfort Jenny.

'Yes, of course,' he agreed, standing up looking grim. 'She wants me like teenagers want acne.' He sighed deeply and Ruth could see real pain in his eyes. 'It's no more than I deserve, I suppose.'

'She's at a difficult age to deal with something like this,' Ruth pointed out. 'She isn't young enough to accept the situation without question, but neither is she quite old enough to understand how things work for adults.'

'The last thing I wanted to do was to hurt her,' said Paul with a worried shake of the head. 'But that's what I seem to have done.'

'She's still of an age where I can assert my authority and force her to see you,' Ruth told him. 'But I'm not going to do that.'

'I don't want that, but I *do* want her in my life, Ruth . . . so *very* much.'

'Be patient,' she said, showing him to the door. 'I'll talk to her . . . tell her how it was between us.'

On impulse, he reached across to her and took her hand in both of his.

'Please help me, Ruth,' he entreated. 'Help me to win back the daughter I've lost, even though I don't deserve her.'

'I'll do what I can,' she said, managing to stifle the urge to put her arms around him and hold him close. 'No promises, though. I'm not going to force her into anything.'

'So I take it you're not pleased to have met your real father at last?' Ruth said to Jenny.

'Not particularly,' she said, sitting hugging her knees while her mother perched at the foot of her bed. 'Why should I be when he's never bothered about me before?'

Jenny was growing up. She had started her periods

and been given a sensible account of the facts of life by her mother, who had been determined not to leave her in ignorance as she'd been when she was growing up. People were much more outspoken about sex these days. The world was a different place for 1960s youngsters. Ruth decided that Jenny was old enough to be told more of the events that had brought about this painful situation.

'Paul knew nothing of your existence until the other day,' she said.

Jenny gave her mother an enquiring look, waiting for her to continue.

'I didn't realise I was pregnant until after he'd gone to Australia, and he left no forwarding address,' Ruth explained. 'He couldn't because he didn't have one. Anyway, we decided not to keep in touch because it would have been too painful.'

'Did you love him?'

'Very much.'

'And him?'

'He loved me too.'

'Why did he leave you then?'

'He had no choice. His family was emigrating and he had to go with them. We were both still at school when all the arrangements were made. We had to do as we were told. Paul isn't to blame for the fact that you've never had a real father.'

'Oh.'

'So, knowing this, will you give him a chance to make up for all the years you've both lost?'

Jenny shrugged her shoulders as though she couldn't have cared less.

'It might be fun, having your dad around, making a fuss of you.'

'Like Uncle Larry used to . . .'

'You're afraid that you'll get to like him and he'll go away like Larry did?'

'Maybe.'

'He can't earn your trust unless you give him a chance.'

'Do I have to get to know him?' asked Jenny, looking peeved.

'No, you don't have to.'

'You want me too, though?'

'Only because it might be nice for you,' explained Ruth. 'Not just because he wants it. I've told him I'm not going to make you do anything, if that's what's worrying you.'

'That's good,' said Jenny, ''cos I'd really rather not.'

Ruth felt a sharp pang of disappointment which surprised her for she had nothing to gain personally from Paul and Jenny's being friends. In fact, she'd been having serious doubts about sharing the role she'd had to herself for so long.

'Any particular reason why not?'

'I don't need him,' she said. 'You're the only parent I need.'

An inspired guess told Ruth that Jenny thought a relationship with her father might come between herself and her mother.

'It won't make any difference to you and me,' she assured her daughter, 'I can promise you that.'

'I still don't want to get to know him, Mum.'

'He'll be very disappointed,' said Ruth, hoping to persuade her.

'He'll get over it.'

'Okay, love, as you wish,' she said, determined not to put pressure on her. 'Now, how about joining me in a mug of hot chocolate?'

'Yes, please,' said Jenny.

Paul phoned Ruth early the next morning and was devastated to hear that Jenny didn't want to see him at all.

'I can't give up, Ruth,' he said urgently. 'What can I

do to make her change her mind? Do you think I should write to her?'

'I'm not sure it will make any difference at this stage.'

'What can I do, then?'

'You'll have to leave the next move up to her, I'm afraid,' she advised him. 'Jenny might change her mind of her own accord eventually.'

'I can't bear to lose her now that I know about her,' he said, sounding really distressed. 'Can I keep in touch with you to find out how she's getting on?'

'Of course you can,' she said, feeling frighteningly happy at the idea of regular contact with him.

'Thanks.'

For all the complications of Paul's reappearance, it gave Ruth a warm feeling inside to have someone else care about her daughter almost as much as she did. No matter how much her family loved Jenny, there was nothing quite so powerful as the empathy of a parent, even one who'd been absent for so long.

It was the twins' thirtieth birthday that same Saturday and there was a family gathering at Nutley Road that evening. Ruth thought a party was just what Jenny needed to take her mind off the trauma of meeting Paul. Jenny adored her Nunks, as she still called her uncles, and enjoyed playing mother to her cousins Tom and Gary.

There was food and drink galore and everyone over-indulged, chattering all at once. Audrey, who had taken the night off from the pub, was flushed and happy with her family around her. She was looking smart in her new blue dress in the latest wonder fabric called Crimplene, which was all the rage. Even Dan had marked the occasion by wearing a jacket and tie – it was a rare occasion indeed for him to dress up indoors.

'You're getting on a bit now, boys,' Ruth teased her

brothers, 'Pat and Peggy will be wanting to trade you in for younger models soon.'

'Leave it out, Ruth,' protested Ray lightheartedly, patting his hair in mock vanity. 'What have the Beatles got that we haven't?'

'Bags of talent, plenty of money and most of the teenage girls in the country drooling over them,' she said with a laugh.

'Watch it, sis,' laughed Ray. 'You might give our wives ideas.'

'Don't you believe it,' grinned Jack. 'They both know when they're on to a good thing.'

This was received with jovial protests from Pat and Peggy and the evening flew past in similar jocular vein. When they were all about to depart and were standing around chatting in the hall, Audrey took Ruth aside and asked her about the dinner party the night before.

'Oh, it was a bit of a disaster really,' she confessed.

'Well, I can't say I'm surprised,' said Audrey. 'But what actually happened?'

Before Ruth had a chance to reply, Ray intervened. He'd been standing in the hall near the kitchen doorway and had caught enough of the conversation between his mother and sister to know that something important was going on.

'What are you two talkin' about?' he asked. 'What's goin' on?'

Ruth tapped her nose with her finger. 'Mind your own,' she said jokingly because there was no point in seriously demanding privacy – not in the Brooks family.

'Come on, sis, you might as well tell me. I'll only pester the life out of you until you do,' he threatened. 'Something happened last night and I wanna know what it was.'

'My father came to visit us,' said Jenny, who had been standing unnoticed by her uncle's side and had overheard his question. Although the child was obviously unaware of it, Ruth perceived a note of pride in her voice. 'I bet that's what they're talking about.'

'You mean that Larry's come back?' said Ray in surprise.

'No, not Uncle Larry, Nunkie, it was my *real* father,' announced Jenny.

'Not Stoneway?' said Ray, aghast.

'Blimey,' gasped Jack.

Ruth knew there was no point in trying to keep it from them since they would find out soon enough anyway. In fact, she was very surprised they didn't know already.

'Yeah, that's right . . . didn't Mum tell you that Paul's back in London?' She turned to her mother and grinned. 'You're slipping, aren't you, Mum? News usually travels through this family faster than a rumour round the market.'

'I hadn't got round to telling them,' explained Audrey. 'I only heard about it myself a couple of days ago, didn't I?'

'Is he back here for good or just visitin'?' asked Ray.

'He intends to stay, I believe,' said Ruth. 'He's got a job here anyway.'

'He said that he's buying a house,' said Jenny, and again there was more than a hint of childish boastfulness.

So . . . Jenny did like the *idea* of having a daddy even if she wanted nothing to do with the man himself, thought Ruth. Interesting!

'What happened to the good life down under then?' said Ray cynically. 'He came a cropper, I s'pose, like so many of these people who bugger off to other countries because the grass seems greener – and find it isn't all that it's cracked up to be when they get there.'

'He's doing very well for himself by the sound of it,' said Ruth.

'He's staying in a posh hotel until he can move into his house anyway,' said Jenny proudly. 'What's the name of it, Mum?'

'The Lambert Star,' supplied Ruth.

'He's not short of a few quid then?' remarked Ray ponderously.

'Doesn't seem like it,' Ruth replied.

Tom and Gary called Jenny to the front door to see how frosty it was outside and she trotted off to join them.

As soon as she was out of earshot, Ray turned to Ruth.

'What's Stoneway's game then?' he demanded.

'He hasn't got one so far as I know,' she replied evenly.

'He must have if he's been sniffing around you and Jenny,' he said. 'Is he trying to get his feet under the table after all this time?'

'No, nothing like that,' Ruth quickly assured him. 'He's a happily married man.'

'That doesn't stop some blokes.'

'No, it isn't me he's interested in.' She gave her brother, who had now been joined by his twin, a brief report on the events leading up to Paul's visit last night. 'It's Jenny he came to see. He wants to take a fatherly interest and try to build some sort of relationship with her.'

'He's left it a bit late to play Daddy, hasn't he?' declared Ray dryly.

'Jenny certainly seems to think so. She isn't having any of it,' explained Ruth. 'She just doesn't want to know.'

'You can hardly blame her,' said Ray.

''Course you can't,' agreed his echo.

'Well, that's peculiar,' said Audrey with a puzzled frown, ''cos I could have sworn she seemed dead chuffed about him coming to see her when she mentioned it just now.'

'Yeah, I noticed that too,' remarked Ruth thoughtfully. 'I was surprised because she's quite adamant about not wanting to see him. She was very offhand with him once she knew who he really was. I'm not going to force her into anything either.'

'I should hope not,' said Ray.

'Me too,' said Jack.

With a mother's perception, Audrey saw a look pass between her sons that would have gone unnoticed by anyone else. She'd been economical with the truth when she'd said she hadn't got around to mentioning Paul Stoneway's return to the twins. She'd held the information back deliberately. All those years of trying to keep them out of trouble when they'd been young hellraisers bent on mischief had made her cautious.

But they were thirty years old now and respectable married men, long past their wild days. She recognised that look though. It had 'hidden agenda' written all over it.

Seeing them off the premises a few minutes later with their wives and children, typical family men, she thought she must have been imagining things.

A feeling of uneasiness lingered, though. Surely they wouldn't . . . would they?

Chapter Twelve

The Brooks twins didn't let the fact that they had never met Paul Stoneway deter them in their pursuit of revenge.

One evening the following week, unbeknown to the rest of the family, they drove to Marble Arch in Ray's Ford Cortina. With the confidence that comes from great physical strength, they swaggered into the Lambert Star Hotel as though they owned the place.

A female receptionist, with good manners and immaculate grooming, was informed that they were colleagues of Mr Stoneway from Shaldrake's and would like to see him on a matter of business. Having listened to their explanation that they preferred not to inconvenience his wife, the receptionist spoke to Mr Stoneway on the internal telephone and arranged for him to meet them in reception in a few minutes.

They were pleased about that. The last thing they wanted was to cause Stoneway's wife any distress. After all, Ray and Jack had standards.

Paul walked into the spacious reception area glancing around expectantly for a familiar face, and surprised when none appeared. Surveying the marble-floored expanse, tastefully furnished with soft leather sofas and a great deal of greenery, he was about to ask the receptionist for an explanation when two large men in dark overcoats strolled over to him.

'Paul Stoneway?' said Ray enquiringly.

'That's me,' he said, looking from one to the other,

thinking he must be seeing double. 'I'm afraid you have the advantage . . .'

'Ray Brooks,' he said gruffly, and glancing towards his twin added, 'This is Jack. We're Ruth's brothers.'

'Of course, I can see the likeness now,' said Paul in his usual amiable manner. 'You all have the same dark colouring.' His expression hardened. 'Has something happened to Ruth . . . or Jenny?'

'Not that we know of,' said Ray.

'They were both fine when we last saw 'em,' confirmed Jack.

'Good.' Paul gave them an enquiring look. 'So how can I help you?'

'We'd like a few words in private,' explained Ray.

'Sure,' said Paul. 'Let's go into the bar, shall we?'

'No, not in here,' said Ray. 'We'd rather take a walk.'

Paul cast a shrewd eye over them. He knew exactly what they had in mind and wasn't in the least perturbed.

'Okay, boys. But give me a minute while I nip upstairs to get a coat, will you?' he requested because he was only wearing a fine-knit sweater over a pair of casual slacks.

'No. We're going straight away,' Ray firmly informed him.

Paul hesitated only momentarily.

'As you wish,' he said with a sang-froid that surprised the brothers. 'Let's go then.'

Flanked closely by the twins, Paul walked out of the hotel into the bitter street, the sub-zero temperature manifest in the sugary white coating of frost on the rooftops and parked cars.

'Are we going anywhere in particular?' he asked evenly as they gripped his arms.

Receiving the distinct impression that Paul Stoneway was laughing at them, Ray said, 'Just walk and cut the chat.'

'I hope we're not going far,' he said, ignoring Ray's

request because the raw cold was penetrating to his bones and making him shudder. 'It's freezing and I'm not used to such cold weather, 'specially without a coat.'

'The weather is the least of your worries, mate,' Ray told him.

'Yeah,' echoed Jack.

'So you intend to beat me up, then, do you?' said Paul in a matter-of-fact tone.

'We don't go out walking in brass monkey weather for the benefit of our health,' said Ray.

'You think I did the dirty on your sister, is that it?'

'Glad to hear you admit it,' said Ray, astonished by the man's nerve. Tougher men than Stoneway had been reduced to snivelling helplessness by the Brooks twins in their heyday.

'Why wouldn't I admit it?' he said. 'When I happen to think it's true.'

'You're a cool bugger,' said Ray. 'But it won't be the cold you'll be shivering with in a minute, I can promise you that.'

'Two against one doesn't seem fair to me,' Paul declared.

'Neither was what you did to our sister,' Ray told him.

'If you say so,' said Paul, having the temerity to sound bored.

'We wanna make sure you don't cause any more trouble for Ruth,' announced Ray.

'Really?' said Paul, completely unruffled.

'Young Jenny doesn't wanna see you, so you stay away from her.'

Before Paul could reply he was steered off the street into a small pub car park, deserted on this freezing night. Ray dragged him into a corner out of the light, shoved him against the wall and squared up to him.

'You stay away from our sister and our niece, do you understand?' he said, aiming his fist in Paul's direction while Jack stood poised, ready to assist if necessary.

In two swift movements Paul brought them both to the ground, Ray with a neat judo kick to his legs and Jack with a similar action to the shoulder. Able to see them in the moonlight, Paul stood over the astonished pair as they sat, dazed, on the frosty tarmac.

'I didn't mention that I'm a black belt in judo, did I?' The twins didn't reply.

'If either one of you tries to get up before I've finished what I have to say, I'll give you another practical demonstration of my skill in the noble art.'

Neither Ray nor Jack said a word. Such effective opposition wasn't something they were used to and they found it humiliating.

'Right. Let's get this damned business sorted once and for all,' said Paul grimly, glaring down at them. 'No one regrets what happened twelve years ago more than I do. I didn't know Ruth was pregnant when I went away. I only found out about Jenny a few weeks ago. Okay, I shouldn't have got Ruth pregnant in the first place, I know that. But these things happen to the best of us, as you know. I can't change what happened but I can do my best to make up for it. I want to get to know Jenny and be a father to her. I also have every intention of taking my share of the financial burden.'

He paused, rubbing his arms against the cold and shivering.

'At the moment Ruth doesn't want my money and Jenny doesn't want anything to do with me at all. But I shall keep trying. I'm *going* to take an interest in my daughter whether she likes it or not, in the hope that one day she'll allow me to play a part in her life, however small. You two gorillas won't frighten me off, so you might as well give up the juvenile heroics.'

They didn't reply or try to get up but just stared at him, angry to be belittled but impressed by him despite themselves.

'Okay,' said Paul. 'Now that you've had the situation explained to you, are you gonna stop impersonating the Kray twins and come for a drink with me?'

'A drink – with you?' exclaimed Ray.

'Nothing wrong with that, is there?' said Paul, looking towards the pub. 'I don't know about you two but I could murder a pint.'

Ray scrambled to his feet, keeping a wary eye on Paul. But he was beginning to think that he might not be such a bad sort of a bloke after all.

'You can relax,' said Paul, sensing their uneasiness. 'You'll get no more judo unless you start on me. I only use it in self-defence.'

The brothers brushed the dust off their overcoats with their hands.

'Well, are you coming for a drink or not, you daft pair?' said Paul. 'I'm not standing out here all night turning blue with the cold.'

They exchanged an uncertain look.

'After all,' continued Paul, stamping his feet as his toes and fingers turned numb, 'I'm Jenny's father and you're her uncles, so I suppose that makes us sort of related, doesn't it?'

'That's really pushing it,' said Ray, but it was only a token protest.

'Well, whatever . . . we all care about Ruth and Jenny and that has to count for something.'

'S'pose so,' grunted Ray.

'Oh, and by the way,' said Paul, 'no one will hear about what happened between us tonight from me.'

Ray looked at his brother. 'I could do with a pint, couldn't you, bruv?'

'Not half.'

'Come on then,' said Paul with a violent shudder. 'Before we're frozen to the pavement.'

And the three men walked towards the pub together.

★ ★ ★

Paul telephoned Ruth regularly to find out how Jenny was. Occasionally he called at the shop but only when he knew Jenny would be at school, to avoid embarrassing her. Ruth thought it important to keep Jenny informed of his continuing interest in her, even though she remained outwardly indifferent. But Ruth suspected that her daughter was secretly rather tickled, even if only because having a father gave her more credibility with her peers.

This suspicion was confirmed when Ruth overheard a conversation between Jenny and a schoolfriend who came home with her after school one day.

'My dad's got a really good job,' said Jenny.

'Has he?'

'Yeah, he's very high up in his firm.'

'Does he earn lots of money?'

'I expect so,' said Jenny. 'I bet he'll get me something really fab for Christmas.'

She was right. He gave her an expensive record player with radio combined. Naturally she was delighted and pleased her father by writing him an effusive letter of thanks.

Ruth thought Paul was treading on dangerous ground with such extravagant generosity and warned him to be careful he didn't slip into the habit of spoiling her.

'I'm just trying to make up for all the Christmases she didn't get anything from me,' he explained.

'Just so long as you don't try to buy your way into her affections.'

'I'm not that stupid.'

As the year ended with the central figure in a sensational sex scandal, Christine Keeler, being sent to prison after pleading guilty to perjury, and the Beatles preparing to take their music to America, this odd situation between Jenny and Paul continued, with Ruth acting as go-between.

The New Year got underway with Ruth being forced

to accept that her friendship with Kitty was over. It was the last thing she wanted but when all her telephone calls to Kitty were received with hostility, she was forced to admit defeat. Ruth was deeply sorry to have hurt her closest friend. But, in all honesty, she couldn't backtrack on her objections to Kitty's interference and give her the apology she knew it would take to rekindle their friendship.

So they were stuck in a position of stalemate. Ruth missed her dreadfully: the chatter, the gossip, the sharing of problems. Just knowing that Kitty was no longer there for her cast a dark shadow over Ruth's life.

The business continued to flourish. From time to time she and Vince discussed the idea of opening another shop. But, put off by the fact that they would have to employ a qualified chemist, they never did more than discuss it.

Jenny was doing well at school and had an exemplary report at the end of her first year at Redfern. As time passed she grew curves and a bust, and became besotted by teenage clothes and pop music. She cast off her childhood like yesterday's knickers – though Ruth was relieved to notice that she retained her academic prowess.

It was when she was in her fourteenth year that she expressed a wish to see her father.

'What's changed your mind, all of a sudden?' enquired Ruth.

'No particular reason. I just thought it might be fun to go out with him sometimes,' she explained. 'So I think I'll write to him and suggest that we get together sometime soon.'

Naturally Paul was delighted that his persistence had been rewarded and arranged to see Jenny the following Sunday.

Being a realistic sort of a person, Ruth wondered if the usefulness of an indulgent father to a fashion-conscious teenager had become apparent to Jenny and was the reason for this sudden change of heart.

* * *

Having no experience of children, Paul found it difficult to sustain a conversation with a thirteen year old over a long period.

'What are your favourite subjects at school?' he asked over tea in a West End hotel, having trailed around Regent's Park Zoo in the spring sunshine making conversation with someone who was a complete stranger to him and who, moreover, had lectured him about the cruelty of keeping animals in captivity.

'Maths and biology,' she said.

'Maths . . . my word. That's most people's worst nightmare.'

'I don't have any problems with it.'

'And what are you interested in outside of school?' God, he sounded as though he was interviewing one of the hopefuls in a beauty contest.

'Pop music and clothes . . . seeing my friends,' Jenny said. 'I can't wait to be old enough to go out to discotheques.'

Thirteen years old and she wanted to go out dancing? 'Struth! He'd have to have a word with Ruth about this.

'You're not old enough yet, though.'

'Not for proper discos, worse luck,' she said, pulling a face. 'But I can go to the one at school at the end of term.'

'School disco?' he said, astounded. 'They didn't have anything like that when I was at Redfern.'

'Well, they do now,' she said brightly. 'Luckily for us.'

'We used to have to organise our own entertainment,' he said, and felt quite sick with worry when he remembered what had happened at that last fateful end-of-term party. Panic rose within him as he realised that at that time Ruth hadn't been much older than Jenny was now. God, what a worry this parenting lark was.

'Things have changed a lot since then,' said Jenny in a

worldly wise tone. 'Mum's always saying so. She thinks it's mostly for the better. You know, with the pill and everything.'

'Does she really?' said Paul, hardly able to believe his ears. What *was* Ruth thinking of, talking to the girl about such things?

'Yes, she does. Most people do. It'll save a lot of unwanted babies being born.'

'Mmm,' was all he could manage. How old was his daughter – thirteen or thirty?

Jenny finished a cream bun, wiped her fingers on a napkin and said, 'Have you heard about the film *The Sound of Music*?'

'That's the one with Julie Andrews, isn't it?'

She nodded. 'It's on in the West End. My friend's been to see it. She says it's fab.'

'We could go and see it together, if you like?' Paul suggested.

Jenny's answering smile was wide. 'Oh, yes. That would be really great,' she said. 'But it's a very popular film. I've heard the queues are a mile long at every performance.'

'I'll see about booking in advance then, shall I?'

'Ooh, thank you, that would be lovely,' she replied happily.

While Paul was congratulating himself on having won over his daughter, Jenny was having some thoughts of her own.

Having a father who would do anything to please you was terrific. She couldn't think why she'd waited to long to have him in her life.

'I understand you've been talking to Jenny about the contraceptive pill?' declared Paul with a disapproving ring to his voice.

Having been brought home by her father, Jenny had

gone straight upstairs to the flat, leaving Ruth and Paul to talk at the front door.

'Yes, that's right,' Ruth said. 'She'd heard about it and wanted to know more.'

'And you told her?'

'Certainly. I wouldn't fob her off on a subject as important as that. Actually, I was pleased she came to me rather than picking up unreliable information from the other kids.'

'She's much too young to be burdened with that sort of information.'

'If I hadn't told her, she'd soon have found out elsewhere. As I've just said, that was what I didn't want.'

'She's just a child.'

'She's an adolescent,' Ruth corrected him sharply. 'She's started her periods and knows about the birds and the bees.'

'Thirteen and you've talked to her about sex!' he said accusingly.

'I've also answered her questions about hippies,' Ruth said. 'That doesn't mean she's going to run away to live in a commune.'

'There's no need to be facetious . . .'

'Look,' she cut in, beginning to feel irritated, 'I answered her questions in what I consider to be a responsible manner and was careful to emphasise the question of morality.'

'Humph!'

'We're living in a different world from the one we grew up in, Paul.'

'So it seems.'

'Anyway, teenagers talk about sex all the time among themselves . . . or what they think happens. Even in our day that went on. Surely you haven't forgotten?'

'I don't remember being as young as that when it started being important.'

'Well, I do. Anyway, what I choose to say to my daughter is not your concern.'

'She's my daughter too.'

Oh, terrific, thought Ruth. One outing with Jenny and he's already an expert on child care. She slowly counted to ten.

'You've spent one afternoon with her, I've spent thirteen years,' she said in a manner that prohibited argument. 'So don't tell me what I can and can't talk to her about. Because when it comes to parenting, you're a complete novice!' She paused to draw breath. 'The only rights you have so far as Jenny is concerned are the ones I allow you to have. I'm in charge and I'll thank you to remember that.'

His face tightened and she knew her message had hit home.

'I'm sorry. Perhaps I did speak out of turn,' he said, sounding genuinely contrite.

'I'll say you did, mate. And I hope you're not going to make a habit of it.'

'I don't think I dare,' said Paul, managing a watery grin.

'What *have* you got on, Jenny?' asked Ruth a month or so later when she opened the front door to her daughter who was just back from a Saturday afternoon out with her father. She was carrying a store bag which, presumably, contained the clothes she'd been wearing when she went out.

'It's a new outfit Dad's just bought for me,' Jenny said excitedly. 'Isn't it terrific?'

'The outfit is lovely,' said Ruth, casting her eye over the miniest of mini-dresses with a bodice which hugged Jenny's bosom. She was wearing pale, lacy tights and buckle shoes with a smallish heel. 'And on someone a bit older it would be perfect.'

'You don't think it looks good on me, then?' she said, looking hurt.

In actual fact she looked wonderful, slender and bright-eyed, her golden hair tumbling to her shoulders. But she looked about eighteen and ready to go out to a nightclub.

'I think the dress looks lovely.'

Jenny brightened immediately. 'Oh, good. I'm glad you like it.'

Knowing how sensitive girls of that age are, Ruth chose her words carefully because she didn't want to damage her daughter's confidence. But there was clearly a need for her to exert some discipline.

'But don't you think it's just a teeny bit too grown-up for you?'

'No! Twiggy dresses like this and she's not very old,' Jenny declared. 'I was reading about her in a magazine.'

'She's older than you are, though.' Ruth cut the conversation short as Paul appeared after parking the car. 'But we'll talk about it later. You go on upstairs.'

As soon as she was out of earshot, Ruth turned on Paul.

'What on earth do you think you're playing at?' she demanded to know.

'What do you mean?' he asked innocently.

'You know very well what I mean,' she blasted. 'You attack me for talking to Jenny about the pill, and here you are letting her dress as though she ought to be taking it!'

'She said she wanted some new clothes so I decided to treat her,' he explained lamely.

'But that outfit is completely unsuitable for someone of her age.'

'I thought it was a bit grown-up too,' he admitted wryly. 'But she didn't like any of the ones I suggested.'

'She wouldn't! You should have been firmer with her.'

'I saw no point in buying her something she didn't want and would never wear.'

'Oh, really. She only has to bat her eyelashes at you and you let her have whatever she wants,' said Ruth, keeping her voice down so that it didn't reach Jenny's ears. 'Can't you see that she's using you?'

'The least I can do is to buy her a few presents to make up for all the things she didn't have when I wasn't around,' he protested.

'For heaven's sake, Paul! You can't make up for thirteen lost years . . . they've gone and there's nothing you can do about it. You certainly won't earn her respect by giving her every single thing she wants the instant she asks for it. Trips to the cinema, meals out, records, clothes, too much pocket money . . . It's ridiculous. The girl only has to mention that she wants something and it's hers.'

'She can be very persuasive, you know, Ruth,' he explained feebly. 'And I really am trying to get to know her better.'

'She knows you are desperate for her to like you and she's milking it for all she's worth,' Ruth told him brutally.

'You make your own daughter sound like a monster!'

'Not at all. Jenny is my life and I love her more than you could possibly imagine. But adolescents are all self-centred. We were too in our day, even if we can't remember it now. It's just a phase, and Jenny is no different from anyone else,' Ruth tried to explain.

'Oh.'

'In you she has found an endless source of treats that I won't always let her have,' she continued. 'Jenny can twist you round her little finger and she knows it.'

'Oh, dear. Surely she isn't really as mercenary as that?'

'She's a young girl with a lot of peer pressure on her,' Ruth explained patiently. 'Her friends have something so she wants it too. It's human nature. I've tried never to spoil her. In the early years I couldn't because money was short. Obviously now, with the business doing well, there is more cash about. But I've brought her up to appreciate things and not lose the pleasure of anticipation with excess. Then you came along and destroy all my hard work without a second thought.'

'Oh, dear,' he said again.

'What sort of hell do you think my life's going to be, trying to maintain discipline while you give in to her at every twist and turn?' Ruth said to hammer home the point.

'Do you think the reason Jenny suddenly wanted to see me was because she thought I'd be a soft touch?' Paul asked.

'That thought did occur to me,' she replied candidly.

'Did it?'

'Mmm. It did happen at about the same time as she got into the teenage culture thing and was wanting all the latest fashions, didn't it?'

'It wasn't me she was interested in at all then?' said Paul, looking cast down by her frankness. 'Just my wallet.'

'Be realistic, Paul. She wouldn't have had a sudden desire to see you out of love for you because you were a stranger to her. She could hardly have been expected to feel affection for you just because she was told that there's a biological link between you. Those sorts of feelings come from knowing someone . . . they have to be earned. But no matter what her original intention was, she *has* given you the chance to build a relationship with her. But you won't build a satisfactory one by giving her every single thing she asks for.'

'It seems I've a lot to learn about being a parent,' he said gloomily.

'Join the club.' Ruth smiled suddenly, lightening the atmosphere. 'There are times when I feel like an amateur and I've been at it for more than thirteen years. Each new stage brings a fresh challenge. The most important thing in your case is not to be so anxious to please her that you lose your head.'

'She'll probably not want to carry on seeing me if I stop coming across with the goodies,' he said miserably.

'If that's the case, then you're better off not seeing her. But I don't think it'll come to that because basically Jenny is a sweet-natured girl. She's just young and a bit dazzled by the power she has over you, that's all.'

'It's ironic really,' he said with a watery grin. 'I'm in charge of a large sales team and can be really tough when I need to be. I'm known for it in the firm . . . it's what pushed me up through the ranks into the position I now hold. But I can't say no to my own daughter.'

'You're going to have to learn if you want to earn her respect.' Ruth gave him a wicked smile. 'And if you want to carry on seeing her . . . because I can be tough too, if I need to be.'

A few weeks later, Jenny and Paul were in a fast food restaurant in Leicester Square having hamburgers. They had been to see *Mary Poppins* and Jenny was full of pleasure. He felt quite overwhelmed to see her so happy. He usually let her choose where they would go. That was just good sense and not indulgence, he told himself, since it would be pointless to take her somewhere where she'd be bored.

He'd have preferred something a bit more refined for tea than a hamburger place but Jenny had said that posh restaurants weren't cool and she wouldn't be seen dead in one. He hadn't argued – on that one he felt he must concede to youth.

'Can I ask you something?' said Jenny, squirting ketchup on to her hamburger.

'Of course.'

'Well . . . there's these machines you can buy that record things,' she said.

'Ye-es?' said Paul, waiting.

'They're called tape recorders . . . you can record

people's voices and records and that.'

'Yes, I know what a tape recorder is,' he told her with more than a suspicion of where all this was leading.

'Everybody's getting them,' she said.

'Everybody?'

'Well, some of my friends at school anyway,' she said.

'And you want me to buy you one, I suppose?' he suggested, his stomach churning at the idea of refusing her.

She put her head on one side and smiled in an appealing way that made mincemeat of his good intentions.

'Ooh, would you?' she said, as though his agreement was already a fait accompli.

'Have you asked your mother if you can have one?' enquired Paul.

Jenny looked taken aback by the question.

'Well, no . . . not exactly.'

'Why?'

'Well, because . . . because . . .' she muttered, her voice tailing off.

'Could it be because you know she'll say no?' Paul suggested, hiding his nervousness.

A strawberry flush crept up her neck and suffused her face. She wasn't used to her father putting up any sort of opposition to her requests.

'Well . . . she never lets me have anything,' she muttered.

'Now you know that isn't true, Jenny,' he admonished, frowning deeply. 'Your mother is one in a million.'

'Yes, I know, I didn't really mean what I said,' she mumbled, feeling guilty and confused by his change of manner. 'But she just doesn't understand about young people.'

'That I find very hard to believe,' he said. 'She's still young herself.'

Jenny gave him a pitying look and said, 'Mum's thirty.'

'That's young.'

'For a mum maybe,' she agreed flatly. 'But she doesn't know about teenagers . . . things were different in her day.'

'They didn't have tape recorders then,' he said teasingly.

'Exactly,' said Jenny, far too intense to see the joke.

He steeled himself for what he was about to say, though it was already becoming easier now that he had begun to take a firmer line.

'No, I am not going to buy you a tape recorder,' he said. 'Not for the moment anyway.'

'Oh.' Her face fell into a pout. 'I was relying on you. I'll be the only one in my crowd who doesn't have one now.'

'If you still want one at Christmas, I'll think about getting you one then.'

'They'll be out of fashion by then,' she said sulkily.

'In that case, you can have whatever the latest fad is,' he said. 'Within reason.'

She pushed her hamburger away.

'Oh, please, Dad,' she coaxed. 'I really *must* have one.'

'No, Jenny.'

'But it's *really* important.' She looked at him with tears in her eyes.

'There's no point in turning on the tears,' he said, 'because I'm not going to give in to you on this one.'

'Oh, Dad . . .'

Suddenly he could see how he was being manipulated and knew Ruth had been right to insist that he make a stand. If he gave in to Jenny over this, there would be no end to it. She would become a spoiled brat, unhappy and disliked by everyone.

'I am *not* going to buy you a tape recorder until Christmas,' he said in the gruffest tone she had ever heard him use. 'And I don't want to hear another word about it.'

She was very quiet after that and responded to his

attempts at conversation with the utmost brevity.

'How's your burger?'

'Fine, thank you.'

'Would you like another milkshake?'

'No, thank you.'

He was thoroughly relieved when it was time to drive her home.

When Ruth answered the door to them, he expected Jenny to go straight upstairs in a huff without a word to him and without making any further arrangements to see him. But although her manner was still a bit frosty, she surprised him.

'Thanks for the film and tea out,' she said casually. 'See you in a couple of weeks, yeah?'

'I'll look forward to it,' he said, with a warm feeling inside.

Things were much easier for Ruth after Paul put his foot down because Jenny stopped behaving like a spoiled child. Having told Ruth all about the tape recorder incident, Paul promised to consult her if he wanted to buy Jenny anything major.

All through the summer, the meetings between father and daughter continued and Ruth began to feel more confident of a permanent relationship developing between them.

As autumn approached, she decided to kill two birds with one stone – to do something she had been wanting to do for a long time, and at the same time show Paul she was beginning to trust him to be a good father to Jenny.

'I'd like to go to evening classes in dispensing,' she told him one day in early September, 'and I wondered if you might be willing to stay with Jenny while I'm out? She'd probably be all right in the flat on her own for a couple of hours, but as we live over the shop I'd rather not leave her on her own . . . even though we do have Ringo.'

'Sure, Ruth, I'll be happy to,' he said, flattered to be asked. 'I do occasionally have to go away on business during the week but perhaps your mum could stand in for me then?'

'So long as I know in time to make arrangements,' she said.

'I won't let you down,' Paul promised, almost childishly thrilled by Ruth's request which made him feel like one of the family.

Watch it, Stoneway, he warned himself, you're a married man, remember.

Chapter Thirteen

'So this baby-sitting is going to be a regular thing then, is it?' said Leila the next morning over breakfast, having been told of Paul's arrangement with Ruth.

'Hardly baby-sitting but, yes, it will be once a week,' confirmed Paul, feeling the sharp tug of divided loyalties.

They were eating in the dining area of their kitchen, a gleaming expanse of formica and floor tiles overlooking a small secluded garden screened by trees and shrubs, already aflame with autumn berries. Early sunlight flickered through the foliage and cast pale undulating shadows on the walls.

'Surely the child is old enough to stay at home on her own for a couple of hours?' said Leila, pouring more coffee.

'If they lived in an ordinary house, it would be different,' he said. 'But living over the top of a chemist's shop . . .'

'What about Jenny's grandmother?' Leila suggested. 'Can't she stay with her?'

'I'm sure she could,' said Paul, 'but it's up to me, as her father, to help out if I can.'

'Ruth managed perfectly well all those years without you.'

'And she'd continue to do so if that was what I wanted.'

'But it isn't?'

'No, Leila, it isn't,' he confirmed. 'And, to be perfectly honest, I think Ruth has asked me to do this for my sake rather than hers . . . to get me more involved with Jenny. It's her way of saying she trusts me not to let Jenny down. I told you how wary she was at first about my taking on

231

the role of father, in case I disappeared when the novelty wore off.'

'That's all very well but you do have a responsibility towards me, Paul.'

'And have I ever shirked that?' he asked, riddled with guilt for upsetting his wife with something that he could never share with her. 'You're not kept short of money or freedom. I take you out to plenty of nice places. And I don't come home drunk or chase other women.'

'I'm not denying any of that. But you are very taken up with that daughter of yours.'

'I've explained to you how much having a child means to me.'

'How do I know it is just your daughter you're so keen on seeing?'

The accusation touched a raw nerve because she was nearer to the truth than he cared to admit.

'If you're suggesting there's something going on between Ruth and me, you're wrong,' he told her.

'Am I?'

'Yes, you are. I only see Ruth briefly when I collect Jenny,' he said. 'You'll just have to take my word for that.'

'Okay, I'll accept that,' she said. 'But you must admit that you are becoming obsessed with your daughter.'

'I wouldn't call seeing her every two weeks being obsessed.'

'Now it's going to be once a week as well.'

'Well, yes . . . but that isn't going to inconvenience you,' he assured her. 'It just means I'll be later than usual getting home from work on Wednesdays.'

'Supposing I want you and me to go out together somewhere?'

'We hardly ever go out during the week.'

'Something might come up.'

'Now you're just looking for problems.'

'I'm just thinking ahead.'

'You don't have enough to do with your time, that's your trouble, Leila,' he told her, hackles rising. 'You need some sort of an interest outside the home.'

'Such as?'

'Why not take a leaf out of Ruth's book and join a class?'

'Doing what?'

'I don't know but I'm sure there are plenty of options available,' he said. 'You could make some enquiries . . . see what's on offer in the way of adult classes.'

'So you can feel okay about all the time you spend with Jenny?'

'No. So that you can have a fuller life,' he corrected, irritated by her negative attitude. 'Take up a hobby, get a job, do *anything* you like, Leila, but for Pete's sake, get off my back.'

The tears in his wife's eyes filled him with remorse.

'I'm sorry, love,' he said, going to her and standing behind her with his hands resting on her shoulders. 'I know it can't be easy for you, my having a daughter who isn't yours. But I'll get home as soon as I can on Wednesdays. We'll go out for a late supper somewhere, if you like?' He leaned down and put his lips against her hair, feeling a familiar tension vibrate within her, an instinctive drawing back that he was aware of whenever he touched her. It had been happening for so long, it no longer upset him unduly. 'The last thing I want to do is put you out.'

'You'd sooner put me out than Jenny or Ruth,' she accused.

'That isn't fair and I think you know it,' he said softly. 'I'm helping Ruth in a very small way. It's the least I can do when you think of what she had to give up because of me.'

'Yeah, that's true enough, I suppose,' agreed Leila, feeling better for having made a stand, just in case Paul thought he could take her for granted.

Leila knew he was right about her having too much time on her hands. It was many years since she'd been out to work. She'd been employed as a shorthand typist when she'd met Paul, an occupation she'd found boring but had drifted into after leaving school in the absence of other options. She'd stayed on at work for a while after marrying Paul but as soon as he'd become a high earner and they'd stopped relying on her salary, she'd seized the opportunity to give it up.

In the Sydney suburb where they'd lived, on a newish housing estate among other young couples, she'd not been short of company because most of the wives had been at home during the day looking after the children. As the only childless wife among them she'd felt even more set apart than usual, but she still hadn't wanted to start a family. She didn't know why.

Here in their select London avenue, sociality among the neighbours was at a minimum. The other residents were mostly business and professional people, out at work all day and fiercely protective of their privacy when they were at home. That suited Leila. Privacy was something she valued. Far better to be lonely without people than with them, in her opinion.

But that didn't make the days any shorter while Paul was out at work. She occasionally toyed with the idea of getting a job. She sometimes even scanned the Situations Vacant columns in the paper. After all, she had easy access to central London and a secretary in the West End would earn a good salary. But when it came to actually applying for a job, she could never pluck up the courage – something that wasn't helped by the fact that she didn't really want to be a secretary. Why should she be a glorified nursemaid to some executive male when she didn't even need the money?

The truth was, she didn't know what she wanted except

that there must be more to life than waiting for Paul to come home every day.

'If you don't fancy getting a job or taking up anything too serious in the way of a hobby, why not take something up just for fun,' he was suggesting now. 'Painting or pottery or a foreign language. You might enjoy it and it would be a way of making friends.'

He was a good man, a thoughtful and caring husband, there was no doubt about that. Casting her eyes over him she saw a tall, solidly built man with clear-cut features and dazzling blue eyes, a perfect specimen of maleness, looking terrific in his smart business clothes. He would be much desired by other women, that was obvious.

So why couldn't she fancy him as she should? Why was their lovemaking, for her, just a dutiful ritual which left her empty and unsatisfied even though she had become an expert at pretending otherwise?

'I'll think about it,' she said, knowing she would do nothing about it at all. She'd been down this road before. It always followed the same pattern. She got all the relevant information and pored over it for days, chose something she thought she might enjoy, then did nothing more.

'I hope you will,' he said with genuine concern. 'You need some sort of an outlet.'

'Yeah . . . I know.'

He returned to his seat and drank his coffee. 'In the meantime, you'll bear with me about Wednesday nights?'

'I'll try not to throw a fit every week,' she agreed.

Paul smiled gratefully. 'Thanks, Leila.' He finished his coffee and got up. 'And in the meantime, I must go. I've a busy day ahead of me.'

As the front door closed behind him, Leila poured another cup of coffee. She sat at the table daydreaming of the new and interesting things she could do with her life, knowing she would do none of them because she just didn't have the guts.

* * *

One Saturday afternoon in July of the following year, Kitty and Tim Barrett were ensconced in their living room, glued to the television set watching the World Cup Final between England and West Germany.

On the edge of their seats with tension as the game went into extra time, they watched Geoff Hurst score a goal in the final second which put his team's victory beyond doubt and set the whole country celebrating. England had won the World Cup for the first time!

When the final whistle blew, Kitty and Tim leaped up and hugged each other, jumping up and down and shrieking victoriously. Tim lifted her from her feet and swung her round. The quiet cul-de-sac of executive-style houses where they lived took on a party atmosphere as people rushed outside to share the good news and talk about the game.

On the way back indoors, Kitty felt a familiar griping sensation in her stomach. Hurrying upstairs to the bathroom, she greeted her period with a mixture of relief and disappointment.

From the point of view of pleasing her husband, which she tried to do whenever possible, she was deeply disappointed. From a personal aspect, it was as though an enormous burden had been removed from her shoulders – for at least another month anyway.

It wasn't that she didn't want a baby exactly; more that she didn't want to share Tim with anyone, for she was just as besotted with him now as she'd been when she'd married him nearly seven years ago. She couldn't deny that their comfortable lifestyle came into her reasoning too. All-night parties, holidays abroad at luxurious hotels, her job and the freedom to come and go as they pleased – children would put an end to all of that.

For about the last three years Tim had been keen for

them to start a family. He saw it as a natural progression, the manifestation of their love. For about two years she'd stalled him. Suggested they leave it for a while because she didn't want to get pregnant until after their next foreign holiday – until after the New Year's Eve Ball with the airport crowd – until – until – until . . .

Finally last year, when she hit thirty, she'd known that in fairness to Tim she must make a decision. It was time either to tell him she didn't want children at all or agree to come off the pill. He'd been thrilled when she'd chosen the latter and since then they had lived from month to month in a state of high expectancy.

The fact that nothing had happened amazed Kitty. She'd thought getting pregnant would be an alarmingly simple matter; avoiding it had always seemed to be the difficult part. Now they were a year on and she was beginning to think something must be wrong with her. Or him.

'It'll happen,' Tim constantly reassured her. 'Don't worry about that. And in the meantime we're having a whale of a time trying.'

Now, she sat on the bed feeling her sense of relief ebb away to be replaced by the dull ache of disappointment. Having decided to try for a baby, a decision that had been partly influenced by memories of Ruth's daughter Jenny, it was disheartening to find that she apparently lacked the basic human capacity to reproduce. Yet there was a confusing ambivalence within her because part of her still wanted everything to stay as it was.

She was suddenly imbued with an overwhelming need to talk to Ruth about it. It was three years since they'd parted company and she still missed her. Kitty's new friends were good fun – she enjoyed their company – but there was no one in her new circle in whom she wanted to confide about something as serious and personal as this.

It was all superficial stuff with the new crowd: holidays, houses, who was sleeping with whom among the flight staff. They were fun friends with whom you had to stay on top; to admit to any kind of problem would tarnish your image and lower your status among the smart set whose wagging tongues would have a field day.

Ruth was the only woman friend to whom Kitty had ever felt able to bare her soul. Only to Ruth could she admit her self-doubt and confusion, knowing her friend would think no less of her and the information would go no further. But she could no longer confide in Ruth. She was past history.

But despite that fact, Kitty felt suddenly compelled to speak to her old friend, an urge so powerful she leaned over to the telephone extension on the bedside table. With a trembling hand, she picked up the receiver, held it for a moment feeling her heart race, then replaced it. With a second burst of courage, she picked it up again and dialled Ruth's number, one she knew off by heart.

'Brooks and Todd, chemist's,' said a pleasant male voice. 'Can I help you?'

It was Vince. *Of course*, she'd forgotten that the shop would still be open at this time on a Saturday afternoon and the phone rang downstairs in the dispensary as well as upstairs in the flat. In a moment of utter confusion, she found herself wanting to speak to Vince – achingly nostalgic suddenly for her old friends.

'Hello . . . is anyone there?' came his voice down the line.

Kitty's mouth was very near the mouthpiece. She parted her lips to speak but no words were uttered. Slowly, she replaced the receiver, her eyes filling with tears. It was too late – too many bad things had been said – too much time had passed. There was no way back. She'd lost Ruth's friendship for ever.

Biting back the tears, she brushed her hair and touched

up her make-up. Then she made her way downstairs to tell her husband that he wasn't going to be a daddy. Maybe next month . . .

Ruth was alone in the flat in the aftermath of the World Cup Final, making tea and feeling curiously lonely and nostalgic. National events were like that: they evoked feelings of patriotism and triggered off memories of other big events spent with old friends and loved ones.

It had been very quiet in the shop this afternoon. People were either at home watching the match on TV, or at Wembley Stadium. This meant that both she and Vince had been able to sneak upstairs to watch the match, albeit only in between dealing with queries from their assistant Madge who was covering for them downstairs. When the victory had come, the two of them had danced round the room, squealing and shouting excitedly.

'It's a good job Jenny's round at her gran's,' laughed Ruth. 'She'd die of embarrassment if she was here. Mothers of teenagers aren't supposed to let their hair down, according to her.'

But now Vince had gone back to work and Ruth was going to follow when she'd made some tea for them all. Standing by the worktop in the kitchen, waiting for the kettle to boil, she found herself wondering if Paul had watched the match with Leila. He would probably be at home this afternoon as this wasn't his weekend for seeing Jenny. Experiencing an unreasonable stab of jealousy at the idea of him and Leila celebrating together, she thought about the real reason for her lonesome mood.

She missed her evening classes which had finished for the summer break. She'd enjoyed the mental stimulation. It had felt so good to stretch her mind – to be working towards a goal. She had also, and this was the crux of the matter, enjoyed the weekly meetings with Paul. She liked coming home to find him and Jenny waiting for her, at ease with each other and pleased to see her. It had given her a warm feeling inside. For a brief interlude each week the three of them had felt like a family.

Jenny always had coffee and biscuits ready for her and Paul stayed and had some, seeming genuinely interested in her class. It had been lovely. He never stayed long because of Leila. But, without her realising it was happening, these snatched moments had become the highlight of Ruth's week.

But there would be no more of them until the autumn when classes resumed. She still saw Paul when he collected Jenny for their outings, of course, but he never lingered on those occasions and she never suggested it. A chat after class was somehow permissible because he was already installed in the flat, but to create a social occasion every time he appeared would be asking for trouble.

The worst thing she could possibly do was to allow her feelings for him to develop. He was a married man and strictly off limits. Nevertheless Ruth was increasingly drawn to him.

She felt a sudden overwhelming need to talk to someone about her troublesome emotions. Her mother was usually a good confidante but Ruth couldn't go to her on this occasion. The idea of her daughter fancying a married man would give Audrey sleepless nights, especially as the man in question was one she strongly disapproved of anyway.

Ruth's one-time soulmate Kitty came into her mind and she ached with regret for the loss of her friendship. This particular problem, however, was one she wouldn't have been able to discuss with Kitty either. Ruth gave a wry grin, imagining her fierce disapproval at the very idea of Ruth's harbouring amorous feelings towards a man Kitty had despised for years for what he had done to her friend. But even though Kitty couldn't help with this dilemma, Ruth longed to have her back in her life.

The sound of the telephone ringing interrupted her reverie. She was on her way to the landing to answer it when it fell silent and she guessed that Vince had picked it up downstairs in the dispensary. When he didn't shout upstairs to her, she assumed the call was for him and went back to the kitchen to make the tea, thoughts of Kitty lingering.

With a sudden hunger to put things right between them, even if it meant she must lose the argument, Ruth went to the telephone and picked up the receiver. Checking the number in her personal phone book, she dialled with nervous butterflies fluttering wildly in her stomach, her hands shaking slightly.

A male voice answered.

Ruth couldn't utter a sound.

'Hello, this is Tim Barrett . . . is there anyone there?'

Her courage faded and she replaced the receiver with a pain in her heart for she knew she wouldn't find the nerve a second time. It had been left too long. Too much had been said, they couldn't rewrite history. That friendship must stay where it belonged – in the past.

Swallowing a lump in her throat and blinking back the tears, she went to the kitchen, poured tea for Vince, Madge and herself and set it out on a tray with some cakes. Then she made her way downstairs to Vince – dear, caring Vince of whom everyone took advantage.

But for all that he was a dear friend and confidant, she didn't feel able to discuss her feelings for Paul with him. Best she keep them to herself and push them to the back of her mind out of harm's way. People could get hurt by desires of the sort she harboured for Paul, and she was determined that wasn't going to happen.

Paul looked worried when he brought Jenny home from their outing one wet Saturday afternoon a month or so later. They were back earlier than usual and the shop was still open.

'Back early because of the rain?' Ruth said, glancing up at the black clouds rolling across the metallic grey sky.

'No, not really.'

'Oh?'

'She doesn't seem very well,' he confided after Jenny had disappeared through the door behind the counter. 'She's been complaining of pains in her stomach.'

'Really? She didn't say anything just now,' said Ruth.

'The pain seems to come and go,' Paul explained grimly. 'I suggested we come straight home when she first mentioned it but she seemed to perk up and wanted to stay out. But she didn't seem any too bright in the car on the way home.'

'Don't look so petrified, Paul,' Ruth advised him lightly. 'It'll just be some sort of a tummy upset . . . kids are always getting those. I'll give her something for it when I've found out exactly what the symptoms are.'

'I do hope she'll be all right,' he said, face creased with worry.

'She'll be fine,' Ruth said reassuringly. 'If I had a shilling for all the tummy aches she's had in her life, I'd be a rich woman now.'

He smiled weakly.

'How can you be so calm?'

'Practice,' she said. 'If I flew into a panic every time she had a pain, I'd be a complete loony by now.'

'Oh, Ruth, you are funny sometimes,' he said, smiling.

'I'm glad your sense of humour hasn't completely died the death under the heavy weight of fatherhood.'

'Not quite,' he said grinning.

'That's better.'

'Look, I'd like to stay longer and make sure she's okay but I really must go,' he said, looking anxious again. 'Leila and I are going to the theatre and I promised I wouldn't be late home. She wants to get there in plenty of time . . . so that we can get a programme and have a drink before the show.'

'Stop worrying and go home to Leila,' said Ruth. 'Let me worry about Jenny.'

'I'll give you a ring tomorrow to see how she is, shall I?'

'If you like.'

'See you.' He turned to go then swung round. 'If anything happens, you will let me know, won't you?'

''Course I will,' she assured him.

'Cheers – see you,' he said, but seemed very reluctant to leave.

'Enjoy the show.'

'Thanks . . . I'll try.'

Leaving Madge to cover for her, Ruth hurried upstairs to the flat to find her daughter sitting on the sofa watching television. She wasn't her usual exuberant self but didn't seem to be in any real distress.

'The pain comes and goes,' she explained. 'I've had it occasionally before but never as bad as it's been today.'

'Is it a griping pain or more of an ache?'

'It's really sharp . . . like a knife stabbing in my side,' Jenny explained. 'But it's gone now and I feel okay.'

'I'll get the doctor to have a look at you if it comes back.'

Ruth gave her some Milk of Magnesia and settled her on the sofa with some pillows and a blanket to watch Juke Box Jury, which they both thought would take her mind off the pain.

By the time Ruth had closed the shop, cashed up and settled down for the evening, Jenny seemed perfectly all right. It must just have been a touch of wind, thought Ruth.

★ ★ ★

Paul stared at the stage, seeing nothing except frightening images of Jenny in a hospital bed with doctors battling to save her life. He knew he was letting his imagination run away with him but he seemed to have lost control.

So this was what they meant by parental empathy. This was what being a parent was all about – being constantly vulnerable, never being free from worry and feeling someone else's pain as though it was your own. Having now experienced it for himself he realised how hard it must have been for Ruth, having to go through this on her own for so long. Her parents would have been supportive but it couldn't possibly be the same as having the help of the other parent. Having been so relieved to have Ruth to turn to this afternoon, he could vouch for that.

Since he'd been seeing Jenny, Paul had been in a permanent state of inner conflict, torn between his wife and his daughter. His uneasy conscience was not so much a result of the time he actually spent with Jenny. It came more from the fact that he found himself wanting to spend more time with her as his affection grew.

The sounds of applause and movement recalled him to the present to realise that it was the interval. He and Leila made their way to the crowded bar.

'What do you think of the show?' she asked, taking a sip of gin and tonic.

'Good,' he said absently.

'Fibber!' she said. 'You've done nothing but fidget all through the first half.'

'Sorry.'

Leila gave a weary sigh.

'Why don't you go to the telephone in the foyer and give Ruth a ring?' Paul had told her all about Jenny's tummy ache on the way here. 'If she tells you that Jenny is all right you might be able to enjoy the rest of the show.'

He gave her a grateful look and hurried to the telephone, looking much happier on his return.

'She's fine,' he said.

'Good.'

'She and Ruth are watching television.'

'There . . . she isn't even in bed so she must be okay.'

'I feel better now.'

'Thank God for that,' she said. 'Perhaps we can enjoy the rest of the evening now.'

'Thanks, Leila.'

'What for?'

'Suggesting that I go and make that phone call.'

'My reasons were purely selfish, I can assure you,' she admitted candidly. 'I knew neither of us could have any sort of an evening until you'd put your mind at rest.'

'Thanks anyway,' he said, squeezing her hand affectionately.

'Oh, go on with you,' she said dismissively, surprised by her own tolerance. Perhaps she was getting used to having his daughter encroach upon her life. Or was it just that it didn't matter to her what Paul did or for whom else he cared?

Ruth came to with a start to find her light was on and she was being shaken.

'Mum, I don't feel well, I've got that pain again,' Jenny was saying in a strangled voice.

'Oh, you poor love . . .'

'It really hurts.'

Ruth was instantly awake and reassuring her daughter, a glance at the clock telling her it was 1.30 a.m.

'Okay, love, you go back to bed,' she said, gently and calmly. 'I'll phone the doctor . . . middle of the night or not.'

An hour or so later Ruth was sitting in a corridor outside

a surgical ward after a traumatic journey in an ambulance during which Jenny had writhed and sweated in agony. Ruth could do little except hold her hand and whisper encouragement. Her daughter was now being examined by a doctor.

Ruth stared at the polished floor, the sickly smell of disinfectant, floor polish and the clinging odour of some earlier meal making her want to retch. Her clothes were damp and felt sticky to her skin. The heavy downpour that had soaked her on the way out to the ambulance had penetrated through her dress to her underwear. She'd been far too worried about Jenny even to think of a raincoat or umbrella.

The doctor appeared and Ruth leaped to her feet.

'It's a burst appendix,' he said. 'We need your permission to operate.'

'A burst appendix?' she gasped. 'Is that more serious than . . .'

'We need to operate,' he quickly informed her again.

She signed the permission form and began the nail-biting wait as they prepared Jenny for theatre. Ruth's stomach was churning and her muscles ached with tension, a damp, solitary figure in the reception area of the sleeping hospital. Her parents were at home in blissful ignorance of this desperate situation. She'd not wanted to alarm them in the middle of the night, had thought it best to wait until there was some definite news before she contacted them. She would have to phone them first thing, though, to ask them to go to her place to feed Ringo and let him out into the yard for a while.

Suddenly, the significance of the fact that she was no longer the only parent hit her. Should she let Paul know? She'd promised she would if anything further happened. She glanced at her watch. It was nearly three o'clock in the morning. He and Leila would be asleep. Should she disturb them at this hour?

She felt she had no choice. Paul had a right to know that his daughter was about to have major surgery. If the worst happened and he hadn't been told, he'd never forgive her.

With her heart pounding, Ruth hurried to the public telephone.

They sat in silence, locked together by love for their daughter and fear for her life, his hand gripping hers almost subconsciously. His clothes also were wet from the rain but the fact went unnoticed. The reception area was almost deserted at this time of night, with just one or two other worried people waiting for news.

Now and then a nurse walked by, rubber soles squeaking on the polished floor. A doctor hurried past clutching some papers. There was a sudden flurry of activity when stretcher bearers brought a new patient in.

'I wonder how much longer we'll have to wait before there's any news?' said Ruth, her mouth parched, head aching.

'I don't expect it'll be too long.'

'It seems like for ever.'

'Yes.'

'Oh, God.'

Paul turned to her and put his arm around her for comfort.

'Hey, come on, Ruth. She'll be all right,' he said reassuringly. 'She'll come through this. She's a fighter.'

She looked into his face, seeing the grey pallor of his skin, the grim set of his mouth, and knew he was just as terrified as she was and just putting up a front to make her feel better.

'Of course she will,' said Ruth. 'She's our daughter . . . a survivor.'

He gave a half smile, feeling very close to her at this moment.

'I'm glad you came, Paul.'

'A whole herd of wild horses wouldn't have kept me away.'

Time passed and still they sat there, rigid with tension and hardly uttering a word. A nurse brought them some coffee which was swallowed without their even tasting it.

When the doctor appeared with the news that the operation had been successfully completed, Ruth broke down in tears, the tension of the last few hours overwhelming her.

Paul's arms were quickly around her and she luxuriated in the feeling of warmth and comfort this gave her. When she drew back she saw that he was crying too and she tenderly wiped away his tears with her hanky in a spontaneous gesture.

The doctor said they could see their daughter for a few minutes, even though she was sleeping. They went in together and just stood by the bed looking at her, the precious gift they'd thought they might lose, alive and on the mend.

Outside in the corridor, they clung together, sobbing with joy and gratitude. They stayed like that for a long time.

Because they both wanted to be at Jenny's bedside when she came round, neither of them went home. Paul telephoned Leila and Ruth called her parents who agreed to see to the dog. She also rang Vince. They were due to open the shop for a couple of hours this Sunday morning because it was their turn on the duty rota. Vince was very concerned about Jenny and said that of course he'd manage without Ruth in the shop.

After going to the Ladies to freshen up she sat in the reception area with Paul, waiting to be told when Jenny was conscious.

'So you've had your first taste of the down side of parenthood, then,' she said.

'Not half! It does terrible things to the nervous system, doesn't it?'

'I'll say.'

'I didn't know I was alive until Jenny came into my life.'

'This is the first serious illness she's had, actually,' said Ruth.

'Let's hope it's the last.'

'You came on to the scene just in time,' she said. 'It helped me a lot, having you there.'

'I'll always be there for you, Ruth,' he said huskily. 'For you and Jenny.'

She stared into her lap because she was feeling so emotional. Clearing her throat, she said, 'How does Leila feel about that?'

'She's pretty good about it now that she's used to the idea.'

'It can't be easy for her,' said Ruth. 'Suddenly having your daughter turn up out of the blue.'

'No, I don't suppose it is easy for her,' he agreed.

They chatted about this and that. She wanted to know about his life in Australia but he seemed more interested in talking about her. He asked about her marriage.

'Larry came into my life like a hero in a romantic novel,' she said.

'Yeah?'

'Yes, he literally swept me off my feet,' Ruth explained. 'Unfortunately, he let me down with one hell of a bang.'

'You were left high and dry for the second time then?'

'I suppose you could say that,' she replied. 'But the way in which my marriage ended was really crippling. It was enough to put me off men for life.'

'You came through it, though.'

'I had to because of Jenny,' she said. 'I felt as though I was falling apart but I couldn't let it destroy me. It really toughened me up.'

'So you fought with him for the shop?' said Paul, having heard about it from Vince.

'That's right. It was something I felt I had to do. At least I've been able to keep myself and Jenny.'

'And the evening classes will help with the business.'

'Only up to a point,' she explained. 'I still can't dispense drugs without a qualified chemist's being on the premises.'

'You'll have to get fully qualified then, won't you?' he said lightly.

'If only . . .'

'Why not?'

'I'd have to get a pharmacy degree and I think I've missed the boat for that by a good few years, don't you?'

'Not necessarily. You could do it as a mature student,' he said. 'Get someone in to replace you at the shop temporarily.'

'I wouldn't even be able to apply for a place on a course,' she told him.

'Why not?'

'You have to have 'A'-levels and I left school without mine.'

'Oh, yes, of course,' he said, assailed by guilt. 'That's a pity.'

'It is, but you can't have everything you want in life.'

'I suppose not.'

'And having Jenny get better is quite enough for me at the moment.'

'Me too.'

The nurse appeared and told them that Jenny was beginning to come round and they could see her briefly. Together they walked along the corridor to the side ward where she'd been placed while she was on the critical list.

Ruth knew that a lasting bond had been formed between herself and Paul this last few hours. She could feel it like a warm hand around her heart. It mustn't be allowed to develop into anything more, of course, but it had carried her through the night and she valued it.

Walking along the corridor with Ruth by his side, Paul felt as close to her as he had the night Jenny had been conceived. *Then* had been fun and magic – *now* was serious and real. A palpable force bound them together, making him want to laugh with the joy of its existence and cry because it must go no further.

He took his commitment to Leila seriously and would never renege on it. But the closeness he had felt to Ruth tonight was something he knew he would never experience with his wife.

As Ruth had just said, you can't have everything you want in life. He accepted that without question. But not being able to have Ruth as his partner in life made him feel very sad as they went to their daughter's bedside together.

Chapter Fourteen

Finishing her dispensing course proved to be an anti-climax for Ruth. The qualification was useful, of course, and gave her a sense of achievement but the end of classes left her with a void in her life. So much so that she even found herself missing the much-maligned homework as well as her Wednesday class. And, most of all, she missed her weekly meetings with Paul.

The end of these made her realise just how tenuous her connection with him was. Jenny was growing up fast. Although still the hedonistic teenager up to a point, she was serious about her future and had set her heart on getting a place at medical school. When she left home there would be no legitimate reason for Ruth and Paul to meet. And that was something Ruth couldn't bear to think about.

Although she and Paul hadn't discussed the bond that had grown between them during Jenny's illness a year ago, it was there, in the background, waiting to grow even stronger.

When Ruth was with him everything registered with more intensity, as though he sharpened her senses and increased her ability to feel. Not all of those feelings were platonic, either, though they got on well in other ways too, sharing a similar sense of humour and many opinions.

Although her sense of decency cried out against it, she was in love with him and there wasn't a damned thing she could do about it. The love that had begun back in 1951 had rekindled and grown since he'd been back in London. She could remind herself of the hopelessness of loving a married man a million times a day but the feelings wouldn't go away.

Now, as she worked in the dispensary on this summer morning, counting tablets into a bottle and mulling over the situation rationally, she thought it was probably just as well that the regular Wednesday meetings had finished before his marriage was seriously jeopardised.

'I suppose the hippies really believe they have found the answer to the problems of the modern world,' remarked Vince, who was finishing his coffee break and reading in the newspaper about the Festival of the Flower Children at Woburn Abbey. 'With their flower power theory.'

'They would claim to have found some sort of a solution, I expect.'

'They're calling this the Summer of Love, apparently.'

'The mind boggles!'

'It certainly does.'

'Most of them are high on LSD from what I've read about it.'

'Mmm.'

'All this stuff they spout about "make love not war" sounds very worthy and idealistic but I reckon it's just an excuse for carte blanche with sex . . . and drugs, of course. No wonder it's catching on with the young,' said Ruth. 'But as the mother of a teenager, I would say that, wouldn't I?'

'You and the rest of the world's parents, I should imagine.'

'Jenny wanted to go to this festival at Woburn, you know,' she told him. 'Paul and I had to take a really firm line with her on that one.'

Vince took another look at the paper and read something aloud. ' "Turn on, tune in and drop out", that's their gospel according to this report. Not Jenny's sort of thing at all, surely? She's much too sensible and keen to get on.'

'You're right. It isn't her scene. I think she just wanted to go and see what it was like out of curiosity and because her friends were talking about going,' explained Ruth. 'But I wasn't prepared to take the risk. Once they get a taste for something like that, who knows where it will lead? She's at an impressionable age and far too young to go to a hippie festival.'

'I agree.'

'As you say, she's keen to get on and knows what she wants to do with her life,' Ruth continued. 'Paul and I were saying the same thing only the other day . . .' Her voice tailed off as it occurred to her that twice in the last few minutes she had said 'Paul and I'. It felt so natural and sounded so right.

'You were saying?' Vince prompted her.

'Oh . . . just that she's a young woman with a mind of her own,' said Ruth absently, sticking a label on to a tablet bottle.

What an ironic situation she was in. She was in love with her daughter's father – which would have been perfect had he not been married to someone else!

One December evening of that same year, Kitty sat in an armchair in her ultra-smart lounge with its contrasting walls and deep pile carpet, staring at the early television news. It was dominated by an account of an amazing breakthrough in medical science: the world's first human heart transplant had been successfully carried out in Cape Town.

Ye gods, what will they think of next? thought Kitty. But although she was impressed, this breakthrough of major benefit to humankind was overshadowed for her by progress of a more personal nature. Today her doctor had confirmed her pregnancy and her unexpected reaction to this news led her to believe she must be seriously deficient as a woman.

Her initial euphoria on hearing it had been followed by a sudden change of mind born of panic and feelings of intense doubt about her ability to take on such a responsibility. It was crazy. After nearly two years of disappointment, she had finally conceived and all she wanted to do was to turn the clock back!

She had grown up to believe that pregnancy was a condition into which a woman slipped with ease and confidence, having found her true role in life. There was never any mention of doubt and uncertainty. Or, for that matter, breasts as hard as footballs and perversely tormenting hormones that made you feel sexy whilst at the same time producing heartburn, nausea and exhaustion, which meant you were barely able to make the effort.

Kitty knew lots of women who'd had babies – their social group was becoming practically non-existent as friends headed en masse for the labour ward and a life of domesticity – and all of them had seemed to sail towards motherhood without so much as a trace of apprehension.

So why did Kitty feel so depressed about it? It wasn't as though she was carrying the result of some hideous mistake. This was a lovingly conceived baby, the product of a happy marriage. She was thirty-two years old, for heaven's sake. It was time she stopped being so self-centred and shouldered some real responsibility.

She wondered if perhaps her parents had made life *too* easy for her. She'd never had to struggle as Ruth had. Ruth . . . oh, if only she could talk to her about it. Ruth had had a child. She might briefly have experienced what Kitty was going through now. And even if she hadn't, she could be relied upon for reassurance. Ruth could always see the positive side of a situation.

But that friendship was a luxury no longer available to Kitty. That was a stage in her life from which she had departed.

She cheered up at the thought of her husband. Darling

Tim would be so thrilled by the news. Maybe if she'd waited until she'd felt broody herself instead of trying for a baby because it was what *he* wanted, she wouldn't be so traumatised now? Perhaps that was nature's way. But it was all irrelevant. She was pregnant and there was no turning back.

A glance at her watch told her it was time to make supper. Tim was on the Rome to London flight and should be home soon, though she never knew exactly what time he would appear because of unexpected delays.

Her raised spirits were dashed by a powerful wave of nausea when she went to the kitchen to grill some chops. She didn't think she was actually going to be sick but broke out in a cold sweat and felt faint. Sitting down to recover, she mopped her brow with a handkerchief, wondering how she was going to stand another seven months of this.

She'd just put the chops under the grill when she heard Tim's key in the lock, earlier than she'd expected. She had planned to tell him about the baby over dinner, when he was feeling relaxed and replete. But the instant she saw his towering figure, so strong and handsome in his uniform, she fell into his arms sobbing.

'I'm pregnant, Tim,' she said, hugging him tight. 'We're going to have a baby.'

'Oh, Kitty,' he said, his voice deep and husky with joy. 'That's wonderful news. You can't know how happy you've made me.'

'I knew you'd be pleased.'

'I am, I am,' he said, kissing the top of her head, his warm eyes lustrous with tears as he looked down at her affectionately. 'But what's the matter . . . why are you crying?'

With his arms around her, she felt safe and happy, fear dissolved by the strength of his love. It was going to be all right. With Tim by her side there was nothing she couldn't do, no situation with which she couldn't cope. She and her husband and their baby were going to be a family and Kitty was suddenly quite ecstatic about it.

She drew back and looked up into that reassuring face, those lovely tender eyes that had captivated her from the first moment she saw them.

'I'm crying because I'm so happy to be having our baby, Tim,' she said, and meant every word. 'So very, very happy!'

Jenny was developing a strong social conscience as she grew up. Although Ruth was proud of her for her sense of justice and feeling for other people, there were times when it caused friction between them.

The anti-Vietnam demonstration in central London the following spring was a typical example. Ruth thought Jenny was too young to take part and forbade her to go anywhere near Trafalgar Square on that Sunday which made her about as popular with her daughter as the American Government. But it was a decision that proved to be wise in the event.

'I bet you're really glad your mum made you stay away now, aren't you?' said Audrey as reports of violence outside the American Embassy between police and protestors dominated the television news on Sunday night. The demonstrators had marched from Trafalgar Square to Grosvenor Square, intending to storm the embassy in protest against US military involvement in the Vietnam War.

'No, not at all,' declared Jenny loftily.

'But it's a bloomin' battlefield,' said her grandmother as scenes of chaos filled the screen. 'You could have been seriously hurt in that crowd. Or even got yourself arrested.'

'You don't think about yourself if you believe in something, Gran,' Jenny informed her primly.

'Ooh, pardon me for breathin', I'm sure,' retorted Audrey lightly.

'Your mother was quite right to stop you from going,' Dan told Jenny. 'That sort of caper isn't for a slip of a girl like you.'

'I *am* sixteen,' she reminded him with an eloquent sigh.

'Exactly,' said her grandfather 'You're sixteen – not twenty-one.'

'Thanks for the support, Dad,' said Ruth with a grateful smile.

She and Jenny had joined the rest of the family for Sunday tea at Nutley Road as usual. If Jenny was seeing her father, Ruth would go alone because it was expected. The twins and their families had just left and Ruth was thinking about making tracks herself soon.

'I'm outnumbered among you lot,' protested Jenny without serious rancour. 'It isn't fair – three against one.'

'Four if you count your father,' said Ruth, winking at her mother.

'I think you'd better give up the fight, Jenny,' Audrey agreed with a smile.

'Dad always agrees with Mum when it comes to my doing anything the slightest bit interesting or adventurous,' announced Jenny with a sigh.

'He's a sensible man, that's why,' said Ruth with a lilt to her voice.

Audrey gave her daughter a sharp look at the sudden change of tone when she mentioned Paul. Her eyes were very bright and she had a soppy grin on her face that she was obviously unaware of. She was still carrying a torch for that bugger if Audrey wasn't very much mistaken, and that was a tragedy because no good could come of it. Audrey had to admit to being surprised at the success of the arrangement between Jenny and her father, though. She had been certain his interest would be just a passing fancy.

But, credit where it was due, Paul had stayed with it and seemed genuinely fond of Jenny. He offered much needed support to Ruth too – taking her side over the anti-Vietnam demo was a typical example. It couldn't be easy bringing up a child on your own. The adolescent stage must be hell without a partner to back you up.

Apparently, Ruth allowed him to help financially now, too. He gave Jenny a regular allowance which took the burden off Ruth because Jenny's clothes cost a fortune now that she was almost a grown woman and wanted all the latest things. Paul's contribution would certainly come in handy if she achieved her ambition and got into medical school too. Audrey lingered for a moment on the thought; a doctor in the family – well, fancy!

For all Audrey's preconceived ideas about Paul Stoneway, she had to admit to finding him a very pleasant man, on the odd occasion when their paths crossed – usually if she happened to be at Ruth's when he came to collect Jenny. He did seem keen to make amends to Ruth too. She frowned at the idea of her daughter hankering after a married man, though. What Ruth needed was someone who was free to marry her. It was time she found a partner. She'd been on her own for quite long enough.

'Don't worry, love,' Dan was saying to Jenny. 'It won't be long before you can go wherever you please, without asking permission.'

'It can't come quick enough for me, Granddad.' She stood up. 'And talking of going, I think we ought to be on our way, Mum. The dog will be wanting his evening constitutional.'

'Yes, we mustn't forget Ringo.'

'Oh . . . can you hang on a minute, Ruth?' said Audrey, remembering something. 'I'd like your opinion on a couple of summer dresses I'm thinking of ordering from my catalogue.'

'Sure.'

'I think I'll go on ahead, Mum,' said Jenny. 'And take Ringo out for his walk.'

'All right, love. You've got your key with you, haven't you?'

'Yeah.'

Jenny left and Ruth spent a short time helping her mother to choose some dresses before she departed too. It was already dark. One of those blustery March evenings with the smell of spring but a bracing wind to remind you that winter isn't quite over. It blew right through Ruth's blue and white anorak which she was wearing over a sweater and jeans.

There were only a few people about as she turned into the Uxbridge Road and walked towards the Green. She met Jenny coming towards her with the dog on the lead.

'I'll just take him across the Green and round the block,' she said. 'Shan't be long.'

'Okay,' said Ruth and continued on her way.

She had just turned her key in the lock and was about to step over the threshold when she froze at the sound of a footstep right behind her. A sour whiff of unwashed clothes turned her stomach and she could hear the wheezy rattle of someone breathing close to her.

As she turned to investigate, a gruff male voice issued an order: 'Don't look round, just act normally and go inside.'

Even as she hesitated, she felt him pressing against her. Before she had a chance to gather her wits, she was pushed unceremoniously inside and told to switch on the light. As her assailant became known to her, she recognised him as a young local man, a customer in the shop.

'What the . . .'

'Don't make a fuss,' he said in a jerky, breathless voice. 'I don't wanna hurt you. Just do as I say and you'll come to no harm.'

'There's no money on the premises,' she told him. 'All yesterday's takings were put into the night safe at the bank.'

'I don't want money,' he said, and she could see that he was ill. He looked to be in his twenties and was pale-faced with stubble on his chin and greasy dark hair. 'I need some stuff.' His voice rose urgently. 'Can't you see I'm desperate?'

'The controlled drugs are all in a locked cupboard,' she informed him.

'Where?'

She nodded towards the dispensary and he opened the door with a shaking hand and pushed her inside, told her to turn on the light and closed the door after them.

'Which cupboard?'

A glance answered his question.

'Open it,' he demanded, looking towards the metal cabinet on the wall.

'I don't have the key.'

'Don't give me that rubbish,' he said, his mouth twitching. 'Of course you've got the key.'

'I haven't.'

'You own the shop,' he said, a greasy film of sweat suffusing his skin and beading his hairline. 'I've seen you in here enough times. It's common knowledge you're the owner.'

'You've been waiting for me to come home, have you?' she said, playing for time.

'Yeah . . . I knew you were out 'cos there were no lights on upstairs,' he said. 'I saw your daughter come in and go out again with the dog.'

'So I can thank my lucky stars you didn't do this to her then?'

'I wanted the organ grinder, not the monkey,' he said. 'She might not have known where the drugs are kept.'

'You need help.'

'Which is why I'm here,' he said shakily, 'So get it for me from that cupboard – *now*.'

'Help with your addiction, I mean . . .'

'Just get the stuff and forget the lecture, will you?'

'I've told you, I don't have the key,' Ruth lied, because to give him the drugs was tantamount to inflicting upon him an early and painful death. He needed medical help and she intended to get it for him, whether he wanted it or not.

'Stop messing me about,' he demanded. 'Whoever heard of a shop owner not having keys to their own cupboards?'

'Although it's my shop, I'm not a qualifed chemist,' she explained, stalling him while she tried to think of a way out of this without giving in to his demands. 'My partner is the qualified one. He keeps the key with him at all times.'

'You must have a spare.'

She shook her head. 'We only have the one key, for security reasons.'

'Oh, I've had enough of this,' he said, his breathing loud and erratic. 'If you won't do it, I'll smash the bugger open.'

'You'll never do it,' said Ruth. 'It's as strong as a safe . . . built to withstand unauthorised people like you.'

While his attention was focused on the cupboard she darted towards the door but he was quicker then she'd thought he'd be. He grabbed her and held a knife to her throat.

'I told you to do as I say and I meant it,' he growled, and Ruth knew he was losing control which meant she was in *real* danger. 'I don't wanna hurt you but I've got to have something to put me right . . . can't you see that?'

'Yes, I can see you have a problem,' she said, knowing he would stop at nothing to feed his habit. 'So I think I'd better telephone my partner and ask him to come over and open the cupboard.'

'Do it then, for Christ's sake,' he demanded in a ragged tone, the knife moving as his hand trembled. 'But don't tell him why you want the cupboard opened or he'll call the Old Bill. At the first sign of a copper you'll get it with the knife.'

Inwardly quaking, Ruth went over to the telephone on the workbench and dialled Vince's number. The intruder stood nearby, still pointing the knife at her.

'Hello,' said Vince.

'Hi, Vince, it's Ruth,' she said through dry lips. 'I've got a bit of an emergency on my hands here at the shop. One of the doctors urgently needs something from the drugs cupboard for a patient. Can you come over and open it?'

'Why can't you open it?' came the puzzled response which she'd expected and knew the intruder couldn't hear.

'Yes, it's very urgent, Vince,' she said, hoping he would guess from her senseless dialogue that all was not well. 'So if you could get here as soon as poss, I'd be very grateful. Thanks. See you.'

And she hung up.

Jenny let herself in through the front door, took the dog off his lead and went upstairs, surprised to find the flat in darkness. Her mother must have been home after Jenny had seen her because the hall light was on downstairs and Jenny remembered turning it off when she went out with the dog.

Deciding that she must have gone to visit one of the neighbours, Jenny took off her coat and turned on the TV. She was about to sit down in the armchair when she realised that Ringo hadn't followed her upstairs. This was most unusual because the dog liked his home comforts and only stayed downstairs in his basket when Jenny and her mother were out or in bed at night.

Even as the thought came, she heard Ringo barking downstairs. What *is* the matter with him? she wondered, listening hard. Another sound was discernible above the canine commotion – she could hear her mother's voice, muffled as though from behind a closed door. She must be on the phone in the dispensary.

There was nothing particularly unusual about Ruth's being in the shop or dispensary in the evening – she often pottered about down there at night, filling shelves and tidying up. Perhaps she'd gone down to get something from the shop and decided to make a phone call while she was there, thought Jenny. She doubted if she would have started work after getting home from Gran's on a Sunday night.

But why was Ringo making such a racket? Deciding to investigate, Jenny was halfway down the stairs when he came bounding up to meet her. He seemed disturbed about something and was making small whining noises in his throat. Jenny shouted down to her mother.

'Are you all right down there, Mum?'

Relief flooded through her at the sound of her mother's reply.

'Yes. I'm fine, love. I'm just getting something from the dispensary. I'll be up in a minute. You can put some coffee on if you like.'

'Okay,' she called, but for some reason she was still uneasy.

She'd just got to the top of the stairs when she heard the low sound of a man's voice downstairs. Hesitating for only a moment, she headed down the stairs to find out who it was. Something stopped her before she reached the bottom, some sixth sense that warned her of danger for them both if she continued. With heart pounding and nerves taut, she crept back upstairs and telephoned the first person who came to mind.

'Dad,' she said in a hushed tone.

'Jenny . . . what's the matter?' he asked, sensing her urgency.

'I'm not sure . . . but I think there might be an intruder downstairs in the dispensary.'

'Where's your mother?'

'In the dispensary too. I think there's someone in there with her,' Jenny explained anxiously. 'It might be nothing . . . could just be a neighbour, or Vince come over to do something. But I've got this awful feeling . . .'

'I'll be right over,' he said. 'You stay where you are. Don't go downstairs.'

'But she might need help.'

'Leave it to me. Promise me you'll stay in the flat?'

'I promise,' said Jenny, feeling so much better for having spoken to him. There was something very reassuring about having her father around. She was so glad to have him in her life and not just from a selfish angle – not any more.

'You're quite safe . . . my daughter won't come down here,' Ruth assured the intruder as they waited for Vince to arrive.

'Are you sure?'

'Quite sure. I come down here for various reasons of an evening. She won't find anything unusual in my being here.'

'What about when your partner arrives, won't she come down to let him in?'

'No. He's got his own keys to the shop.'

'Oh.' He put a quivering hand to his mouth and bit his thumbnail, shivering violently. 'How long will it take him to get here?'

'Not very long . . . he only has to come from Fulham.'

The addict put the knife into the pocket of his filthy brown leather jacket, pacing up and down.

Sick with fear for herself and concern for him, Ruth

watched the demented creature, his visibly increasing discomfort reminding her of the dangerous situation she was in.

Paul and Vince drew up outside the shop at almost the same time.

'What are you doing here?' asked Paul.

They exchanged information.

'That settles it,' said Paul, having heard about Vince's odd phone call from Ruth. 'There's definitely something dodgy going on in there.'

'Looks like it.'

'We'd better find out what it is then, hadn't we, mate?' said Paul. 'I thought I was going to have to force my way in rather than bring Jenny downstairs, but as you've got the keys . . .'

They made their way through the shop into the hallway and found the dispensary locked. Jenny appeared with the dog and was immediately ordered back upstairs by her father.

Paul rattled the dispensary door handle. 'Ruth, are you in there?' he called.

'Paul . . . what are you doing here?'

'Who's in there with you?'

'I'm alone.'

'Why are you locked in then?'

'Is there any sign of Vince?' she asked, ignoring his question.

'I'm here, Ruth,' said Vince. 'With the keys to the cupboard.'

The door was opened slowly by Ruth who was being held from behind by the intruder, with one arm gripping her and a knife in his other hand pointed at her throat.

'Two of you, eh?' he said.

'That's right,' said Paul, looking at him and considering tactics.

'I need some stuff,' he informed them. 'And if I don't get it, and fast, she's gonna get it with the knife.'

'Is that so?' said Paul, staring directly into the man's face.

'Yeah,' he replied, meeting the gaze despite his agitation.

While the intruder's attention was focused on Paul's face, he brought up his foot and knocked the knife out of the man's hand with a neat judo kick. Taken by surprise he lost his hold on Ruth, enabling Paul to drag her out of the way before grabbing the man and holding him in an armlock.

'He needs medical help urgently,' said Ruth anxiously.

'I'll ring for an ambulance,' said Vince.

'Get the police while you're at it,' suggested Paul.

'Don't bother about that now,' said Ruth. 'Treatment is what he needs.'

'The man has forced his way into your home, threatened you with a knife, and you don't want the police involved?' said Paul incredulously, holding the man firm while Vince dialled 999.

'I didn't say I didn't want them involved,' she said. 'I'm more concerned about the medical side of it, that's all.'

'We'll have to report it to the police, Ruth. It's our public duty,' Paul pointed out, still gripping the shaking man who had fallen silent and looked terribly ill. 'He's committed an offence . . . forced an entry into your property and used threatening behaviour. He mustn't be allowed to get away with it, for the sake of other people's safety.'

'I know,' agreed Ruth wearily. 'But getting him some treatment is the main priority so far as I'm concerned.'

'What do you think will happen to him?' she asked much later that night as she and Paul sat drinking coffee by her living-room fire.

The intruder had been taken away in the ambulance and the police had finally left after recording details of the incident. Vince had gone home and Jenny was in bed. Paul had stayed on because he thought Ruth needed company after such an ordeal.

'He'll probably get away with just a fine,' Paul informed her.

'I meant about his habit.'

'Who knows?' he said. 'If he's lucky he'll get on to a rehabilitation programme. But how long he'll stay off the drugs after that is anyone's guess.'

'Let's hope he's one of the lucky ones who manage to succeed.'

'Yes, let's hope so,' Paul agreed because Ruth had been through a lot tonight and he thought a positive attitude was what she needed. But he'd heard too many horror stories of this modern curse on society to feel optimistic. He was terrified his daughter might be tempted to experiment. Her generation had been made so vulnerable by the drugs craze.

'Did Leila mind your staying with me for a while?' asked Ruth because he'd phoned his wife to put her in the picture.

'She didn't seem to.'

Ruth brushed a weary hand over her brow. She looked tired and dishevelled. Her hair was sticking up, her mascara was smudged. But she still looked beautiful, he thought, and very sexy with her dark eyes heavy and shadowed, and her face flushed from the fire. The whole miserable incident had obviously shaken her up, even though she tried not to show it. Seeing her so close to having a knife plunged into her throat had scared the living daylights out of him too.

It was an ill wind though. Because, despite all the trauma of the last few hours, Paul couldn't help but be warmed by the fact that Jenny had turned to him at a time of trouble. It made him feel like a proper father. Helping Ruth and being with her in the aftermath gave him a sense of belonging, too. It was just like being one of the family and he couldn't get enough of it.

'That's good,' said Ruth. ''Cos I wouldn't want to put her out.'

'Let me worry about Leila.'

'She must get fed up with having to share her husband.'

'She's used to it.'

'I suppose she would be by now.'

'Anyway, you look as though you ought to be in bed,' said Paul.

'They say there's nothing more tiring than tension, don't they?' she agreed. 'I'm whacked but I don't think I'll sleep.'

'You really ought to think about getting this place properly alarmed, you know.'

'Who do you think I am, the owner of Harrods or something?'

He looked at her.

'It costs a fortune to have a burglar alarm installed,' she informed him. 'Not many small business people like us can afford one.'

'Oh.'

'Anyway, an alarm wouldn't have prevented tonight's incident because the bloke came in when I opened the door.'

'I suppose you're right,' he admitted. 'But I really do worry about you . . . you and Jenny, here on your own at night.'

'We're not on our own,' she said. 'We have Ringo. And, in the normal course of events, he's better than any alarm system. The slightest sound at night and he barks the place down.'

'Okay, Ruth, I believe you.'

She was exhausted and unnerved. She wanted nothing

more than to curl up in bed – with Paul beside her. But she just said, 'You'd better go soon. Or Leila really will have cause to be angry.'

He stretched and yawned. 'Yeah, I suppose you're right.'

They both stood up. He picked up his sports jacket from the back of the chair and put it on. He wanted to take Ruth in his arms and tell her he didn't want to go home – not now, not ever. He wanted to stay with her and Jenny and be a permanent part of their lives. He looked into her eyes.

'Ruth, I . . .'

'Yes?'

'I . . .'

She waited, buoyant with a hope she knew she shouldn't feel.

How he managed it, he never knew but somehow Paul found the strength to deny his instincts.

'Er . . . do you think you'll be all right now?' he asked.

She wanted to tell him that she'd never be all right, not without him as her partner in life. But she just said: ''Course I will. I was a bit shaken up but I'm fine now.'

'I'll be off then.'

'Okay. Thanks for everything, Paul,' she said at the front door.

'It's my pleasure.'

He brushed her cheek with his lips and hurried out into the gusty street. Walking away from her tonight was one of the most difficult things he'd ever had to do and he felt weak and shaky from the effort it had taken.

Shutting the door behind him and pushing the bolts across, Ruth felt utterly bereft.

Chapter Fifteen

'Here you are, darling . . . breakfast in bed for you and our favourite bump,' said Tim Barrett one morning in early summer, sailing cheerfully into the bedroom with a breakfast tray.

'You're spoiling me rotten,' said Kitty, sitting up and leaning back against the pillow. 'I won't half miss it after the baby's born.'

'I'll have to make sure that I don't stop doing it then, won't I?' he grinned, settling her with her tray then perching on the edge of the bed for a cup of coffee and a chat with her before he left to go on duty.

'I'd better have that in writing, I think,' she laughed, anticipating her boiled eggs and toast with relish, the nausea and sickness having abated after the first three months.

'Oh ye of little faith . . .'

'Just being realistic.' She grinned. 'I can't see either of us being able to have breakfast in bed when we've a new baby to see to.'

'We might.'

'Oh, Tim, I'm *so* lucky,' she said with strong emphasis. 'What would I do without you?'

'You won't have to do without me, so we'll never know the answer to that.'

She cut the top off her boiled egg and dipped her toast in it.

'I seem to have been pregnant for ever,' she remarked. 'And there are still five weeks to go. Now I know what people mean when they say that the last couple of months seem longer than the whole of the first seven.'

'Just enjoy being a lady of leisure, now that you've finished work.'

'I am enjoying it. But I can't help wishing the time onwards to when the baby is actually here,' she said. 'And, *boy*, will I be glad to be slim again.'

'The time will soon pass,' he said, stroking her arm.

'Oh . . .' She put down her spoon. 'It's kicking again.' She took her husband's hand and placed it on her swollen stomach.

'Definitely a footballer in the making,' he said. 'He'll play for England one day.'

'It might not be a boy.'

'I think it will.'

'Yes,' she said thoughtfully. 'So do I. It's funny that.'

'Boy or girl, we'll love it to bits,' he said.

'You bet.'

She finished her egg and spread marmalade on some toast. 'So you're off to Madrid today then?'

'That's right.'

'You'll be back tonight, though?'

'Mmm, but I'm not sure what time,' he said. 'I'll phone you as soon as we get back to the UK to let you know that I'm on my way.'

'Okay.'

'What are you doing today?' he asked.

'I've nothing special planned. I prefer not to drive far with the bump making it so uncomfortable or I'd go to see my mother.'

'Mmm.'

'I might invite a neighbour in for coffee or something.'

'Good idea. So long as you take it easy,' he said. 'Remember you're supposed to have a rest every afternoon.'

'I intend to, don't worry,' Kitty told him lightly. 'I can't do much else but take it easy with my own personal mountain slowing me down practically to a standstill.'

He stood up purposefully.

'Well, I suppose I'd better be making a move,' he said. 'Since they haven't yet invented passenger planes that fly without a pilot.'

'I'll come down and see you off,' said Kitty, putting her tray on the bedside table.

'There's no need, love,' he said. 'You stay and finish your breakfast.'

But she was already heaving her great weight out of bed and reaching for her dressing gown.

Downstairs in the hall, she felt quite overcome with emotion.

'Oh, Tim,' she said, clinging to him, her eyes brimming with tears.

'Hey.' He looked concerned. 'What's all this about?'

'I'll miss you.'

'But I'll be back tonight.'

'I know, I'm just being silly.' She felt ridiculously senti-mental. Her love for him was so intense it hurt. 'I don't know what's the matter with me. It must be my condition.'

He held her close, gently stroking her hair and telling her that he loved her.

'I'm so lucky to be married to you, Tim,' she whispered.

'I'm the lucky one,' he said, and kissed her hard on the lips.

Watching him stride down the front path, an impressive figure in his dark uniform, her heart swelled with pride. He got into the car, blew her a kiss out of the window and started the engine.

As the car rolled out of the Close, she felt a shiver of fear and a pang of loneliness, almost as though they had parted for ever.

Chiding herself for allowing her pregnancy to make her so emotional, Kitty went inside to finish her breakfast.

* * *

The day had a dawdling quality about it for Kitty, pleasant enough but lacking in purpose. Routine domestic chores, a sociable coffee with a neighbour and a long telephone conversation with her mother took up most of the morning, and the mandatory lie-down after lunch used up a large chunk of the afternoon.

Deciding that a breath of fresh air wouldn't go amiss, she set off for a stroll to the local shops for a few items. It was a fine afternoon, sunny and warm with a light breeze keeping it comfortable for someone in Kitty's condition, wispy white clouds racing across the sky.

This leafy suburban area had only been developed in the last fifteen years or so and was made up of privately owned houses, many of them detached. The streets were mostly well-kept avenues with grass verges and glorious young poplars reaching up above the ubiquitous lilacs and laburnums.

Judging by the number of women drivers ferrying cargoes of children, school must be out, thought Kitty, also noticing groups of pram-pushing mothers with schoolchildren in tow.

That'll be me one day soon, she thought. But it was still too early to think of it as a reality. At the moment she couldn't even imagine herself pushing a pram, let alone having a child of school age. Try as she might, she found it impossible to think of her unborn baby as a living, breathing human being – something she guessed wouldn't happen until it actually put in an appearance.

The awful doubts that had plagued her early on in the pregnancy hadn't troubled her again. Nourished by Tim's love and support, she'd felt deliriously happy during this waiting period. They talked about the baby all the time, anticipating its presence in their lives and making plans for its future. She'd spent hours in baby stores while Tim made the spare bedroom into a nursery.

Reaching the small parade of shops, she bought a

birthday card for a friend, a few groceries, a white cabbage for coleslaw to which she had become addicted throughout her pregnancy, then ambled home, stopping for a chat with someone she knew on the way.

Back home, she began chopping cabbage for the coleslaw which she and Tim would have later with spare ribs cooked in a deliciously sharp sauce which she made with lemon juice, vinegar and brown sugar. Clearing up a few bits of ironing, she went upstairs to put the clothes in the airing cupboard. A sudden feeling of weariness forced her to lie down on the bed where she fell instantly asleep, waking with a start to realise that it was nearly eight o'clock.

Happiness dawned gently with the realisation that Tim would soon be home. Mentally checking that everything was ready to cook as soon as he phoned from the airport, Kitty got up slowly and made her way downstairs to put on the television in the lounge.

Still feeling a bit drowsy, she sat in the chair watching 'Coronation Street' until a newsflash sent her heart leaping to her throat. Gripping the sides of the chair, she watched the newsreader's mouth as he said that there had been a serious aircrash. Reminding herself that she always overreacted to this sort of report and that there were literally thousands of planes in the skies at every moment of the day, she steeled herself to hear more.

'Details are just coming through of a plane crash in Madrid,' said the newsreader. 'The plane crashed shortly after taking off from Madrid airport en route for London. The plane burst into flames as it hit the ground and there is no hope of any survivors . . .'

Shaking and sweating and wanting to be sick, Kitty managed to get herself into the hall. With terror in her heart she dialled the number of the airline that Tim worked for.

★   ★   ★

Ruth was in reminiscent mood as she drove home from Redfern, having delivered Jenny to a fifth-form disco in celebration of the fact that the exams were over. Where had the time gone? she asked herself. It certainly didn't seem seventeen years since her own 'O'-levels.

Having responded to Ringo's slobbering welcome as she opened the front door, she made her way upstairs to the flat and turned on the TV, just in time for the closing credits of 'Coronation Street'. 'Damn,' she muttered, because she enjoyed the goings on in the 'Street'.

Deciding to spend some time downstairs in the shop, making a display of sun tan creams and lotions as they were currently enjoying a spell of warm weather, she switched off the television and headed for the stairs.

The telephone rang just as she was passing it on the landing.

'Hello.'

'Ruth?'

'Yes,' she said, her heart lurching as she recognised the voice.

'It's Kitty.'

'Yes, I thought so,' she said, delighted to hear from her but curious as to what had initiated the call. 'This *is* a surprise.'

She waited for Kitty to speak next but all was silent.

'Kitty . . . are you there?'

Still there was no sound but there was no dialling tone either so she hadn't hung up.

'Kitty . . . is there something wrong?'

'Tim's been killed,' she said in a thick, bewildered voice.

'What!'

'He's dead . . . and I don't know what I'm going to do.'

'Oh, Kitty . . . *love*.'

'His plane crashed.'

'My God!'

'I need you, Ruth.'

'Are you still at the same address?'

'Yes.'

'I'm on my way.'

She telephoned Paul with the dreadful news and asked him to collect Jenny from the disco later on.

'I'm not sure what time I'll be back . . . depends what sort of a state poor Kitty's in.'

'Don't worry. I'll stay at the flat with Jenny overnight if you're not back . . . if she isn't happy about being there on her own.'

'She can go to my parents,' suggested Ruth.

'I'll sort it,' he said. 'You concentrate on Kitty.'

'Oh, and Paul . . . could you make sure the dog gets a bit of a walk before bedtime?'

'Sure.'

'And can you ring Vince and tell him what's happened?' she requested. 'I think he would want to know.'

''Course I will.'

'Thanks.'

Within minutes, Ruth was in her car heading for Staines.

When Kitty opened the door to her old friend, it was as though the years between had never passed and there had been no rift. They fell into each other's arms. Ruth wept, Kitty sobbed uncontrollably. It was a long time before she was able to speak.

'You're pregnant then,' said Ruth eventually.

'I wish to God I wasn't now,' wept Kitty.

'When are you due?'

'Five weeks' time,' she said, her words barely audible.

'Well, at least Tim will live on in the baby,' said Ruth.

'Tim's dead and all the baby will do is make life more agonising for me,' cried Kitty hysterically.

'You must have been looking forward to it before . . .'

'We both were,' she sobbed. 'Now I couldn't care less about it.'

Ruth had just managed to get her distressed friend into an armchair and was about to make her some tea when the telephone rang.

'Don't answer it,' said Kitty, panic-stricken. 'I don't want to speak to anyone. You're the only person I can face at the moment.'

'But it might be your mother,' Ruth pointed out worriedly. 'The plane crash will have been reported on the telly – she'll be wondering about Tim. So will other people . . .'

'Oh, all right, answer it and tell whoever it is what's happened,' she said, her voice thick from crying. 'But I don't want anyone to come visiting.'

'Not even your mother?' said Ruth.

'No.'

'But she'll want to be with you.'

'Not now – not yet,' said Kitty. 'I know there are things to be done and people to see but I can't face any of it tonight.'

The caller on the telephone was Kitty's mother. Ruth persuaded her not to come over until the morning, assuring her that she would stay the night with Kitty herself. During the evening Ruth also dealt with a stream of calls from friends and relatives who had heard about the tragedy.

When she telephoned her own flat, Paul answered, having brought Jenny home. He agreed to stay with her and said he would arrange for Vince to get to the shop in time to open in the morning in case Ruth couldn't get there herself.

'Thanks, Paul,' she said. 'I really appreciate your help.'

'If we can't help each other at a time like this . . .'

'Yeah, I know.'

* * *

'I can't even get drunk to blot out the pain because of the baby,' said Kitty in the early hours of the next morning. 'God, what a mess!'

She and Ruth hadn't gone to bed because Kitty said she wouldn't be able to sleep. Exhausted from weeping, she was lying on the sofa, Ruth was in the armchair. The only thing she could do to help her friend was to be there, awake and listening to her grief-stricken monologue. Now, seeing Kitty's lids droop, she knew that nature was about to take its course.

Ruth herself could barely stay awake. When Kitty's eyes finally closed, she got up and covered her with a blanket. Then she lay back in her chair and went to sleep.

She came to with a start to hear Kitty crying out in pain.

'It's all right, love,' she said, instantly at her friend's side, assuming her cries were those of grief. 'I'm here with you . . . one day it won't hurt quite so much.'

'I bloody well hope not!' said Kitty. 'It's the baby, Ruth. I think I've started, I'm going into labour . . .'

'But you're not due yet.'

'The baby obviously doesn't know that,' said Kitty.

Seeing the agony on her face, which was beaded with sweat, Ruth hurried to the phone and called an ambulance.

The following evening, Kitty lay in her hospital bed staring at the ceiling. She hurt inside and out. She was sore from the birth, heartsick at the loss of her husband, and her nervous system was so badly ravaged that even the rustle of the sheet felt like needles piercing her skin. Her eyes were sore from weeping, her head ached and she had a tight knot of tension in her stomach that destroyed her concentration and wouldn't let her rest. She'd been in this wretched state ever since the birth of her son that morning.

She was in one of the side rooms attached to the main

maternity ward. The staff had thought she would be more comfortable away from the noise and chatter in the ward, given her tragic circumstances. Being premature, the baby was underweight and in an incubator being cared for by nurses.

His absence was an enormous relief to Kitty. She was in no fit state to be responsible for anything so fragile as a newborn baby. *A newborn baby.* He could be anyone's child for all the feeling she had for him, apart from terror at being his mother.

The door opened and Ruth came in, carrying a bouquet of flowers.

'Hi,' she said, putting the cellophane-wrapped display on the locker.

'Hi,' said Kitty, her mouth so dry her tongue felt heavy. She took Ruth's hand, eyes filling with fresh tears.

'How are you feeling?'

'Oh, Ruth, thank goodness you're here,' sobbed Kitty. 'I feel terrible.'

'Still weak from the birth?'

'It's more than just that,' she said, wiping her eyes with a handkerchief, too deeply distressed to realise how she appeared. 'I feel awful . . . completely isolated from the rest of the world.'

'Shall I ask them to move you into the general ward with the other mums?'

'It wouldn't help,' she said. 'Something peculiar has happened to me. I feel so strange . . . so jittery and deperately alone . . . I just don't know what I'm gonna do.'

'I managed to persuade them to let me in to see you, despite the fact that I'm not a relative,' said Ruth, trying not to show how worried she was by her friend's state of mind. What should have been the happiest day of Kitty's life had been destroyed by the cruellest of fates and Ruth's heart went out to her. 'But I'll have to disappear as soon as your other visitors arrive 'cos of hospital rules. Your mum said she and your dad will be coming to see you, when I spoke to her on the phone earlier.'

'Yeah, I got a message from the nurse about that,' said Kitty without much interest.

'Good.'

'Thanks for coming, Ruth,' she said, tears streaming down her cheeks again. 'You were so good to me last night, I don't know what I'd have done without you.'

'Don't be silly . . . it's what friends are for.'

'I've missed you all these years,' Kitty sobbed. 'I'm sorry for what I did. I shouldn't have told Paul about Jenny.'

'That's all in the past,' said Ruth soothingly. 'And I missed you too. I nearly phoned you several times.'

'I got as far as dialling your number,' admitted Kitty, 'but I didn't have the bottle to go through with it.' She sniffed into her hanky. 'But when I heard about Tim, I forgot all about the quarrel. You were the only person I could bear to see.'

'I'm glad you called me,' said Ruth, meaning every word.

She was feeling both physically and mentally exhausted, having spent the night in the hospital visitor's room. She'd wanted to be there for Kitty when the baby finally arrived. It had been almost lunchtime by the time Ruth finally got home, fit only to crawl into bed and sleep just long enough to be able to function for the rest of the day.

Vince had been only too willing to manage without her in the shop. Both he and Paul had been saddened by Kitty's tragic loss, as had Ruth's family who had known her for many years.

'The baby's still in the incubator then?' she asked now.

'Yeah, thank God,' said Kitty, adding quickly, 'I mean, I'm glad he's not in here with me.'

'You don't want him with you?'

'No.'

'Why's that?'

'I'm afraid he'll cry.'

'It's what babies do.'

'Well, I don't want him crying around me,' she said. 'It would mean he wants attention and I'm not able to give it to him. I'm tired, so very tired, and I haven't slept since he was born.'

'It might be a comfort to have him with you later on, when you're feeling stronger,' suggested Ruth. 'He's a beautiful boy. You'll feel proud every time you look at him.'

Kitty collapsed into fresh tears, heaving deep guttural sobs.

'Everyone keeps telling me how lucky I am to have such a beautiful son,' she wept. 'And I realise how wicked I am because there are thousands of childless couples in the world who would give anything to have what I have. But I don't feel lucky because I don't want a baby – I only want my husband.'

Ruth sat with her arm around her friend's quivering shoulders.

'I know you're grieving, love,' she said. 'But your baby needs you.'

'I don't *want* to be needed,' she sobbed, becoming almost hysterical. 'Don't you understand . . . I'm the one needing someone? I need Tim and he isn't here . . . never will be again.'

'There, there,' soothed Ruth.

'I only got pregnant because Tim wanted a baby,' Kitty wept. 'Now that he's gone, I won't be able to bring up a child on my own. Tim was my strength. Without him I'm nothing.'

'Now that isn't true,' said Ruth gently. 'You're stronger than you think. Anyway, you've parents who care about you and lots of friends. We'll all do whatever we can to help you through this.'

'I feel so ill, Ruth.'

'You're bound to feel weak after all you've been through,' she said. 'Having a baby's enough in itself but losing your husband too . . .'

'I've told you, it's more than that,' Kitty wailed. 'I feel different . . . sort of odd. I'm not the same person any more. Something happened to me when the baby was born . . . everything's dark and frightening. I want to die.'

Now Ruth was really worried.

'I'll go and talk to a nurse,' she said. 'Perhaps they can give you something to calm you . . . make you feel better.'

'They can't bring Tim back, can they?' she cried, her voice rising.

'Well, no, but . . .'

'Tim is the only thing I want in the world,' she cut in through choking sobs. 'I don't want a baby, I just want my husband.'

'But he isn't just any baby, Kitty,' said Ruth. 'He's Tim's child, a part of him, to live on into the future with you.'

'You just don't understand,' she said, and turned away.

As she buried her head in the pillow, heaving fresh sobs, Ruth slipped quietly from the room and went to find a nurse.

No medicine could give Kitty the only thing she wanted but she certainly needed something more than Ruth had to offer. Her heart ached for her friend.

Kitty was very ill in the ensuing weeks. She wept constantly, was unable to eat or sleep and continued to reject the baby. The doctors said she had an acute case of post-natal depression, exacerbated by her bereavement. A psychiatrist was called in and anti-depressants were prescribed. Kitty and the baby, whom she named Timmy, went to stay with her parents in Hammersmith until she felt able to cope on her own.

The fact that she was living nearer made it easier for Ruth to visit and she made a point of going to see her every day. But it was a heartbreaking experience because Kitty was so changed. There was no evidence of the confident and fun-loving person she'd once been in this emaciated woman. The blue eyes that had once shone with vitality were dull and lack-lustre with dark shadows like bruises beneath. She didn't bother with make-up and her clothes hung shapelessly on her because she had lost such a lot of weight. The person who had always had such self-assurance was now a nervous wreck. She seemed so frail, so frightened, so utterly forlorn.

'I can't even get her to go out to buy clothes that fit,' confessed her harassed mother to Ruth, out of Kitty's hearing one day.

'It's so unlike her,' Ruth observed.

'I know it is,' said Mrs West with a sad shake of the head. 'And she barely eats enough to keep a fly alive.'

'How is she with the baby now?' enquired Ruth. 'Is she beginning to take an interest in him now that he's not quite so tiny?'

'Not really. She does what she has to for him, gives him his bottle and baths him and so on, but only if I won't do it for her. She wouldn't get out of bed if I didn't make her,' said Mrs West, a neat, attractive woman with blue-rinsed hair and the same blue eyes as her daughter.

'What a shame.'

'The doctor has told me to be firm with her,' she explained. 'I've been told not to do everything for the baby. Help her with him, yes, but not take over her responsibilities. It's important she does things for him, to build her confidence and help her to bond with him. Though, naturally, I do what I can.'

'Of course.'

'It's breaking my heart to see her like this, Ruth.'

'Mine too.'

'Little Timmy is coming on a treat now and she isn't enjoying him at all. I'm beginning to think my daughter will never smile again.' She looked bleak. 'I can't reach her, you see, and I feel so helpless. That's why it's so hard. She seems locked into a world of her own.'

'Yes, I've noticed that.'

'I'm very grateful to you for coming to see her so often, Ruth,' said Mrs West. 'Your visits are the highlight of her day, even though I know she doesn't always show it.'

Ruth shared Mrs West's feeling of helplessness. This was what made the visits so emotionally draining. Kitty had become so introverted, she took no interest in anything outside of herself and how she was feeling.

One day in the autumn when Ruth was visiting her, Kitty put their friendship to the test when she asked something of her which was completely unexpected.

'I think it's time I moved out of here.'

'Oh?' said Ruth enquiringly.

'Mum and I are beginning to get on each other's nerves,' explained Kitty.

Taking this to mean that she was ready to move back into her own house, Ruth saw this as a hopeful sign.

'There's nothing quite like your own place, is there?'

'Oh, I don't want to move back to Staines yet,' she explained.

'What do you have in mind then?'

'Well . . . actually, I was wondering if I could move in with you and Jenny?'

Completely flummoxed, Ruth could see a multitude of problems to such an arrangement.

'But I'm working all day, Kitty,' she pointed out. 'So you'd be upstairs in the flat on your own with the baby.'

'But you'd be on the premises,' she said. 'And that would give me confidence.'

That was a very good point. Although initially the idea of Kitty and the baby moving into the flat had sounded like a recipe for disaster, Ruth now thought it could be a good thing for Kitty at this stage, a sort of halfway house until she was ready to go home to Staines. Living with Ruth would mean she'd have people around her if she needed them while at the same time having to look after her son without her mother on hand to use as a fallback.

Ruth knew instinctively that Jenny would be pleased to have them as lodgers, especially as there were no crucial exams in the offing that had to be swotted for.

'I do have a business to run though, Kitty,' Ruth reminded her because she wanted to make things clear from the start to avoid problems in the future. 'I won't be able to come rushing upstairs every time Timmy cries and sends you into a panic.'

'I realise that.'

'Well, what can I say then?' Ruth was delighted to be able to make some practical contribution to Kitty's recovery. 'Except that we'll be happy to have you and Timmy . . . and you can move in as soon as you like.'

Chapter Sixteen

Audrey Brooks hurried into Ruth's shop one wet November morning, eager to get inside out of the rain.

'It's bucketing down out there,' she said to anyone who cared to listen, shaking the worst of the rain off her umbrella outside the door before closing it behind her.

There was a general nod of agreement from waiting customers as she made her way to the back of the shop which was damp and steamy, the air thick with the rubbery smell of rainwear.

'Am *I* pleased to see *you*,' said Ruth who was serving at the counter.

'Kitty's not so good then?'

Ruth waited until the shop had emptied then turned to her rainsoaked mother who was standing beside her in a plastic mac and a headscarf, flattened to her head by the rain.

'She's having a really bad time this morning,' said Ruth. 'I was worried about leaving her upstairs on her own but I had to come to work.'

''Course you did,' said Audrey, shaking her head worriedly. 'Don't worry, I'll stay with her for a while. She usually calms down when I'm there.'

'Thanks ever so much, Mum,' said Ruth. 'I really appreciate your help.'

'Think nothing of it, love,' said Audrey cheerfully 'That's why I'm here . . . to try and help the poor soul through this awful thing.'

As the door to the hallway closed behind her mother, Ruth felt her own tension ease slightly. Audrey had been an absolute diamond this last couple of months, spending time with Kitty while Ruth was working, for Kitty had an irrational fear of being alone with the baby. Although Ruth was overwhelmed with pity for her friend, having her in residence was proving to be extremely stressful.

Timmy was an absolute joy. Now nearly five months old, he was bright-eyed and sunny-natured. The entire Brooks family was in thrall to him, even the twins who often saw him at their mother's house where Kitty was a regular visitor. Vince made a great fuss of him too whenever Kitty was passing through the shop with him.

But she was still suffering dreadfully from depression. Living with her in this state was an appalling strain, mostly because Ruth felt so powerless to help. The illogical nature of Kitty's behaviour made it difficult for the lay person to understand. Whilst she still hadn't taken the baby to her heart and saw him only as a frightening responsibility, she was abnormally protective, constantly terrified he would come to harm. Although she feared and disliked motherhood, she was excessively conscientious and overly sensitive to Timmy's every heartbeat. The doctor had warned her that constant observation wasn't good for her or the baby but she couldn't stop doing it.

There was no shortage of impatience from the 'pull yourself together brigade' who denied the existence of post-natal depression and thought Kitty was making a fuss about nothing. But Ruth knew better. She saw her friend in the mornings, shaking and sweating and being physically sick.

The doctor had told Ruth not to feel guilty about leaving her to go to work because she wouldn't be doing Kitty any favours by staying with her all day. Apparantly only by fully accepting her responsibilities would she overcome her fears and lead a normal life again.

So Audrey's frequent visits were an absolute godsend,

especially as Kitty's own mother had taken umbrage when her daughter had moved out of her house into Ruth's and couldn't be called upon to help.

'Oh, Audrey, thank goodness you've come!' said Kitty who was sitting by the fire in the living room, still wearing her dressing gown, with Timmy in her arms. She looked very anxious.

'Why, what's the matter, love?'

'I think the baby's temperature is up.'

'He looks all right to me.'

'You feel how hot he is.'

Seeing only a healthy baby who was warm from being near to the fire and was giving her a gummy smile to prove it, Audrey put her hand on his forehead which made him chuckle.

'He feels perfectly normal to me.'

'Don't you think he feels as though he's burning up?'

'He's warm from being near the fire, you daft cat,' said Audrey.

Kitty wasn't convinced. 'I'm not so sure, you know.'

'I think I can recognise a sick child when I see one,' said Audrey. 'I have brought up three kids of my own, you know. Anyway, he'd soon let you know if he was off colour, believe me.'

'I suppose so,' said Kitty, her disturbed state of mind making her unaware of how exhausting she was to other people.

'The best thing you can do is to go and get yourself dressed,' said Audrey, knowing how important it was to be firm with her.

'In a minute.'

'It's turned ten o'clock, you know,' Audrey reminded her determinedly. 'High time you were washed and dressed.'

'I haven't had time to bother about myself this morning,'

said Kitty distractedly. 'What with the worry of the baby being poorly.'

'You must find time to look after yourself,' said Audrey in a kind but definite tone. 'Anyway, there's nothing wrong with the baby.'

'I'm not so sure . . .'

'You go and make yourself decent,' she suggested, grinding her teeth because Kitty could be so exasperating. 'I'll look after this little fella while you're gone.'

Casting her eye over Kitty, she saw a sad creature who was obviously bruised and broken inside. Audrey recalled how glamorous she'd once been. But now her cheeks were sunken, her eyes heavily shadowed and her lips chapped and dry.

'Would you?'

''Course I will,' said Audrey, taking the baby from her. 'Go on, love, you go and get dressed. It'll make you feel better.'

Kitty went, returning promptly wearing a baggy polo-necked sweater and jeans which were several sizes too big. She was without make-up but had combed her hair which hung limply to her shoulders, greasy and unstyled.

The baby was growing tired and fretful so Audrey persuaded Kitty to put him in his cot for a sleep while she made them both some coffee.

'Why don't you go out on a shopping spree one afternoon soon?' suggested Audrey companionably as they drank their coffee.

'I'm not in the mood.'

'You could go up West and get some clothes to fit your new ultra-slim figure,' persisted Audrey. 'Maybe get something done about your hair an' all, while you're at it.'

'I'm not dragging the baby round the West End,' said Kitty.

'I'll look after His Nibs,' Audrey offered. 'It'll do you

good to have a break from him and he'll be fine with me.'

'Thanks for offering but I don't think I ought to go out and leave him,' said Kitty. 'Not while he's still so little.'

'Tim must be turning in his grave,' said Audrey, taking a harsh line to try to oust Kitty from the trough she was in.

'Why exactly?'

'The way you've let yourself go, o' course.'

'I haven't . . .'

'Oh, not much,' cut in Audrey. 'The woman Tim married was pretty and smart. Now look at you. You're a bloody disgrace and that's the truth. It isn't as though you're short of money. He left you well provided for.'

'Tim loved me whatever . . .'

'He'd soon have gone off you if he'd seen you going about in this state for any length of time.'

'I will get myself sorted . . . sometime,' she said absently.

The conversation was interrupted by the sound of the baby crying upstairs. Kitty looked immediately stricken and leaped up in a state of high agitation, her face pale, neck suffused with bright red blotches.

'I knew there was something wrong with him,' she declared.

'He's only crying, love,' Audrey pointed out. 'It doesn't mean that he's ill. He probably just wants his nappy changed.'

Unconvinced, Kitty tore upstairs as though the infant's demise was imminent, returning with him in her arms. As cute as they come, he'd stopped crying the instant he was picked up and was now smiling.

'Maybe I should call the doctor,' said Kitty, far too harassed to accept that there was nothing wrong with the child.

Audrey looked at Timmy whose face was wreathed in smiles.

'You can't call the doctor out to a perfectly healthy child,' she said, because the doctor had already been pestered with a stream of false alarms from Kitty. 'It isn't fair to the doctor or to the other patients . . . people who are genuinely sick and really need attention.'

Kitty still looked uncertain. 'I need reassurance,' she said.

'There is nothing wrong with that child at all,' said Audrey forcefully. 'Is that reassuring enough for you?'

'I mean from someone with medical qualifications.'

'Oh, well, in that case . . .'

'Do you think Vince would come up and have a look at him?'

'He isn't a doctor.'

'No, but he is a qualifed chemist and does have a certain amount of medical knowledge,' said Kitty hopefully. 'People are always asking his advice about their ailments.'

Kitty might have hit upon the answer, thought Audrey. Better to bother Vince, who was on hand and a friend, rather than call the doctor out for no good reason. One thing Audrey did know for sure: Kitty wasn't going to stop fretting until she'd had some sort of professional advice. She certainly wasn't going to take any notice of Audrey.

'It won't do any harm to let Vince have a look at him,' she said thoughtfully. 'Shall I nip down to the dispensary and ask him to come up when he's got a minute?'

'Yes, please,' said Kitty gratefully.

Even though Vince was used to seeing a very different Kitty from the one he'd fallen in love with as a boy, it still broke his heart to find her looking so sickly and lacking in spirit, her eyes dull with pain and worry.

'If I was half as healthy as this little chap, I'd be a happy man,' he said, having cast a professional eye over Timmy.

'Really?' said Kitty.

'Yes, really.' He threw the child up in the air and made him chuckle to emphasise the point and put Kitty's mind at rest. 'He's as fit as a flea in my opinion.' Vince paused, aware of the ethics of the situation. 'But I am only a pharmacist and not a doctor. If you're really worried about him, I should take him to the afternoon surgery.'

'There'll be no need,' she said, visibly relaxing. 'If you think he's fine, that's good enough for me.' She heaved a sigh of relief. 'I feel ever so much better now. Thanks for coming up to look at him, Vince.'

'My pleasure,' he said, handing the baby back to her and tickling him under the chin. 'I'm glad of the chance to see him.'

Seeing what a calming effect Vince had on Kitty, Audrey had an idea.

'Have you time for a cup of coffee with us, Vince?' she asked.

He looked at his watch.

'I'd love one,' he said. 'Ruth will soon let me know if I'm needed urgently.'

'I'll put the kettle on then,' said Audrey with a meaningful look.

'I've been telling Kitty she should go out shopping for clothes and get her hair done,' said Audrey to Vince as the three of them had a companionable cup of coffee, Timmy now asleep in his cot. 'I think it would do her good, don't you?'

'I certainly do,' he agreed, nibbling a ginger biscuit. 'They say new clothes are better than a tonic, don't they?'

'I've offered to look after the baby while she goes but she doesn't trust me with him.'

'It isn't that I don't trust you, Audrey,' Kitty denied. 'It's just . . .'

Vince exchanged a knowing glance with Audrey.

'I'll be on hand if there's any sort of a problem,' he said. 'And Ruth is around as well. I think between the three of us, young Timmy will manage to survive for a couple of hours while you're out.'

'Well . . .' She was still hesitant.

'We all want the old Kitty back,' said Vince with brutal candour. 'The girl who could knock spots off Marilyn Monroe in her heyday. The sexy blonde your husband married.'

Usually nothing outside her own grey world, containing herself and the baby, registered fully with Kitty. But for some reason Vince's comments made quite an impact. She remembered the last time he'd spoken his mind to her, after she'd told Paul the truth about Jenny. She'd argued with him then and had later realised he'd been right.

'Are you saying I look dowdy, Vince Todd?' she said.

'You don't really want me to answer that, do you, Kitty? You only have to look in the mirror.'

'Well, you certainly don't mince your words, do you?'

'Not when plain speaking is needed,' he said. 'I agree with Audrey. You owe it to yourself to get smartened up. If you carry on like this, you'll lose all your self-respect.'

'My word, we are forceful today.'

'Not without reason.'

Watching this exchange, Audrey saw a spark of vitality in Kitty for the first time since Timmy's birth. It was only a glimpse but enough to give Audrey hope.

'Oh well, since you're both going to nag me until I do as you say, I suppose I'd better do something about the way I look,' she said. 'Perhaps a haircut and some clothes that fit might be a good idea.' She turned to Audrey. 'Could you look after Timmy for a few hours . . . say, tomorrow?'

'It'll be a pleasure,' said Audrey, exchanging a smile with Vince.

* * *

No one was more surprised than Kitty when she found herself drawing strength from such an unexpected source. But Vince became her salvation during the weeks that followed.

Having once experienced the benefit of his reassurance, just knowing that he was downstairs in the dispensary made her feel less vulnerable. If she was having a particularly bad time she would go downstairs to see him. She usually had to wait for his attention while he got on with his work but she always felt better for having talked to him. After all these years, she could see why Ruth valued him as a friend.

He didn't always gave Kitty an easy time, though. If he thought it was necessary he could be very blunt indeed. But his warmth and good nature never failed to strengthen her. Although she still inhabited a world of darkness where everyday life seemed to be beyond her, she did begin occasionally to glimpse the light.

One afternoon in the New Year, she experienced more than just a glimpse. It happened when she was on her own with Timmy in the flat. He was sitting on the floor, supported by cushions because he wasn't yet able to sit up on his own. Kitty was having a cup of tea.

When one of the cushions fell away from him, she instinctively dived to the floor to replace it before he fell. But he didn't fall. He stayed sitting, firm and solid, waving his arms and chuckling.

Warmth and light flooded Kitty's being with such brilliance, it was almost like a spiritual awakening. The tension that had plagued her for so long dissolved, leaving her clear-headed for the first time since Timmy's birth.

She wanted to cry – but with joy, not sorrow. Her son could sit up unaided. It was a miracle! She wanted to tell the world. Scooping him up into her arms and smothering him with kisses (an unprecedented event), she hurried downstairs to the shop.

The customers were delighted to hear of this major development and made a great fuss of Timmy, enjoying this pleasant diversion while they waited to be served. Hearing all the noise in the shop, Vince appeared from the dispensary to see what was going on.

Seeing Kitty's animated face, he exchanged a glance with Ruth. They both knew that it probably wasn't permanent – that tomorrow could hold all the old demons for Kitty, such was the fluctuating nature of her illness. But they were of one mind in believing that she had taken that first vital step out of the darkness into the light.

It was a gradual process and Kitty still had setbacks and bad days. But an improvement was clearly discernible to Ruth as the days lengthened and spring flowers brightened the Green with glorious splashes of white and yellow. Not only did Kitty begin to enjoy her son at last, she also began to take an interest in life again and regained her appetite. She even put on a little weight and got some colour back in her cheeks.

Now that she was less introverted, she did her share around the flat, preparing the evening meal and keeping the place tidy while Ruth was working. Although she was much more like her old self, she'd become softer, somehow, and lost some of her arrogance.

Ruth enjoyed having her around now, especially as Jenny had a busy social life and was out a lot in the evenings. After they had settled Timmy down for the night, Ruth and Kitty would sit down to watch the TV but usually chatted instead. On a Saturday night they'd get a bottle of wine and have it with a TV supper. It was fun.

One Saturday evening in April, however, Ruth introduced a more serious note by raising a subject that was worrying her – Kitty's relationship with Vince.

'I should hate to see him get hurt,' she remarked.

'Why should he be hurt?'

'Well, he's always had a bit of a thing about you, hasn't he?'

'A hundred years ago he might have,' said Kitty. 'But not now.'

'I think it's still there . . . just as strong as ever.'

'You're imagining things.'

'I don't think so,' said Ruth, peering at her friend over the rim of her wine glass. 'You only have to look at him when the two of you are together to see it.'

'Vince and I are good friends,' she protested. 'There's no more to it than that.'

'Not on your side maybe . . .'

'Well, I've done nothing to encourage anything other than friendship.' She paused, looking at Ruth questioningly. 'Have I?'

The old-style Kitty would never have burdened herself with anything so tiresome as self-doubt. It was strange to see evidence of it now, but she was all the nicer for it.

'Not intentionally, perhaps,' said Ruth. 'But in as much as you've been seeking him out such a lot, I suppose it would be easy for him to read something more into it. I mean, he wouldn't say anything to you about it. Vince is far too much of a gentleman to do anything that isn't quite proper . . . with Tim not having been gone a year yet.'

'Oh, Ruth,' said Kitty, sounding genuinely distressed, 'I really value his friendship and I can't bear the idea of not being so pally with him because he might get the wrong idea. And if I say anything to clear the air, it might embarrass him. It could seem patronising.'

'It's tricky,' agreed Ruth.

Kitty sipped her wine thoughtfully.

'Honestly, Ruth,' she said after a while 'I think you're wrong. There's no hint of romance between us at all. Even if he does have a lingering pash for me, he isn't expecting our current friendship to develop, I'm sure of it.'

'So long as you're sure, that's all right then,' said Ruth.
'I am.'

'Good. Only Vince is a dear friend and people use him. They can't get enough of him when they're down – but give him the elbow as soon as they're feeling better.'

'He's a dear friend to me too, Ruth, and I don't want to hurt him,' said Kitty. 'I know I used to be a real bitch about him but I've seen him in a new light.'

'You don't think he's the twerp of all time, then?'

'Far from it. Now that I've got to know him better, I can see that I was miles out,' she confessed. 'He's strong and very reassuring. A really good bloke, in fact.' She looked misty-eyed. 'I just don't know what I'd have done without him this last few months.' She paused. 'Or any of you, for that matter. You . . . your mum . . . Jenny.'

'We've enjoyed having you,' said Ruth, with a touch of wistfulness because she knew it wouldn't go on for ever. Sooner or later Kitty was going to want to move back into her own place – she'd stayed longer than any of them had expected as it was. Once she was really back on her feet, she was going to want her independence.

Vince was thinking much the same thing about Kitty. Being an altruistic type, he was waiting for a suitable moment to bring up the subject because he thought it was time she had her own place again, for the sake of her self-confidence. He certainly had nothing to gain by her moving back to Staines.

His chance came one fine day in early summer. It was Vince's lunch hour and he'd spent a pleasant interlude in the park with Kitty and the baby. They'd had a picnic and played on the grass with Timmy who could now manage a few staggering steps on his own.

Walking back across the Green with Kitty pushing the

pram, he said, 'It'll be Timmy's birthday soon.'

'Yes.'

'It doesn't seem possible that a year has passed already.'

'It does to me.'

He looked at her profile as she stared ahead thoughtfully. Her bobbed hair was shiny, her skin had regained its bloom. But there was still an air of sorrow about her.

'I suppose it would do for you, having had such a tough year.'

'A year since Tim died.' She sighed deeply. 'In some ways it feels as though it was only yesterday that I last saw him. Other times it seems so long ago, I can hardly picture his face. When that happens I panic and stare at his photo for ages. I'm scared of forgetting what he looks like.'

'That's a common fear for people who have lost a loved one, I should imagine.'

'Mmm.'

'Anyway,' he said after a pause, 'I suppose you'll be moving back to Staines soon?'

'What makes you say that?' she asked, turning to look at him sharply.

'Well, you can't stay with Ruth for ever, can you?' he said.

'Has she said something to you about it, then?'

'No.'

'Is she fed up with having us staying with her? Is that it?' asked Kitty, overreacting because she was still feeling insecure. 'I'd rather you were straight with me about this, Vince.'

'Ruth loves having you staying with her,' he assured her. 'It's company for her. I think she gets lonely now that Jenny has a life of her own outside the home.'

'Oh . . . so long as she's not finding it too much, having us.'

'She most definitely isn't, I can promise you that. But it is a year since you left your home,' he said as a gentle reminder. 'So I suppose it is about time you moved back into your own place. Had your own space again . . . your independence.'

'Yeah, I know.'

'You don't sound too keen.'

'I can't face going back to that house and living there without Tim,' she confessed. 'And being so far away from all my friends.'

'You've lots of friends in Staines, surely?'

'I know quite a few people. But since I've been back here among my real friends, I've realised that the others are just acquaintances,' she told him. 'They're nice enough people but not the sort you turn to when you're in trouble.'

Vince gave this some thought.

'Why not sell the house in Staines and move back into London?' he said after a while. 'If that's the way you feel about it.'

'Sell up altogether?' said Kitty, surprised at the suggestion.

'Yes, why not?' he said. 'Get a place near here. Then you'd have your independence and your friends around you.'

'Wouldn't that be a bit of a cop out, though?' she said. 'You know, not going back and facing up to life without Tim.'

'You'll have to do that wherever you live,' he said. 'You're already doing it.'

'I've always thought I'd have to go back to the home Tim and I made together,' she said. 'To soldier on without him . . . all part of the grieving process, you know.'

'Why did you think that?'

'I don't know . . . because it's my home, I suppose.'

'Home shouldn't be a place you dread going back to, should it?' he said frankly.

'No, I guess not.'

'There are no ties for you in Staines now. It isn't as though you have a job to go back to or anything.'

'That's quite true.'

'Once Timmy starts school it won't be so easy to up sticks and move,' he said. 'But at the moment you are in the happy position of being able to please yourself.'

'Ooh, Vince, you've really given me something to think about,' she said, feeling as though a weight had been lifted from her shoulders. 'I don't know why I didn't think of it myself. Well, I do know . . . it's because I haven't been thinking straight about anything lately.'

'Well, it's an option worth considering, anyway,' he said. 'And I'll do anything I can to help if you do decide to move nearer to here.'

'Thanks, Vince,' she said. 'You really are a true friend.'

She was feeling quite excited as they made their way back to the shop. The thought of returning to the house in Staines had filled her with dread for the past year. Now it was over. Thanks to Vince.

Chapter Seventeen

The Hong Kong 'flu epidemic which had started towards the end of the year reached its peak in January, getting the new decade off to a miserable start for many people. Business boomed for Ruth and Vince, though, and the shop was permanently packed to the doors.

As well as a huge increase in the sales of prescribed medicines, purchases of patent 'flu remedies rocketed as overcrowded doctors' waiting rooms sent people hurrying to their nearest chemist's shop for alternative means of relief. Reports of deaths in their thousands from this cruel virus caused panic among some of the customers and Vince's reassuring manner was in constant demand. Ruth spent a fair amount of time heartening people too.

When Vince fell victim to the disease himself and was forced to stay at home, Ruth took on a locum to cover for him, once again having cause to regret her lack of qualifications

No sooner was he back at work than Ruth succumbed to the bug, and had a particularly virulent attack which left her low in spirits as well as health. Even after she'd returned to work she was still tired and depressed. Her state of mind wasn't helped by the fact that she missed the company of Kitty and Timmy in the flat.

Kitty had sold her house in Staines and now lived nearby in Brook Green in a traditional semi with a big garden by London standards. She called in at the shop to see Ruth and Vince most days, often around lunchtime so that they were free to spend time with her and Timmy.

Ruth was delighted that her friend was more like her

old self again after such a traumatic period. But Kitty wasn't the woman she'd once been. Although she'd regained her self-confidence to a certain extent, she'd lost that harsh assertiveness and wasn't quite so sure of herself as she used to be. Ruth thought she was a much nicer person for it.

This made it even more of a wrench when she moved out because Ruth had got used to the chats, the gossip, the at-home companionship. Jenny would be going away to medical school in the autumn, provided she achieved the necessary exam grades, so Ruth would really be on her own then. She knew she must adjust to this next stage in her life but it wasn't something she looked forward to with any degree of pleasure.

Paul had visited her during her recovery period, armed with fruit, flowers and magazines. He was sweet and sympathetic and Ruth had enjoyed his attention. But knowing he could never give her the love and companionship she needed only added to her feeling of emptiness. After all, she wasn't yet thirty-five, it wasn't surprising she didn't relish the prospect of spending the rest of her life alone.

She was in this rather disconsolate frame of mind when she first met Bob Bridgeman who came into the shop one blustery day in February to introduce himself. He was a cheerful, ebullient man with a squarish countenance, a weatherbeaten sort of complexion and an untidy shock of sand-coloured hair streaked with grey. He wasn't much taller than Ruth but was chunky and muscular.

'I've just moved into the parade,' he explained, having politely stood aside and waited until she'd finished serving a customer before engaging her in conversation. 'So I thought I'd pop in to say hello . . . as we're gonna be neighbours.'

'You must be the owner of the new wallpaper shop

that's just opened next door to the dry cleaner's,' said Ruth, after shaking his hand.

'Home decorating store, if you don't mind,' he said, teasing her, shandy-brown eyes sparkling with exuberance. 'Wallpaper, paint, brushes, paste . . . everything the punters need to give their gaff a face lift.'

'You've made your shop look really smart,' she remarked. 'I noticed it when I passed the other day. It's very light and modern.'

'You need an eye-catching shopfront to draw people's attention, don't you?' he said. 'Yours looks nice too.'

'We like to keep it up to scratch.'

'We?'

'My partner and I,' she explained. 'He's the pharmacist.'

Turning away, Ruth poked her head through the doorway behind her and called to Vince in the dispensary. He hurried into the shop and was introduced to the newcomer.

'Do you live over the shop?' asked Bob, directing the enquiry to them both.

When they each gave different answers, he looked puzzled.

'I do, Vince doesn't,' explained Ruth.

'Oh, so you're not . . . ?'

'No, we're just good friends and business partners,' Ruth explained.

'I'm living over the shop too,' Bob informed them chattily.

'That's good.' Some of the living accommodation above the shops was used for offices and storage which meant there weren't too many people in residence after the shops closed at night. The more the merrier in Ruth's opinion. She liked to know that there were people around her. 'I know where to come if I run out of sugar then.'

'I'm more likely to be the one on the cadge,' he confessed with a wry grin. 'Housekeeping isn't my strong point.'

'No?'

'No. My wife looked after me rather too well, I'm afraid, and I've never managed to get to grips with the job since she died.'

Unless he'd married a much older woman, his wife wouldn't have died of old age, thought Ruth, because he couldn't be more than about forty. He was quite attractive in a rough and ready sort of way.

'Cancer,' he explained as though reading her thoughts.

'I'm sorry,' said Ruth.

'I was devastated. It took me ages to recover.' He shook his head gravely. 'It was an experience I *never* want to go through again. It was too much for me to cope with.'

Ruth nodded sympathetically.

'That's why I decided to open a shop, actually,' he continued. 'To give me a new interest and stop me from moping about. Sold my house to get the capital. Well, I don't need a house now I'm on my own . . . the flat above the shop is plenty big enough for me.'

'The retail trade is a new venture for you then?' said Ruth conversationally.

'Yeah. I'm a jobbing builder and decorator by trade.'

'You're well placed to advise your customers, then.'

'Not half,' he agreed. 'It'll be a nice change to be on the other side of the business, selling the stuff instead of buying it.'

'Anyway, welcome to the parade,' said Vince as the shop began filling up with customers and he had to get back to his work.

'That goes for me too,' said Ruth. 'I hope you do well. I should think you will because this is a busy shopping area.'

'Thanks for your good wishes, folks,' said Bob, stepping aside to make way for the influx of paying customers.

'Anything you need,' said Ruth, 'you know where I am.'

'I might take you up on that,' he said with a grin and a wink, his head cocked at a jaunty angle. 'So don't be surprised if I come knocking at your door for some milk or something after the shops are closed.'

'I'll be happy to oblige,' she said casually, turning her attention to a customer who was handing her a prescription.

'Cheers then, see you around,' called Bob from the door.

Ruth smiled across at him in a friendly manner and their eyes met. Much to her surprise she realised that he fancied her. She wasn't sure if she reciprocated but it was flattering to know that she could still produce that sort of a reaction in a man.

Kitty pushed Timmy on the swing in the park one April afternoon, seeing his chubby face light up with smiles and feeling a surge of warmth just looking at him. He was so much like his father it was quite uncanny. People had been right when they'd said that Tim would never be forgotten while his son was alive.

It was nearly two years since his death and hardly a day went by when she didn't see him in their son. But she could think of her husband without pain now. She tended to remember the good times they'd had when he'd been alive rather than the tragedy of his death.

Mercifully, the post-natal horror that had driven her to the brink of insanity was over, apart from the occasional bad day. Now that the baby stage was behind them and she could communicate with Timmy, she was much more relaxed, albeit still turning to Vince when she felt panicky. It was wonderful not to wake up to terror and blackness every morning, but to pleasurable anticipation of the day. At nearly two Timmy was great fun, running around and chattering, his vocabulary increasing practically by the hour.

The only negative aspect of her new independent life with Timmy in their own home was not having Vince close at hand as she had when she'd been staying at Ruth's. She missed Ruth's company, of course, but not to the same extent as she missed Vince, and not only as a means of reassurance either. He was a dry old stick and he'd made her laugh. She'd felt almost happy when she was with him.

Pushing the swing, she knew that she wanted more than just a few minutes' chat with Vince in the dispensary or a quick cup of coffee in Ruth's flat. She wanted to spend proper leisure time with him, to invite him round to her place for supper and Sunday lunch every so often, in the way that friends did.

'Friends' being the operative word and the root of her problem. She had never been sexually attracted to Vince and didn't want that sort of a relationship. But she had grown to like and respect him very much. Something about the capable way he conducted himself, the sure way he had of helping and advising people, stirred something deep inside of her which made her enjoy being with him and want to develop their friendship further. But it wasn't a physical thing and she didn't want to give him the wrong idea.

'Vinth,' muttered Timmy as she lifted him off the swing. 'See Vinth.'

'Yes, we'll go and see Vince now,' she said, strapping him into the buggy. 'We'll pop along to the shop and see Ruth and Vince.'

'Vinth . . . Roose,' he chanted happily.

As she walked through the streets towards Shepherd's Bush, the sun came out from behind a cloud, illuminating everything and making her aware of the uplifting presence of spring. Clusters of daffodils shook their yellow heads in numerous front gardens, clean washing billowed and flapped in the breeze at the back, and people had shed their winter clothes. Mini-skirts, which were supposed to have died the death, were out in force in much larger numbers than the calf-length midi which was so ageing to most women.

Kitty dressed for comfort these days, usually in jeans and a shirt or sweater. Quite a contrast to the sophisticated suits she used to wear for work and the glamorous evening clothes she'd once had so many opportunities to show off. How long ago all of that seemed now.

Her thoughts drifted back to Vince. She decided that the best thing she could do was to be open and honest with him, tell him how important their friendship was to her and how she'd like to socialise with him sometimes in the way that real friends did. She'd invite him to the house for a meal on Saturday evening so that they could talk the whole thing over. Vince was a very understanding bloke – he'd know exactly what she meant and probably want the same thing himself.

Kitty found herself hurrying as she got nearer to the shop, her spirits lifting at the idea of having him over to the house on Saturday.

Preparing the meal on Saturday evening, Kitty felt young and frivolous again, as though she had a proper date, which was quite ridiculous since she was only seeing Vince. It was so long since she'd done anything other than watch television in the evening. Hers was strictly a daytime existence now. She occasionally had people in for lunch but she hadn't done anything to get dressed up for in the evening since before Tim died.

Tim . . . Just when she thought she was over him, a stab of pain caught her unawares and told her otherwise. She doubted if she ever would get over him and wasn't sure she wanted to. But she guessed the reason for her current lighthearted mood had something to do with the fact that preparing to entertain was reminiscent of a time when she'd felt like an attractive woman rather than just a mother, and had enjoyed her femininity. If nothing else, having someone to dinner was a reason to make an effort with her appearance.

She'd prepared the meal as far as she could during the afternoon and got Timmy bathed and ready for bed early. She'd intended to keep him up to see Vince but he'd fallen asleep on the sofa so she'd taken him upstairs to bed.

Humming the tune of Elvis's latest big hit, 'Suspicious Minds', she prepared the melon and put it in the fridge, prodded the spicy chicken dish in the oven and made sure the vegetables were ready for cooking later, checked the wine, put the last-minute touches to the dining table and hurried upstairs to get ready. It was fun to take special care with the way she looked, she thought, slipping into a pale lemon trouser suit.

When Vince arrived, armed with wine and flowers, Kitty was flushed and quite unaware of how stunning she looked, her hair worn short and simple, her eyes glowing.

'You look lovely,' he said.

'Thank you. You look nice too,' she replied, casting an approving eye over his crisp white shirt and smart jacket, chin freshly shaved, hair neatly combed into place.

They chatted non-stop over the meal. He poured the wine and the mood was happy and relaxed in the candlelit dining room. Timmy woke up once and they went to him together. A few gentle words soon lulled him back to sleep.

Vince was very complimentary about the meal.

'I'm glad you enjoyed it,' said Kitty graciously. 'It wasn't anything too fancy . . . I didn't want to get too ambitious. I'm out of the habit of entertaining. In fact, you're my first dinner guest since Tim died.'

'I'm flattered,' he said, smiling warmly at her. He felt very happy.

Clearing the table was a joint effort but they left the dishes until later. Kitty made coffee which they took into the lounge, a tasteful room furnished in various shades of green with pale pink walls and a redbrick fireplace with little nooks and shelves containing books and ornaments.

'I'm really enjoying myself, Vince,' she said, as they settled into armchairs to either side of the hearth, a vase of spring flowers filling it on this mild spring evening while the chill was taken off the house by the central heating.

'Me too,' he said softly.

'I've missed having you around since I moved out of Ruth's.'

'I've missed you too.'

'It isn't quite the same now that I have to go out to see you.'

'Isn't it?'

'No. I feel as though I have to have a genuine excuse to come and clutter up the dispensary now,' she continued. 'And you're always so busy there we can't talk properly.'

'I've always managed to deal with your problems, though,' he said. 'And you could never clutter up the dispensary... only enhance it.'

'Yes, well, I don't have so many problems now, do I?'

'No, you don't,' he said. 'It's great to see you looking so well.'

'Anyway, Vince,' said Kitty, wanting to get to the point of the evening, 'missing you as I have has made me think that it might be rather nice if we could go on seeing each other.'

'Oh, Kitty,' he breathed, his voice trembling slightly.

'I thought we might get together like this on a regular basis,' she said. 'You know... have a proper friendship.'

He didn't reply at once, but narrowed his eyes enquiringly. 'A friendship?'

'That's right.'

'What do you mean exactly?' he asked in a cautious manner.

'Well . . . just for us to see each other sometimes,' she said. 'Spend some evenings together, you know . . . be like proper mates.'

'Mates?'

'Yes. I want us to see something of each other,' she tried to explain. 'I don't want our friendship to end now that I'm better and don't need to rely on you any more.'

His eyes were dark with pain.

'I don't want to be your *friend*, Kitty,' he said grimly. 'Surely you must realise that?'

'But, why, Vince . . .'

'I don't want to be your friend because I do want to be your lover, your husband, your other half . . . anything except your friend. Don't you know that I'm in love with you? Have you become so immersed in your own feelings you've stopped noticing other people's altogether?'

Kitty turned pale. Ruth's warning came into her mind and she felt terrible. How could she have been so thoughtless?

'Oh, Vince,' she said, eyes cast down with shame.

'You're an intelligent woman . . . you must have had an inkling . . .'

'I knew you had a bit of a thing about me when we were at school but that was years ago,' she said. 'I thought it was over long ago.'

'It was,' he said, so hurt and disappointed his voice was clipped and breathless. 'I haven't been mooning about for nearly twenty years, hankering for a girl I once fancied at school. I'm not that stupid.'

'But . . .'

'But I've fallen in love with you all over again this last two years,' he interrupted. 'And now I wish to God I hadn't. I certainly wouldn't choose to love a woman who sees me only as a shoulder to cry on. Unfortunately none of us has a choice when it comes to falling in love.'

'You've never said anything to me about it, all this time we've been friendly...'

'Because I knew romance wasn't what you wanted from me,' he explained. 'But when you needed me so much and we got on so well together, I began to hope for something more. But I knew that any initiative in that direction had to come from you, I wasn't going to embarrass you by saying anything. When nothing happened and you got better and moved out of Ruth's, I accepted it wasn't to be. I've always known you didn't fancy me anyway. Then you invited me to dinner . . . and, well, I'm only human, I couldn't help hoping.'

'I'm so sorry, Vince,' she said, through dry lips, her heart like lead. 'I should have realised what I was doing to you in the first place. But I was sick when I turned to you for comfort. I was in a world of my own. I couldn't see outside my own problems.'

'But you're not sick now, are you?' he said bitterly. 'People can't be expected to make allowances for ever.'

'I never meant to take advantage of your good nature,' she said, realising just how much she had taken him for granted. 'I suppose I was desperate. And you did seem to enjoy helping me.'

'I did, I did,' he said, eyes full of anguish. 'And I'll always be there for you if you are in trouble and need me. But *please, please* don't ask more than that of me because I just can't give it to you. I can't take intimate dinners with wine and candlelight. Don't you know what that does to me, feeling how I do about you and knowing that you'll never care for me in the same way?'

Kitty stared at him with guilt-ridden eyes.

'When you opened the door to me tonight and I saw you looking so lovely, having taken the trouble to look good, *for me, or so I thought* . . . Naturally I assumed . . . what man wouldn't?'

'You thought I'd invited you because I wanted more from you than friendship.'

'Of course I did,' he said sharply. 'Who wouldn't have?'

'Oh, Vince I'm so sorry.' Kitty was full of remorse. 'I've been out of circulation for so long, I've forgotten the rules.'

'I'd better go . . .'

'There's no need.'

He gave a humourless laugh. 'Oh, yeah, I'm sure to want to stay, having made a complete fool of myself,' he said grimly.

'I'm the one who's made a fool of myself, not you,' Kitty told him. 'I've been a complete and utter dimwit.'

'Please don't humiliate me even more by being kind,' he said grimly.

'There's no reason for you to feel humiliated,' she said sadly. 'I'm very flattered to have you love me. I only wish I could feel the same.'

'Like I said just now, we don't have a choice about that sort of thing,' he said. 'If it isn't there, it can't be forced.'

'More's the pity,' said Kitty, hating herself for causing him such pain.

'I'd like to go now, if you don't mind doing the dishes?' he said.

'Of course not.'

At the front door, Kitty said, 'There is one thing I would like to say before you go, Vince.'

'Fire away.'

'I'm very grateful for everything you did for me when I wasn't well,' she said gravely. 'Without you I don't think I'd have got better.'

'Nonsense . . . it was just a question of time,' he said.

'No.'

'You'd have come through it whether I'd been around or not, once Timmy grew out of the baby stage.'

'That's something we'll never know, isn't it?'

'Maybe not.'

'But I do know how I felt when I was in that hell, and I know how much better it was for me having you to turn to.' Tears burned under her lids. 'I thank you for that with all my heart.'

She brushed his cheek with her lips and watched him walk down the path to his car with a feeling of profound sadness because she knew she had lost a very dear friend.

One evening a week later Ruth telephoned Kitty.

'Is everything all right?' she asked.

'Of course, why shouldn't it be?' Kitty was rather too quick to say.

'We haven't seen you all week,' said Ruth. 'You've not been near the shop. I thought perhaps either you or Timmy was sick.'

'We're fine,' she said. 'I've been a bit busy just lately.'

'Too busy to call in and see us?' said Ruth. 'That isn't like you.'

'Well, I . . .' Her voice tailed off and Ruth sensed something was wrong.

'I've missed seeing you . . . and Timmy.'

'I haven't been around your way this week.'

'You sound odd, Kit, what's the matter?'

There was a silence. Then Kitty said, 'Oh, Ruth. I've been really stupid.'

'I'll pop over and you can tell me all about it,' said Ruth.

'So you're keeping away from the shop because of Vince?' said Ruth, having heard the whole story over a cup of coffee at Kitty's kitchen table.

'That's right,' she confessed. 'It seems the most sensible thing.'

'He hasn't said a word.'

'He's probably feeling too rotten about it to want to say anything.'

'It's a pity it's turned out like this for the two of you.'

'Yes.'

'I suspected something like this might happen, though,' said Ruth. 'I guessed Vince was in love with you even though you were so sure I was imagining things.'

'I know you did. Perhaps I guessed, too, in my heart, but I didn't want to admit it because it complicated everything and I was enjoying being his friend.'

'Could be.'

'Anyway, I think I'd better keep away from him altogether, for the time being,' was Kitty's opinion.

'I think that's best.'

'So you and I will have to meet outside your working hours.'

'I'll come round here to see you, don't worry about that,' said Ruth. 'Best you keep away from the shop, at least until the dust has settled. You can always get back to normal later on.'

'Things will never be the same as they were between Vince and me now that his true feelings are out in the open,' lamented Kitty.

'Not even when all this has faded into the past?'

'No. I would always feel as though I was hurting him just by being there and not being able to return his feelings.'

'Inviting him to dinner was a definite mistake,' said Ruth.

'Yes, it was,' admitted Kitty.

'Poor old Vince seems destined to remain a bachelor and he's got all the qualities to make a wonderful husband. If Larry had been half the man Vince is, I would have been saved a whole lot of heartache.'

'I miss seeing him,' said Kitty. 'He was really good for me.'

'Sex usually gets in the way in the end, doesn't it?' said Ruth.

'Seems like it,' agreed Kitty gloomily. 'I really did think Vince was the exception, which was very naive of me.'

'Not necessarily,' said Ruth. 'It is possible for a woman to have a platonic relationship with a man.'

'You reckon?'

'Yes. Vince and me for example . . .' said Ruth.

'I'd not thought of that.'

'But the sexual element very often messes things up, I should imagine.'

'It certainly ruined my friendship with Vince,' agreed Kitty.

'Mmm.'

'And the silly thing is, I feel so lost without him in my life.'

Ruth gave her a sharp look.

'Are you sure you aren't just the tiniest bit in love with him?'

Kitty shook her head.

'I only wish I was,' she said sadly. 'That would solve everything.'

'Yes, it would,' Ruth agreed thoughtfully.

They fell silent, drinking coffee and eating biscuits.

'Talking of men,' said Ruth, looking at Kitty with a smile in her eyes.

'Ye-es?' queried Kitty.

'I'm going out on a date myself on Saturday night.'

'Good God!'

'There's no need to sound quite so surprised,' said Ruth. 'I can still manage to inspire the odd wolf whistle.'

'I know that, you fool,' she said. 'It's just that, well . . . since Larry, you haven't seemed interested in men.'

'I've no intention of jumping into bed with this one either,' she said lightly, though her heart ached as she thought of Paul, who was out of reach for her. 'But a spot of male company might be fun.'

'Who is he?'

'His name is Bob Bridgeman. He's recently moved into the parade. Pops into the shop for a chat every so often. He called round to the flat the other night to ask me if I knew anything about the Chamber of Commerce because he's thinking of joining. We got chatting and he ended up inviting me out. I think the Chamber of Commerce was just an excuse to call, though, because he'd done his homework about me. He knew I was divorced and I hadn't told him. I was quite flattered actually, that he was interested enough to bother.'

'So what's he like?'

'Quite ordinary, fortyish . . . he's a widower.'

'Sounds promising.'

'He's okay.'

'I can't wait to hear how you get on.'

'It's been so long since I've been out on a date, I've forgotten what do do.'

'You'll soon get the hang of it again,' Kitty reassured her.

'I'll probably be so nervous, I'll talk too much and he'll think I'm deranged.'

'Stop putting yourself down,' admonished Kitty. 'You'll be your usual charming self and he'll be smitten.'

'I haven't had as much experience with men as you have,' Ruth reminded her lightly. 'Don't forget that my prime dating years were taken up with motherhood.'

'So they were.' Kitty dunked a biscuit in her coffee. 'Where's he taking you?'

'Oh, just out for a drink somewhere,' said Ruth. 'It's all dead casual.'

'I hope you have a good time, anyway.'

'Thanks. I'll let you know how I get on.'

Although Ruth had made light of it, she actually wished she hadn't agreed to go. Chatting to Bob Bridgeman for half an hour or so was one thing, spending a whole evening with him quite another. She didn't feel like making the effort to get to know a new man when the only man she wanted was Paul. Oh, dear, what had she let herself in for?

Chapter Eighteen

'This is really good,' enthused Ruth on Saturday evening as she and Bob Bridgeman tucked into home-cooked ham and salad with chunks of fresh bread and butter, whilst cosily ensconced at a window table in a Thameside pub near Kew.

'Not bad, is it?' he agreed. 'Just right if you don't want a full-scale meal.'

'I didn't think I was hungry until I started on this,' she said. 'I had something to eat before I came out.'

'That was a long time ago,' he reminded her. 'Another half hour or so and it'll be closing time.'

'Is it really as late as that?' she remarked, glancing at her watch. 'The evening has absolutely flown by.'

'Time flies when you're enjoying yourself, so they say.'

'That's certainly true in this case.'

'For me too.'

Ruth was amazed to be having such a good time. She'd felt at ease with Bob as soon as she'd got into his silver-grey Ford Capri outside the shop. He'd swept her along with lighthearted conversation, eliminating any possibility of self-consciousness between them.

During the course of the evening, she had learned that he was originally from Hackney, one of seven children and the son of a dockworker. He'd established himself as a jobbing builder and decorator in the early 1950s when there had been a big demand for property renovation. He had no children of his own, apparently, but 'a positive army' of nephews and nieces in East London whose collective birthdays cost him a fortune, albeit gladly spent.

'Next time perhaps we'll go to a restaurant,' he suggested lightly. 'I didn't want to arrange anything too formal for our first time out together . . . before we'd broken the ice.'

Ruth looked up sharply. 'You're assuming there will be a next time then?'

He pulled a face. 'Sorry. I'm taking too much for granted,' he apologised. 'I just thought that as we seem to get on quite well together, we might want to go out again sometime, that's all. But if you'd rather not . . .'

'I didn't say that.'

'Am I moving in on someone else's territory, perhaps?' he asked.

'Not at all,' she assured him. 'I'd like to go out with you again, actually.'

'Good.'

'It's just that I'm not looking for anything too heavy, Bob,' she explained, instinctively feeling the need to hold back. 'I've been through a very painful divorce and it left me wary of serious relationships.'

He sipped his drink, observing her thoughtfully over the rim of his glass.

'I wasn't thinking of rushing you up the aisle or moving in with you,' he replied evenly. 'A night out was all I had in mind.'

'Oh.' She felt very stupid. 'So I'm the one who's being presumptuous?'

'I think we're about even on that one,' he said with a half smile.

Ruth managed a wry grin.

'The way I see it,' he said, putting his beer down on the table and addressing her with a serious look on his face, 'I'm on my own, you're on your own. We can both do with a spot of company now and again. Right?'

'Definitely.'

'So let's do each other a favour but keep it casual. Go

out together now and then and see how it goes from there,' he suggested. 'No strings on either side . . . for the time being.'

'That's fine by me,' she said, delighted with such an uncomplicated arrangement. Now that that was settled, she could have stayed here all night, enjoying his conversation and absorbing the warm, cosy atmosphere of the pub in the full flow of a Saturday night. It was so crowded in the bar, some of the clientele had spilled out on to the tow-path on this mild spring evening. Ruth could see them in the light from the window, a vociferous gathering, laughing and joking against the dark, misty backdrop of the river. 'I must say, I'm having a smashing time tonight. It's so good to get out of the flat of an evening for a change.'

'I expect your daughter has a busy social life of her own, doesn't she?' he suggested. 'Teenagers usually do.'

'Normally she does but she's swotting hard for exams at the moment so she's not going out quite so much as usual.'

'How old is she?'

'Just eighteen.'

'She seems nice.'

'She's lovely but there's no living with her at present,' Ruth explained with a grin. 'It's vital that she achieves certain grades to be able to accept her place as a medical student and she's terribly on edge about it.'

'Going into medicine, eh! She *is* doing well,' he said. 'You must be very proud of her?'

'You bet I am. And I think my parents will probably explode with pride once her place is assured at medical school. In their wildest dreams they never imagined having a doctor in the family one day. When they were young it was unheard of for someone from the working classes to go away to university.'

'Things have changed a lot since the war in that respect.'

'Fortunately.'

'So Jenny will be leaving home soon then?' remarked Bob.

'In the autumn.'

'You'll miss her?'

'Not half.'

'Don't worry, I shall make it my business to see to it that you don't get too lonely,' he casually informed her.

Looking at him with a woman's eye, she saw a moderately attractive man, squeaky clean and well turned out in a blazer and tailored grey slacks. She thought something might possibly develop between them – given time.

'It's still quite a long way ahead.' She met his eyes candidly. 'Let's do as you say and see how it goes.'

'Yeah, sure,' he agreed.

Through the window she saw the lights go on in a houseboat moored nearby, making the vessel instantly come to life. It seemed in tune with her own feelings at this moment. She was imbued with a sense of inner warmth and well-being. She hadn't felt this carefree in a very long time. And it wasn't all due to the gin and tonic either!

Kitty awoke one summer morning to the sound of birds singing and sunshine pouring in through a gap in the curtains, a slice of pale light striking the wall and ceiling. A look at the bedside clock told her it was seven-thirty. Seven-thirty and the house was still silent which meant she'd beaten Timmy to it this morning for a change.

With wakefulness came a feeling of gloom: not the biological blackness of her illness, more a feeling that something wasn't quite right in her life. She lay on her back watching the flickering shadows on the wall made by the trees outside, and was overcome with guilt because really she had nothing to feel miserable about. The post-natal horrors had gone, she'd come to terms with Tim's death and her little son was a constant source of joy to her. But all of this was spoiled by a vital missing element which she became more aware of with each day that passed.

Too restless to lie still, she slipped into her dressing gown and went downstairs where she made a pot of tea and sat at the kitchen table drinking it, deep in thought.

Finally, driven by instinct, she decided to do something she should have done a long time ago. She went to the telephone on the wall and dialled a number.

Kitty's hands trembled slightly as she prepared a light supper and her heart was racing as she went upstairs to get ready. She didn't dress up too much but greeted Vince in a crisp white shirt and jeans.

'Thanks for coming,' she said anxiously when she opened the door.

'That's okay.' He looked wary, his eyes resting on her suspiciously.

'Come on in and sit down,' she said, showing him into the lounge.

'Timmy asleep?' he asked, sitting down in an armchair near the glass doors that opened on to a small paved terrace. The last of the evening sunshine turned the balustrade a brilliant white and enriched the colours of the scarlet and pink potted geraniums.

'Yes,' she said.

'Ah . . . bless him.'

'Supper is ready, but would you like a drink before we eat?'

He looked at her, his brow deeply furrowed.

'No, thanks,' he replied.

'I'll go and see to the food,' she said, nervous about his reaction to what she had to say.

'Bugger the food,' he snapped. 'Just tell me why I'm here.'

Kitty looked at him uncertainly, then perched stiffly on the edge of a chair opposite him, biting her lip.

'Well, I'm not sure how to put it into words,' she began.

'That isn't like you,' he said. 'You're one of the most articulate women I know.'

'The fact is, Vince, I'm utterly miserable now that I don't see you.'

'You know where to find me,' he pointed out briskly. 'You can call into the shop any time you like. I'm always willing to help out with your problems. I told you that three months ago.'

'My problem is missing you,' she said, her eyes full of tenderness.

'Oh . . . oh, I see.' He sounded surprised and looked hard at her, remembering his last painful humiliation. 'I'm not sure I can help with that. I told you before . . .'

'Oh, Vince, please don't make it hard for me,' she urged him. The atmosphere was so tense, even the twittering of a bird in the garden set her nerves on edge.

He stood up and thrust his hands into his trouser pockets. She noticed how tall and clean-cut he looked in sports shirt and casual slacks.

'I'm not quite sure what you're trying to tell me, Kitty,' he confessed evenly. 'I got it *so* wrong last time.'

'All I know, Vince, is that I can't bear not to have you in my life,' she tried to explain. 'I thought I could get along without you but I can't, and I don't want to try any more.'

Staring at her, he waited to hear what else she had to say, his heart beating with excitement.

'Not seeing you has made me realise just how much you mean to me.'

'I can't believe I'm hearing this. Are you trying to say . . . ?'

'Yes.' She gave a helpless little shrug. 'A part of me will always belong to Tim,' she said, 'I'm not going to lie to you about that.'

He still didn't move – just stood where he was, waiting for her to continue.

'But Tim is dead . . .' she began, her voice tailing off.

'Yes, sadly.' Still he waited, wanting to be absolutely certain he wasn't misunderstanding before he responded.

'And I want you to be a part of my life – my life and Timmy's.'

'Someone to lean on,' he said, still not convinced of her motives.

'No . . . well, sometimes I expect I shall need your support,' she said. 'But I want to be there for you too, Vince.'

'This isn't just a whim?'

'No, not a whim.'

'But you told me you didn't feel that way about me,' he said, afraid to believe this wonderful news. 'We agreed it couldn't be forced.'

'I haven't forced anything. It was there all the time, inside me,' she told him. 'I was just too confused to see it.'

'But what made you . . . do you mean what I hope you mean?'

'If missing someone so much when they're not around that life feels empty, and wanting to make them happy, adds up to being in love, then that's what I feel for you,' she said, her voice wobbling.

'Oh, Kitty.'

'So if you can find it in your heart to give me another chance after the appalling way I've treated you, you'll make me the happiest woman alive.'

He smiled – that wide, lop-sided grin that had become so dear to her.

'Come here, you complicated, infuriating, tantalising and adorable woman,' he said, opening his arms to her. 'Come here.'

Kissing him felt so perfect – so right – she wondered

how it could have taken her so long to respond to his unwavering devotion.

Audrey Brooks was having a wonderful time. Her home was full of people – family, friends, relatives, neighbours. The table was laden with party food, pop music beat cheerfully from the record player, the furniture in the back room had been pushed aside for dancing and Audrey had had several gins.

There was nothing she liked better than a knees-up, and this one was in celebration of something really special. After all, it wasn't every day your granddaughter got the exam results she needed to study medicine.

'You enjoying yourself, Mum?' asked Ray, appearing at her side. With a drink in one hand and a cigarette in the other, she was smiling as she watched the guests dancing to a Beatles number.

'Not half.'

'She's done really well, hasn't she?' he said, looking across the room at Jenny who was talking to her father, who had been invited at her request.

Audrey nodded. 'I'll say she has. Ruth's done wonders, bringing her up on her own. Jenny's a real credit to her.'

'No doubt about that.' He swigged his beer while Audrey sipped her gin and tonic. He looked across at Ruth who was dancing with Bob. They were laughing, obviously happy and at ease with each other. 'What do you think of Bob Bridgeman?'

'He seems a decent enough chap to me,' replied Audrey.

'Yeah, I think he's okay, too,' said Ray. 'But are they a couple?'

'Seems like it,' said Audrey. 'She's been going out with him regular for a few months and they get on very well.'

'Do you think they'll get spliced?'

'I'm not sure about that,' said his mother, 'but I think it would be a very good thing if they did. It's time Ruth had someone by her side, 'specially as Jenny's gonna be away most of the time.'

'Mmm.'

'Trouble is, Ray, there's only one man Ruth really wants,' she said, looking across at Paul.

'Stoneway?'

'That's right.'

'Has she told you that?'

'She doesn't have to,' explained his mother. 'You only have to see them together when he comes to collect Jenny . . . or see her eyes light up when she mentions his name.'

Ray tutted. 'That's pointless as the geezer's married. He's a good bloke, but not for Ruth.'

'Exactly. I'm hoping she'll realise what a waste of time it is and grab her chance of happiness with Bob.'

Ray's twin and both their wives appeared by his side.

'Smashing party,' remarked Peggy to her mother-in-law.

'Thanks, love, I think people are enjoying themselves.'

'Three cheers for Jenny, I say . . . for providing us with an excuse for a party,' said Peggy.

'One thing's for certain, Peg,' grinned her twin sister Pat, 'we won't be celebrating her cousins getting into medical school.'

They all laughed because, although Tom and Gary were the sharpest, most streetwise of boys, they were about as scholarly as frogspawn.

'You never know, they might surprise us all,' smiled Audrey. She was very fond of her tearaway grandsons who got into just as much trouble as their fathers had at that age. 'They are only ten.'

'There would have to be a bloomin' miracle,' laughed Peggy. 'They'd never go to school at all if we weren't behind 'em with a whip . . . metaphorically speaking, of course.'

'That's a big word,' joshed Ray. 'You been watching BBC2 or something?'

'Some of us have more than a dozen words in our vocabulary,' she countered good-humouredly. 'And that's another big one for you.'

'Where are the little horrors, by the way?' interrupted Jack, scanning the room.

'That's a point,' said his wife. 'I haven't seen them for a while.'

'Which means they're up to some sort of mischief,' said Jack, going to look for them.

When the music ended, Ruth and Bob wandered over to Kitty and Vince.

'I haven't seen you two dancing much,' said Ruth lightly.

'We're waiting for a nice smoochy number,' laughed Vince, who had been like the proverbial Cheshire Cat ever since he and Kitty had become a couple. 'So that we can have a cuddle.'

'I remember a time when Kitty would have sooner died than sit a dance out,' said Ruth.

'You're going back a while, Ruth,' she said. 'I'm a bit past that sort of enthusiasm.'

'You poor old thing,' teased Bob.

'Your neighbour is baby-sitting for you tonight, then?' remarked Ruth.

Kitty nodded.

'At least you don't have to drive them home,' said Ruth.

'I know . . . it's really handy.'

Bob excused himself to go to the bathroom and Vince wandered over to Paul, leaving the two friends alone.

'It's lovely to see you and Vince so happy together, Kitty,' said Ruth.

'It feels right, Ruth, I can't believe it took me so long.'

'He's like a dog with two tails.'

'I know.'

'Who would ever have thought you two would get together?'

'Definitely not me,' said Kitty with emphasis. 'If I'd have speculated on any of the four of us pairing off, I'd have put my money on you and Paul, never Vince and me. It's funny how things work out.'

A shadow passed across Ruth's face. 'Yes, it certainly is.'

'Actually,' said Kitty with a sparkle in her eyes, 'Vince and I are planning on getting married early next year.'

'Oh, that's wonderful news! Congratulations,' said Ruth hugging her.

'No definite date yet,' she said. 'Just let's say it's on the cards.'

Ruth smiled in reply.

'What about you and Bob?' asked Kitty. 'You seem to be getting on well.'

'We are. He's great fun to be with and I like him a lot.'

'He certainly seems to have got his feet under the table with your family.'

'Bob's a good mixer, he gets on with everyone,' said Ruth.

'So is there a future for the two of you?' asked her friend.

'Who knows?' said Ruth. 'I'm just enjoying the present for now.' She looked thoughtful, cheeks flushed against her dark hair which she wore in a smart classic bob. 'I'd forgotten how good it feels to be part of a couple, to have someone to go out with and share things with.'

'Yes, I'm finding the same thing myself,' said Kitty.

Their conversation was interrupted by the return of Bob, frowning darkly.

'Would you believe it?' he said to Ruth. 'I just caught those nephews of yours smoking.'

'I'd believe anything of that pair of devils,' she said. 'If there's any mischief to get into, they'll find it.'

'I went out into the back garden to get a breath of air,' he explained, 'and there they were . . . puffing away like a couple of old chimneys.'

'Experimenting.'

'They'd pinched the fags from their dads' packets apparently.'

'I hope you read them the riot act?' she said seriously.

'You bet I did. I don't think they'll do it again in a hurry.'

'You scared the life out of them, did you?' said Ruth.

'It had more to do with the fact that Jack appeared while I was in full flow,' he explained. 'Both lads were a delicate shade of green by then anyway, and serve 'em right.' He grinned and sighed. 'We've all been there.'

'These days you have to worry about youngsters experimenting with more than just ordinary cigarettes,' remarked Ruth.

'Leave it out. I don't think things are so bad that ten year olds are in danger from pot,' he said lightly. 'Even a pair of dedicated rebels like them couldn't get hold of that.'

'I meant older children.'

'Yes, drugs are an increasing problem,' he agreed. 'There's no doubt about that.'

The conversation was interrupted by a call for silence from Ruth's father who had turned off the music and was standing in the centre of the room with Audrey at his side.

'I'd like you all to raise your glasses to Jenny who is such a credit to the Brooks family,' he said in a serious voice.

There was a roar of agreement and all eyes turned to the guest of honour who was standing by the record player looking slim and lovely in a sage-green mini-dress, her straight blonde hair falling to her shoulders, her naturally pale colouring brightened by flushed cheeks.

'You'll make me big-headed, Granddad,' she said with a smile.

'I never thought a member of our family would rise to such heights,' he continued undeterred. 'She's a clever girl.'

A cheer went up.

'She's worked very hard and I think I can speak for us all when I say we're proud of her and wish her all the luck in her chosen field. To Jenny . . .'

As she raised her glass, Ruth was caught in a blast of emotion. A powerful tide of maternal love and pride swept through her, catching in her throat and stinging her eyes with tears, her profound joy tinged with sadness as she recognised the fact that she and Jenny had reached the end of an era. Swallowing hard, she caught her daughter's eye across the room and smiled.

She recalled once being asked by Kitty if she felt bitter about having her youth destroyed by motherhood. She'd told Kitty she couldn't regret having been given such a precious gift. That was still as true today as she and Jenny faced a parting of the ways.

They had had their differences like any other mother and daughter but they were about as close as it was possible to be. Now their life together in its present form was drawing to a close.

Jenny would soon be setting off on her own and Ruth had to let go of her little girl and respect her as a woman with opinions of her own. She must allow her to live her own life and make her own mistakes, however hard that was, and hope that the values she had instilled in her remained constant and helped her as she found her way in the world. Ruth realised the importance of letting Jenny know that she would always be there for her no matter how adult and independent she became. Ruth also knew that she herself must make a life of her own so that Jenny could feel free to enjoy hers with an easy conscience.

But now Ruth was recalled to the present by the fact that her daughter had joined her grandparents in the centre of the room, and was about to make a speech.

'Thank you, Gran and Granddad, for having this super party for me, and thanks everyone for coming,' she said in her high-pitched youthful voice.

Everyone cheered.

She looked across at Ruth.

'I'd also like to thank my mother for all the support and encouragement she has given me over the years, helping me to achieve my goal.'

Another burst of applause.

'My arrival meant that Mum wasn't able to go to university herself,' she continued, flicking back her curtains of hair. 'Though, from what I've heard, she was more than capable.' She cleared her throat. 'Anyway, I hope I can repay her for all she's done for me by getting qualified.' She made a face. 'I'm only too well aware that this is just the beginning. I've a good few years of hard work and study ahead of me before I actually qualify.' She gave a wicked grin. 'I hope to have some fun, too, along the way.'

There was a burst of laughter.

'Seriously, though, I'll really try to prove myself worthy of your celebrations tonight.' She looked across at her mother and there was an electric silence as mother and daughter were drawn together in a moment of unity which was felt throughout the room. 'Thanks, Mum. You're the best.'

As the cheers rose, Ruth's heart was so full she stumbled from the room in a blur of tears.

Paul found Ruth at the bottom of the garden, crying silently.

'I'm being ridiculous, I know,' she said as he handed her his handkerchief in the dim light. 'But I feel so damned emotional.'

336

'You're not the only one,' he said gently. 'I had a lump in my throat when Jenny was giving her speech.'

''Cos you're so proud of her?'

''Cos I'm so proud of you both,' he said. 'You've done a wonderful job.'

'You've done what you can this last few years, too,' she said.

'But you've brought her up.'

Ruth didn't deny it. 'I'm glad you came tonight, Paul,' she said, 'It meant a lot to Jenny.'

'I wouldn't have missed it for the world.'

'Leila didn't come, though,' she said, knowing her mother had invited his wife too, out of courtesy.

'She said she'd rather not,' he explained. 'Probably thought she'd feel a bit out of it. After all, Jenny is nothing to her.'

'That's true.'

'Feeling better now?' he asked.

'Yes, I'm fine now,' she said, sounding more composed. 'We'd better go back inside. Someone will come out looking for us in a minute.'

Sure enough, voices rose from the house.

'Mum, are you all right?' called Jenny.

'Ruth, what are you doing down there?' came her mother's enquiring tones.

'We're coming back in now,' replied Ruth. She was glad to have had a few moments alone with Paul. It seemed right they should share such an emotional highpoint. They were Jenny's parents, after all.

Chapter Nineteen

Paul Stoneway found his wife in a very good mood when he got home from the office one evening in the autumn.

'Your dinner's in the oven,' Leila cheerfully informed him, 'I'm not sure what time I'll be home. Some of us might go for a drink or a coffee after class.'

At his enquiring look she explained: 'My yoga class, remember . . . it starts again after the summer break tonight. I did tell you.'

'You did too,' he said, remembering. 'It slipped my mind.'

There was nothing unusual about that, he thought, for he and Leila grew ever more distant with each day that passed and were both extremely vague about each other's arrangements. Oddly enough, though, the more separate their lives became, the better they seemed to get along.

Leila had changed, very much for the better in his opinion. There was a sparkle about her lately; she seemed to have acquired a new zest for life. She was certainly easier to live with now that she had her own outside interests.

No one had been more surprised than Paul when she'd gone out and made friends of her own. It had all started because of a book she'd read early in the year – a self-improvement publication about yoga. Instantly enthused by the subject, she'd practised with the book at home for a while but had soon begun to look for a class locally.

Having tried to persuade her to take up a hobby for years, he'd been amazed when she'd suddenly joined an evening class of her own volition. He could only assume that her interest in the subject had been strong enough to galvanise her into action. Other outings had followed: theatre and cinema trips with friends she'd made at the class, discussion groups about self-awareness, coffee mornings . . .

Paul was delighted to see her taking an active part in things after so many years in the shadows. The fact that her new lease of life had nothing to do with him didn't inspire him to jealousy. Why would it when the quality of his life had improved along with hers now that she no longer relied solely on him for companionship?

She even looked different, he thought now, noticing the sage-green track suit, the trendy sports shoes, her lustrous red hair worn short and casual, eyes shining with vitality.

'So don't wait up for me,' she said, giving him a dutiful peck on the cheek.

'Okay,' he said, anticipating the evening alone with pleasure, such was the emptiness of their relationship. 'Have a good time.'

'I'll do my best,' she said, and left the house smiling.

He was smiling too, pleased to see her so happy. A few moments later, however, as he glanced out of the window to see her drive away, he was unexpectedly touched by sorrow – for something that he and Leila had never had.

Leila drove to the school tingling with excitement. It was so good to be back at class. She'd been lost without it during the summer. Fortunately, some of her classmates had felt the same and they'd been out together some evenings, for a meal and a chat. It was hellish to have organised activities stop when you'd got used to regular female company.

Now she felt revitalised, imbued with the energy that

autumn always inspires – the smoky hint of mist, the chill in the air, dusk already gathering. It was wonderful to go out without Paul, to have friends of her own. It kept her sane in an otherwise empty marriage.

Her face creased into a frown. Poor Paul. How hurt he would be if he knew what really went on in her mind on the rare occasions when they made love, and what an accomplished actress she had become. Fortunately sex wasn't a problem these days. Paul didn't seem interested and she certainly didn't encourage him.

Parking the car outside the school, she made her way inside, among the throngs of people heading through the gates. The corridors smelled of paper and plimsolls, disinfectant and school dinners, and echoed with chatter and footsteps as people hurried to their different classrooms.

In the hall, the women of the yoga class were talking about summer holidays and catching up on news as they stripped down to their leotards. There were twenty or so in the group, ranging in age from about thirty to eighty.

Noticing a new face, Leila went over to introduce herself.

'Hi, I'm Leila,' she said, smiling at a tall, willowy woman who looked to be in her mid-thirties. 'You're new, aren't you?'

Nodding, she returned Leila's smile. 'Yes, I'm Marsha Brown.'

'Welcome to the class,' said Leila, her own sense of well-being filling her with generosity towards others.

'I thought I'd give it a try,' said Marsha, shedding her track suit to reveal a dazzling pink leotard which looked stunning with her dark colouring. 'Yoga is supposed to improve the concentration as well as keep you in trim. Does it work?'

'It's done wonders for me.'

'That's encouraging,' said Marsha, who exuded style

of the unconventional sort, her long, straight black hair, enormous round eyes and dramatically bright lipstick giving her an exotic, bohemian look. 'I'm a businesswoman so I can do with something to help me unwind.'

'I'm sure you'll find it beneficial.'

'I hope so.'

The lesson got started and Leila closed her mind to everything else, concentrating on her deep breathing and the exercises which were carried out very slowly and smoothly.

At the end, a few of the regulars decided to go to the pub round the corner to finish the evening off. Leila asked Marsha if she'd like to join them. 'Unless there's someone waiting for you to go straight home?' she added, grinning.

'No, there's no one,' said Marsha. 'And, yes, I'd love to join you.'

In the pub, they gathered around a table, talking among themselves. Leila found herself making sure she was sitting next to Marsha. They each had a glass of white wine and exchanged a few personal details. Marsha was divorced, apparently.

'Do you have a job?' she enquired casually, leaning towards Leila who noticed the smooth texture of her skin. She was confident and imposing with a disconcerting gaze that both excited and frightened Leila because of the effect it had on her.

'No, I'm a kept woman, I'm afraid,' she said lightly. 'You're in business, you say?'

'Yes, I have a health food shop in Richmond,' Marsha explained.

'Sounds interesting,' said Leila. 'You mean, vegetarian food?'

She nodded. 'Yes, and various kinds of vitamins . . . everything you need for a healthy diet without meat.'

'I presume you're a vegetarian yourself?' remarked Leila.

'Naturally,' she said with emphasis. 'I haven't eaten meat in years.'

'You sell wholemeal flour and prunes?' said Leila with interest. 'That sort of thing?'

'Well, yes . . . but obviously there's a great deal more to it than that.'

'I should imagine there is,' said Leila, 'but I must admit to knowing very little about vegetarianism apart from understanding it's something hippies are into in a big way.'

Marsha gave a rich throaty laugh, throwing back her head and emphasising her long slender neck.

'So much for the public perception,' she said. 'In actual fact, my customers come from all walks of life.'

'Really?'

'Yes, really,' she confirmed. 'You must call in and see what we have to offer sometime, if you're ever in the area.'

'I'd love to,' said Leila casually. 'But my husband wouldn't be too pleased if I started serving nut cutlets for dinner.'

'Don't worry, I promise not to try to convert you.'

'I doubt if you could,' said Leila lightly, 'I'm a very conventional sort of a person.'

'A meatless diet doesn't make you a crank, you know.'

'I wasn't suggesting that it did.'

'I know you weren't, but a lot of people think that's what vegetarians are.'

'Yes, I know.'

'The day will come when it won't be considered odd because so many people will be doing it,' said Marsha with conviction. 'More and more people are coming over to our way of eating. I know that from the increase in our turnover.'

'Do you run the shop on your own or do you have a partner?'

'It's my shop but I do have some staff,' Marsha explained.

'It must be very satisfying to be in business for yourself.'

'I enjoy it, and it gives me a reasonably good living, which is important as I'm on my own. It's only a small shop but you'd be surprised how much business goes through our till . . . and it's growing all the time.'

'Some of the big pop stars are vegetarians, aren't they?' said Leila, searching her mind for a crumb of knowledge that would allow her to make an intelligent contribution to the conversation.

Marsha nodded and drank her wine.

'Your turn now . . . let's hear something about you,' she invited after a while.

'There isn't much to tell really,' said Leila. 'I lived in Australia for a while. I'm married. As I said, I don't have a job.'

'Children?'

'No. There's just Paul and myself. How about you?'

'No. No kids.'

'Been divorced long?' asked Leila, surprised at the strength of her own interest.

'Six years.'

'It must have been a painful thing to have to go through?'

'Yes. But not nearly so painful as living a lie.'

The remark registered like a thunderclap with Leila because it was something she did every day of her life. She found herself wanting to bare her soul to Marsha but just said, 'Were you both pretending everything was all right?'

'Yes, sort of muddling along, day after day, hoping it would get better but knowing it never would,' she said. 'The fault lay with me, not my husband. I should never have married him. It could never have worked. He deserved better.'

It sounded intriguing and Leila wanted to know more but she just said, 'But you're both over it now?'

'Oh, yes. He's remarried and happy, so far as I know.'

'Will you get married again, do you think?' asked Leila chattily.

Marsha gave her an odd look, as though she had suggested the unthinkable. 'Well, no . . .'

'Oh.'

'I have . . . er . . . friends, from time to time,' she said. 'But not marriage. Never again.'

The conversation was interrupted by the group beginning to disperse. Leila and Marsha got up and left with the others.

'Will you be coming to class next week?' Leila asked outside, rummaging in her bag for her car keys.

'Will you be there?'

'Oh, yes, I come every week.'

'In that case I'll definitely be there,' said Marsha, putting her hand on Leila's arm in a friendly gesture and letting it linger for just a moment longer than necessary.

'I'll see you next week then,' replied Leila, still breathless from her touch.

'I hope she'll be all right,' Ruth said to Paul one autumn Sunday as they began the long drive back to London from Manchester in Paul's Volvo Estate, having installed Jenny in her college room with all her luggage.

'She'll be more than all right . . . she'll have a whale of a time,' he said reassuringly. 'Medical students are known for it.'

'Yes, so I've heard,' said Ruth. 'They play hard to relieve the stress of working so close to sickness and death, I suppose.'

'Exactly.'

'I feel quite bereft,' confessed Ruth. 'As though I've lost a limb.'

'I can imagine,' he said. 'I'll miss her too, but obviously it's more of a wrench for you, as you live together.'

'Still, I've got Bob to stop me moping about. He said he's gonna keep me so busy I won't even notice she's gone.'

'Good for him,' said Paul, seething with jealousy and knowing he was being unreasonable.

'Jenny's leaving home is a natural progression,' remarked Ruth as they left the city and headed on to the open road, 'and I know I have to get used to it. But we've always been so close. I suppose because there was just the two of us for so long.'

'Mmm.' He cleared his throat and changed the subject. 'It's getting serious between you and this Bob Bridgeman then, is it?'

'He does seem keen, I must admit.'

'And you?'

'I like him . . . he's a nice bloke, and very good company.'

'Do you like him enough to marry him?'

'Hey, hang on,' she said in joking admonition. 'There's been no mention of marriage.'

'He might soon start to think along those lines, though.'

'Yes, he very well might.'

'And if he does . . .'

'I shall give it careful consideration,' Ruth told him.

'You're probably a bit wary after the experience of your first marriage,' Paul suggested.

'It has left its mark, of course. But Bob is a different kettle of fish altogether. Larry swept me off my feet at a time when I was hungry for love and romance. Bob and I are good mates as much as anything. We have lots of laughs and I trust him completely.'

'Sounds as though you will marry then, if he asks you?' persisted Paul.

'I might do,' she told him. 'But why the sudden interest?'

'I just want to know that you're going to be okay,' he said.

How could he tell her that he hated the idea of her marrying anyone else when he was in no position to marry her himself? How could he tell her that he was in love with her and it didn't decrease with the passing of time? Ruth deserved some happiness and from what he'd heard of Bob Bridgeman, from both Ruth and Jenny, he seemed like the sort of bloke who would give her that.

'Oh, I'll be okay, Paul, don't you worry about me,' she said brightly. 'I'm an expert at being okay whatever fate has in store for me, because I'm a survivor.'

'I know that,' he said, 'but don't you want more from life than just to survive?'

'I'll settle for survival. Not many people get what they really want from life. Most people have to accept compromise at some time or another.'

'You think so?'

'I do. I mean, take Kitty for example. She had a marriage made in heaven, but not for ever . . .'

'But through Tim's death, Vince got what he's always wanted. It's an ill wind . . .'

'Yes, okay, I accept that. But it was a long time in coming for him, wasn't it?' said Ruth. 'I think he went through hell over the years.'

'Mm . . . I think you're probably right.'

Thinking back over these last few months, Ruth thought it was true to say that Bob had improved the quality of her life. He said she'd done the same for him. They were two lonely people who enjoyed each other's company, that was the essence of their relationship. She was not in love with him and didn't pretend to be but she would be a fool to refuse him if he did want to make things permanent between them. There was no point in spending the rest of her life alone just because she couldn't have Paul.

They were both subdued for the rest of the journey. Even when they stopped for tea, neither had much to say. When Paul drew up outside the shop, there was no avoiding the reason for their gloom.

'So I don't suppose you and I will be seeing each other again until Jenny comes home for the Christmas holidays?' said Ruth.

'There won't be a particular reason to see each other,' he said, staring ahead of him so that she couldn't see the sadness in his eyes. 'But I'll keep in touch.'

'Yes.'

'I'll want to know if you've heard from Jenny,' he said.

'Of course.'

Ruth was longing to tell Paul how she really felt about him. She wanted him to stay with her tonight. She was tired of doing the right thing. Just for once she wanted to please herself.

'I'll come and see you safely inside,' he said, opening his door.

'Thank you.'

The dog almost knocked them over with his exuberance on their way in.

'Calm down, boy,' said Ruth soothingly as he nuzzled her. She patted and stroked him before they all went upstairs to the flat which felt chilly from being empty all day.

'Ringo hasn't been cooped up here all day,' she explained unnecessarily to avoid putting into words what was really on her mind. 'Mum and Dad were going to come round to take him out. I wouldn't leave him here all day on his own.'

'I know that, Ruth.'

She shivered.

'Shall I put the fire on?' he offered.

'Please.'

He leaned down and switched it on.

'Have you time for a coffee?' she asked, as he stood up.

'Well . . . all right,' he said, his voice sounding hoarse. 'I'll go and make it then.'

But she didn't move. They both stood transfixed, looking at each other across the hearth, now emitting the orange glow of simulated coals. Suddenly she was in his arms.

'Oh, Ruth,' he whispered into her hair. 'There's never been anyone else but you for me. I've loved you for all these years.'

'Paul, I . . .'

There were no further words as they embraced. He drew back and looked into her face, the years fading away so that she was a sixteen-year-old girl again. He'd done wrong by her once – he wouldn't do it a second time.

'I must go . . . I won't have that coffee.'

'Stay, Paul, please,' she urged him, seizing the moment. 'I want you to stay so much. I need you tonight, I really need you.'

It was a struggle both mentally and physically. But somehow he managed to let go of her and move away.

'No, Ruth,' he replied softly, voice hoarse with emotion.

'I want you to stay . . . please.'

'As much as I want to stay, and believe me there's nothing I want more, we'll both regret it.'

'No, we won't.'

'You'll get hurt, Ruth,' he said. 'Stick with someone who's free to be with you legitimately and all the time.'

She didn't move or utter another word, just stayed where she was by the fire listening to his footsteps on the stairs. She was bitterly disappointed but pleased, too, that Paul had shown what he was really made of by doing the honourable thing.

It was better that things were left as they were, she knew that in her heart, however it felt now. Apart from the betrayal of Bob and Leila, Ruth knew she wasn't cut out to be any man's mistress.

* * *

Outside in the car Paul was feeling wretched in mind and body, emotionally and physically drained, and tortured by regret. Weighed against all of this, the fact that he had actually done the right thing gave him little comfort.

How he had managed to leave without succumbing to temptation was something of a mystery because he'd never considered himself to be any kind of saint in that direction. But he'd had to do it. He had to let Ruth go so that she could find happiness with Bob who was in a position to love her in an honest and proper way. She deserved better than an affair with a married man.

His thoughts turned to his own marriage. It wasn't a loving one but Leila didn't deserve to be ditched. He couldn't be that cruel. Even though he and his wife were growing increasingly distant, she would be lost without him, for practical reasons if nothing else for she depended on him heavily. It was only recently she'd had any friends of her own. So any idea of Ruth and him getting together wasn't even worth considering.

It was probably just as well they wouldn't be seeing each other until Jenny came home for Christmas, however bleak that prospect was. At least he couldn't be tempted into something he would later regret. He'd telephone her regularly, though, to make sure she was all right because that was something that mattered a great deal to him. Jenny's leaving home had been a real wrench for her mother.

When Paul felt calm enough to drive home, he started the engine. Something made him glance up at the lighted windows above the shop. Ruth was standing at the living-room window looking down. It was as much as he could do not to rush back and hammer at her door. But he just waved his hand in farewell and drove away with tears running down his cheeks.

Chapter Twenty

True to his word Bob spared no effort to fill the gap in Ruth's life left by Jenny, providing her with company and a social life without making her feel suffocated. He was a more down-to-earth type of man than Larry had been – more like her brothers and father, a working-class man's man who liked football, darts, and a pint at the local with his mates.

This made him easily accepted into the Brooks family, which created a happy background to their relationship. Ruth grew increasingly fond of him as their life fell into a comfortable routine.

On Saturday evenings they usually went out somewhere special, to a theatre, a film or restaurant. Sundays they always joined the family at Nutley Road. Sometimes during the week they had a companionable meal at home together after work, either at his place or hers. Theirs was an easy-going, undemanding relationship which Ruth valued. As well as taking the sting out of Jenny's absence, it helped her to come to terms with the fact that Paul was not for her.

Being kept so busy, it seemed no time at all until Jenny arrived home for the Christmas holidays with a huge appetite, a holdall full of dirty washing, a new air of confidence about her and a whole lot of student jargon. Ruth loved having her back and made a great fuss of her, but she knew this would never be her daughter's full-time home again.

'Are you trying to stock your system up for next term or something?' teased Ruth as her daughter munched

351

her way through the contents of the fridge and larder with gusto.

'Oh, if only that were possible,' Jenny said with a sigh. 'It's great to get some decent nosh again. The food at college is disgusting.'

'Being away has made you appreciate the comforts of home, then?' said her mother.

'I'll say.'

Jenny was full of stories about the new friends she'd made and how they stayed up into the small hours talking and drinking coffee. There were parties too, apparently, but she was understandably less forthcoming about these to her mother. The profits of the telephone company soared as she maintained new friendships long-distance. Ruth was forced to ask for a little restraint during shop hours in case business calls were being blocked. It was wonderful to have her youthful exuberance about the place again, though, and Ruth savoured every moment.

She was pleased to find that Jenny wasn't caught up in her new life to the exclusion of all else.

'You and Bob are still going strong, I notice,' she said breezily one day.

'Yes.'

'I'm pleased for you, Mum,' she said. 'Bob's a smashing bloke.'

'I'm glad you like him.'

Bob joined the family at Nutley Road on Christmas Day. It was the same as ever, noisy and crowded, with an abundance of food, drink and bonhomie. After an enormous lunch, with crackers and lively conversation, everyone was too replete to do more than lounge around. Tom and Gary managed to recruit enough players, albeit reluctantly, for a trial run with their new board game after tea. The evening's entertainment consisted of a cold supper, charades and some TV.

It was a happy day which was rounded off by Ruth

and Bob's announcing their engagement. It hadn't been the most passionate marriage proposal but it came straight from the heart . . .

Ruth and Bob had taken the dog for a walk after supper and were heading back across the Green, bleak and deserted on this cold and damp Christmas night, when he said, 'You've come to mean a lot to me, Ruth.'

'I'm glad about that, Bob,' she said, 'because the feeling's mutual.'

'It's been good for us both this last few months, hasn't it?'

'Yes, it's been lovely.'

He tucked her arm under his.

'I was wondering what you'd think about us getting married?'

Although she'd suspected this would happen eventually, she hadn't expected it at that precise moment and was lost for words.

'It seems the most logical thing to do,' he said, stopping and looking at her. 'I mean, we get on well, we spend all our spare time together, so why don't we share our lives?'

'I'd be honoured to marry you, Bob,' she said quickly, before she had time to change her mind.

He beamed. 'Oh, that's wonderful,' he said, hugging her. 'The sooner the better so far as I'm concerned.'

'Hang on, Bob,' she protested lightly, instinctively drawing back from that final commitment. 'I'd like to enjoy being engaged for a while.'

'Then that's what you shall do,' he said. 'As soon as the shops open again after the holiday we'll go up West and get you a ring.'

'Wonderful,' she said, reaching up to kiss him on the lips.

Kitty and Vince finally tied the knot early in February. It was a small church wedding with a reception at a hotel afterwards, attended by close relatives and friends, including the entire Brooks family.

It was one of those deceptive February days with bright sunshine and a punishing wind that cut right through to the bone. Kitty wore a thick winter suit in cream with royal blue accessories, Vince looked smart in a dark lounge suit and Timmy was cute in a little suit with flared trousers, though he wore a fur-lined coat over the top at the church.

Ruth was there with Bob, complete with diamond engagement ring.

'I hear congratulations are in order,' said Paul, shaking Bob's hand and kissing Ruth on the cheek when everybody had arrived at the reception and was having a sociable drink before sitting down to the meal. 'You should have made it a double wedding.'

'It's a bit too soon for us,' Ruth informed him. 'I expect we'll get married sometime in the summer.'

'Jenny couldn't make it today then?' remarked Paul.

'No, not in the middle of term,' she explained. 'It's a long trip from Manchester and she'd have had to stay overnight. She'd have missed some important lectures.'

As Ruth and Paul lapsed into talk about their daughter, Bob wandered off to mingle with the other guests.

'Leila's not with you today, then?' remarked Ruth casually.

'No, she couldn't make it.'

Ruth peered at him.

'Paul . . . are you all right?' she asked. 'You look a bit drawn.'

'I'm fine.'

She didn't believe him.

'Tell me to mind my own business if you like but you look as though you're in a bit of a state,' she said. 'Has something happened?'

Something had happened all right, but it wasn't anything he wanted to talk about.

Ruth was looking at him enquiringly.

'Paul . . . what's the matter?'

He sighed deeply. 'Oh, well, everyone will get to know sooner or later, so I suppose you might as well be the first.'

She waited.

'Leila's left me.'

'Oh, dear,' she said, feeling immediate empathy. 'When did this happen?'

'A couple of weeks ago.'

'Oh Paul, I'm so sorry. Is it permanent? Or can it be put right?'

'Oh, it's permanent all right,' he said grimly. 'She wants a divorce. She's already moved in with someone else.'

Shaking her head, Ruth's eyes were full of sadness as she remembered how devastated she'd been when Larry had done the same thing to her.

'I know how agonising it feels,' she said.

'I'll get over it,' Paul told her with typical male bravado.

'Was it completely unexpected or did you suspect she was seeing another man?'

'It isn't a man.'

'Not a man?' Ruth looked bewildered.

'No.'

'You mean . . .'

'Yes, it's a woman,' he confirmed grimly. 'She's always been that way inclined, apparently.'

'Oh, Paul.' Ruth's voice was full of compassion. 'I know that you're hurt but it must have been awful for her too, all these years.'

'All that time and I had no idea,' he confessed.

'I suppose she felt she had to keep it secret because of people's attitude towards that sort of thing, especially when you married back in the 1950s.'

'She didn't even admit it to herself, apparently.'

'Personally, I think it's a good job it's out in the open now, for both of you.'

'Talk about irony,' he said bitterly. He could hardly turn Ruth's life upside down by asking her not to marry Bob just because he himself had suddenly become free. It was too late for Ruth and him. She was happy and settled with Bob now. 'While you're about to embark upon marriage, mine has fallen apart. If that isn't the ultimate in bad timing, I don't know what is.'

Ruth didn't reply for fear she would say something that would ultimately lead to her letting Bob down. She couldn't do that to him.

One evening in April, Ruth telephoned Paul and asked him to come over and see her because she needed a favour from him.

'I've a slight medical problem,' she explained, over a cup of coffee in her living room.

'Oh?' he said, observing her from his armchair on the opposite side of the hearth where he was sitting with his legs stretched out in front of him. 'Nothing serious, I hope.'

'I hope so too,' she said, her calm manner belying the fact that she'd been in a state of terror for weeks. 'I don't think it's anything to worry about but my doctor referred me to a specialist whom I went to see this morning. He wants me to go into hospital for tests.'

Paul couldn't hide his sharp intake of breath as he put down his coffee cup and leaned towards her in concern.

'You know how thorough doctors are these days,' said Ruth.

'Yes, they check the slightest thing out, just to be on the safe side,' said Paul reassuringly.

'Exactly.'

'Would it be too rude of me to ask what the problem is?'

'I've got a lump in my breast,' she said, just saying the words out loud making it feel horribly real. 'It's probably nothing . . . just a harmless cyst or something . . . but it's best to get it looked at.'

'Definitely,' said Paul reassuringly though he had turned cold with fear. 'It'll be nothing but it will put your mind at rest.'

'I'm sure it will,' she continued, stiff with fear. She'd noticed the lump quite accidentally one night in the bath. She'd told herself she was imagining things, tried to convince herself there was nothing sinister there at all. It had been weeks before she'd plucked up the courage to go and see her GP. 'Anyway, this favour I want to ask you . . .'

'Of course. Anything at all I can do to help.'

'It's Jenny,' she informed him gravely. 'I don't want to worry her at this stage because it's probably nothing, so I'm not going to tell her that I'm going into hospital.'

Paul's brow furrowed. 'Is that wise?'

'I think so. She has quite enough on her mind with her studies,' said Ruth. 'I don't want her worrying about me unnecessarily.'

'Even so, Ruth, you are her mother. She would want to know.'

'If I tell her, she'll feel she has to come rushing home and she's only just settled back after the Easter hols.'

'Supposing she tries to get hold of you on the phone?'

'That's unlikely as I'm going in on a weekday,' she told him. 'Jenny usually rings at the weekend.'

'I see.'

'If it proves to be nothing serious, I'll only be in hospital for a day or so and I won't be missed,' she explained. 'In the unlikely event of something more serious emerging, then she'll have to know because I shall be in there for longer.'

'And if that does happen, you'd like me to tell her?'

'If I'm not in a position to do so, yes,' she said. 'I think they'll do a mastectomy while I'm still under the anaesthetic from the biopsy if the tumour is found to be malignant. I'm not sure what sort of a state I'd be in if that were to happen. But I don't want Jenny upset if there's no need.'

'Of course I'll tell her,' he readily agreed. 'That's no problem at all.'

'Thanks.'

'But what about Bob?' he enquired. 'As your future husband, won't he expect to be the one to tell her?'

'I'd rather she heard it from you, Paul,' she said. 'You're her father . . . she's close to you.'

'I'm sure it won't be necessary,' he said stoutly, hoping to convey a calmness he didn't feel. Ruth was so precious to him, he couldn't bear to think of the worst possible scenario. 'But you can rely on me if it is. Just let me have all the details so I can keep up to date with the situation.'

'Will do.'

'Bob knows you're going to ask me, I assume?'

'He doesn't know anything about it yet,' she told him.

'Really?' said Paul in surprise.

'I didn't know I was going to have to go into hospital myself until this morning when I saw the consultant,' she explained. 'You're the first person I've told, as a matter of fact. I'll tell Bob and the family tomorrow.'

'I'm sure you've nothing to worry about,' Paul said gently.

'I hope you're right.' Ruth was feeling a lot stronger somehow for having shared her secret with him.

Bob froze as he listened to what Ruth had to tell him the next day.

'I know what you went through when your wife died of cancer and I'm sorry to have frightened you,' she said, noticing his sudden pallor. 'But it's probably just a harmless cyst.'

'Yes . . . yes, bound to be,' he said, unnerving her with his overt fear.

'I'll be glad when it's over though and I know one way or the other,' she confessed.

'I bet,' he said, struggling to pull himself together for he didn't want Ruth to see how devastated he was by her news.

'Honestly, Bob,' she said, making light of it because his attitude was making her feel worse, 'anyone would think *you* were the one going into hospital, from the look on your face.'

'Sorry.'

'Squeamish about hospitals, is that it?' she asked with deliberate levity.

'Yeah, I am a bit,' he said, managing a smile whilst feeling sick with misery and fear.

'Don't worry, you can get into bed with me if you come over queer when you come visiting,' she teased him.

'Oh, Ruth, I'm not that bad.' She couldn't know the horror she had just inflicted upon him. She had no idea of the memories her news evoked. 'I'm concerned about you, that's why I seem worried.'

'I appreciate your concern,' she said, 'but this time tomorrow night, you'll realise you had nothing to worry about.'

He really did hope so because he'd watched one woman die. He didn't think he could go through that a second time.

When Ruth came round after the operation, her first feeling was relief that it was over. All the fear of the last few weeks seemed to have melted away. She felt quite elated, in fact. She was still a bit drowsy and drifted in and out of sleep, only vaguely aware of her surroundings: a row of beds opposite, voices, nurses, the rattle of crockery. She'd known it would be all right. Thank God for that. Now she could get on with her life.

Feeling relaxed and sleepy from the lingering effects

of the anaesthetic, she slipped her hand between the harshly laundered sheets and felt for her left breast.

Shock reverberated through her in an icy blast as her hand found only flatness. There was nothing there except a dressing over the wound. She'd tried to prepare herself for this, she'd signed a form giving the surgeon permission to remove the breast if necessary. But to *actually lose it* was *terrifying*!

'God help me,' she muttered to herself.

Chapter Twenty-One

Bob Bridgeman was in tears at Ruth's bedside, having managed to pluck up the courage to tell her about his true feelings.

'I'm so ashamed,' he wept, hardly able to look at her, 'but I just don't have the strength to go through with our marriage, not now.'

'You want to break off the engagement . . . ?'

'I'm so sorry,' he sobbed. 'I'm weak. I'm not good enough for you. I just don't have the strength to cope with cancer again. I couldn't give you the support you deserve.'

Still reeling from the blow she'd received yesterday, Ruth found that this second shock seemed like just another part of the general disintegration of her life. Naturally she felt betrayed but she could see why Bob felt as he did.

'I understand, Bob,' she said wearily.

'You do?'

'If I could run away from this thing, that's what I'd do.'

'Maybe if I hadn't been through it all once before, I'd feel able to cope.'

'I *do* stand a good chance of a full recovery, you know,' she pointed out. 'The doctors have assured me of that.'

'I know, I know,' he was quick to say, tears streaming down his cheeks, 'but because of what I've already been through with my wife's illness, I'd be living in fear and it wouldn't be fair to you. I just can't go through that again.'

'Well, I appreciate your telling me and not just disappearing,' she said.

'I'm so ashamed,' he said again, staring at the floor.

She was disappointed in him in one way but admired him for being honest with her. It must have taken courage to come here and break off their engagement the day after her operation.

'Don't upset yourself, Bob,' she said. 'I'm glad you've been straight with me.'

'Oh, Ruth,' he said, looking up at her, eyes red from crying, 'you're so brave. I hate myself for doing this to you.'

'I'll be all right,' she said. 'I have my family around me.'

'They'll want to see me in hell for doing this to you.'

'I'll explain to them how it is for you, don't worry.' Her eyes filled with tears as the pain of his rejection finally hit home. 'But I'd like you to leave now.'

'Sure,' he said, standing up quickly, obviously relieved that the visit was over.

He didn't kiss her. Just held her hand for a second or two and hurried out of the ward. Ruth watched him go through a mist of tears.

Paul was looking at the managing director of the Shaldrake Drug Company across his desk but his thoughts were miles away.

'Well, Stoneway,' boomed the MD expectantly, having just imparted some very important news. 'Doesn't that bring a smile to your face?'

'Um . . . yes, of course,' he muttered through a preoccupied haze. 'Naturally I'm pleased. It's wonderful news.'

'I take it you accept then?'

Silence.

'Stoneway,' said the MD with a look of irritation, 'is there something about the offer you're not happy with?'

'No . . . er . . . nothing at all,' Paul assured him vaguely.

'What gives you that impression?'

The MD, a florid mountain of a man with an immense stomach, an oversized moustache and abounding enthusiasm for his business, looked at his sales manager in astonishment.

'Well, maybe I'm expecting too much,' he said with withering sarcasm, 'but when I offer my sales manager promotion to sales director, I expect a bit more than the halfhearted reaction I've had from you.'

Dragging his thoughts away from the subject that had dominated them for the last few days, Paul said, 'I'm sorry. Naturally I'll be honoured to accept a seat on the board of Shaldrake's.'

That was more like it and the MD beamed complacently.

'You've worked damned hard and proved yourself worthy over a number of years,' he said, leaning back with his fingers laced together and his hands resting on his stomach. 'Both in the UK and in Australia.'

'I've enjoyed the job,' said Paul, 'and hope I can make a further contribution to the company in my new position.'

'I'm sure you can. Shouldn't have promoted you otherwise.'

The MD got up and waddled over to the filing cabinet from which he produced a whisky bottle and two glasses.

'Glad to have you on the board, Stoneway,' he said, returning to his desk and pouring them both a drink. 'We need some new blood at that level.'

Paul raised his glass, forcing enthusiasm into his tone. 'I'm really looking forward to getting started on the job.'

'Good.'

In fact, right now Paul couldn't care less about his promotion. He couldn't think further than Hammersmith Hospital where he'd spent every second he possibly could this last few days, giving Ruth moral support as she came to terms with her illness. She would never know just how frightened he'd been on hearing that the tumour had been malignant, but he'd managed to conceal his true feelings and keep up a positive front for her sake.

Her courage had humbled him. Whenever he visited her, she was sitting up looking calm and pretty, hair freshly combed, face made up. She'd even cracked jokes with her visitors. He wondered how much of it was real and how much was an act. But the nurses had told him that her morale was excellent, considering the shock she'd had.

The doctors were confident of a full recovery. Obviously there could be no guarantee that the disease wouldn't recur but, because they had caught the growth early, she had every chance of a normal lifespan, though they advised her to undergo radium treatment as an outpatient for a short while after she left hospital.

Paul clung to the positive aspect as though Ruth's life depended on it, refusing to allow any dark thoughts to linger.

Breaking the news to Jenny had been an emotional experience. She was brave but devastated as was the entire Brooks family with whom Paul was getting quite pally, through seeing them at the hospital so often. Ruth had such a crowd at visiting times, they had to take turns by her bedside.

'This is such a gathering of the clans, it feels like a party,' she had laughed the other evening. 'The only one missing is Ringo. I can't wait to get home to see him.'

He smiled at the memory. His admiration for her knew no bounds.

One person who was conspicuous by his absence was Bob Bridgeman. He'd been to see Ruth just once since the operation to break off their engagement. Everyone was being very diplomatic about it, telling Ruth that it was probably all for the best if Bob didn't feel able to stand by her. But she must have been deeply hurt even if she didn't show it.

Bob had already left the area. He'd closed the business and paid the staff off so there was little likelihood of his ever coming back. How he could have deserted the woman he professed to love at a time of such dreadful adversity was quite beyond Paul. But Bob had been through a lot when his wife had cancer, apparently.

He was recalled to the present by the sound of the MD's voice.

'So I suppose you'll be doing some heavy celebrating tonight, eh, Stoneway?' he suggested heartily.

A week ago, that would probably have been true because this promotion was something Paul had wanted for a very long time. At last he had achieved the goal he had been aiming for. Now it meant nothing to him. He had room in his heart for only one thing at the moment and that was Ruth.

'No, not tonight,' he said.

'Oh? I *am* surprised.'

'A very dear friend of mine is in hospital,' he explained, finishing his whisky. 'So that's where I'll be this evening.'

'Ah . . . I see,' said the MD, his tone respectfully subdued.

Ruth's parents and Jenny were with her when Paul arrived at the ward that evening but they left soon afterwards.

'I hope I haven't chased them away,' he said lightly.

'Of course you haven't. I expect they were relieved to go,' said Ruth. 'We'd exhausted just about every topic of conversation.'

'How are you feeling?'

'Not too bad, considering. I'd been so sick with worry before the operation. At least now I know the worst and something has been done about it.'

'Yes.'

'The staff here are terrific, they do everything they can to keep us patients cheerful.'

'That's good.'

'It's very kind of you to visit me so often, Paul,' she said, her brow furrowing. 'You mustn't feel obliged to, you know.'

Because she meant so much to him, the remark seemed odd.

'I wouldn't dream of not coming to see you,' he told her.

'I wondered if you visited me to make up for the fact that Bob and I have split up.'

'Not at all. I come because I want to see you,' he said, and meant it.

'You mustn't think too badly of Bob,' she told him. 'He suffered a great deal when his wife had cancer.'

'I suppose so,' said Paul. 'It seems so hard on you, though.'

'I'll get over it.'

He took her hand and held it gently between both of his.

'I won't leave, Ruth,' he said. 'I'll always be here for you.'

Tears sprang to her eyes. 'That's kind of you, Paul.'

'I'm not just being kind,' he said with infinite tenderness. 'I want to be with you.'

She didn't reply. The pain of Bob's departure had already faded. She didn't have the spirit left in her to feel much about anything, presumably because of the medication she was on. Nothing seemed to register with any degree of reality. Except Paul. He seemed very real indeed.

'I'm so glad you're here,' she said, holding his hand until the bell rang to indicate visiting time was over.

Bob Bridgeman sat at the bar in an East End pub knocking back whisky in the hope of drowning out his guilty conscience. Running away from Ruth's illness was the cruellest thing he had ever done and he despised himself for it.

But he wouldn't go back. He was *never* going back to her. He couldn't live with all that fear and worry again, the punishing isolation of sickness, the threat of death and the sheer loneliness of the whole thing. He remembered vividly the horror of living with his wife's wretchedness, watching her deteriorate until that final desolate parting. Oh, no, never again.

His fevered mind drifted back to Ruth and the last time he'd seen her when he'd told her it was all over between them. He'd known he had to do it because when he'd looked at Ruth, he'd seen his wife and had broken out in a cold sweat. He was glad Ruth had asked him to go. He'd not been able to get out of that hospital quick enough.

With the utmost speed, he'd employed an estate agent to sell his shop and closed the business, all his hard work wasted. He would lose a lot more than Ruth over this but there was no alternative. Deeply ashamed, he'd left his flat under cover of darkness, taking as much as he could stuff into a suitcase, and gone to an old mate in Hackney where he'd been staying ever since.

It would have to be a very dark night indeed for him to go back to collect anything else he needed from his flat. Ruth was very popular in that area – her shop a focal point in the community. People would hate him for what he'd done to her. He'd have to ask one of his mates to go over and get the rest of his stuff and to see the furniture out of the flat when the business was eventually sold. He wouldn't dare face the people of that neighbourhood again.

Maudlin with alcohol, he sank into a mood of self-pity. How unfairly life had treated him, robbing him of his wife and then his second chance at happiness. He'd fitted in well with the other business people in the parade on the Green. He'd made a lot of friends and enjoyed

PAMELA EVANS

being a shopkeeper. He'd been looking forward to the future with Ruth. Now, because of that bastard illness, he was alone again and would have to start from scratch in business when the shop was sold and he got the cash to buy another.

He had no heart to start again, though. There seemed no point in anything now that he'd lost Ruth. He ordered another treble whisky and swallowed it quickly, needing to blot out the memories and self-recriminations. But the vivid mental image of Ruth in that hospital bed just wouldn't go away.

The guilt and self-loathing were overwhelming. He'd done an atrocious thing to Ruth and living with the misery of knowing that would be his punishment for the rest of his life. But no matter how low he sunk or how much he missed her, he couldn't go back.

'Make Jenny go back to college, will you, Paul?' said Ruth a few days later as father and daughter visited her in hospital.

'Huh, that's a joke. Since when did she take any notice of me?' he asked with a grin for the atmosphere this evening was lighthearted. Ruth was in good heart. She seemed to be taking Bob's departure in her stride, along with everything else she was having to endure at the moment.

'You're her father,' said Ruth, 'so exert your authority.'

'Are they giving you LSD or something?' he teased. 'You must be having hallucinations if you think I have any authority over her.'

'Well . . . she certainly won't listen to me,' pronounced Ruth, giving her daughter an affectionately disapproving look. 'I've begged her to go back to Manchester and get on with her studies.'

'I wouldn't dream of going back for the time being,' said Jenny.

'Look, love,' said Ruth in a firm but persuasive manner, 'I'm fine and I'm being very well looked after here. There's nothing you can do except visit me.'

'That in itself makes it worth staying a while longer.'

'As much as I enjoy seeing you, I don't want you to fall behind with your work.'

'I'll soon catch up.'

'Anyway, it isn't much fun for you, hanging about a hospital every day.'

Jenny laughed gently, holding her mother's hand. 'And it's a barrel load of laughs for you, I suppose?'

'It isn't at all bad, actually, lying around like a lady of leisure all day being waited on hand and foot,' said Ruth, making a joke of it. 'I really think you should go back and get on with your course.'

'You'll be coming out of here soon,' persisted Jenny. 'You'll need someone around then, for a while anyway.'

'It's a nice thought and I really appreciate it,' said Ruth warmly, 'but your gran is only round the corner and she'll be in and out to see me. And the hospital will arrange for an ambulance to take me to outpatients for the treatment. Kitty will be hovering near, I should imagine. There'll be no shortage of offers of help.'

'Don't forget me,' said Paul lightly. 'I'll be around too.'

Jenny looked thoughtful, as though she could be persuaded.

'Yes, there is that . . .' she began but still seemed uncertain.

'I think you can go back to college safe in the knowledge that your mother won't be neglected in any way,' declared Paul. 'Not with her family and myself around.'

He thought it was typical of Ruth to be worrying about her daughter even at a time of personal trauma. Understandably, her own thwarted youthful aspirations had made her overly concerned about Jenny's education. He also suspected that Ruth might be finding it something of a strain to keep up the cheerful front she put on for her daughter. It might fool Jenny but it didn't convince him. Ruth was going through hell right now.

'Okay,' said Jenny, brightening. 'I suppose you're right. I ought to go back.'

'At last you've seen sense,' said Ruth, her voice warm with relief.

'I'll find out about the train times and go back tomorrow.'

'There you are, Paul,' Ruth joked. 'Your daughter does take notice of you. This change of heart is down to you.'

'A fluke,' he answered. 'I shouldn't think it'll be repeated in this lifetime.'

'Come on, Dad,' joshed Jenny, 'I'm always ready to listen ... if you talk good sense.'

'It depends how you define good sense, doesn't it?' he said with a smile in his voice. 'It tends to differ with the generations.'

'You can say that again,' confirmed Ruth with a grin.

In the midst of this banter, Paul had to look down at the floor to hide the tears that burned beneath his lids in a moment of intense and unexpected happiness. Through all the recent blackness and anxiety, something priceless had emerged – a feeling of togetherness with the two people he loved most in the world. This illness had created a profound sense of unity between himself and Ruth and their daughter, which he knew would be permanent.

He wanted them to be a real family and planned to ask Ruth to marry him, but this wasn't the time. Not while she was feeling so vulnerable. If he broached the subject now she would probably mistake love for pity. For the moment he had to be content just to be by her side, helping her to get well again without putting her under any sort of emotional pressure.

The sense of closeness was strengthened when he and Jenny left the ward together.

'I'm so glad you're here, Dad,' she said to him as they walked along the corridor.

'I'm glad too.'

'I don't think I could have got through this without you.'

He turned to her, seeing the tears in her blue eyes.

'Yes, you would,' he informed her without hesitation.

'How can you be so sure?'

'Because you've inherited your mother's courage, that's why.'

'I haven't, you know. I'm absolutely terrified,' she confessed, face crumpling as the tears began to pour down her cheeks. 'I'm scared stiff that the cancer will come back.'

'I know you are, love, and I'm frightened too,' he admitted, holding her close and letting her cry. 'But the doctors are optimistic and so must we be. Together we can be strong. We have to be, for your mother's sake.'

'I'll try,' sobbed Jenny.

'And bear in mind that lots of people live to a ripe old age after the same operation as your mother has had.'

'Yes, they do, I know,' she agreed. 'I'm just being pathetic. Sorry.'

'Apologies aren't necessary.'

'Thanks for being here.'

'Thanks aren't necessary either,' he said, 'because I want to be here with you and Ruth.'

He gave her a handkerchief and they left the hospital together, arm in arm, each comforted by the other.

When Kitty had been ill after Timmy's birth, Ruth had been there for her. When Ruth returned from hospital, the situation was reversed. Every afternoon Kitty was in the shop helping Vince while her mother looked after Timmy.

Kitty's services weren't necessary to the business

because Vince had managed to get an experienced temporary assistant until Ruth was well enough to return to work, but his wife had been so keen to help, he hadn't the heart to tell her that she wasn't really needed.

'At least it makes me feel as though I'm doing something for Ruth,' she said to Vince. 'I want to be on hand if she needs me while she's fresh home from hospital, but I don't want to stay upstairs with her in case it's too much for her.'

'Her mother's in and out a lot during the day,' he pointed out. 'And Paul goes to see her straight from work.'

'That's true, but knowing I'm down here if she needs me in the afternoons will give her an added boost,' said Kitty staunchly. 'Plenty of company is what she needs right now.'

'She seems remarkably cheerful whenever I see her,' said Vince.

'Yes, I don't know how she does it. She's making a wonderful recovery,' agreed Kitty. 'And never a word of complaint. I doubt if I'd be so brave if it happened to me. I think she's marvellous the way she's coping.'

Kitty had no idea how keenly Ruth craved for solitude so that she could let go and drop all the pretence.

Chapter Twenty-Two

That summer the fashion craze for trendy young women was tight-fitting shorts, known as hot pants, worn with platform-soled shoes. Many of the girls wore plain shorts in the daytime and satin disco pants for dancing at night.

One Saturday afternoon in May, Ruth was standing at the living-room window idly watching a group of snazzy young females in hot pants strutting boldly across the Green in the sunshine. She observed them with envy, not because of their youth but because their figures were complete. Even the girls who were rather too generously endowed for this revealing style, and whose thighs and bottoms bulged and wobbled hideously as they walked, had the basic female requirement of two breasts.

They weren't deformed like she was, with only one boob. Admittedly the deficiency wasn't noticeable to other people because she had been fitted with a false one before leaving hospital. But it felt odd and alien to her and she was extremely self-conscious about it.

Her mother's voice broke into her thoughts. 'Fancy coming for a mooch round the shops, Ruth?'

Setting her features into a smile, she said, 'I'm not really in the mood, Mum.'

'It'll do you good,' said Audrey, who had come to visit as she did every day. 'It's a lovely afternoon . . . much too nice to be stuck indoors.'

'There isn't really anything I need at the shops,' said Ruth.

'I don't actually *need* anything either,' said Audrey, 'but we can both do with some fresh air.'

'I took the dog out earlier.'

'Another outing can only be a good thing,' persisted her mother, who was concerned about Ruth's tendency to shut herself away since she'd been home from hospital. 'We can do some window shopping and have a wander down the market to see what's on offer.'

'I really don't feel like it.'

'You might as well make the most of having some time to yourself,' continued the indomitable Audrey. 'Once you're back at work there'll be precious little of it.'

'But I . . .'

'Come on, love,' she urged. 'We won't be out more than an hour – we'll come back as soon as you feel tired.'

Ruth finally conceded defeat rather than have her mother fretting about her. Over the last month or so, since she'd been home from hospital, Ruth had put enormous effort into trying to convince everyone that she was feeling fine and in good spirits. They were all so kind to her and she was moved by their concern. But constantly pretending she was in good heart was exhausting when all she really wanted to do was to succumb to self-pity. Facing up to having cancer felt like crashing into a wall at high speed.

She continually reminded herself of the blind and the helpless, of terminally sick children and the starving people of the third world. But no amount of compassion for those poor unfortunates made her feel any the less sorry for herself. It was dreadful. She was so ashamed.

'Okay, I'll get my jacket,' she said, forcing a smile and going upstairs to the bedroom to get the jacket of her trouser suit.

Outside in the street, the glaring sunshine and the vitality of the Saturday crowds seemed harsh and excessive, aggravating her black mood. They ambled around the shops, looking in the windows, had a wander round Marks and Spencer, then made their way through the market which was teeming with noisy, vociferous crowds.

This ambience, so familiar to Ruth, seemed oddly foreign and unreal, as though she'd never been here before. The blare of pop music from the record stall hurt her head: the lively spiel of the traders shredded her nerves; the colour of the fruit seemed agonisingly bright, as did the loose sweets and the clothes hanging up in rows.

She could feel a scream rising in her throat at the terror of these strange new thoughts and feelings which were completely beyond her control. Once she had been a part of this community – now she felt like an outsider, a stranger locked in a world of her own because she had a death sentence hanging over her.

A quarrel was in progress between a crockery seller and a punter.

'This teapot you sold me last week is bleedin' rubbish,' claimed the punter, holding the item out for the trader to see.

'Whassa matter with it?'

'The handle fell off as soon as the missus put hot water in it.'

'It never did. There was nothing wrong with that pot when I sold it to you . . .'

'It was faulty and I want me money back.'

'Piss off or I'll call the police and have you done for causing a public nuisance.'

'I'll be the one to call the law, mate, if you don't cough up . . .'

Ruth and her mother walked on, Audrey lingering at every stall as was her habit, Ruth pretending an interest to please her. There was a much more multi-ethnic flavour to the market now than there had been when Ruth was growing up. A wider range of goods was available to cater for the many people from foreign shores who now lived in the area. Exotic foods created a rich, spicy aroma which mingled with the more traditional smells of fruit and fish and hot dogs and hamburgers.

It was the smell of town life, an integral part of Ruth's existence. But today it seemed overpowering, clinging to her clothes and hair and making her want to retch.

The sense of disorientation was making Ruth panicky and she struggled to calm herself so that her mother would see no outward sign of the turmoil within her. Everything here is the same as it was before the operation, she told herself. It only seems different because you've had a shock that's changed your life.

When they got back to Ruth's flat, Audrey asked her if she would like to spend the evening with her parents.

'I'd rather stay here, if you don't mind, Mum,' she said. 'I'll be round tomorrow as usual for Sunday tea, though.'

'Well, if you fancy some company tonight, you know where we'll be,' said Audrey. 'I'm doing my shift at the Rose and Crown and Dad will be coming down later on for a drink. You're welcome to join us.'

'I'll see what I feel like,' said Ruth, knowing she wouldn't change her mind.

'Do you good to get out.'

'I know, Mum,' she said, weary of her mother's unremitting efforts. 'And I'll bear it in mind, I promise.'

'Will Paul be calling in to see you?'

'Probably,' she said absently. 'He comes most days and I haven't seen him yet today.'

'He's a good friend to you.'

'Yes, he is.'

Paul Stoneway had gone up in Audrey's estimation this last few weeks. He'd been a tower of strength to Ruth through this ordeal, and to young Jenny.

'I'll be off then.'

'Okay, I'll see you tomorrow.'

Alone at last Ruth sank on to the sofa in a state of

nervous exhaustion, relieved that she could now stop pretending to be cheerful. She put on her happy face when Vince and Kitty came up to say they'd closed the shop and were going home, then sat back down, vaguely aware of the fact that Paul might call in to see her. He never telephoned first but just turned up. Probably so she didn't have the chance to tell him not to come, she thought.

Miserable and lethargic, she sat staring into space until the sound of the dog barking and bounding down the stairs made her realise there was someone at the door.

It was Paul, clutching a bottle of wine and a box of chocolates.

'I hope you haven't eaten,' he said cheerfully, putting the wine and chocolates down on the kitchen table, ''cos I thought you might fancy a takeaway later on.'

'Oh, Paul, there's no need for you to give up your Saturday evening for me.'

'Anything good on the box tonight?' he said, ignoring her comment.

'I've no idea.'

'I'll have a look in the paper then,' he said, going into the living room, whistling a tune.

It was his breezy manner that made something snap inside Ruth. She rushed into the other room and snatched the newspaper out of his hands, throwing it on the floor.

'Stop it!' she screamed. 'Stop it – stop it – stop it!'

'Stop what?' he said, looking startled by this sudden outburst. 'What on earth's the matter with you?'

'Will you stop behaving as though nothing's changed?' she yelled. 'Everyone is behaving as though everything is just the same and it's driving me mad.'

'Nothing has changed so far as I know,' he said calmly.

'How can you say that?' she shrieked, on the verge of hysterics. 'When I have a death sentence hanging over me?'

'We all have one of those,' he said with determined calm. 'None of us is immortal.'

'You know perfectly well what I mean,' she shouted. 'Why can't you say it? Are you afraid of the word? I've got cancer, Paul. I'm going to die.'

'You've *had* cancer,' he corrected, standing up to face her. 'It's been dealt with and you're getting better. You could see us all out. The doctors have told you that.'

'They can't guarantee it though, can they?' she said, face distorted with anguish.

'Of course they can't,' he admitted. 'Any more than they can guarantee that I won't die of a heart attack during the night or get killed in a road accident on the way home.'

'That isn't the same thing at all and you know it!'

'Come on, Ruth, this isn't like you,' he said patiently. 'You've been so brave . . .'

'It's all been an act,' she interrupted, her voice quivering. 'I haven't been brave at all and I don't *want* to be brave. I'm angry and afraid and very sorry for myself. I don't *want* to have my life cut short, I don't *want* to have a scar where my boob used to be and have this illness hanging over me day after day like a black cloud, colouring everything I do. It's my first thought when I wake up in the morning and my last thought before I go to sleep at night.' Her breathing was rapid, her chest heaving, her face deathly white and stained with red blotches. 'And I know I'm being pathetic and it's all *me-me-me*, so don't bother to remind me about all the people who are much worse off . . . all the sick children who won't even have as much time as I've already had . . . because that doesn't help. At this precise moment, all I can think about is myself . . . and don't tell me that's wrong and I'm the most selfish woman alive because I already know that . . . and that makes me feel even worse too . . .'

Her voice faltered and died as her face crumpled and she collapsed into tears, heaving deep guttural sobs, sinking down on the sofa and weeping loudly and without inhibition, almost as though she'd forgotten that Paul was there. All the tension and fear she had suppressed for so long flowed out of her unabated.

She cried for a long time. Paul sat quietly beside her with his arm gently around her shoulders, saying very little – just keeping her well supplied with clean handkerchiefs. The tears finally subsided, leaving Ruth exhausted.

'So now you know the truth about me,' she informed him, her voice thick and muffled from crying. 'And I'm so ashamed.'

'I'm no expert,' he said, deeply moved but managing to stay in control, 'but I doubt if the way you are feeling is unusual. Other cancer patients probably feel the same in the early stages of recovery. I don't think you should be too hard on yourself.'

She turned to him, her dark eyes raw and swollen, her hair damp with sweat and tears, her green and white checked shirt crumpled and stained with black marks where her mascara had dripped on to it. She looked wild and unkempt and he ached with love for her.

'I always credited myself with having my fair share of guts,' she told him, 'but this thing has knocked me sideways and I can't seem to do a damned thing about it.'

'What you're feeling is only natural,' he said firmly. 'Can't you see that?'

'No.'

'The people you read about or meet in the street who are being so brave when faced with some dire fate . . . you don't know what they are really feeling, or how they behave when they're on their own. That's what courage is – facing up to adversity with dignity for the world to see even though you're feeling frail inside yourself. You're only human, Ruth, you're bound to feel sorry for yourself. I'm sure it will soon pass.'

'You can't imagine how bad I've been feeling these last weeks, especially since I've been home from hospital.'

'Doesn't the fact that the doctors are so optimistic give you any relief?'

'Not really,' she told him. 'I'm haunted by the idea that it will come back somewhere else in my body. I can almost feel it starting – the slightest ache or pain and I think it's creeping through me. I can't bear to think of the future because I don't seem to have one.'

'Every moment of life is a gift for every single one of us,' he pointed out. 'While you're worrying about not having a future, precious moments are ticking away.'

'I know all about that,' she said with an eloquent sigh, 'but it just won't go away, this constant grinding fear. It wasn't so bad when I was in hospital. I felt secure there, being looked after by professionals. But as soon as I came home, I just fell apart inside, though no one realised it.'

'I guessed you were putting on a show,' he told her. 'I'm relieved it's out in the open now.'

She looked worried.

'Paul, I don't want anyone else to know about this, particularly Mum and Jenny. They'd be worried to death if they knew how I was really feeling. Besides, I hate self-pity in other people and loathe it even more in myself. Everybody would be so disappointed in me if they knew the truth.'

'Nobody will blame you for being human but I won't say a word,' he assured her. 'You can sink to your lowest ebb with me and no one else will ever know about it.'

She managed a watery smile and took his hand.

'Thanks, Paul.'

'There's no need to thank me,' he said. 'Just promise me that you'll call me when you're needing a shoulder to cry on?'

'You'll probably regret saying that,' she said with a

wry grin. 'Your clothes will shrink to nothing in the constant floods.'

He smiled. 'That's better. You've got your sense of humour back.'

'A bit of a feeble effort.'

'It's a start.'

'Things don't seem nearly so bad when I'm with you,' she confessed.

Taking both her hands in his, he said, 'As I've told you before, Ruth, I'll always be here for you. I left you once but never, *ever* again.'

'I'm glad.'

'While we're on the subject, there's something I've been wanting to say to you for a long time, long before you got sick,' he told her gravely, 'but it was never the right time. First because I was married to Leila, then because you were engaged to Bob, and then because you were ill and I was afraid you would misunderstand my motives. Now I'm going to say it to you anyway because I've realised that the time will never be exactly right . . .'

Her dark, tear-rinsed eyes looked expectantly into his.

'I love you, Ruth.' He raised a hand to stop her as she tried to speak. 'I never forgot you when I was away in Australia. But what we felt for each other as teenagers is nothing to what I feel for you now that I've got to know you over a long period of time. And I know that feeling will stay with me for life. I want to marry you more than anything else in the world, when my divorce from Leila comes through.'

'Oh Paul . . .'

'But I don't want to press you for an answer until you're ready,' he cut in softly. 'I know you've enough on your mind at the moment. I just want you to know how I feel.'

'You still want me, even though I'm not a complete woman?'

'Of course you're a complete woman.'

'I'm minus a boob.'

'Oh, Ruth, how could you even think that would matter to me?'

'You're a man,' she said, her mouth drying as she thought of her disfigured body.

'So?'

'Breasts are important to men. It's a recognised fact,' she said. 'They've always got plenty to say about them.'

'A lot of that's just fun and fantasy.'

'Even so . . .'

'Okay, so men are turned on by women's breasts and I'm no different,' he admitted candidly. 'But don't you realise, Ruth, that I love you because you're you? One boob or no boobs at all, it doesn't make a scrap of difference to me.'

She was more touched than he would ever know. But she was feeling far too vulnerable and unsure of herself to enter into such an important commitment as marriage. For one thing she was afraid she would become ill again and he would be lumbered with an invalid for a wife. Even as the thought came, she felt the blackness descend. It hovered constantly, just a thought away.

'I've loved you for a very long time, Paul,' she said. 'The schoolgirl crush I had on you has developed over the years into real love since you came back into my life. All the time you were with Leila I tried not to let my feelings emerge but they did anyway. But this isn't the time for me to decide about anything so important as marriage. I'm feeling too mentally fragile and lacking in confidence. I need to feel strong again before I can even consider making such an important decision.'

'I understand, Ruth,' he said, gently kissing her. 'Just keep it in mind that I want you as my wife whenever you're ready.'

'I will,' she said, smiling tenderly at him.

Later they dined on Chinese takeaway in the living room in front of the TV.

'Do you think you might feel better once you've started back at work?' asked Paul, munching a spring roll.

'I honestly don't know.'

'When will you go back?'

'As soon as the radium treatment is finished, I hope,' she said. 'I only have to go twice a week now instead of every day. The treatment will be finished altogether soon.'

'Do you feel up to going back to work yet?' he asked.

'I'm not sure.'

'Perhaps you could go part-time at first.'

'I expect that's what the doctor will suggest,' she told him.

After the meal they had coffee and chocolates and he remarked on how much more relaxed she seemed.

'I do feel better. It must be your influence,' she said lightly. 'You seem to have the knack of cheering me up.'

'I'm glad about that,' he said. 'Perhaps your illness won't be the last thought on your mind when you go to sleep tonight.'

'If it isn't, I expect it'll be there when I wake up,' she said. 'Mornings are hellish for me.'

'Perhaps I should stay...'

Up went her brows.

'Just so that I'm around, if it'll help,' he said. 'I didn't mean...'

'I wish you did. At least an improper suggestion might make me feel like an attractive woman again,' said Ruth with a hint of her old spirit. 'Instead of an invalid.'

'You're a very attractive woman and there's nothing I'd like more.'

'But?'

'But I'll sleep on the sofa just the same,' he said with gentle firmness. 'I wouldn't dream of ... not so soon after your operation. I'm not a complete moron.'

'I think I would like you to stay tonight, though, Paul,' she told him.

'Then that's what I'll do.'

When Ruth woke the next morning, her first feeling was the usual panic. Then she remembered that Paul was downstairs sleeping on the sofa, and she relaxed. For the first time since she'd left hospital, she was able to lie still in bed without tension knotting her stomach. He was such a calming influence.

For a while she lay still, looking at the ceiling and enjoying this rare moment of peace. It felt so good having Paul close by when she woke. It was something to which she could easily become accustomed. But she didn't want him only as a prop during her post-operative depression.

It was high time she dragged herself out of the doldrums and took each moment as a gift as Paul had suggested. This morning, for the first time, she felt positive enough to believe that it wasn't a complete impossibility.

One thing she did know for certain: the next time Paul stayed the night with her, he wouldn't sleep on the sofa!

Chapter Twenty-Three

'It's nice to see you back, Ruth,' said a harassed young mother, coming into the shop one summer morning with a baby in a pushchair and a lively two year old, Wayne, who immediately escaped from her clutches and ran wild among the toiletries. Brenda Barnes was a regular customer, usually for baby products. She'd grown up in the area and Ruth knew her and her family well. Her eyes lingered on Ruth inquisitively. 'You're looking *really well*. This is the first time I've seen you since . . . er, well since before you were . . . um . . . ill.'

'I'm feeling fine now.' Curiosity was a common reaction among people seeing Ruth for the first time since the operation. Some were too embarrassed to comment at all and made things worse by not looking at her directly, as though afraid of what they might see. They meant no harm but she couldn't help being affected, even though she concealed her feelings well. 'And how are you?'

'Knackered,' was Brenda's way of putting it as she recaptured the struggling toddler and bent down to wipe the baby's nose. 'I feel as though I could sleep for a week.'

'The kids wearing you out then?'

'Phew, not so you'd notice,' said Brenda dryly. 'I've been up all bloomin' night with the baby . . . he's teething again, poor love.'

'Ah, bless him.'

'That's what I've come in for, actually, something to put on his gums.'

Ruth turned to a drawer behind her and produced a tube of teething jelly. 'We've had very good reports of this one,' she said, handing it to Brenda.

The young woman glanced briefly at the product, reading the instructions.

'This'll do. If you say it's okay, that's good enough for me.'

Ruth put it into a paper bag while Brenda dragged the squealing Wayne away from the door where he was perilously close to being knocked over as people tried to come in.

'The little devil's into everything,' she tutted as she handed Ruth the money. 'I need eyes in the back of my head.'

'I can imagine,' said Ruth, melting in the beam of a heart-stopping smile from the toddler who had a mop of dark curly hair and mischievous brown eyes. 'He's lovely though.'

'*And* he knows it,' said Brenda, lifting him up and smothering him with kisses. 'I'll take a couple of tins of baby food an' all, while I'm here. And a bottle of Ribena . . . Wayne's favourite.'

The transaction complete, Ruth exchanged a few more pleasantries with Brenda and gave Wayne one of the glucose sweets she kept on the counter for customers' children.

'Well, I hope you manage to get some sleep tonight, Brenda,' said Ruth as the young woman grabbed Wayne's hand and headed for the door with the pushchair.

'You and me both. In the meantime I'd better finish my shopping and get home before I fall asleep on my feet,' she said, holding tight to the little boy who was squirming to get free. 'Thanks, Ruth. See you again soon.'

''Bye, love. Take care.'

Ruth proceeded to work her way through the queue that had formed, wishing her own cheery persona was more natural. She'd been back at work for nearly a month and was now fully involved in the business again. Her state of mind had improved since her outpouring to Paul, even more so since she'd been back in the shop and didn't have so much time to dwell on her personal situation. But despite her very best endeavours, the blackness descended as soon as she wasn't fully occupied.

Although she was able to grasp the obvious truth of Paul's 'every moment is a gift' dictum, she still found herself wondering how many more times she would see the changing of the seasons or if she would live long enough to see Jenny qualify and marry. And with these thoughts came a depression which she could not conquer.

Paul remained a constant source of strength. He was kind but firm with her when she was feeling down, and always there when she needed him even though she still didn't feel able to commit herself to a full relationship with him.

'Why don't you find a fit and healthy woman to take Leila's place?' she'd told him the other day while in low spirits. 'Instead of waiting around for a beaten up old crock like me who's too frightened to get up in the mornings sometimes.'

'If you're an old crock, that doesn't say much for the rest of us.'

'You *would* say that . . .'

'Even if you were an old crock, I'd still be hanging around 'cos it's you I want,' he'd told her simply. '*Not* a replacement for Leila who was never the right woman for me anyway. I've waited this long, a bit longer isn't going to hurt me.'

'Humph.'

'Anyway, you're perfectly healthy,' he pointed out. 'You've *been* ill. Your illness is in the past tense, Ruth, you have to keep remembering that.'

But as much as she tried to discipline her mind to this fact, the all-pervading gloom still consumed her rather too often. The only antidote seemed to be work, and since she couldn't keep herself employed during her every waking moment, it wasn't an ideal solution.

Over coffee that morning with Vince in the dispensary, he said, 'Kitty asked me to invite you and Paul over to lunch on Sunday.'

'I can't speak for Paul, of course, but I'd love to come,' Ruth told him. 'I'll mention it to him and let you know.'

'Funny the way things have worked out, isn't it?' he remarked, looking at her over the rim of his mug, 'You know . . . the four of us, all ending up together.'

She and Paul weren't a couple in the true sense but Ruth just said, 'Yes, it's quite a coincidence.'

They drifted on to business, chatting about various new drugs and the shop in general. Ruth felt her depression ease as she escaped from herself in thoughts of the business.

The sudden appearance of their assistant Madge, whey-faced and trembling, brought the conversation to an abrupt end.

'Ring for an ambulance, quick,' she said in a shaky voice. 'A kiddie's been knocked down by a car just outside.'

Even as Ruth dialled 999, Vince was already on his way outside to see if there was anything he could do to help. As soon as she'd finished on the phone, Ruth followed him, leaving Madge to cover in the shop although everyone was far too caught up with the accident to want to buy anything.

Illustrating the macabre side of human nature, people appeared from nowhere as they always do at an accident and Ruth couldn't get through the crowd to offer assistance. When she did manage to see through the crowd of people to the scene of the accident, her heart lurched at the sight of Brenda Barnes kneeling down in the road, beside a child.

'Oh, no, not Wayne,' Ruth muttered almost to herself.

'Poor little soul,' said Reg from the dry cleaner's, who

happened to be standing next to Ruth.

'She was in our shop with him not fifteen minutes ago,' said Ruth.

'Oh, yes?'

'He ran off, I suppose?' said Ruth. 'He's always doing that.'

'Yeah. His mother was in the butcher's, apparently,' said Reg. 'I suppose she took her eyes off him for a second and he was off . . . straight into the road in front of a car.' He shook his head sadly. 'Can't blame the driver, though.

'Poor Brenda, and that poor little boy,' she said. 'Is he . . . ?'

'Dunno.'

'Here comes the ambulance anyway,' said Ruth, and went back into the shop because there was no good reason for her to stay out there. She was shaking all over and collapsed into a chair in the staffroom before her legs gave out on her.

When Paul called to see Ruth that evening, she seemed a bit down.

'What's the matter?' he asked, fearing some sort of a relapse.

'A little boy was knocked down and killed this morning outside the shop.'

'*Oh, no.*' He winced. 'What a dreadful thing.'

'He was only two.'

'Poor little chap,' he said. 'It makes your blood run cold to think of it, doesn't it?'

'I'll say. I've known his mother for years. How will she ever get over a terrible blow like that?'

'I don't suppose she will,' Paul said gloomily. 'Not entirely. But she will learn to live with it after a while.'

'Which is what I have to do.'

He waited, knowing that Ruth wasn't talking about the road accident now.

'This has put my own situation into perspective quite dramatically. None of us knows what's round the corner, do we?' she said. 'Brenda Barnes could never have predicted this.'

'I thought you said that that kind of sensible reasoning doesn't help?'

'It didn't until today,' she tried to explain. 'Since my operation I've reminded myself about people who are worse off than me 'til I've nearly gone mad thinking about it. I've read in the paper about famine and wars in distant places, and I've felt sorry about the sadness and tragedy . . . and still felt sorry for myself. But having something so terrible happen outside the shop has really got to me. I can't stop thinking about little Wayne, snuffed out just like that.' She paused. 'And poor Brenda . . . how she must be feeling.'

'Now you can see how important it is to take each day as it comes.'

'I've already seen thirty-six summers, which is a lot more than Wayne.'

'Yes.'

'This has made me realise just how small and insignificant we all are in the scheme of things. The future is out of our hands.'

'Exactly, which is why you must try to live each moment to the full.'

'I'm going to try, Paul,' she said. 'I'm *really* going to try.'

'Here's to us, the fifties foursome gloriously reunited,' smiled Vince, raising his wine glass at lunch the following Sunday.

There are five of us now, though,' Kitty pointed out, looking proudly at her three-year-old son who was dutifully attending to his roast lamb, accepting it as a mere obstacle on the way to the yummy-looking trifle on the sideboard.

'If you're counting our second generation, then it's six,' Ruth reminded them chirpily, though she was still full of sorrow about Wayne's death.

'Of course,' agreed Kitty lightheartedly. 'We mustn't forget Jenny.'

'She'll be home for the summer holidays soon,' remarked Ruth casually.

'And looking for ways to earn some pocket money, I shouldn't wonder,' added Paul.

'I'm sure Vince and I will be able to find her something to do at the shop, won't we, Vince?' said Ruth.

'We'll do our best.'

'Studying to be a doctor, eh?' said Kitty with a touch of awe. She looked at Timmy. 'I wonder if he'll aspire to such heights.'

'I don't see why not,' said Ruth. 'There's a lot more opportunity now for youngsters than there was when we were at school.'

'Attitudes have changed since then, too,' said Paul.

'I'll say,' said Ruth. 'I was considered something of a novelty in our street because I had university potential. But going away to college and university is becoming quite commonplace for ordinary working-class people nowadays.' She paused, looking from Kitty to Vince. 'Not that you're working-class, of course, but I am.'

'Was,' corrected Kitty.

'Still am inside, you don't lose the class you were born into,' pronounced Ruth. 'But I was speaking generally about things being better ... especially for women. The fact that Jenny is at medical school is proof of that. Women doctors were almost unheard of when we were children.'

They were all in agreement about this.

'Maybe Timmy will follow in his father's footsteps and become a pilot,' said Vince, returning to the original topic.

'I'd like that for him in a way ... 'cos it's glamorous and exciting and all of that,' said Kitty, glancing at her husband thoughtfully. 'But being cautious and a bit mumsie, I think I'd rather he followed you into pharmacy, Vince. I'd sleep easier at nights with my son safely on terra firma.'

'I'd like that too.' Vince looked at Ruth. 'We could take him into business with us, perhaps. Open another shop.'

'Now you're entering into the realms of fantasy,' she laughed. 'Who can say what he'll want to do? It's much too far ahead.'

'True,' said Kitty, adding thoughtfully, 'I don't know why you two don't open another shop though . . . now.'

'We've often thought about it,' said Vince, 'but it would mean putting one of the shops under management because Ruth isn't qualified.'

'That doesn't matter, does it?' said Kitty. 'Lots of chemist's shops aren't owner-run these days.'

'That's true enough,' agreed Ruth, 'but bringing a manager in from outside has never really appealed to us for some reason.'

'You know what the solution to that is then, don't you?' said Paul.

All eyes turned to him questioningly.

He looked at Ruth. 'The answer is for you to get qualified.'

There was silence while they all digested this suggestion.

'You know that isn't possible, Paul,' said Ruth eventually.

'I know no such thing.'

Kitty looked at him enquiringly. 'You're not serious?'

'I'm deadly serious.' He turned to Ruth. 'You've always regretted not finishing your education. Now's your chance to put that right. And for sound business reasons as well as personal fulfilment. Even if you didn't open another shop, your being qualified would be an enormous help. As it is now you have to get a locum to cover for Vince when he's off sick or on holiday. Many times you've said what a nuisance it is. You're already a dispenser which would cut down the study time. You told me once that you have the right 'O'-level subjects to take pharmacy further if you ever had the chance. Well, now's the time to go for the big one . . . get your pharmacy degree.'

'He's right,' said Vince.

'Yeah, what about it, Ruth?' said Kitty eagerly.

'I think you've all gone raving mad,' she said in good-humoured astonishment. 'I'm thirty-six years old, for heaven's sake.'

'So you'll be a mature student,' said Paul. 'People a damned sight older than you are doing degree courses, you know.'

'You have to go away to university to get a degree,' she wisely pointed out. 'Not to mention the 'A'-levels I'd need to get on to a degree course.'

'It's one hell of a challenge, I admit,' said Paul. 'But you could study for the 'A'-levels at home in your spare time.'

'And what about the university course?' she said. 'I do have a business to run and I can't be in two places at once.'

'We'd get someone in to cover for you while you were away,' suggested Vince. 'It would be worth it because the business would have so much to gain if you were qualified.'

'It's a nice idea,' said Ruth, 'but we all know it's just a fairy tale.' She grinned. 'Now, can we change the subject . . . and would you pass me the mint sauce, please, Vince?'

A few evenings later Paul called at Ruth's place, bursting with information.

'I've been making enquiries,' he said, standing beside her as she made coffee in the kitchen.

'Oh, *have* you?' she said, looking at him suspiciously.

'You can do your 'A'-level course at home,' he

announced excitedly. 'Provided you actually sit the exams at an authorised centre.'

'In other words a school . . . with all the eighteen year olds?'

'That's right.'

'That's bit daunting.'

'A minor consideration,' he said, brushing aside her objections. 'The important thing is that it's possible for you to do this.'

They took their coffee into the living room and sat down in armchairs near the window.

'You're getting completely carried away with this whole thing, Paul,' Ruth reproached him, but she was excited by the idea despite herself. 'Your enthusiasm is blinding you to the practicalities.'

'A challenge like this is just what you need right now,' he stated categorically. 'It would keep those morbid thoughts at bay. You'll be far too busy to think about being ill.'

'Oh, Paul, do you really think I could do it?' she asked, a gleam coming into her eye that he hadn't seen for a long time.

'I know you can.'

'But I do have a full-time job.'

'There are evenings and weekends,' he pointed out. 'You could get up earlier in the mornings and do some studying while you're fresh.'

'Slave driver,' she laughed.

'Don't worry, I'll see to it that you take time off for relaxation.'

She bit her lip.

'Can you honestly say you wouldn't like to get a pharmacy degree?' he asked.

'Of course I can't say that,' she told him. 'You know I'd love it.'

'Well, then . . .'

'I've already told you, Paul, there are too many factors against the idea. The shop being the main one,' she explained candidly. 'Anyway, the whole thing would be a fairly long-term project.'

'That doesn't matter.'

'But what if . . .' she began, her expression darkening.

'Then you don't finish your course,' he said, knowing what was on her mind. 'But you can't spend the rest of your life asking yourself what will happen if you get ill again. That's pointless.'

'You're right,' she said. 'I just need reminding fairly often.'

'So will you take steps towards getting on to an 'A'-level home study course?'

'Why are you so keen for me to become a student, anyway?'

'Because it's the right thing for you,' he explained. 'And because it was my fault you didn't finish your education at the usual time. The least I can do is to encourage you to finish it now.'

'But I'm so rusty and out of the habit of learning anything.'

'You'll soon get into it.'

'I wish I was as confident in myself as you are in me.'

'Trust me, Ruth,' he said gently. 'I know you can do it.'

She looked at him, sitting in the chair with his legs sprawled out in front of him, a fine figure of a man in denim jeans and a blue and white checked shirt that brought out the colour of his eyes. Now in his late thirties Paul had even more charisma than he'd had when he was younger. He was still quite slim but solid and muscular. He wore his hair longer than he used to, in common with most other men, and it suited him.

He inspired such confidence in her, she felt as though there was nothing she couldn't attempt. She *really* wanted to try for a pharmacy degree. In fact, she was more excited by the prospect than anything in a very long time. With this feeling came a rush of love and gratitude to Paul who had come up with the idea in the first place. He'd done so much for her during her illness. He'd seen her sink to the very depths, but had never lost patience, always remained positive. Never demanded anything more than her company.

Now he was encouraging her towards new and difficult horizons. But with him beside her, anything seemed possible.

'I think I will give it a try,' she said. 'I'll get in touch with the Pharmaceutical Society tomorrow and find out exactly how to set about it.'

From the width of Paul's smile she could have been forgiven for thinking that her decision was going to benefit him personally.

'Oh, I'm so pleased, Ruth, I know you won't regret it.' He got up. 'I think this calls for a celebration. What say I pop down the off-licence and get a bottle of wine?'

A feeling of acute tenderness for him overwhelmed her.

'Let's wait until we have something to celebrate, shall we?' she said with a smile in her voice. 'You know, like me actually passing some exams or something.'

'Ah, but this is an important landmark,' he said. 'Your agreeing to do it. A definite cause for celebration.'

Ruth's profound tenderness was turning to desire and she was taken aback because tension and fear had destroyed any stirrings in that direction for a long time. With enormous joy, she realised that she felt normal again and it was like being reborn. She knew in that ecstatic moment that deciding to study for her pharmacy degree wasn't the only event that today would be remembered for.

She stood up and hugged him.

'Yes, I agree with you . . . we should celebrate.' She kissed him deeply on the lips. 'So you go and get a bottle of wine.'

'Okay,' he said, breathless at the message in her kiss, 'I'll go right away.'

'And, Paul?'

'Yeah?'

'You don't have to go home tonight, do you?'

'Not if you'd like me to stay.'

'I would, very much,' she said. 'But this time the sofa is off limits.'

Ruth began her studies that autumn on a home study course for 'A'-levels. Good grades would get her a place on a degree course at one of Britain's university-based schools of pharmacy. She intended to try for a place at one of the London colleges so that she could live at home.

Her alarm clock was set for 5.30 every morning which gave her a reasonable study period before business started for the day. She also worked at her books during the evenings and Sundays. Discipline was paramount. It was extremely hard going but very satisfying.

Paul was wonderfully supportive, keeping her supplied with coffee, dragging her off to the pub or a restaurant for a break, walking the dog for her of an evening. He was one in a million and her love for him grew with every moment that passed.

After they had become lovers that night in June, they planned to marry as soon as his divorce came through. He stayed overnight quite often but still didn't move in. They were mutually agreed about setting up home in a place neither of them had previously shared with another partner, after they were married.

Now that Ruth's life was so full of purpose and mental stimulation, the dark thoughts came less often and her illness faded into the past. Time brought its own reward too. As she grew in health, so she was able to see the future ahead of her.

One bitterly cold morning the following February, she was made to realise just how complete her recovery was . . .

The shop was packed with customers in the medical section, some waiting for prescriptions to be dispensed as the season produced its usual crop of 'flu and bronchitis, others wanting patent medicines for coughs and colds. Every seat was taken and people were squashed together. The air was ringing with coughs and sneezes, and heavy with the scent of Vick. There was also a strong smell of paraffin from the oil heater which they were using to heat the shop in place of the electric fire, rendered useless by yet another power cut as the crisis over the miners' pay dispute deepened.

Ruth and Vince and their staff were working flat out to clear the queue and dispense the medicines as quickly as possible. Extra time was spent accounting for all the transactions by hand because the electrically operated till was out of action.

People were chatting among themselves to pass the time. The topic was the one on everybody's lips at the moment – the electricity blackouts that were being caused by the miners' strike.

'That's all you need when you're feeling poorly, innit?' said someone. 'No light or heat for up to nine hours at a stretch.'

There was a general murmur of agreement.

'The three-day week in industry will do the country no favours either,' said someone else.

'I blame the government,' said a man with a rattling cough.

'Useless bunch!'

'What about the miners?' came a loud, dissenting voice. 'They should get back to work and give us all a break.'

'They're entitled to decent pay...'

And so the debate continued in a lively manner and a community atmosphere prevailed. Busy serving at the counter and dashing to and from the dispensary with the medicines, Ruth was listening with only half an ear. She was about to go back into the dispensary with yet another prescription when an urgent call held her back.

'Excuse me,' said Mrs Brown, an elderly lady who had been standing quietly in the corner with her husband and had now pushed her way to the counter. Her husband followed slowly, obviously in distress. His face was grey and screwed up with pain and he held his chest, wincing when he breathed and groaning softly. The couple were local and had been customers at this shop for as long as Ruth could remember. 'Sid's got much worse, dear. So could you make up his medicine next?'

'Yes, of course we can.' Observing the condition of the man who was shivering violently, Ruth added, 'Come on through to the back. I think you need to sit down while you're waiting, Mr Brown. You'll be more comfortable away from the crowd.'

Vince said he would get the old man's medicine ready right away and Ruth took Mr Brown into the staffroom and helped him into a chair near a small paraffin stove. But he seemed to get worse by the second, sweating and shaking and complaining of pains in his lungs.

Mrs Brown was beside herself. 'Sid's not the sort to make a fuss,' she confided to Ruth. 'I reckon there's a bit more wrong with him than just a touch of 'flu like the doctor said. Sid wasn't nearly as bad as this when we set out for the surgery, or I'd have got the doctor to come to the house.'

When Sid stood up then passed out cold, Ruth was really worried. After a brief consultation with Vince, she telephoned Mr Brown's doctor and was advised to call an ambulance. 'Better get him into hospital, just to be on the safe side,' said the GP. 'I'll get on the phone to them, let them know he's on the way and give them some background details.'

Ruth's heart went out to this couple. They looked so frail and frightened.

'I think I'd better go with them in the ambulance to give Mrs Brown some support,' she said to Vince. 'If you can manage here without me? She needs someone with her.'

'You go, I'll be all right.'

In the ambulance, Ruth concentrated on keeping Mrs Brown calm while the ambulance man tried to make her husband more comfortable.

At the hospital he was whisked away and Ruth sat with Mrs Brown in the waiting room, having got her a cup of tea.

'Is there anyone you'd like me to telephone for you?' she asked. 'Any children you'd like to be here with you?'

She shook her head, crying silently. 'No, there's only me and Sid.'

'Oh.'

'What am I gonna do if he dies?' she said. 'I've always hoped I'd go first.'

'Hey, slow down,' said Ruth gently. 'It might not be anything too serious. And doctors can do wonderful things these days.'

It was some sort of a virus and Sid's lungs were badly congested, they were told. His age didn't help because he didn't have the strength to fight back. But they'd put him on medication and were doing everything they could. They were hopeful but couldn't guarantee anything.

Ruth telephoned Vince.

'I can't leave Mrs Brown here on her own and they have no family,' she said. 'So I don't know when I'll get back to the shop.'

'Stay there as long as you need to,' he told her. 'We'll manage here.'

The next few hours were traumatic for Ruth as she tried to keep up the old woman's spirits. They let her see her husband for a while and it was both pitiful and heartwarming to watch her at the bedside talking to him, though he was only half-conscious.

Somehow the afternoon passed in an agony of suspense and in the evening Mrs Brown was told that there was a slight improvement in Sid's condition. He was going to be all right!

'Oh, thank God,' she sobbed with relief in Ruth's arms. 'I don't know what I'd have done without you today, I really don't. Thanks for being here with me, love.'

'I'm glad to help.'

'Yes, I really believe you are too,' she said, her faded blue eyes shining brightly again in her thin face. 'I've watched you grow up, Ruth, and I know you haven't always had it easy.'

'Who has?'

'But you've come through all your troubles and your shop is a valuable part of our community – a really caring local chemist's.'

'We do our best to please.'

'I'll say you do! Mind you, I think you went a bit over the top with customer service today, don't you?' cackled Mrs Brown, her sense of humour returning along with the colour in her cheeks.

Ruth had to smile.

'It was worth it,' she said. 'Sid's going to be all right, that's the important thing. I can't tell you how pleased I am.'

'I think I can guess.' She gave Ruth a grave look. 'I'm glad you came through your own illness an' all. You gave us all a few sleepless nights, I can tell you. You're very well liked in our neighbourhood.'

With a shock Ruth realised that she had forgotten all about her own illness and almost had to ask the old lady what she was referring to.

Now Ruth knew she had *truly* found the way forward. She no longer consciously had to cast her fears from her mind. It was happening naturally and was an exhilarating feeling.

'You'll give me a swollen head with all this praise, Mrs Brown,' she said, hiding her emotion with a grin. 'So go and see your Sid . . . then we'll go home.'

Chapter Twenty-Four

Britain was sweltering in the drought-ridden summer of 1976, an endless stream of sunny, scorching days. Lawns turned brown, tarmac melted, flowers died, reservoirs dried up, and dogs and cats languished in the shade. Water rationing had been introduced in some parts of Wales and the West Country, and forest fires had destroyed hundreds of acres of woodland in the New Forest.

Making the most of the sunshine, however, Londoners had gone continental with alfresco meals, Mediterranean-style clothes and bikinis in Hyde Park. People couldn't sleep so rose earlier to get the chores done before the temperatures soared, and retired to their suffocating bed-rooms later than usual at night. It was all rather uncanny and extremely unBritish.

On this particular August evening, the entire Brooks family and friends had gathered at the family home in Nutley Road for Dan Brooks's seventieth birthday party. All the windows and doors in the house were open and many of the guests had drifted out into the small back garden, neat and well-kept now that Dan had retired and had time to look after it properly. The lively sound of Abba's 'Dancing Queen' resounded from the house as dusk began to fall with refreshing coolness.

'We should have had this shindig in a hall and got outside caterers to do the food to save Mum slaving away in this heat,' Ray said to Ruth. 'I told her that us kids would foot the bill between us but she insisted on having the party here.'

'That's understandable,' said Ruth. 'It wouldn't be the same anywhere else.'

'No, I s'pose not.'

'She's in her element tonight, anyway,' remarked Jack.

'You know Mum,' said Ruth. 'There's nothing she likes better than a party *and* all the preparation that goes with it – heatwave or not.'

There was a general murmur of agreement from her brothers and their wives.

They were standing on the terrace by the French doors leading to the back sitting room. Their parents were mingling with the guests on the small lawn. Ruth looked across at her father, his once-black hair now pure white, his skin deeply tanned. Old age suited Dan. He'd lost his sallow factory complexion and looked fit and chipper. Audrey was standing beside him, clutching a gin and tonic and talking to some of the neighbours. She didn't seem to have changed much over the years so far as Ruth could see. Obviously she'd aged but she was still full of life, her hair still red, albeit out of a bottle.

A surge of affection for her parents washed over Ruth and she reflected on all the good things they had done for her: supporting her as a teenager in trouble, being there for her when her marriage broke up, and more recently when fate had sent her to hell and back. She hoped that achieving her pharmacy degree had made up for the disappointment she'd inflicted on them as a schoolgirl.

It was more than five years since Ruth's operation and she was enjoying good health and a happy marriage. She and Paul had made it legal as soon as his divorce had come through two years ago. They'd had a small wedding with just close friends and family, but it had been the happiest day of Ruth's life.

As a graduate, she had now completed her on-the-job training, passed the registration examination and was registered to practise as a pharmacist. She and Vince had recently opened a shop in the Notting Hill area which Vince managed while Ruth looked after things at Shepherd's Bush. She had mixed feelings about this. The expansion made excellent business sense but she missed Vince's jovial company during the day.

Kitty came over to her.

'Enjoying yourself?' she asked.

'Yes, are you?'

'I'm having a smashing time.'

'Where's Timmy?'

'He's around somewhere . . . with Jenny,' explained Kitty.

'She's always had a soft spot for him,' smiled Ruth

'That's true.' Kitty sipped her lager. 'Vince and Paul are talking cricket so I thought I'd take the opportunity to come and have a chat with you.'

'All the men are obsessed with the Test Match at the moment.' Ruth looked thoughtful. 'But Paul's supposed to be looking after the bar and making sure everybody has a drink.'

'He is doing,' said Kitty. 'With Vince's help.'

'Those two are as thick as thieves . . . just like when they were boys.'

Out of the corner of her eye Ruth saw her mother hurrying into the house, and wondered why.

Audrey went upstairs to the back bedroom and stood in the dark by the window, looking out across the familiar urban landscape, the amber-tinted sky above the rooftops, the lit windows in rows.

A need to be alone had driven her here. She wanted a few minutes in quiet contemplation on the day her husband achieved his three score years and ten. The window was open and the cool evening air felt soothing to her face. Already there was a spicy tang of autumn in it.

Party sounds drifted up from below – talking, laughing,

pop music beating through the house, and the thump of dancing feet. A lot of the guests were still standing around chatting in the garden, illuminated by the lights from the house. Everyone seemed to be having a good time.

Dan was seventy. It didn't seem possible. Or that their children were now middle-aged. It didn't seem five minutes since they'd been under her feet. She was *so* proud of her family. All of them, no matter what their achievements.

Naturally she was very proud of Ruth for becoming a qualified chemist and Jenny who was now a junior doctor in a London hospital. But Audrey didn't think less of the twins or her grandsons, Tom and Gary, who had just left school and started work at the latest import from America: McDonald's.

The twins were still as closely bonded as ever, but it didn't seem to have harmed their marriages. They'd struck lucky with Pat and Peggy and Audrey was fond of her daughters-in-law.

All things considered, she thought she was a very fortunate woman. They'd had their differences, like any other family, but they'd stayed together – and not just in the geographical sense. The Brooks family would be together in their hearts if they were spread to the farthermost corners of the globe.

Yes, I'm very lucky indeed, she thought. Smiling, Audrey went downstairs to rejoin the party.

Paul appeared at his wife's side.

'Fancy a walk?'

She looked at him enquiringly. 'Had enough of the party already?'

'No . . . I just want you to myself for a little while,' he said. 'And I need to stretch my legs. Only round the block.'

'Okay, we'll take the dog with us.'

Unnoticed, they slipped away and ambled down the

street towards the Green in the cool night air, midges swarming at the street lights, privet hedges glistening with dew. People were standing at their gates chatting, conversations from inside drifting out through the open windows.

After they'd crossed the road to the Green, Ruth turned and looked across at the shop.

'I still can't get used to the idea that I don't live there any more,' she remarked, glancing up at the flat.

'No regrets though?'

'Not likely. I adore our little house in Holland Park,' she said.

'At least there are no ghosts from the past there.'

'That's right. And it's good to get right away from the shop when I've finished work at the end of the day.'

'It worked out well, with Jenny taking the flat on,' he remarked.

'The perfect arrangement. She needed a place of her own and the shop-flat is really convenient for the hospital,' Ruth said. 'I wouldn't have felt happy about her living there on her own if we hadn't had the place properly alarmed, though. Fortunately it isn't quite so expensive these days.'

Ruth stared in thoughtful silence at the shop for a moment. 'I haven't really gone anywhere when you think about it, have I? I mean, I still work in the same chemist's shop where I went as a teenager – an unmarried mother as they called single mothers in those days. I was so grateful to Mr Grover for being kind enough to give me a job.'

'In geographical terms you haven't gone anywhere,' Paul agreed. 'But in real terms you have come a very long way indeed. I'm so proud of you for getting your degree.'

'I had no choice with you nagging me silly,' she reminded him.

'You're glad I did . . . admit it?'

'I am, I am,' she emphasised. 'It still gives me a thrill

to be the registered pharmacist for this shop.'

'With good reason.'

'The job is so right for me,' she said. 'I enjoy being a community chemist, advising people and listening to their problems. I've known some of our customers all my life. I wouldn't want to move away. That's why I wanted Vince to run the new shop, so that I could stay on my own patch.'

They strolled on, arm in arm across the Green, the grass like burnt straw, the traffic roaring around them, Ringo sniffing the ground.

'But the best thing of all is being alive and married to you,' she said.

He squeezed her arm. 'Oh, Ruth . . . you say the nicest things.'

She stopped walking and flung her arms around him with the sheer joy of living.

'I think we'd better go back to the party soon,' she said, drawing back after a while. 'Before someone misses us and sends out a search party.'

'Yeah, sure.'

He slipped an affectionate arm around her shoulders and together they walked back to Nutley Road in the balmy evening air.

A selection of bestsellers from Headline

LAND OF YOUR POSSESSION	Wendy Robertson	£5.99 ☐
DANGEROUS LADY	Martina Cole	£5.99 ☐
SEASONS OF HER LIFE	Fern Michaels	£5.99 ☐
GINGERBREAD AND GUILT	Peta Tayler	£5.99 ☐
HER HUNGRY HEART	Roberta Latow	£5.99 ☐
GOING TOO FAR	Catherine Alliott	£5.99 ☐
HANNAH OF HOPE STREET	Dee Williams	£4.99 ☐
THE WILLOW GIRLS	Pamela Evans	£5.99 ☐
A LITTLE BADNESS	Josephine Cox	£5.99 ☐
FOR MY DAUGHTERS	Barbara Delinsky	£4.99 ☐
SPLASH	Val Corbett, Joyce Hopkirk, Eve Pollard	£5.99 ☐
THEA'S PARROT	Marcia Willett	£5.99 ☐
QUEENIE	Harry Cole	£5.99 ☐
FARRANS OF FELLMONGER STREET	Harry Bowling	£5.99 ☐

All Headline books are available at your local bookshop or newsagent, or can be ordered direct from the publisher. Just tick the titles you want and fill in the form below. Prices and availability subject to change without notice.

Headline Book Publishing, Cash Sales Department, Bookpoint, 39 Milton Park, Abingdon, OXON, OX14 4TD, UK. If you have a credit card you may order by telephone – 01235 400400.

Please enclose a cheque or postal order made payable to Bookpoint Ltd to the value of the cover price and allow the following for postage and packing:

UK & BFPO: £1.00 for the first book, 50p for the second book and 30p for each additional book ordered up to a maximum charge of £3.00.
OVERSEAS & EIRE: £2.00 for the first book, £1.00 for the second book and 50p for each additional book.

Name ....

Address ....

....

....

If you would prefer to pay by credit card, please complete:
Please debit my Visa/Access/Diner's Card/American Express (delete as applicable) card no:

.... Expiry Date ....